Also by Julia Gregson

East of the Sun

Band of Angels

A Novel

JULIA GREGSON

A TOUCHSTONE BOOK
PUBLISHED BY SIMON & SCHUSTER
NEW YORK   LONDON   TORONTO   SYDNEY

Touchstone
A Division of Simon & Schuster, Inc.
1230 Avenue of the Americas
New York, NY 10020

Copyright © 2004 by Julia Gregson
Originally published in Great Britain in 2004 by Orion, an Hachette Livre UK company

First Touchstone trade paperback edition May 2010

TOUCHSTONE and colophon are registered trademarks of Simon & Schuster, Inc.

For information about special discounts for bulk purchases, please contact Simon & Schuster Special Sales at 1-866-506-1949 or business@simonandschuster.com.

The Simon & Schuster Speakers Bureau can bring authors to your live event. For more information or to book an event contact the Simon & Schuster Speakers Bureau at 1-866-248-3049 or visit our website at www.simonspeakers.com.

Manufactured in the United States of America

10 9 8 7 6 5 4 3 2 1

Library of Congress Cataloging-in-Publication Data

Gregson Julia.
    Band of angels : a novel / Julia Gregson.
        p. cm.
    1. Young Women—England—Fiction. 2. Nurses—Fiction. 3. British—Ukraine—Crimea—Fiction. 4. Crimean War, 1853–1856—Fiction. I. Title.
PR6107.R44494B36   2010
823'.92—dc22
                                                            2009042198

ISBN 978-1-4391-0113-1 (pbk)
ISBN 978-1-4391-1778-1 (ebook)

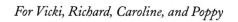

For Vicki, Richard, Caroline, and Poppy

Acknowledgments

I'd like to thank Daphne Tilley, for taking me on a long-distance ride across Snowdon to the Lleyn Peninsula, where I discovered the drovers' roads and the beginnings of my story. Jenny and David Clifford, for lending me their house. Turkish Airlines, for flying me to Istanbul, where I took a boat across the Bosphorus and saw Florence Nightingale's room at the Barrack Hospital; Alex Attewell, director of the Florence Nightingale Museum at St. Thomas's Hospital in London for his advice. Special thanks to Delia.

For love and support, thanks to my late mother, Vicki Sutton; to my sister Caroline; to Sarah, Charlotte, Hugo, Natasha, and Poppy; and, of course, Richard, for patiently reading all those drafts. I owe Kate Shaw a big debt of gratitude for her advice and support, and many thanks to my agent, Clare Alexander, for her professionalism and encouragement.

Prologue

Wales 1844

When I say 'Charge,'" said Deio, "Charge!"

She hesitated for a moment. The sea was high and her pony already excited. She leaned forward.

"Wait! Wait! Wait!" he bellowed against the wind. "Not till I say."

The flounces on her pantaloons were streaked with mud and the dark stains from her stirrup leathers would not wash out. Mair would be so angry.

"Now," he said. "Go!"

It was always the same, the split second between the order and its execution, the moment when she saw it all: her pony red-eyed, iron-mouthed, out of control. The shock of falling, the crunch of her bones. Mother and Father, Eliza and Mair, trudging behind her small coffin. Mother's one red rose hurled into the raw earth.

"I am coming," she shouted into the snarling wind. "For Wales, for glory."

Now that they were galloping, the wet sand made a thrumming sound under Plover's feet and the waves crashed like falling buildings.

"I am flying," she thought. "I am God and I am flying." Ahead, in a cloud of sand, was Deio's pony, and beyond him the waves and the cliff.

They were turning now, jumping the swirling eddies, jumping through air, around the curve of the beach, faster and faster. When he wrestled his pony to a halt near the rock pools his face was wet with wind tears.

"Oh Deio," she said. "She flew. I could hardly hold her."

His pony, a mad little black thing scarcely broken, snatched at its bit and showed the whites of its eyes.

"Again," she said. "Come on."

"No."

"Why not, peasant? You are not the boss of everything."

"Don't call me that. The charge is over. We won. You don't keep doing a thing once you've done it."

She watched him pull an old fob watch from his buckskin breeches. Almost everything he did had magic for her. He was twelve years old, with jet black hair and dark green eyes. A cast in his right eye, more pronounced when he was being perverse or was tired, gave him a certain air of the gypsy.

"Oh goddamn and blind it. 'Tis half past one," he said.

"Please, Deio, don't tease, don't. If I'm late, I'll get a lathering."

"Caw, caw, caw," he cried at a group of seagulls flying above his head. He leaned over his pony's shoulder and flicked her with the length of elder he used as a crop. It hurt a bit, but she wouldn't tell-tale-tit any more than she would about the other tests.

"I am going with Da to the blacksmiths." His father was a drover, he always had interesting things to do.

Now they were climbing up the narrow sheep path that led to the bad stretch of cliff that they called Giant's Mouth, and the wind was tugging at her hair with a ferocity that pleased her. They loved this place, forbidden to all local children ever since Ceris Jones, a fisherman's daughter from Abersoch, had gone over the edge during a picnic and been carried home stone-cold dead on a sheep hurdle.

Up here the air was pure and earthy, with the boom of the sea below and waves bashing and bubbling like great gobs of spit between the black teeth of the rocks, and you could hardly breathe for fear that your foot would catch a loose stone or a piece of wet grass and you'd go plunging and cartwheeling down through space, down and down and down forever.

They got off their ponies and stared toward the horizon. It was clear enough to see Bardsey Island. Without looking at her and with no change of expression he put his arm around her.

"There's an apple tree in the Dinas Field," he said. "We'll get some tomorrow. I'll hold you up to the branches."

They cantered to the top of the track where it joined the main road to Aberdaron. He was always in flight and she was always half glad. At the top he made a comrade's clenched fist. His house, Pantyporthman, the Drover's Hollow, was two miles to the left, up a track gouged with cattle hooves.

After she caught up with him and they'd said good-bye, there was a pain in her chest as she watched him canter back down the road. His words—bugger bastard—but she needed them now and it was a bugger wanting to go back with him and wanting to go home, too. "I'll hold you up to the branches," she whispered.

Now she stood with her back to the sea and looked down on the green blur of hills dotted with whitewashed cottages. The Lleyn Peninsula. Deio, who had ridden to London on a drove and who knew, said this was the end of Wales.

Then Mair ran up the lane shrieking. Mair was their maid, fat and with wild, red, frizzy hair.

"Are you insane completely, Catherine Carreg?" she shouted. "Your poor mother's frantic. Where have you been?"

"Down to Whistling Sands. I'm allowed."

"Only a few times when your mam was ill—and don't you ever dare tell her I said you could."

"More like fifty, a hundred, two hundred times, when Mama was ill," thought Catherine giving back a crafty look.

"And what sort of state is that to come home in with your auntie coming for lunch? Did ye fall in the cow muck?"

From her pony, she could see inside Mair's mouth, the place on her lower jaw where she had lost two teeth and the spittle ballooned.

"Eliza is washed and dressed already and looking a perfect picture, and look at you!" She wondered how fast he was riding home and if he would jump the fallen log near the gate. Another test. If he'd get her a horseshoe from the blacksmiths so she could hang it in the tack room at home. If she could see him tomorrow and the day after that and was it a sin to hope Mama would carry on having rests in the afternoon?

"Oh Mair." She put her maid's hand on the pony's sopping neck. "I went so fast."

Their eyes locked for a moment in perfect complicity. They were both in their own way trapped.

"Don't give me fast, madam," said Mair with a spiteful look. "One day you'll go down there and the Water Horse will get you, it happened to another little girl I knew."

Catherine shivered. "Don't Mair, please!"

"He'll come out of the water, all beautiful and wet, and you'll want to ride him, and you will, and then he'll bite your neck with his big teeth and then he'll drown you."

"No he won't," shouted Catherine. "He knows where I am and he doesn't come. He likes me."

"Oh, well he will," said Mair in a mysterious voice. "He'll come."

"Don't Mair, please stop. You're frightening me." She put her hand into the maid's rough red one and gave it a squeeze. "And keep my great big magic secret."

"You silly little girl." Mair's eyes were unsmiling as she bounced down the hill toward Carreg Plâs. "It won't last long."

Part One

Chapter 1

She so wanted her mother to be happy, but she never really was, and for the four years that her mother had suffered from the variety of illnesses, the headaches and bad backs and bouts of insomnia that were really all a kind of anguish, it had suited her parents to drop her next door, and Pantyporthman had become her second home.

There she met Deio. He was a few years older than she and, at first, tried hard to ignore her. Then, because the drovers were always busy, he'd let her tag along. She'd backed ponies, gone fishing, learned to stalk, to make a fire out of nothing, and, in between, they'd taken the tests: the breakneck gallops down the steepest paths, the sickening jumps, hair flying above her head, from the cliffs into the sea. He taught her to swear and told her matter-of-factly one day while they were out on the horses what men did with women. He brought her a piece of amber from London when his dad took him there on a drove. He'd carved her a lapwing out of driftwood that she wore around her neck. She shivered when she looked at him, at his careless grace on a horse, his dark hair against the sky. Nothing at home made her feel so alive, so free.

And then, a few months after her sixteenth birthday, it stopped.

The gossip began when Catherine—who had wild tawny hair and a spirited, mobile face—grew, it seemed overnight, from a curious-looking child into a beauty. Local opinion thought it "a bit whatsname" to see her still riding out with Deio Jones, who frequently traveled to London and who was known to be wild. Eventually it fell to the vicar, the Reverend Hughes, to saddle up his skinny horse and ride the eight miles from Sarn to Aberdaron in order to have "a little, ahem, talk" with her father, "in a private place so to speak."

It was glorious that early spring morning; the air smelled of salt and wildflowers and the Reverend, who lived on his own in a dark damp cottage, enjoyed the chance to get out and to observe the Carreg family at closer quarters. They were a curious tribe; Huw Carreg, Catherine's father, came from a family who had lost a great deal of money in lavish improvements to a series of houses and at the gambling table. Either way, the money had gone. Huw, had he not then married Felicia, might have been allowed to reinvent himself in the community as a hardworking farmer, which was all he ever wanted to be. But Felicia, Catherine's mother, had sealed his fate. She was beautiful and strange and, once he had got her home, confused him and them and made him, forever, not exactly foreign, but never really local.

The house he rode toward, Carreg Plâs—the name in Welsh meant place of stones—had been Catherine's home for as long as she'd been alive. It was the last remnant of her grandparents' once-flourishing estate, a no-nonsense L-shaped farmhouse, built of brick and stone, with slate walls on the Atlantic side to withstand the worst of the winter gales. In the twelfth century, it had been the home of the abbots of Bardsey Island, where thousands of saints were said to be buried. Thousands of pilgrims had come here, their last resting place before they took the boat to Bardsey. They'd washed their bruised feet under the pump in the herb garden—for them a place of joy or relief, for her mother a prison.

Hidden by trees, the house, dark and with higgledy-piggledy rooms, was designed to endure rather than impress, but upstairs, from its different windows, you saw wonderful things—the foothills of Snowdon, the Atlantic Ocean, Cardigan Bay—lit up with the hard sparkle of diamonds on this spring morning. The Reverend had been having trouble with his false teeth. A dentist from Rhyl had come in his horse and trap, given him a whiff of chloroform, and filed down the roots and affixed the new teeth, but they still seemed to wobble slightly as he sucked them in now, for duw, how the place had run down over the last ten years. He frowned at the tangle of bramble near the gate, the messy circle of grass at the end of the drive, the two stone greyhounds on either side of the front door with their heads half-eaten away.

Later, over a drop of Bristol in the parlor, the Reverend—a stoop-shouldered man with a perpetual dewdrop at the end of his nose, and a manner both snobbish and servile—talked about the great harvest that year, and the high prices cattle were fetching in Caernarfon; the lower classes seemed to be getting a taste for meat. Then, seeing Mr. Carreg look wistfully toward the door, he grasped the nettle. There was talk in the village that Catherine, a fine girl, had been riding out with the Jones boy. Now, as far as he knew, he was a fine boy, too—although he'd have to take this on hearsay as the family were not regular attenders of the church. He had thought hard about coming up, he said. After all, if the tongue told all the bosom knew, none would be neighbors, but in a small community like this, and with the Carregs being such a fine old family, the best candle surely, was prudence?

Father, who had a gentleman's disdain for gossip, could not bring himself to confide in this man any details of his wife's illness or the chain of circumstances that had led his family into such an intimate relationship with his neighbors. He thanked him for his visit and showed him the door.

Shortly after the Reverend Hughes had gone, Father had a sharp and urgent discussion with his wife, then called Catherine and her sister, Eliza, into the parlor. One look at his face made Catherine's heart thump.

"Catherine," he said, "I expect you had a nice day today, did you?"

"Yes, Father," she said. "I think so."

He put his cheek closer to her, he'd shaved for this and his skin smelled of witch hazel. Then he said, in the same dull voice, he was glad she had had a nice day because he was working hard on the farm all day, and now that Mother was much better and she was growing up, it was time for her to spend more time at home, helping. At this, Eliza, always the peacemaker, had made gentle, encouraging noises.

"And of course"—Mother gave a pleading look to her husband—

"we'll have some fun, too. It has been quiet for you girls and you have been so patient, so good."

"Patience be damned!" Father's shout made them all jump. "I should have put a stop to it years ago; we've let her run wild. Riding around with Deio like a hoodlum." He opened his legs, a surprisingly coarse gesture meant to mimic a girl riding astride.

The sharp cuff he gave her behind the ear made Eliza cry out, and Catherine feel like a dog sent clattering across the floor when it had done its necessaries inside.

"Don't do that, Father," she'd said, determined not to cry, "I am too old for that."

He gave her the look she feared most, as if all the words in the world would not be able to contain his rage and disappointment.

"Do not be too sure of that, missie," he said. "I'll do what I damn well please in my own house, and what I want is for you to stop seeing that boy and the rest of them."

"Stop seeing them?" she whispered. "How can I? They are my friends, and he is hardly ever home now."

This was true. That week, he was away in Ludlow at a horse fair, but they'd arranged a ride for when he got back.

"It's not right," her father repeated. "It sits all wrong, does it not, Felicia?" Mother's face, so bad at lies, flickered with distress. She was afraid of the drovers, linking them with her times of greatest unhappiness, but on her own she would never have forbidden it.

"Well, Huw, they have indeed been kind, but we . . . I . . ."

"We what Father? Say it? Do not need them anymore?"

"Catherine"—he balled his big red hands—"that is quite unnecessary."

"If it is, I am sorry, Father but . . ."

Eliza's round blue eyes were pleading with her to stop now and say the gentle, womanly things that would end this horror.

"You are deliberately missing the point," he hammered out. "Those men are capital men and I will continue to do everything we can to help them, but your time with them is over. Do you understand that?"

"I do, Father." *And wish to God I had been born a man.* For one moment she imagined herself looking down at him from a horse and knocking him down without a word.

She had to tell them the very next day. Pale with shock, she took the shortcut to Pantyporthman, across the two fields and down by the river. In her basket was a jar of Mair's elderberry jam and some pickled onions. In Meg Jones's kitchen she put the basket on the table.

Meg had Deio's wide-set green eyes; she wore bangles on her strong brown arms. "Well, there's kind." Meg took a cake out of the oven and put it beside the jam on the table.

"Now give me your cloak, set down there tidy, and have a piece of this."

"The preserves are from Mother," Catherine lied. She didn't want her mother to be blamed for this. "With her most cordial good wishes."

If Meg was surprised by this formality she did not show it. She shooed a cat away from the bench and told her to sit down and eat and stop dithering like an old sheep.

"No thank you." She felt tears rising. "I am expected at home."

"You all right, love?" Meg looked at her sharply, and said, "Deio's away this week with his father. There's a sale on Ludlow way. He's got a grand new horse, I expect he'll show you."

"How is he?"

Meg lit a pipe and looked at her. "He misses you. He never says so but he always does. You met each other too young."

"Too young for what?" She put her head in her hands.

"Don't! Don't, love." Meg looked shocked at her distress. "There's always time," she said, "but he's like his father, he needs to live a bit first."

"But we do live," she sobbed. "We do. I would never stop him doing that." She could do nothing now to stop the tears.

"I know you do, love, I know you do, but this sort of love at your age—it does hurt so."

"Why does it have to hurt?" she almost shouted.

"It's too much and I should shut my trap." Meg knocked out her pipe and stood up, now almost as pale as Catherine. "Deio would tell me to shut it."

"Finish what you were saying." Catherine felt in this moment that she hated Meg.

"There's nothing to finish, love. All I was trying to say is he'd hate a life too settled."

"And do you think I want that?"

"No, but it's what you will have."

"I don't think I will." Catherine stood up and put on her cloak. "But you have no need to trouble yourself with this anymore." This was coming out so wrong, but she pressed on. "You won't see me here again. I won't be coming back."

"Love, calm down." Meg took her hand and, for a moment, she grabbed it like a lifeline. "All I was saying was be patient, give it time."

"I won't be coming back. I can't." It was Meg's turn to look confused.

"So where are you going, love? Somewhere exciting?"

"I don't know. Nowhere," she stammered. "Mother is much better, you see, and now I can't come back. But thank you very much anyway."

"I see." The penny was starting to drop. She could see it in the stiff way Meg took her cake away from the table and placed it on the shelf. "I thought you'd come for something else." Later, she'd led her to the door and, in a polite voice Catherine had never heard before, thanked her for coming.

Running home along the riverbank, Catherine, her empty basket in her hand, felt shocked and unreal. She cursed herself for her abrupt treatment of Meg, wished she had had the courage to at least sit and eat the cake and explain things more fully. She imagined a scandalized Meg explaining the scene to Deio and Lewis in the English accent she often teased her in.

"Stuck up little madam, comes in and says, 'Sorry we won't be needing yew anymore thank yew,'" and cringed to imagine their response. Lewis, who had started with nothing and worked his way up by selling hunters to the gentry, was a proud and prickly man, even more so now he had real power in the community. Deio was his father's son. She would not be forgiven, she knew that. But what was so unfair, what made her pant with agitation as she ran, was that Father would stay friends with Lewis, maybe even with Deio. The big world of men's work would go on. They dip each other's sheep, meet in the tavern, lean over gates together and smoke pipes as if nothing of any importance had happened and they were all still brothers under one skin.

A catastrophe for her, nothing to them. Her world suddenly shrunk to the kitchen, the dairy, the parlor: the whole world of footling tasks that made up being a woman. And there, barring a miracle, she would stay.

Chapter 2

$\mathcal{P}$oor Mother looked excited when Catherine got home. She had left the door to the parlor slightly ajar so that she could hear her coming. A fire crackled in the grate, the beaded lamp was lit. She had the *Caernarfon and Denbigh Herald* on her lap.

"I've been making a list of all the things we can do now I'm feeling better," she said.

Her face, pretty and flushed, had taken on the rose and amber colors of the lamp beads. "Look!" She handed over the newspaper. "There is sea bathing in South Wales. Sea bathing! We can take the coach from Caernarfon at"—she peered at the advertisement—"at the Uxbridge Arms. It leaves at seven o'clock in the morning. We really could swim and eat ice creams and walk along the beach and be back on the following day. I'm also determined on you and Eliza having a new dress each," she prattled on gaily, "something in satin I fancy—Father's hay crop was so good he will not object—you are old enough now for puff sleeves, at least I think you are."

She looked over the newspaper for Catherine's reaction.

"Oh my darling." She held out her arms. "Oh my God, I'm so sorry. It's all my fault."

"It is not," wept Catherine. "I am glad you are so much better and we will have fun."

"I should have gone and explained myself."

"But you do not know them like I do."

"Did you say how extremely grateful we have all been, how highly we esteem them as neighbors. I should not have left it all to you. I shall write to them myself."

"She can't read in English," said Catherine forlornly, "so there is no point."

"Oh Weddy Bloodstairs!" Weddy Bloodstairs was Mother's all-purpose Welsh swear word. Usually it made her laugh, for Father was very solemn about them learning Welsh and it was deliciously sacrilegious, but today, at this precise moment, the memory of Mother halfheartedly toying with her Welsh lessons like a child forced to eat its greens annoyed Catherine.

"It is too difficult," Mother would protest, after her teacher, the small and bossy Miss Davies, had left the house. "The sounds are awful, like a cat about to be sick." Father had been humorless about it, but he was right. You could not live in a place and ignore its language—or you could, but you could expect to be, as Mother had been, lonely. "Well, it is done now and I don't want to think about it." Catherine tried to sound cheerful. "I'll draw the curtains; we can have tea by the fire."

And so their lives took on a new routine. In the mornings, she and Mother and Eliza helped Mair in the kitchen with household tasks: they made butter, washed dishes, waxed, bottled, and cooked. Eliza, dear Eliza, so gentle and blond and lovable, performed these tasks with a grave absorption that sometimes wrung Catherine's heart. Eliza wanted nothing more from life than to be a farmer's wife and to have as many healthy children as possible. Why was she so different? Why, in the middle of polishing silver or podding peas, did she feel at times a wild surge of outrage that life, after all, was nothing more than a series of endlessly circulating, footling tasks that made you feel like a donkey tied to a wheel.

And what about Mother? Once, long ago, when Father had talked and laughed, he'd described his moment of magic: seeing Mother, aged nineteen, in the moonlight on the veranda of his parents' house in the foothills of Snowdonia. He'd remember what she'd worn: a long silver dress with a row of pearl buttons down the front. It was a summer ball; there was money for such things in those days. She was the daughter of a friend of his father's, a land agent. Her name was Felicia. She'd come from London. And Catherine, forever after, had imagined her sitting there in the moonlight under the dark of the mountains, a transplanted creature like a mermaid.

Now, she watched her mother's long dreamy fingers patting butter in the dairy, or folding up the umpteenth sheet on washing days. How did she stand it, and how did Mair? Mair, who believed that the fairies would come if you left your kitchen clean. You could hear her at six o'clock in the morning singing as she cleaned out the hearth. Did she never want to throw her brush down and shriek, at the top of her lungs, "I need more."

In the afternoons, Father took them on short outings—somehow the longer trips had not materialized. Catherine, who was still angry with him, suspected that the trips were really only for him. He was helplessly in love with Juno, his dark bay cob, and the spanking little governess cart he kept in the cowshed that, with its brasses and gleaming mahogany sides, was a relic of grander days. He almost smiled at Catherine as he brought the horse to a halt, knowing that normally she would have shared this moment of pure pleasure at the perfection of the horse. The carriage jingled faintly as her mother put her foot on the step. She tried to smile back but already felt the claustrophobia of a family outing. The sun was out, the waves danced in the distance; just the kind of day to gallop full pelt down the beach at Whistling Sands.

While the carriage made its way through the high hedgerows she glanced at her father's back and wondered what had happened to them. Father, with his red whiskers and faint smell of tobacco, had once been the rock her life was built on: a permanent statement of power and intent, like the sea, like Snowdon. He had lifted her onto her first pony, plucked her from the apple tree when she got stuck, walloped her one afterward and cheered her up later with a peace offering of a barley sugar. He kept them in a tin in his smoking cabinet, and distributed them to his children with a grave impartiality so much more thrilling than mother's nervous, openhanded generosity.

Catherine had loved him once, and hoped to love him again in spite of the cold draft of dislike she sometimes now felt as she watched him chewing or sitting reading *Farmer's Almanac* by the fire or talking—or usually not talking—to Mother. Now you had to watch him as carefully as you might watch an aggressive dog or a stallion too free with its heels, or perhaps it had always been so but she was only starting to notice. Now when he walked into the house, you had to watch his heels: laugh at his jokes, pick up on his few-and-far-between remarks, not forget his strictures about closing doors or leaving dogs out or not coming to the table with dirty hands, or else the reaction would be swift and sure and Mother would get sad and pale and sometimes have to go to bed for the afternoon.

Father dropped them off in the small seaside town of Pwllheli. The plan was a short walk to a shop where they were to search for bonnet trimmings. At Siop Sion's, the haberdashers, they had not got the precise shade, "almost a robin's egg blue," as Mother said to an assistant whose head was shaking almost as the words came out. "Thank you anyway," said Mother. The jangling bell at the door of the shop seemed to mock them as they left. Mother and Eliza seemed quite content as they swung arm-in-arm down the cobbled street that led to the harbor, but Catherine felt quite dizzy with futility. How could some doodle on a hat take up the entire morning for three grown women?

Father was irritable with them as they drove home. The beautiful day had not lasted and a faint mizzling rain was making him anxious about the haymaking planned for the next day. When the door of the governess cart was shut behind them and the green rug settled over their knees, he set off toward home without a word. A mist had rolled in off the water, blurring the point where sea met sky and making the occasional farm, glimpsed through a wet hedge, look dreamlike; nothing seemed real except the small enclosed world of their cart and the clip-clop of Juno's heels. The sound was soporific, and Catherine, leaving her parents to their awkward communications, dozed for a while. When she woke, they had reached the main road to Aberdaron. The countryside had darkened around them, and in one or two of the houses up on the hill lights flickered uncertainly like fireflies.

Catherine's spirits were so low that she missed the sound that made Juno's ears prick and Father sit up straighter. Then she heard it, "Hip Hop Tro," at first faintly, then louder, "Hip, Hop Tro-oooh!" Then a burst of singing, and the metallic clatter of horse's hooves.

Out of the mist came the shapes of two dozen or so Welsh Blacks, then two men on horseback, whose song came to a ragged halt. Deio's father, Lewis Jones, tipped his hat briefly toward her and Mother. Deio's brother, Rob, pointed an imaginary gun at Father in a joking, oddly debonair gesture.

"Off tomorrow lads, is it?" said Father, smiling and talking to them in Welsh. "Not a bad life, eh? Where to?"

"Gloucester, Northleach, Redland, Thame, Hampstead, Pentonville, Smithfield," Lewis recited.

"Don't drink all your money on the way home then," said Father.

"What about you, neighbor?" said Rob. "Watching your weeds grow?"

"I'll be here," said Father, with a patient shrug that made Catherine recoil.

Then Deio rode out of the mist, and came alongside her. He did not look at her but sat loose-limbed on his horse, a damp wind playing with his hair. He was close enough to touch and Mother saw the look that passed between them. "My dear," she said to her husband, "I'm feeling rather tired, could we . . ."

She could have jumped on his horse from where she sat.

"Aye aye." Father dragged himself back into the world of tiresome women and afternoon teas. "We'll go home and have tea by the fire." He was gentle with his daughter who had grown quite pale. He could afford to be now he'd won that battle. She did not hear him; her eyes had locked with Deio's. "Take me away," they said.

The year passed. She heard through the grapevine that the drovers were much in demand and away most of the time. It was easier when they were gone. She also preferred the winter months when the wind blew off the Atlantic and bent the trees on the Lleyn like little old men and it got dark an hour or so after lunch and there was no possibility of going anywhere. Then the light died, first in the wet trees outside their windows, then in the distant peaks of the mountains beyond. They'd build up a fire in the parlor and close the shutters, and Mair would bring them tea and toast sprinkled with cinnamon and sugar. Mother seemed so happy. Sometimes, her eyes would fill with tears and she would look at them as if for the first time and say, "I have wonderful daughters. I have done nothing to deserve them."

At other times, after tea, she would make them laugh by dragging out what she called her Road to Hell box, a small carved box full of spools of cotton and tangled skeins of silk and her pile of unfinished projects: a tray cloth that only needed a handful of stitches to be finished; the tapestry for a footstool that had waited three years to be mounted. Sometimes she would hold up these items and attempt a serious lecture on the importance of finishing things, but her nature was too fluid and subtle for sermons and she often ended up making them hoot with laughter. It was something about the disparaging way her long fingers held up the trolley cloth and the beaded tray, the way her voice tailed off as she tried to work up enthusiasm for the idea that God was up there, waiting impatiently for the beaded tray.

What they most looked forward to was the moment when Mother's needle dithered over the canvas and she began to tell stories. One afternoon when it was pelting with rain and the mountains just a gray blur in the distance, she told them, Catherine was never to forget it, in a voice steely with self-control, about her own mother who had died of tuberculosis. She was seven years old. She'd been in trouble the day before, she'd torn her dress and been whipped severely, three times on each hand. Mother held out both her hands, and such was her power as a storyteller that both Eliza and Catherine leaned forward, mingling their red and fair hairs in the lamplight, sure the marks would still be there. Mother had been naughty, she'd been attempting to fly with an umbrella over the henhouse and she was sure it was her fault when, a few days later, the sanatoria's gray cabriole arrived at their door. She remembered everything: the coachman's umbrella swooping down like a terrible bird. The sound of rain on the tarpaulin. The flutter of her mother's hand as she drove away. The look on Mother's face as she told this story, pierced Catherine to the heart. Normally, Mother tried so hard to make her stories have happy endings and to tell them only about nice things. Sometimes, when they were young, this had ludicrous consequences. "Don't look, my loves," Mother would say if they passed a squashed squirrel or a rabbit on the road. "It's sleeping, it was going to a party and it is having a sleep." And Mair, if she was with them, would look at her in astonishment and say, "That ain't asleep, Mrs. Carreg, that's dead as mutton."

Silly as these attempts were, her determination not to inflict her own sufferings on her children was heroic. For her spirits were either very high or unfathomably low. She swung on a seesaw that seemed to get higher and lower as the years progressed, and later she was quite unreachable in her sadness, sometimes for months on end. There were one or two terrible "cures," many afternoons in darkened rooms, and yet Catherine, when young, had had very little understanding of her mother's nerves, which, to say the least, were permanently strained.

Later, Catherine wished she had known more about the bad things. About pain and loss and sorrow. If she had, she would have been more prepared for what happened next.

Chapter 3

𝒯he night when her world started to unravel was innocently beautiful. The spring sky glowed with stars and, outside in the fields, ten new lambs born that day were suckling on their mothers. It was two days before her eighteenth birthday. Earlier in the day she and Eliza had walked along the cliff path to watch the fishing boats setting out for their evening's work. As they walked back arm-in-arm, sunset turned their faces and the sea behind them into liquid gold.

There wasn't enough to do to fill an evening, so she'd gone to bed early, but had woken a few hours later with a feeling of intense foreboding. Hearing a faint scrabbling sound on the landing outside, she'd gone, half asleep, to see what it was, and found Mother on the floor. She was on her knees beside an oak trunk carved with acorns, sifting in a wild, muddled way through what Catherine, moving closer, could see were heaps of baby clothes: tams, woolen boots, jackets smelling of damp and camphor. Clothes she had been saving for her grandchildren.

"Mama?" The candle in Mother's hand was close to a flannel nightshirt. "What are you doing?"

"Can't you see?" There were huge circles beneath her mother's eyes.

"Mama!" Catherine snatched the candle. "Be careful with that. Can't I help you tomorrow?"

"I have no time," Mother said. She looked utterly bewildered.

"Why not?"

"The wretched thing is coming in August."

"What thing?"

"A baby."

"What?"

"A baby."

"A baby! No!"

And then, Mother had bared her teeth and let out a howl, an awful sound in which fury and pain and supplication were all mixed up.

Pregnant. Expecting. With child. In the Lleyn in those days, it was considered a little bit "you know . . . not nice," even to say these words in polite company. You could say, "I hear Ceris Davies (she was the local midwife) has been up to see the so and so's," or "the whatevers will have another mouth to feed," or "someone should pass the box on to Mrs. X soon." The box belonged to the parish, and was full of old baby clothes that were passed from house to house. But the Carregs weren't box people. They lived outside of the village and were considered practically gentry, or had been once. So how was Catherine supposed to find out about how such a thing could have happened to Mother? You could never ask Father. Although he was a farmer, he hated any hint of indelicacy in his women, and besides, he was up now night and day with the lambing and looking almost as wild-eyed as she.

She'd asked Mair, who'd said, "Good Lord, what a thing to ask me," and her little curranty eyes had rolled back and she'd smirked and said something about Father and long winter nights. Eliza was worse than useless, prattling on gaily about taking the little pet for rides in the pram and giving it bottles, until Catherine had felt a strong impulse to slap her.

"Eliza," she said, "it is not like playing dollies. Mother is too old for this, and she is so unhappy."

"Well, Ceris Davies," Eliza had replied, turning pink and coming as close as she ever did toward being cross, "says that sometimes these late babies—she called them 'the last of the golden chicks'— well, I thought it was sweet anyway, can be a great and unexpected blessing, and that God does not send us anything we can't manage.

She said that once Mother's confinement is on her she will feel as proud as a dog with her puppies."

"Chickens! Puppies! Oh don't be such a fool," Catherine had shouted, finally losing her patience. "What does Ceris Davies know about a woman like Mother?"

"Are you a snob, Catherine?"

"Yes," she'd said, breathing heavily, "I expect I am—as well as everything else."

Afterward, Catherine had brooded on the word "confinement" and looked it up in the dictionary. *Confinement: imprisonment, restrictions, limitation, to keep indoors or in bed.* She thought of the way Mother had begun now to walk in the afternoons with a kind of painful energy in a circle in the garden. *My God, who in their right mind would be born a woman?*

And then, because she was eighteen and the most pressing thing on her mind was herself, and because everybody else seemed so keen to forget about it, she put it to the back of her mind, hoping that August would never come. But it had, earlier than expected.

On the day her Mother died, she woke early feeling cheerful. It was dark outside. Under her eiderdown, patterned with red and green cabbage roses, she lay flexing her limbs and listening for the slap and swish of the threshing machine outside and for her father, who lay with her mother in the next room, to stand on the creaking floorboard and yawn, or sometimes, yawn and break wind simultaneously. (Her modest ear only allowed one of these sounds.)

She was excited. Today was market day, held once a month at Sarn, and she had faint, though unacknowledged, hopes of seeing Deio there. He'd been away again and come back. Mair told her all the girls were in love with him now. He had grown so handsome with his remarkable wide-set green eyes and long, slightly bandy legs. The calves of his boots were always blackened and dented with the sweat and shape of horses. She still had dreams about him. Silly dreams. Herself, wind- and rain-swept on the back of his horse, galloping off into the mist and over the mountains to somewhere far from here.

The house that morning felt satisfyingly empty. Mair, who normally slept in a small room under the eaves in the top of the house, had been given her weekly wage of five shillings and left early to walk to market. Eliza was in Caernarfon visiting their grandmother. Two others had made a brief appearance in the house: one born dead, the other dead of diphtheria before his fourth birthday. In one month's time there would be another. Catherine, twisting in bed, could not bear to think of this. Today was Mother's last trip to market before the baby came. A gift from God of course, but also horrible and wrong: a door slamming shut on her mother at a time when she seemed so much better. Now Mother rose heavily from the table after breakfast, walked slowly upstairs, and opened the oak trunk carved with acorns. Nightgowns, woolen boots, jackets, tams. That for the wash, that to throw away, that for a stitch, that for when the sewing lady came. She tried to sing sometimes to show she was all right, but her voice sounded cracked and funny.

Catherine got up quickly. This was supposed to be a happy day. Mother had persuaded Father to give them some money to go to Sarn and buy taffeta or silk for her first grown-up ball in Caernarfon. Father, grumbling but only a bit, had given in to his wife's entreaties that the girls must begin a social life before it was too late. He thrust his big red hand into a leather pouch hidden behind the flour jar on the dresser, drew out five shillings, and said to Mother with a shy look, "You girls bleed me dry." Or maybe he gave in because Mother had sighed and flapped the air as though she had limited breath for an argument.

Walking barefoot toward her wardrobe, Catherine was half at the ball already and half walking across the square at Sarn with Deio's eyes on her. She wondered what he saw when he looked at her: the little girl he'd reenacted Llewellyn's last stand with—she'd been good at that, swiping with her sword and making gurgling cries as she galloped off—or the child who had loved playing hospitals with him, bandaging their obliging cat and putting it to bed, and telling him it may not last the night. She hoped he might forget that now and see her as she was: a woman, or very nearly one.

She selected the smartest of the three dresses she owned (white cambric with a *broderie anglaise* trim and a bodice pintucked into thirty narrow pleats). She hung the dress on the front of the cupboard then poured water into a pretty china basin with a lily-of-the-valley motif and a faint crack down the center. As she washed under her nightgown what Mair, who could be coarse, referred to as "nooks and crannies," a sudden burst of sun sent patterns of light over her skin and made her shiver with pleasure.

She went down to the kitchen, a narrow room on the northern side of the house and always dark. She took a taper to the kitchen fire and lit an oil lamp over the table. It cast a warm glow on familiar objects: the dresser with its green-and-white china, the hearth with its hooks and pans, and beside it the still shocking thing: a baby-chair covered in green velvet, its carved footrest scuffed from generations of kicking babies.

Since it was Mair's day off and they had no other help now, Catherine went into the creamery behind the kitchen to draw off a pint of milk from one of four blue basins. Stepping into a patch of sunlight outside the creamery door, a yellowhammer sang its little-bit-of-bread-and-no-cheese song, and she stood for a moment, jug in hand, listening and smiling. A pretty young woman to whom nothing really bad had ever happened. Then, turning, she saw her father standing at the kitchen window looking agitated. He beckoned her inside, his mouth was moving. She thought she must have done something wrong: worn her best dress outside; left her candle lit; not got his breakfast quickly enough.

"Catherine," he said, when she stood before him dry-mouthed, "go upstairs straight away to your mother, something's happening to her."

"What is it, Father?"

His tone frightened her, reminding her of the blank spots in her childhood: the slammed doors, Mother's long rests in the afternoon. But now, Father was waving his hands in jerky circles, and telling her to take a chamber pot with her and seemed incapable of naming the thing.

She dashed down the path to the necessary, the shed where potties were stacked in a cupboard to the left of the privy. She ran back into the house and up the stairs, frightened to open the door that led into Mother's room. When she did, she saw her mother, half undressed in her bed, her hair undone. Her skin gleamed with sweat. Her favorite gray dress was all undone like a burst doll's. Her bosom and corsets were showing. Whatever was happening?

"Mother," said Catherine, cold with horror. "What is it?"

Mother gave her a distant wave as though saying good-bye to an acquaintance.

"Go away, please," she said. "I want Mair."

"She's not here."

Mother, remembering, started to moan about the market and a green dress before she doubled up with pain.

"Oh Mama!" Catherine was crying with fear. "What shall I do?"

"Catherine," Mama's hands were wet to hold as she sat up and tried to smile. "Don't be frightened, darling, but a silly and awkward thing has happened: the baby has come early. You must"—Mother's calm voice turned into a sharp yelp of pain—"help me!"

Her hand pulled back the sheet. Her dress, her drawers, the sheet were part of a widening circle of crimson.

Weak and giddy with panic, the girl ran at first from one window to another. She could see her father, a stick figure in the yard, feeding calves, with their two laborers, Alun and Twm. She struggled with the window, but the frame was soft and old and the catch sunk into the wood.

"Wait for me," she gasped. She ran downstairs and through the yard until she found him. He was standing near to Juno, half-harnessed for the ride to Sarn. Alun was polishing the governess cart and telling Father they didn't make them like that anymore.

"Well, good oh, Alun," Father was saying, "and now I'd better get my women to the fair else I won't be very popular will I. Not a bit popular eh?" Father's shyness often took the form of an awkward heartiness, particularly when he talked to other men about his women.

"Father," Catherine started to say, "we can't go anywhere."

He took her arm suddenly and pulled her roughly away from Alun and into a nearby feed room.

"Don't talk about it in front of him," he hissed. "It's our business."

"Father," she said, her mouth so stiff with fear it was difficult to make words. "The baby is coming and I don't know what to do. Help me for God's sake."

"I can't help her," he said. All the red had gone out of his face and he looked shrunken and papery. "Do as I say and listen. I can't help her, it would kill her."

"Shall I put the cart on now, sir?" Alun was asking through the crack in the door.

"Not for now thank you, Alun," said Father in a flat calm voice, "go home and have your breakfast until I send for you."

"Right, sir." Alun sounded surprised.

His footsteps receded. Father thought for a moment and then said to Catherine, with some echo of his old authority, "I'll go into Sarn and find Ceris Davies. You stay here and try not to worry. There are often false alarms. That's why it is better the men stay out of it, I'll not be long." He tried to take her hand. "You're a good girl. It's better I go and get help."

She looked at him in appalled disbelief. He was a coward, and he seemed to be pleading with her to understand.

"It's better I go." He repeated stubbornly.

"Why is it better?" For the first time in her life she was shouting at him. "You have done lambing."

"Don't you shout at me, else you will weep for it," he'd shouted back, turning red again. "You go back into that house. Boil some water, tear up some sheets. I'll get Ceris Davies."

Catherine grabbed him by both sleeves of his smock and shook him. "But I don't know what to do. Even Alun would know more," she cried, still shouting.

He'd raised his hand to smack her face then thumped her on the arm. "Stop that and get inside," he shouted back. "You'll soon understand."

Chapter 4

$\mathcal{C}$atherine stood outside the front door and watched her father leave. Fear made her feel numb and slow, as though she were wading against a strong tide, and it seemed a great effort to turn and go back into the house, which, with her father gone, seemed charged with menace. In the kitchen, the clock ticked, the breakfast things lay where they had been left. Mother or Mair would have had them cleared away by now and the floor would have been swept clean.

Unwilling to go upstairs, Catherine ate the half-rasher of cold bacon Father had left on his plate and immediately felt sick. She thought about Mair, who could be brisk and short-tempered but who was kind to her when she felt sick.

"Come home soon, Mair," she prayed. "Help us." She prayed that Ceris, the midwife, the small bossy woman she normally disliked, would be in when Father called. "It's not fair," she thought, for her prayers had made her feel weak and tearful, "I shouldn't have to do this on my own."

Filling a cup of water, she went upstairs. The sky through the landing window looked blue and empty. The door to Mother's room was closed. She hesitated outside then put her cup of water down and pushed hard, for the door was inclined to stick.

"Mother," she said. "Mama?"

Inside the bedroom, the curtains were closed and the room, normally fragrant with mother's lavenders and rosewater, smelled bad. She opened the curtains, and turned to the bed where Mother lay, quite still and very pale, her eyes fixed and open.

"Mother . . . oh please!"

As she flew toward the bed, she stumbled over something soft: Mother's dress—her favorite dove-gray silk—stood up on its own, supported by its hoop petticoats as if it led a separate life, its violet trim now saturated with blood. She lifted the dress and threw it into the corner of the room. Mother cleared her throat.

Catherine wanted to cry. She knelt beside the bed and took her mother's hand, covering it in kisses.

"It's all right, darling," she whispered with more confidence than she felt. "Dada will be back soon. You can tell me what you want."

Her mother tried to speak, but a spasm of pain flung the peach satin of her quilt from her. Catherine put it back, trying not to look.

"Mama," she yelped, "what am I to do?" For the first time in her life she hated herself: her dithering gestures, her cry of weakness and self-pity.

The pain seemed to come in waves that took Mother to terrible peaks of suffering, then to recede into a false calm that left her tousled and apologetic on the pillow and saying "what a to do," and trying to tell her that having *her* had been one of the best days of her life. During a quiet phase, she told Catherine that babies arrived on a cord from down here. She waved vaguely toward the middle of the quilt. If her baby came, Catherine was to take the big sewing scissors, not the little ones, from the green sewing bag with the pink geraniums in the chest near the window, and be very brave and cut the cord. It wouldn't hurt Mama, it would help her.

Catherine turned away almost sick at the thought. "Please God, please Ceris, come," and, turning back, smiled as if Mother's request was the most natural one in the world. A shrill song started up inside her head: "The big scissors not the little ones, I see. I see." She got down on her knees and put her head next to her mother's. Her forehead was waxy now and white and she was breathing through her mouth. She put her hand gently on her mother's face. She wanted more than anything in the world to save her from pain and ugliness. Mama, groaning and panting, began grimacing and pushing her away.

Mother started to scream. "Help me, Catherine, help me." Her mouth was square and purple, her face unrecognizable. "Help me!"

This cry would stay with Catherine forever. She dashed toward the windows and then back toward the bed, shouting, "Tell me what to do!"

Mother was grabbing violently at the quilt again. When she drew it back, Catherine saw her legs were bloody and that the thing lay at the end of a quivering cord. It was hideously ugly, its skin red and flopping, its skull soft and dented like a bad plum.

Catherine took the big scissors from the sewing bag and, shuddering with revulsion, cut the cord and put the baby in the oak cradle at the foot of the bed where it lay without moving. She spewed in the potty underneath the bed and stayed there for a while, hunched and listening with painful concentration for her mother's breath. When she sprang up she hit her head so hard on the iron bed she almost knocked herself out.

Pulling herself together, she put her head on her mother's breast and their red hairs mingled. At last she heard it, the faintest gasp from a face so pale the lips looked like glass. She took a brush and did her mother's hair, hearing her own voice making mad sounds. She got up and ran to the window again. The sky looked thicker and darker than before with rain clouds gathering over Port Iago, and the hills blanked out. "I feel like a pie in the sky," a silly voice inside her sang. She took a cloth and tried to rub some of the mud and blood from her hands and her pretty white dress. "It's no good," she thought. "It will never come out."

Chapter 5

Toward the end of the afternoon, it rained suddenly for half an hour and then the sun came out again, a brilliant, unreliable sort of sun, streaming through the windows and lighting up a huge cobweb Mother had missed. Catherine pushed her fingers through the cobweb, feeling just as weightless and insubstantial. When Mother groaned she held her head up and gave her a sip of water. When a line of grayish dribble fell from her mouth, she wiped it away, past grief, past disgust, locked now into a small world of action and reaction.

"They'll be home soon," she whispered, without much hope. "Home soon: Daddy and Eliza and Mair. Home for Mama."

Mother licked her lips and stared blankly ahead of her.

Catherine lit a candle, and got into bed on the other side of her mother, nearly suffocating now from the bad, sweet smell in the room, and fell into an uneasy sleep. Later, when the sky was black above the line of trees, she heard the rumble of a cart in the yard outside. She flew downstairs and, standing there like another kind of dream, was Deio. There was rain on his hair, and his sleeves were rolled up and the muscles and skin of his arms gleamed. Before she had time to think, she flung her arms around him. He felt so strong, so alive. She clung to him, sobbing and trying to explain all that had happened. They had never touched each other like this before, but she was too far gone to feel the strangeness of it.

He took both her shoulders between his hands and stroked them, murmuring, "Ty Du. Ty Du . . . It's all right. It's all right." He smoothed her hair and held it in a bunch as he gently explained that he'd found her father by the roadside, fallen from his horse but all right; he would be in shortly with Ceris the midwife.

When her father walked into the kitchen, Deio and Catherine sprang apart. Father had torn his clothes and looked ashen with fatigue. She was shocked at the wave of pure dislike she felt at the sight of him. Behind Father, at the kitchen door, was Ceris, carrying a scuffed portmanteau in her hand. She looked curiously at the handsome young couple—she'd heard the gossip, too. Father, sensitive even in these circumstances to that look, bundled Deio out the back door, forgetting to thank him.

When Catherine led them into Mother's room, the stench was overpowering and Father, smelling it and understanding, groaned and put his head in his hands. Ceris threw off her shawl and went straight to the window, forcing it open, tut-tutting, and working her mouth significantly as she did so.

Ceris, the Lleyn's only midwife for fifteen years, had delivered babies in damp sheds behind haystacks, in bedrooms occupied by five people, in the poorhouse sanitoria, and, once, to a screaming girl with snow on her lips on the Bardsey to Aberdaron ferry. She took out of her bag a jar that contained a mixture of goose fat, fresh butter, and hen's fat.

"Right now, Mr. Carreg," she said, walking toward the bed, "I must take a closer look-see . . . so if you don't mind."

When Father had closed the door behind him, she lined up her pair of scissors, her dirty towel, a dark jar, and a vial of laudanum on the bedside table, then drew back the sheets. Felicia made feeble movements with her hands to push Ceris away.

"Come on now, there there." Ceris told Catherine to hold her mother's hands on either side of her. "Come on," she said sharply, "I don't like doing this either, but I must you know."

Catherine watched the midwife lubricate her two fingers with the gray-colored lard from the jar. When her Mother screamed, she joined in. "Leave her alone now, it's no good, I know it isn't."

Ceris looked at her quietly, her two glistening fingers in the air, sad for this pretty girl in her stained white dress, but detached. She saw women every day in a parlous state: some with their pelvises distorted by rickets; others prematurely aged by desperate poverty or heavy physical work; most robbed of any sexual attraction by repeated childbirth. She was as gentle to Felicia as her skill and training allowed, but in her heart she resented her. This English-woman, with her pretty pearl earrings, lying under her satin quilt had had a better life than most of them. Far better.

After the scream there was a timid knock at the door. Eliza, white as a sheet, stood on the landing, Father sitting crumpled in a chair behind her.

With her arms folded, Ceris stood at the door and addressed them. "She's bad, as I don't have to tell you, with the puerperal sepsis, as you may not know."

She closed her eyes for a moment while this sank in.

"All you can do is keep her nice and tidy with this." She gave Catherine a vial of dark liquid, the same liquor of opium that Mother took for her headaches. "If she should by any chance start to come round"—the midwife's look showed them how faint a pos-sibility that was—"beef tea and some of this."

She cast around again in her untidy portmanteau and brought out a small bag of sago and one of arrowroot. "I'll have to make you, um, you know . . . for this—times being hard," she said.

Father gazed stupidly at her outstretched hand, then reached into his pocket for money and paid her.

"Half a crown for the visit," she said. "Extra for the sago." *Let them pay*, thought Ceris, *they can afford it.* "Poor little mite," she said lifting the cover from the baby's face.

She pocketed the money and went downstairs, gazing curiously as she did so at Felicia's pretty arrangement of pictures and at the one or two good pieces of furniture, fixing them in her mind so she could entertain her friends later to a full description of the house, and the look she had seen pass between the drover's boy and Catherine.

When she'd left, they stood in the kitchen together, surrounded by the devastation of the day. The breakfast plates still unwashed, Father's bags dumped by the door. Deio's forgotten coat, which lay over the chair by the range. Eliza, taking Catherine in her arms, saw the look in her eyes of someone too young to have seen so much. She smoothed back her sister's wild hair and hugged her tight.

"Poor darling Catty," she said, "poor love. You were so brave."

"No." Catherine looked straight ahead of her, her mouth struggling. "I was hopeless. I didn't know what to do."

The pain in her eyes was so terrible that Eliza, determined not to cry, said in her grown-up voice, "I'm sure you did, cheer up, we'll get her better."

She looked so forlorn that, in spite of themselves, they both gave strange grimacing laughs, and then hugged again. "How did people live without sisters?" Catherine thought, not for the first time.

"Are you hungry, Catherine?" Eliza was trying in a muddled way to clear the table.

"No," said Catherine. "But I want to change my clothes. Leave that to Mair, she'll tidy up." Her shoulders were very cold, and her teeth were chattering.

Eliza led her upstairs into their bedroom, unhooked her dress and helped her into a clean nightdress; Catherine was still shivering. "We should go in and see her now," said Eliza.

Hand in hand, they walked across the landing. Through the window the stars were coming out and, in the tall trees outside, rooks were settling in their nests. Inside her room, Mother was asleep, a lamp burning on the table beside her. The baby and the crib were gone.

Mother's face was so pale now that her lips looked blue. When Catherine gently stroked her cheek, she butted against her hand like a kitten. And at that moment, it seemed to Catherine that she looked upon the most precious gift of her life, and that all the objects in the room: the bed, the tapestry chair, the sentimental picture above the bed of a lad and lass in an English garden, had become remarkable and touched with an extra light.

"Sit there." Eliza settled Catherine into the blue chair beside Mother's bed. The same armless chair Mother had fed them in as babies.

"I'll bring some bread and cheese. It may be a long night," she said, leaving the room. How grown-up she sounded, all within a day.

Eliza came back with some inexpertly hacked slices of bread and cheese. They ate ravenously for a moment before pushing their plates away. It made them feel sick to eat while Mother lay like that. Also, the smell, sick and sweet.

They sat in silence for a while, as though frightened that words, or even the sound of their own breathing in their ears, might disturb Mother or stop them from hearing something important. Then Eliza got up and busied herself, hanging up Mother's dress, straightening the bed, and putting some primroses in a blue vase on the bedside table.

Watching her through half-asleep eyes, Catherine found these small observances comforting. Sweet Eliza playing dollies. She had a sense of everything being out of her hands now, as though she were a very small boat out on a far larger sea than she had ever imagined: she must wait now for the waves to take her where they would. From somewhere outside in the yard, she heard the honk of a goose. She closed her eyes and slept, dreaming of herself caught in a shop somewhere, wading through a stream of materials—organzas, silks, satins—certain she was urgently needed elsewhere, unable to stop herself twirling and beaming at her reflection in the glass in dress after dress after dress. When she awoke with a start and a stiff neck, the first thing she smelled was her mother dying, and grief flooded in like water in a sinking ship. Eliza stood at the door, a bowl of potpourri in her hands.

"Eliza." Catherine stood up. "Leave the room for a while. I'm going to change Mother's sheets and clean her up. I know what to do now."

Eliza's small white hands plucked at two drooping primroses, threw them into the wastepaper basket.

"Please don't, Catherine, don't touch her, I beg you. Ceris will be back later, or Mair. Let them do it."

She looked so embarrassed that Catherine almost gave in.

"Let her go with dignity," Eliza said.

"Dignity," said Catherine, whispering furiously. "Damn dignity. I want her to live."

They stood on either side of the bed glaring at each other like two strangers who had collided in a freak accident, then Eliza, with a tearing sob, left the room, knocking over the vase of flowers as she went. Catherine, blundering around on the floor in a mess of water and broken pottery and petals, heard a faint cry from the bed and, jumping to her feet and rushing to the bedside, saw a thin line of what looked like black treacle coming from her mother's mouth. She wiped it away with the back of her hand. Life was neither pretty nor fair, she knew that now, all at once: not the dainty little garden in the sampler Mother had embroidered in the picture above the bed, with hollyhocks and delphiniums and roses around the door; not pretty dresses and nice young men and darling babies, but hard and ugly and awkward; from now on, her only hope lay in facing up to this.

She changed the bedclothes, drawing back in horror in spite of herself from the steady stream of green and black lochia that flowed from her mother. There would be no turning back now to the life of beautiful lies. Gently, Catherine touched the tips of her two fingers against her mother's face.

"Don't struggle anymore," she said clearly, without knowing where the voice came from. "Go now."

Once again Mother pushed her cheek against her fingers, like a kitten hungry for affection. Her lips moved slowly and painfully, without making any sound.

"And I love you," burst out of Catherine. "I love you."

A collection of terrible and painful thoughts seemed to be massing behind Mother's skin, exhausting, inexpressible thoughts.

"Don't talk," Catherine begged, "get better."

But there was no getting better, she knew. The dark wave was gaining in speed, poised against the black sky, ready at any moment to roll over all of them. Outside, the sound of animals being fed: the clank of a pail, a pig shrieking with joy. Dawn was breaking in a breathless pink outside the window.

Eliza and Father came in, came to the bed.

"Can she talk to me?" he asked Catherine in a loud boom that made her wince. She shook her head.

He sat down so heavily on the bed Catherine wanted to cry out, "Watch her, you fool. Be more careful."

Father took Mother's hand into his red paw and said in the soft crooning voice he usually reserved for horses, "Don't worry, my darling, we'll soon have you right. You're a good old girl." He raised her hand to his lips. "A very good girl."

It was the closest he'd ever come to saying love words. Felicia seemed to nod, her eyes to flicker.

"Is all well between us?" he struggled on. "Is all well? Squeeze my hand if you say yes."

Whether she squeezed or not, Catherine never knew. She turned away, unable to bear the sight of them slumped on the bed together, head to head, like broken dolls.

A few moments later, the color of Mother's face changed from white to mottled mauve. Her breathing came in several hoarse rattles, and then stopped. As Father plunged down to listen to her breathing, Catherine saw that his breeches were torn, and that she could see straight through to his combinations. She hated him at that moment: hated him, blamed him, pitied him. Herself and him.

Chapter 6

On the day of Mother's funeral, the body was moved out of the front parlor, then carried by a black plumed horse to the top of a lonely hill at Clynnog Fawr, to St. Beunos Church, the only local church that performed English-language ceremonies.

When the door creaked open, the candles flickered and a fresh blast of chill air swept up the aisle. The vicar, Reverend Norman, a thin, high-shouldered man working out his last year before retirement, shuffled up the aisle. Behind him Father and Alun, Twm and Mr. Pitkeathly, the church warden, carried the coffin.

"I am the resurrection and the life," the vicar said in his thin wheezy voice. He cleared his throat and started again.

"I am the resurrection and the life. He that believeth in me, though he were dead, still shall he live."

Catherine, looking through her fingers at the coffin, felt such a wave of anger and despair that she wondered if it would be possible to go on living in such pain. Before, all her griefs had been such little ones—a trifling punishment, the death of a dog, a row with Eliza. She had existed in a bubble of happiness and protectedness, and now the bubble was burst and she was left shivering and defenseless. All at once she felt the desperate loneliness, the unlivedness of her mother's life. She had never fitted in here, never properly been known or loved or understood for herself. Only two people had even come to see her during the three days she'd lain in the front room: Father, of course, and Aunt Gwynneth, his widowed sister, a woman Mother never liked. She'd stood there gazing down at her, reading from a stone-colored book called *The Strength of My Life.* Mother would have hated it.

Catherine cast a wild look in the direction of her father, who stood next to Eliza at the end of the pew. He looked distinguished in the smart frock coat inherited from his own father and worn only once before, at his wedding. Mother from time to time had begged him to dress up and take them out. Such a small thing to ask, but he'd always been so busy with the animals, a deliberate busyness that was part of his determination to throw off his privileged past, to be a proper Welsh farmer who spoke Welsh and had dirt under his fingernails. Determined for himself but not for them, not for his girls. For his girls it was always "be dainty . . . eat like a lady . . . watch your complexion." And for God's sake never have fun. He was a hypocrite, an impostor, and in the end nobody, nobody had been fooled.

"Catherine! Catherine . . ." Her aunt, seeing her look so strangely at her father, touched her sleeve and inclined her head in a significant way toward the vicar.

From the end of the church, the vicar's voice, competing poorly with the wind and the boom of the waves outside, recited in indistinct gasps. "Man born woman . . . hath but a short time to live and is full of misery . . . cometh up." A large wave, rising, falling, crashing on the rocks below washed the words away. "And is cut down like a flower . . . fleet . . . shadow . . . and never continueth in one stay."

And it was there, standing in that dark church, that Catherine prayed the most fervent prayer of her life: "Help me live my life."

When it was over, she followed the coffin down the aisle toward the patch of blue sky outside. At the door, Mr. Pitkeathly was smiling apologetically. "Forgive me, Miss Carreg," he murmured, "but men only to the grave."

She carried on walking, not understanding.

"Ladies stay inside," he stammered, putting his hand up to her arm.

Men only to the grave. She'd stood in the half-dark of the church porch, bewildered, stranded, and then, when she understood, wanted to scream with rage.

"It's a ridiculous convention, isn't it? I've always wanted to know what part of the Bible God said it in."

There was a murmur from inside the church and several people in the rows turned around to see who had spoken. Catherine saw that it was Eleri Holdsworth, a tall woman with wild white hair, an artist who lived on the headland and whom Mother had admired from a shy distance. Now Eleri held out a hand to Catherine in the dark and squeezed her hand with surprising warmth.

Catherine looked at her without speaking.

"Please come and see me, please do, when you are ready," said Eleri quickly. "I have something for you."

Then Aunt Gwynneth, bustling and frowning, had come out and taken her arm and led her inside again.

Deio groaned out loud as she left his sight. He was up on the hill, standing between two ash trees. He'd been there for close to an hour, sure he would not be welcome inside. He'd seen the small party of men walk up the hill, the earth being flung, the church doors opening again. His eyes swept over the mourners, now crunching their way slowly down the hill, heads down against the wind. Then she'd raised her head and looked up without seeing him. He saw the whiteness of her skin and the look in her eyes and, for that moment, felt her wounds. He could have howled; this was not what he wanted; it was everything he wanted. He was so torn, so lost; he wanted to own her, to protect her, to be free. Watching her, he unthinkingly tore a clump of grass from the ground. He picked out a danesberry from the grass; the plant his ancestors said had the power to help souls from one life to another. He took some of the berries in his hand and, squeezing them open, stained the palm of his hand a deep bright red.

Chapter 7

$\mathcal{R}$ iding home, passing a farmyard where sheep were being sheared, Deio felt the same: skinned and undone; calling out in an uncertain voice for something he was not sure of. He couldn't let her do this to him again, he thought, slamming his legs into his horse's side. Never again.

He'd been a boy then; now he was twenty-two and preferred it this way. The next day, he would start the ride across the mountains to London and that always made him feel good. He'd come back from Smithfield, from Kent, from Wrexham, saddlebags stuffed with money and strange food and London linens, new shotguns and bridles, quilts, bits of jewelry for the girls. He'd have stories to tell, stories that kept other men spellbound in the taverns, sagging over their ales and saying "Never! And Duw! Duw! Duw!" Not a sniveling boy exploding with pain in an upstairs bedroom, hoping his parents couldn't hear him; not a dog creeping through the Carreg's backdoor, unsure of his reception.

She'd raised her head, she'd looked at him again with those eyes. He would look away. He had no other choice and that was all it took, a clear decision: she looked, and you looked away, and in time it would probably get easier.

His horse, dapple gray and four years old, shied at her reflection in a puddle. He hardly ever lost his temper with a horse, but now he gave it a sharp one and she cantered for a few strides, stiff-legged and sideways, then he sat deeply and tuned himself to her, gathering her up and making her as calm and comfortable as a rocking chair. He knew about horses, it was bred in the bone. He understood the roots of their terror, their need to escape, and the right degree of force and tenderness it took to get them both to trust and accept you as the man in charge.

It worked with women, too. They were mad for the drovers, waited for them in every town, lay down with them in the night bucking and biting and calling out. You could never tell a woman like Catherine a thing like that. Even now, when he thought of that redheaded girl in Bala—her long waist; her high, hard breasts—he knew he wanted to stay free. He closed his eyes briefly, he pushed his long legs deeper into the saddle and made the gray horse sweat and stretch out and go to the point where fear met freedom. He told himself he felt better already.

But when the horse was walking again, relaxed now and calmly swishing away flies with its tail, he saw Catherine's face looking up at him from the church porch. He saw her eyes bewildered by sorrow and felt her power to wound. It had happened before: *Mother says I can't come anymore.* That night he'd slammed his fist into the wall so hard he'd almost broken it, then his hateful sobs and his father's scorn and, even worse, kindly chat about never letting a woman do that to him, and then the closed door, until now.

Now he was at the duck pond rimmed with feathers, slap in the middle of the boundary line between Pantyporthman, his Da's thirty-acre farm, and Huw Carreg's hundred acres. His home— from here a sprawling series of stone buildings surrounded by stack barns and small wooden corrals—seemed set apart and special, a self-contained island of noise and excitement amid the more peaceful farms of the Lleyn. He loved everything about it: its sweeping views to the east and the west, the fields where they kept their broodmares, their trout stream, the foothills of Snowdon beyond, tonight bathed in pink light after the storm. From where he sat, he could hear the dinning of two hundred head of cattle, pent up and anxious before their journey; the shouts of men, the yaps of the corgis, Nip and Ben, who'd come with them to London; the deeper bark of Fly, their collie.

In the yard in front of the stack house, four men were herding a group of thirty or so Welsh blacks into a small field to the left of the house. His older brother, Rob, stopped when he saw him.

"Where you been, boy?"

"I went to Matthew Butts." Deio named a blacksmith who lived near Nevin.

"Any luck?" said Rob, tensely. If they couldn't shoe their cattle, they couldn't leave for London.

"None at all," Deio teased, glad he'd got one thing done that day. "He can only do it tomorrow if we ride them over."

"Thank God for that," said his brother, smiling. "He's been getting himself in such a lather you could shave with him."

Deio looked swiftly across the yard toward his father, Lewis Jones. He was dosing a heifer and had his arm over its neck and a finger in each nostril. "Yer varmint," he said softly, "ged in there. Give me the horn," he said to Rob. A thick green mixture was poured down the hollow horn. The cow rolled its eyes and coughed.

"I couldn't swear to him having the hoosh," said Lewis in his deep, slow voice, "but I'm not taking no chances."

He loosened the noose, clouted the beast on its rump, and with his eyes half-narrowed took a long measuring look at the other cattle in the yard. Lewis Jones knew just about as much as it was possible to know about a herd of cattle without actually growing horns himself. He saw them with a stockman's eye, constantly on the alert for hoven and hush and garget and pleural pneumonia; for the streaming noses and listless eyes that could decimate a herd and spell their ruin. They were banknotes on four legs: each one of these cows bought at ten pounds apiece in Wales would double in value in London.

It took months of detective work to assemble the group of Welsh Blacks such as he looked at so impassively now. First, the long, carelessly inquiring chats about who was going broke and who was selling cheap, then going to summer fairs and leaning over gates as if you had all the time in the world, until it was the right time for a palm to be slapped and a deal struck and another ten or fifteen cattle entered into his books. His reputation rested on his shrewdness: the locals expected nothing less from a man who held their livelihood in his hands.

When the cow was drenched, he straightened himself up slowly and bellowed at Deio.

"What kept you? You've been hours gone."

"I've been getting a blacksmith," shouted Deio. "*Working*."

Lewis Jones in his worst moods reckoned none of them worked as hard as he did. Once, because Deio was as hot-tempered as his father, this might have led to a fight. Now he knew that on the nights before they left rows sprang up sudden as electrical storms and it was better to keep your mouth shut. He'd learned, too, after three trips to London, the point to his father's tyrannical behavior in the matters of punctuality and oiled leathers and tightly wound ropes and checked supplies of medicine. Out on the mountains, a sick beast, a thrown shoe, a lame horse, could mean ruin.

Ten minutes later, when he walked into the tack room, his father was rolling the tarpaulins up into the tight cigars each man would tie on the front of his saddle.

"There's some ale and bara brith in the kitchen if you want it, lad," he said. "Get it down you while you can."

"Yes, Father," Deio gave him his cocky smile, and his father put his head down, glowering. It didn't do to let a boy like him get too familiar.

Deio walked back into the house, through a door scuffed with dog paws, into the warm heavy, stale atmosphere of the kitchen. His mother, Meg, was surrounded by saddles, canvas bags, men's boots, leather gaiters, cow horns, hammers, nails, flitches of bacon, girths, sacks of flour, and bread. He walked in and smelled bara brith hot from the oven, cats, leather dubbin, cows, old pies and rabbit stews and sticky fruitcakes and new baked bread. The smell of home.

Meg sat by the fire sewing a saddlebag. He looked at her closely; like his father, he missed nothing.

"You are crying because he is going, or crying because he's a mean old bastard?"

"Both," she said. She picked up her pipe, sucked on it, and looked at him, smiling at her own stupidity. "And don't you dare talk about your father like that, even though I may have to kill him one day."

"Well, finish those before you do"—he gestured toward the saddlebags—"or he'll be roaring again."

"Oh will he," she muttered fiercely, dragging away on her pipe.

"Oh will he? We'll see about that." She had his wonderful eyes and brown skin like a gypsy; the kind of woman who belonged outside.

She got up to get Deio some food and then, to make him laugh, clenched her fists and waved them comically in the air. He never worried about her really: she was strong at the center, you could not crush her for long. Out from the oven came some bara brith, moist crumbs of fat gleaming and the currants still hot enough to hurt the mouth. Then she took down her bread from the cupboard, and the butter she had churned in the dairy. She poured him a glass of ale and some for herself and lit her pipe again, watching him from a distance through the smoke. She looked at her boy, wolfing down his bread and cheese as if he couldn't wait to get outside again. Not bred for captivity. Just like his father.

"So where were you this afternoon?" she asked softly.

"Nowhere."

"Nowhere?" she said. She picked up a skein of thread from her basket and knotted it. "Not at her funeral then?"

"Does it matter?"

"Does it?"

"I don't know."

"Catherine," she said, looking directly at her son, "was for a while like another daughter to me. Poor Catherine," she said softly, her brown eyes very dark and still. "Poor love. Whatever will happen to her now?"

Much later that night, after the animals were fed and watered, and the packs checked and rechecked and the leggings oiled and the dry socks soaped and waterproofed and the fodder tied down, the last gate opened and the cattle swept like a dark avalanche down from the hills and into the herding yards.

Then Reverend Hughes, the Methodist minister from Sarn, came into the kitchen, stood at the head of the table and closed his eyes.

"Let us pray," he said, "for these brave men who face danger and cold and hardship to relieve the hunger of the starving men of England."

Meg Jones, almost feverish now from the high anxieties of the day, added two fervent prayers of her own: "Lord," she prayed, looking through her fingers at her husband. "Keep him out of the kitchen but in my heart, and don't let the railways come to the Lleyn."

She looked at her son who was pale and distracted. Normally on the night before a drove left, once everything was done, he got rowdy and his eyes shone with excitement. She closed her eyes again and thought without thinking that it was funny that the clergyboys warned you about sin and temptation, suffering and evil and all the rest, but the flamers never warned you about love.

Chapter 8

A week after Mother's funeral, Aunt Gwynneth took them to Caernarfon to supervise the purchase of black crepe and bombazine. She had insisted on staying on at Carreg Plâs to help the Poor Dear Girls through this Dreadful Time and was very keen for them to do things properly.

Gwynneth's presence in the house made Catherine almost mad with nervous irritation. Restless and wretched herself, her mind endlessly picking over the hours that had led up to her mother's death and the part she had played in it, what she most wanted was silence—a state Gwynneth regarded as most unhealthy. For Gwynneth, with her red-rimmed, sympathetic eyes and her long damp hands, so ready always to stroke a brow or to mix beef tea, had taken up her position in the house as The One Who Understands. She specialized in flavorless sayings. "It's all for the best whatever" was one, pronounced with a sweet wan smile. "There is nothing so certain as death" was another, guaranteed to set Catherine's teeth on edge.

Now, when Father came in from the fields looking numb and exhausted, Gwynneth, who treated men like backward invalids, drew her chair up close and asked her brother lots of questions: "You were haymaking today were you, Huw? That's nice," or more archly, "I know I'm a silly goose but how can you tell a Charolais cow from a Freesian?" Or "Tell me in *detail* now. How is it you make your lovely Lleyn hedges?" He'd never been much for talking, and now she'd listen to his slow, reluctant answers in a bright and bobbing way, like a bird ravenous for the merest crumb of information. Mealtimes had become a particular strain, beginning with

Gwynneth straightening her back and reading in a tremulous voice from her Bible. Then she'd poke through the pots, fussing about "nourishing titbits" for Father—"For a child milk, and for a man meat," she was fond of saying, passing him the sweetest pieces near the bone while ostentatiously reserving for herself and the girls scraps of wing and gristle and skin.

Now Mair sulked and clashed pots in the kitchen and Eliza, poor Eliza, who tried so hard to find nice things to think and say about everyone, sat and burbled helplessly, trying to fill in the gaps. For Catherine loathed the woman and the feeling, as far as she could make out, was mutual.

This tension between them found an outlet in the question of the front parlor. In Mother's day it had been a delightful room—a little jackdawish and untidy, perhaps, with its china jugs and gewgaws, its papier-mâché inkstands and watercolors, but that was Mother. Gwynneth had taken against it from the start.

"How on earth your poor dear mother found anything in here I'll never know," she'd said, removing the odd picture and occasional table, saying it would make it easier to clean. These were preliminary forays. Then, after two weeks in the house, she'd made her frontline attack: dragged a large tin trunk into the parlor and unpacked a pile of antimacassars, a collection of brittle-looking butterflies inside a glass box, and some books. The books, duncolored, damp to the touch, had various inspirational titles such as *The Strength of My Life* and *One Day at a Time*. They were on loan, she said, from the Methodist church to help them all through this Terrible Time. They were to take a particular care not to get them dirty. Catherine shuddered at the very sight of them.

Gwynneth was also a snob. In reduced circumstances herself (her dead husband had owned a failing tanning works near Pistyll), she made it known, at first obliquely and later with needling remarks of the "you can stoop and pick up nothing" kind, that while it was a very great shame that her brother had turned his back on the life of a gentleman, it was by no means irreversible. So began a new campaign to upgrade the status of this branch of the Carreg family, and thus endless conversations about manners and social niceties and what sort of persons it was proper to consort with, and although Gwynneth's Methodist leanings did not entirely square with the more frivolous philosophies of women's magazines, such as the *Welsh Woman's Domestic Magazine* or the *Ladies' Treasury*, several appeared in the parlor.

These magazines, stuffed with hints on how to make jam, to dress one's hair, to dress well, and how to become a stimulating conversationalist, made it crystal clear that the capture—and the continuous captivation—of a man was the point of a woman's life, and Eliza read them, from cover to cover, with a grave absorption that wrung Catherine's heart. Her sister so much wanted a husband.

Catherine had no words yet for the despair she felt on reading these feeble magazines, and had no wish anyway to spoil the experience for Eliza, who still cried herself to sleep. But at night, often rigid with sleeplessness, she thought of the dream she'd had on the night Mother died: of herself twirling and twirling in a sea of organza and lace and satin, of being wound tighter and tighter in choking, confining dresses, utterly panicked and absolutely convinced she was needed elsewhere.

The row, when it came, exploded unexpectedly. It was a mild summer evening and the air from open windows smelled of night-scented stock and new-mown hay. Father was exhausted so they'd gone to bed as soon as it began to grow dark. About ten o'clock, the dogs started barking, at first rhythmically, then hysterically, their noise taken up by a whole circle of dogs around the peninsula. Then she'd heard the thunder of cattle on the move, and the drover's cry of Hip Hop Tro. It was such an odd cry, not like a song or a greeting or a shout, but a statement of approach and right of way, a determination to exist, as simple and elemental as birdsong. She'd lain on her bed listening in the half light, tears pouring down her cheeks. She'd never felt so lost. It was the wrong time for Aunt Gwynneth, who had moved into the spare bedroom next door, to walk in.

"Catherine, my dear," she said, walking toward the window. "Shut that window at once, what a *noise*."

She grimaced in agony.

"*So* inconsiderate of the persons next door." She leaned over Catherine, with a faint smell of face cream and mothballs.

"Don't close the window, Aunt," she said, raising herself on her pillow. "I like it open. Thank you."

"Oh no, no, no." (Her aunt pronounced it noo, noo, noo.) "It is not a matter of thank you, or what we want always, it is a matter"—she had to shout now over the noise of the cattle—"of what all of us want in the house."

"Leave my window open. Leave me alone." Catherine's voice was bloody and screaming with rage. She got on her knees and pounded her fists into the pillow.

Aunt Gwynneth stood over her with her arm raised and her teeth bared.

"Nobody speaks to me like that, My Lady."

Then Father ran into the room.

"I was trying to help," said Gwynneth, clutching the bosom of her nightdress and bursting into tears. "I am trying to help and she shouts at me."

Father looked at Catherine and Catherine looked back with a calmness bordering on insolence. He slapped her once across the cheek, making a livid mark.

And then he hit her again.

Gwynneth began to shriek, "Oh no! Poor child!"

He stood at the door, glaring at both of them. "I do what I like in my own blasted house," he said.

Gwynneth, lopsided and crying, left the room. Father slammed the door behind him. The dogs had stopped barking outside and Catherine lay in the dark with her mouth open, breathing heavily. The indignity of being slapped was unbearable. She felt like a small, soiled, wounded animal, with no pride and nowhere left to run. She wanted to scream, a terrible scream that would make them all dash back into her room and pay attention. To hurt him as he had hurt her. "She was too young to die," she would have told him. "And you and I killed her."

＊　　＊　　＊

The next morning there was a timid knock on the door. She shuddered in case it was Gwynneth, but it was Eliza.

"I've brought you some bread and some jam and some beef tea," said her sister in the grown-up sensible voice she used whenever she felt a fuss could be averted. She put the tray down and seeing her sister's swollen eyes said, "Oh dear. What happened?"

Eliza flung her arms around her sister's neck. They hugged each other tight and Catherine, feeling herself in danger of a flood of tears that would never stop, pushed her gently away and gestured toward the tray. "You are kind."

"Gwynneth made the tea and Father sent me up with it. He wants to see you after breakfast. Why is he looking so unhappy?"

Catherine squeezed her hand and said in a tiny voice. "I can't live like this, Eliza. . . . It's so—I'm so—I shall end up in Clytha." Clytha was the local lunatic asylum.

"Catherine." Eliza's smile was strained. "Don't be cross with me for saying this, but we are all dreadfully worried for you. You seem so particularly out of sorts, and it's starting to upset Father and—" A furrow appeared between Eliza's usually cloudless blue eyes. "*Please* say sorry to him, vex him no further."

"I'm like a prisoner here," said Catherine. "I have nothing to look forward to, nothing to do, and everywhere I go that woman is there, changing things and giving advice and talking to us about Nice Young Men, oh surely Eli, you feel it, too?"

"I do, darling," said Eliza patting her hand. "But I do believe in . . . in . . ." she looked around wildly for inspiration, " 'one day at a time,' and, it may sound awfully silly to say this, but if you put a smile on your face, you will feel better."

Oh my God, her poor little sister, reduced to quoting from *The Strength of My Life*. "Oh Eli"—Catherine grasped her sister's hand—"dear little goose. If only I was as good as you, and as nice."

"I'm not nice." Eliza squeezed her hand again, it was quite an effort talking to her older sister like this, Catherine had been her heroine for so long. "I just think what would Mother have wanted?"

"Not this," said Catherine. "Not for herself or for us."

*   *   *

After breakfast, she went downstairs and found Father in the parlor.

"Sit down, Catherine," he said. He could not meet her eye. He looked around wildly for the green velvet chair Mother had sat in near the window.

"She's put it near the fire," said Catherine. "It's a more *suitable* position."

He smiled at her, in a bobbing reluctant way. "Sit down there then," he said in a low voice.

"Thank you." She sat down and looked straight ahead.

"I was wondering," he said, stroking his beard, "I mean I know— I have been thinking . . ."

He put his head in his hand and sighed deeply. "What's wrong, Catherine? Tell me. Get it out."

She fought an impulse to say the right thing, the loving thing, the thing that would smooth everything over.

"Send her away," she said softly.

"I don't want to yet," he said. "She's a good woman and you and Eliza won't be here forever."

The plain-faced clock over the mantelpiece was ticking, making her feel more nervous than she already was.

"Then send me," she said in a whisper. He didn't hear her. When she looked at him again, his own face was working against tears.

"I am working day and night to try and get the farm back on its feet," he said. "Can't you see that?" His voice wobbled and died out. "She at least is trying to help, and she is my sister."

"You didn't like her when she was little, old snitch, bossy boots," she thought. She'd heard him say it scores of times.

She longed for him to talk about Mother. Say how he missed her, and how both of them in their own ways might have done more. Anything was better than this numb dislike between them. Then they might have kissed and cried and got this sorrow from them. But he was standing up and sighing and talking about the hay in the top field.

"Cheer up." Father picked up his hat and walked toward the

door. "You've got things to look forward to if you think about it—your grandmother's party for instance, you'll enjoy that."

"In six months time," she almost shouted. "What am I to do until then?"

"I'll tell you what you do, madam." His mouth was quivering with rage, and he had his great hands out, ticking off ideas one by one. "Needlework, shopping, gardening, bottling. It was a good enough life for your mother."

"It was not," she shouted inwardly, "she was half mad with boredom and loneliness."

She saw it suddenly with an inward shudder. They were like two small boats adrift on a huge dark ocean. With her last ounce of self-control, she said, "Father, please let me go out this afternoon. I'll take Juno for a ride? I'll help Aunt Gwynneth this morning with the mending and the flowers, but I must have some air."

He had his back to her but she could tell by the set of his shoulders that he was furious.

"You must do as you please," he said.

"I will," a small cold voice inside her said. "I must now."

Chapter 9

$\mathcal{A}$fter an almost silent lunch, Catherine saddled up Juno for the first time in over a year and rode out. It had rained all morning, and the sun shone on wet grass and shorn fields. She rode in the direction of Aberdaron where Eleri Holdsworth lived in a spartan house overlooking the bay. Catherine had roughly three hours between now and suppertime to carry out the plan that Miss Holdsworth was part of.

It was lovely out, with Juno striding beneath her. Beyond the fields, the sea creased out in silver and pearl folds toward the horizon. Thanks to the horses and to Deio, she knew all the tracks and the fields. She rode past the hollow tree where she and Deio used to play animal doctors with Lily, his spaniel, who adored being handled and who rolled her eyes and swooned with pleasure when they wrapped her in sheets and pretended to bleed her, to lose her, to rescue her. And there, near the stream, was the place where Deio had once made her laugh until she'd nearly wet her drawers, by jumping on a stone and holding out his hat and singing *Ooover tha weengs oh the weengs of a doooove* in the warbly voice of Miss Pitkeathly, who did recitals at the church.

Going down the steep, slippery sheep track that led to Eleri's house, she was glad of Juno's sure tread. A foot or so away from the path was a sheer drop down to the beach, and you could hear the sucking and pounding of the surf below. As a child, when sudden moods of voluptuous misery had come without warning, she had loved it up here, where the whole world—the gulls crying in the empty air, the howling wind off the sea—seemed as lost and lonely as she.

Eleri Holdsworth's house was built in the side of a hill, with an uninterrupted view of the sea. As the gate closed behind her with a click, Catherine felt suddenly nervous and almost changed her mind. Then she saw Eleri, sitting on her own outside her cottage, perfectly still in a battered chair. Beside her, a table with a drink on it, some paint, and what looked like a bundle of sketches. It would be rude to turn back now.

"Good afternoon, Miss Holdsworth." She had to shout above the sound of the sea. "Forgive me . . . are you working?"

Eleri looked at her calmly. "Yes, but I'm very happy to see you." The hand she put on Juno's shoulder was sunburned and splattered with paint.

"I'll take him. You go inside and make yourself at home."

She pointed toward the door and Catherine walked into the cottage to find herself in a kind of studio-cum-bedroom with a beamed roof and simple whitewashed walls. The worktable, on which were neatly arranged sheets of paper, pens, and paints, was set in a bay window overlooking a huge sweep of sea and dominated the room. Beside it were bookshelves bursting with books, a collection of bird feathers arranged in three small glass vases, and some seashells.

"I like your room," she said when Eleri joined her.

"I too," said Eleri. "Would you like a glass of elderflower cordial?"

"Thank you," murmured Catherine. She sat down on the bed, but leaped up with a screech as her hand encountered something bristly and alive.

"Oh dear, I'm sorry, it's Flo." Eleri pulled a badger out from under the cushions. "The hunt gave her to me; one of the hounds holed her up by mistake. She likes to get me up at midnight to run around in circles on the cliff tops."

Catherine smiled at the thought of this old lady (Eleri was at least fifty) dancing in the dark with a badger. Mother would have loved that.

"That's better, your face looked as long as a boot before. Now take your hat off and unlace your boots. You're trussed up like a chicken." She smiled as she left the room, and came back carrying a tray with two glasses of cordial and a plate of bread and jam. Then, to Catherine's amazement, she sat down on the floor beside the fire, stretched her legs out like a man, and lit a pipe.

"Now," she said, "we can listen to the waves or we can talk. You choose."

To give herself time, Catherine asked Eleri how she came to live here. Eleri told her that ever since she was about three or four she had wanted to be a painter. Each summer, her family had rented a house in Aberdaron, and one day, while out sketching with her father, a London surgeon, she had seen this house for sale.

"It had six acres and cost twenty-five pounds, and as soon as I saw it, I said, 'Papa, I've found my place,' and to his credit, he gave me the money and allowed me to stay."

"What a very remarkable man," said Catherine. "But, forgive me asking you, why did he let you stay? It must have been very unusual then. I mean . . . now as well, too. But it was a long time ago . . . oh dear."

"It's all right," said Eleri, laughing at her confusion. "He was, *is* remarkable. He's a great supporter of women and a good surgeon and he watches people very closely and with great interest. Do you remember the Parable of the Talents? Well, it's still his favorite. He believes that people who ignore their gifts do so at great peril to themselves. Your mother, incidentally, I might put into this category. Have a look at that picture over there, near the door. She painted it."

"She painted it!" Catherine couldn't have been more amazed. "Are you sure?"

"She came up to sit for me. I liked her a great deal, we talked, and at the end of our sessions she asked if she could sketch me."

"But it's good." It was a charcoal sketch, a few dashed lines, but she'd caught in them the shrewd kindness of Eleri's expression, the wildness of her hair.

"It's very good," said Eleri. "I told her so at the time, but she didn't believe me."

Catherine's hands were trembling with emotion. Her mother had done this painting.

"Was she good enough to be a painter? I mean, more than a woman who painted?"

"I'm not sure." Eleri puffed on her pipe as she thought about this. "Very difficult to say: a gift doesn't just turn up while you sleep like a ha'penny from the tooth fairy. It's a decision, part of the journey of your life, something that you must seek and work hard for and be ruthless about once you have found it. I did some poor man a very great service by not trying to make myself into a wife. I would have been a monster. Now—" Eleri seemed not to do small talk. "What about your mother? I should have painted her more . . . she was so beautiful . . . you, too . . . shame, shame."

Catherine left a gap here for her to say the usual things about going on to better places . . . heavenly rests and so forth, but Eleri just kept on smoking, one hand wrapped around her knee.

"I was with her at the end, when she died."

"Oh good, a great relief, a bonus," said Eleri. "Did you not find it so?"

"No. I was hopeless," said Catherine. "I didn't know what to do."

"A-hum." More smoke curling around Eleri's head and a sudden boom from the waves hitting the rocks outside.

"Now my aunt lives with us. She is . . ." Catherine searched for words that might convey the meals, the sulks, the furniture-moving. "It is so different and difficult. We miss Mother dreadfully." She felt disloyal but had a great need to clear her head.

"I keep feeling I must go away. I'm so restless; I'm driven to distraction by the sound of the drovers leaving. Do you hear them from here? You do! And oh, I don't know, I feel a great longing to go somewhere where I can learn. Where people talk. Nobody talks at home anymore."

Eleri looked at her for a while, then took a long drink.

"Have you ever been to Bardsey Island?" she asked eventually. "You can see it from this window if you stand on a box."

Catherine felt a wave of anger and embarrassment wash over her. She had opened her heart, and now this good woman was going to try and distract her with scenic wonders.

"I will take you there one day if you like," said Eleri.

"That would be very kind," said Catherine numbly. She wished she could leave now.

"It is supposed to be a magic island: twenty thousand saints buried there—or two thousand, depending on who you are talking to—people for centuries walking from all over Britain to get there. They say Merlin the Magician is buried there inside a glass house."

She talked on for a while about other magic islands, places with trees that were always in bloom, filled with birds that never stopped singing. Catherine saw her mouth moving but hardly heard a word. If she was late home Father would never let her out again.

"The Welsh, all of us, love these stories," she went on. "They take our minds away from how hard life really is—again, it's the idea of life suddenly turning up ready-made for you like a present left at the door."

A sharp wind had got up and was rattling the windows and outside, even though the sun was shining, it had started raining.

"Ah," said Eleri, getting up to close the window, "sun and rain together. The Devil, or so another legend goes, is beating his wife." Her eyes were shining now in the darkening room. "But if thunder is heard while the moon is shining, the devil is beating his mother. To a Celt, the Devil is almost as important an idea as the idea of God."

"I think I really must go home," said Catherine.

"And God help you if you find the Water Horse," said Eleri, "he looks so lovely and he's deadly."

"Do you believe in him?" Catherine was interested at last. "I think about him every time I see the sea."

"No." She put down her pipe. "No, I don't. But I do believe he shows us what we fear."

"What?"

"Well, there he is: beautiful, extraordinary. He stands placidly by the water's edge. We try to mount him, and sometimes you can ride him and you feel so powerful, so wonderful, and the next time he bolts back into the sea with you and you die a horrible and frightening death. What could be clearer?" Eleri's eyes were shining in the dusk. "It's our fear of being out of control. He's the one who tells you to stick with the ordinary, don't move, everything else is dangerous and nothing possible, but the problem is that if you fear everything you can't control, you'll never do anything that matters to you."

When Catherine looked up Eleri was frowning at her. "You are very self-absorbed," she said. "Many people of your age are. Let us suppose for a moment that you did have a hand in your mother's death. What have you done about it since? I mean, apart from walking on the cliffs and feeling misunderstood."

"I have a plan," Catherine said angrily. "That's why I'm here."

"All right, I'll keep my mouth shut," said Eleri. "I talk too much. It's one disadvantage of being on your own."

"No, don't." Catherine leaned across and touched Eleri's hand. "Please don't stop."

"Well?"

"Well—" Her mouth went dry. "I want to be a doctor. I do know your father is a surgeon and I want to go to London," she blurted out. "I want to be a doctor. I want to save some woman somewhere from the misery my mother went through. She shouldn't have died like that."

"Lots of women do."

"I know."

The room grew quiet for a while, only the boom of the sea.

"I used to watch you sometimes," Eleri said eventually, "with that drover's boy on the cliff. I heard you once tell him your pony had a toothache, you'd tied its jaw in a bandage."

"Oh no." Catherine covered her face in confusion.

"No, no, no, don't. It was so charming, it made my day to see it, and then you both bolted down the beach to pick up some more patients. How you survived I'll never know. All that rushing into the sea with wooden swords."

"Oh dear." Catherine went scarlet.

"Don't be embarrassed, you were such warriors. It did my heart good to see you."

Catherine looked at her. "So what do you think?"

"Oh Lord." Eleri sighed. "Now you've absolutely ruined the point of my little homily by setting yourself an impossible task. There aren't any woman doctors."

"There must be."

"One, Catherine. One, I think, in the whole of London. My father knows her, she's an ancient spinster like me and as fierce as a man. I'm sorry, there is no point in encouraging you to do something that will ruin you."

"Are there any other proper jobs for women in London?"

"You could be a governess, but again what a life! My father visits at a place in Harley Street. I can't remember the exact name— a something, something, for the care of Sick Gentlewomen in Distressed Circumstances. He says they're such sad creatures— exhausted, poor."

"But at least a life of their own."

"To some extent, though most would prefer someone else's."

"But they earn their own living."

"They earn their own living."

"Who runs that home?"

"I know nothing about her, apart from the fact that father says she is well-born and quite bossy."

"Perhaps I could stay there, a respectable place."

"Yes, respectable." Eleri stood up and lit a lamp.

"You did what you wanted to do, even though it seemed mad to everyone else."

"Look, Catherine," said Eleri. "It's not impossible, nothing is, and if you are not afraid of going down the social ladder you might gain practical experience as a nurse and study as you go along. But I can't recommend it as a way of life—" She broke off. "Have you spoken to your father about the idea?"

"No." Catherine's heart sank. "He won't be in favor of it."

"My father would be," said Eleri suddenly. "He believes that it is high time nursing attracted more respectable people. He is also that rare thing: a man who genuinely admires women."

"Might I speak to him?" Catherine cried.

"Possibly."

"Can I come and see you again?"

"Yes, but don't come in the morning, I like to paint then." It was the first time Catherine had ever heard a woman state how a day could be arranged to suit herself. She took one of Eleri's brown, paint-flecked hands in her own and kissed it. "Thank you," she said.

At the bend in the road, she turned in her saddle to wave. Eleri was at the gate.

"Good luck," Eleri shouted. "Be brave."

The wind blew back her white hair, revealing the pink of her scalp. Against the vast sky and empty fields, even handsome, vigorous Eleri looked small and temporary. But soon she would walk back into her house and turn up the lamp and begin her work.

Catherine rode down the track to the beach where a lump of lichen-covered driftwood, about three-foot high, had washed up on the beach. She shortened her reins and pointed Juno toward it. As they gathered speed, her mind, as it always did, flashed to the shock and the pain of a fall, the sand slamming into her wet face. Then the moment of suspended joy as she and Juno whooshed through the air to an elegant landing. So often, the bad things you imagined happening did not, and now she had a way forward, not clear, not easy, but better than staying and going mad. But first she must speak to Deio.

Chapter 10

When they were children, he liked building fires for her. When they took the ponies out, his pockets were always stuffed with papers and twigs and a tinderbox. They'd find a hollow, get their food out, and he'd lay down a ring of stones and crumple the paper, crisscross the wood, and select this or that bit of driftwood to wedge it all into place. When they sat in front of the flames, he'd take note of the tall cliffs, and the mountains behind them, and the sea below, and a feeling of quiet ecstasy would come to him and an idea that he would protect her forever.

And here he was, waiting for her again, but he felt wrong now, like someone in a dream, sitting here in his clean shirt and his second-best breeches waiting for her, only this time his heart going like a bloody hammer.

The hut smelled of fish and seaweed. Beyond the half-open door he could see the sea flopping and turning and a small boat moving across the horizon. He'd avoided this place, but now, excited, angry, he remembered it: the flat-out gallops down the beach, the jumps they'd set up, the dares about who could ride farthest into the sea. It was here, in a way, that the end came, even before she came to speak to his mother. They'd been playing a fortune-telling game, and she'd grabbed his hands, opened his palm, and leaned forward, her conker-colored hair brushing his face, silky and sweet smelling.

"Young man," she'd said, in the gypsy voice that normally made him laugh. "Sometimes I dinks you a little bit happy, sometimes I dinks you a little bit sad."

But on this day the scent of her, the exquisite trail of sensation her finger had left running down his lifeline, had excited him so much he'd almost cried out in pain. Later, he knew that whatever it was they had together was gone, replaced by nothing that he knew about, or understood.

He took out the same fob watch that had so impressed her years ago. His father's name was engraved on its lid: Lewis Jones, drover, Pantyporthman. Ten to four. He was ten minutes early. The sky was already turning from blue to a deep glowing pink. Later in the day, the fishermen's wives would come down to the beach with their children to check the nets and pick up some wrack for their sacks. Unusually for him, he'd been ahead of himself all day: getting up early this morning to creep around and bathe in secret, then lying to his father about a blacksmith's appointment, and finally rushing here like some great soppy girl, when he'd hoped to arrive late and swing from his horse in a calm manner and be what he normally was with women, the man in charge.

He heard the crunch of her horse's hooves first and then the creak of her saddle.

"Deio?" she called out softly.

"I'm here, Catherine," he called from the dark.

She came into the hut and took off her hat. She wore a blue velvet riding habit, and her skin glowed from the gallop.

"I like your new horse," she said.

"He's all right."

"A very nice one," she said brightly, reminding him of the tone her mother had used to try and bring the locals out.

"A bit too clever," he said, "but I'll sort him out soon."

"On a drove?"

"Yes."

"To London?"

"Yes."

Goddamn her, and her mother. He seemed to have lost the power of speech.

They sat down beside each other on the wooden bench that ran around the walls of the hut, and all he could think about was how once, when they were children and sitting on this same bench, he had made her, for a test, put out her tongue and touch his. The feeling had amazed him—it was like holding a live and landed fish in your mouth. Afterward he'd wrestled her, and they'd raced down the beach on their ponies. She'd never tell in those days, you could depend on her. *Tell-tale-tit your tongue will split, they'll feed it to the puppy dogs bit by bit.* She was a fierce little girl with her own principles.

Memories, half-forgotten now or re-formed into something the mind could manage without shame and denial, a few more stilted words, and then that look of determination he remembered crossed her face, and she looked him straight in the eye and spoke in an attempt at the schoolmarm's voice they'd once used for fun.

"I suppose you're wondering why I asked you here today."

He said no he hadn't given it a thought, he was too busy, and she'd blushed a deep red.

"Well, I have a favor to ask you, a very big favor."

"Oh." His voice implied he owed her none, but his mouth went dry.

But as she talked about her plan, to go with him to London, without telling her father who would forbid it, he became aware of an excitement growing, then a keen disappointment as his mind caught up with his emotions, and he heard her talking about a governess home, and her desire to be anywhere but here, "and on my own," she finished up, "to think my own thoughts." And "I have ten sovereigns saved," she said, as if it was some vast fortune.

"So will you please consider me? I could help with the horses and other things. Please."

She put her fingers over her mouth as though she couldn't bear the suspense, and when she looked at him with those beautiful slanting tawny eyes, a wave of fury swept over him.

"No," he said eventually in a flat voice.

"No?" she was appalled. "Why not?"

"We don't take ladies, not to London. And what about your father?" It seemed to her he was exaggerating his Welsh accent. He gathered up his bridle as though about to leave.

"Look," she said, "wait." Her voice had begun to tremble. "I came here asking for some measure of protection from you. It had not occurred to me that I would have to ask your permission." She stood up from the bench. Her chin, with its small, carved dent, tilted toward him. It flashed through his mind to take her arms, to pin them over her head and still that agitated body with the full weight of his.

"I will tell my father as soon as I am settled. His life will be very much easier without me, I loathe and detest his sister."

A child, he thought, *a spoiled little girl.*

"What are you thinking?"

"That we can't take you. We don't take ladies to London."

"Why so?" Once, a long time ago, when he'd pushed her off her pony into a water bucket, she had got in such a rage with him that she'd stood up and calmly whacked him one around the face. He'd felt the sting for an hour afterward. Now, he saw the same look in her eyes.

"Highwaymen, stampedes, mad bulls, bogs—and that's before you get to the borders."

He was still young enough for his own lip to tremble with pride at all he had already seen and been through.

"How brave, Deio," she said. "I bet all the girls think you're quite the man."

He looked at her with no expression; everybody knew his reputation.

"Stuff and nonsense," she said. "Why do men always pretend the things they do are so impossibly difficult? And what about those women who walk to London every year to pick flowers or take cheese? How ever do they manage?"

"The weeders are not ladies." It took a great effort of will not to shout.

"They are women. And what pray do you mean by a lady?"

He took his hat in his hand and worked it around in his fingers. "I don't have to tell you, Catherine," he said. "People like you are too well bred for the likes of us."

As she closed her eyes to defend herself against accusations she felt he could justly make, he saw the sunlight dapple over her eyelids and, hearing the sucking and the gentle slapping of the waves, he felt his own courage falter and slide.

"They were frightened of us growing up too fast," she said in a small voice. "Can't you understand that?" She blushed and looked away.

"There was nothing not to understand," he said. In the silent moment that followed, there was a commotion outside the hut. They went outside and saw that Jewel had caught his legs in the tether rope and was pulling back.

"Woah, pretty one," she murmured, while he unwound the rope, "calm down now. We'll stay in the sun with you."

On the cliff tops high above them, a row of seagulls followed a pinprick man plowing a field. He saw her look around briefly to check there was nobody else.

"Mustn't let anyone see us," he teased, and for the first time she saw the familiar dimple in his cheek.

As they sat down in the hollow of a sand dune, a dragonfly landed between them.

"The Devil's Messenger," she said softly.

"What?"

"Nothing." She had her back to him; now she turned to face him.

"Do you know something, Deio? I have tried very hard to live the life of a nice young lady here, to be good and modest and ignorant, and I am heartily sick of it. I have none of the fun of farm girls, who have friends and can do proper work on the farm, and none of the privileges of the ladies who are educated and who go on outings. I hate my life and I curse my ignorance. Listen—"

She had drawn so close to him, he could feel her breath on his face.

"If you won't take me to London as a woman, take me as a man. I will dress as a man, work as a man, and take my chances like a man in London."

Now he felt as angry as she was.

"Where would you stay? Think, woman."

"At this home for governesses, a respectable place, or with other friends."

He knew the modulations of her voice well enough to know that the friends had not been asked yet.

"What would you do there?"

"That's up to me."

"Not if you want me to take you, it isn't."

"Work. I want to do nursing or medicine."

"Nursing!" He thought of the nurse he'd met on his second trip to London, in a tavern near Smithfields, slack-faced with drink and wild for it. Her room, her tattered stockings, her moans as she bent forward and he took her without even taking off his britches.

"Oh Deio," she laughed suddenly. "If only you could see your face and the horror on it. Why shouldn't I work as other people do?"

He smiled bitterly.

"Deio." Her arms were about him before he had time to think and, for a moment, her body rested against his. He felt her breath on his face, and smelled her hair. He closed his eyes and breathed out slowly. For a second his hand rested on her face.

"Don't do this, Catrin," he said. "You don't know what London's like."

She took one long breath of him then let him go. "We mustn't do that again," she said in a shaken voice. "It would put quite another complexion on my request."

"Yes," he tried to smile, "quite another." He took a strand of her hair that had escaped from underneath her hat and gave it a small tug before tucking it behind her ear. He sighed and walked away.

"My brother Rob is in charge of hiring now," he said, "and, let me get this straight: you want to go to London to see your aunt and to study?"

"Yes. Yes. I've said all that."

"Wait. I need to get this in my mind."

"On the next drove?"

"The next drove. Which is three days time, from here to Bala, Llangollen, and then London." He heard her catch her breath. It was sooner than she'd expected. "I am not saying yes and I am not saying no."

His face, apart from a muscle working in his jaw, was expressionless again, and she remembered how implacable he could be, even as a child.

"I will ask him and I shall leave my answer in a letter in this hut tomorrow."

"Please say yes." She cursed herself even as the words left her mouth. She sounded like one of those pitiful girls in novels. He stood up and slipped the bit between his horse's lips. Up on the cliff, the man with the plow made his patient way back, the birds wheeling and shrieking above his head.

"I'll leave a note for you here, tomorrow at four," he said.

Chapter 11

When she went back to the hut two days later, there was a bag underneath the bench with some clothes inside it. He'd left a small pair of green wool breeches, patched on the inside leg, which she vaguely remembered him wearing when young; a smock of coarse wool, and a bullycock hat that was black and could be pulled down low over the temples. Inside a pair of battered leather gaiters was a note written in his careless hand: "Rob can see you. He is short one boy to drive the beasts. I said you were from Abersoch."

She squeezed the note into a tight ball in her hand and felt her heart thump. Her life until now had been so carefully orchestrated and planned. In the diaries that Mother, and then their governess, Miss Wilkinson, encouraged them to keep, each hour was accounted for: from eight till nine breakfast; from nine to ten, French; walk after lunch—and so forth. She'd begun to loathe the boredom of routine without understanding how securely it yoked and guided her. Now, even the idea that she could, at least for a while, be free made her shake with fear.

It was twilight by the time she walked up the steep hill toward home. The tip of the peninsula and Bardsey Island were lit up by gorgeous streaks of pink and peach light. On a night like this it was easy to believe in magic, in Merlin and his glass house, in Bran and his perfect island.

When she reached the road, a horse and cart quietly clopped toward her. A man with two collies on either side of him turned and waved. "How do, Miss Carreg. Lovely evening." It was Twm

Gwelog, a neighbor for as long as she had been alive, and soon to be part of her past.

Once home, she crept up to her bedroom via the backstairs and lay on the bed in a panic. What had seemed so clear suddenly seemed madness. What if this was all a silly game? One she might regret for the rest of her life? Her escape nothing more than a showy moment, an empty flourish with no follow-through and no plan of subsequent action? She could lose the love and respect of her family, her security, her place in the world.

She lay for a while, her eyes wide open, breathing rapidly through her mouth. Then she got up and took down the bundle of clothes lying on top of her chest of drawers. She took off her lawn dress, her two petticoats and chemise, and stepped into the green breeches. The material prickled against her soft skin and the waistband swam on her. She swaggered around the room for a while, kicked one leg out, and smiled. She could smell the horses again, and the sea. Him.

The fawn smock was too long in the arms by miles, but as her head came through it she felt funny. She wound her hair tightly around her head, put on the black hat, and gazed long and hard at herself in the mirror. Her face was pink with excitement. She *could* pass as a boy. She wanted to keep the clothes on, but it was nearly seven-thirty, almost suppertime. From the kitchen downstairs she could hear Gwynneth—an angry clanker of pots and pans at the best of times—talking in her sharp whiney voice to Mair, whom she was in the process of retraining.

In the dining room, Gwynneth was sitting in Father's place at the head of the table. He was out harvesting and would not be back until late. Eliza sat beside her aunt, looking hunched and depressed. She straightened up when she saw Catherine, and smiled so hopefully that Catherine wanted to take her in her arms there and then. A new look of wary disappointment had crept into Eliza's eyes of late, and what she was about to do, thought Catherine, would only add to her sorrow.

Now Gwynneth leaned over the ham and the vegetables, thanking God for all his gifts. Her blue-veined eyes were closed. Her head was faintly wobbling.

"We started earlier than usual," she said to Catherine when grace was over. "I've sheets to be hemmed for Reverend Hughes. We are all very worried about Mrs. Williams you see," continued Gwynneth, chewing, to extinction a small slice of meat that had been transferred to her mouth.

"Her husband is taken very bad and somebody has to lend a hand." Gwynneth's proud hard stare seemed to indicate, that wonderful someone would have to be her.

Eliza, who was chewing, too, made a kind of little humming sound. Catherine said, "Oh poor you, Auntie, when must you deliver the sheets?"

"Tomorrow of course—one's promise is a debt," said Gwynneth coldly.

Catherine could feel something funny happening to her lip. Her aunt out of the house all day.

"Oh yes," said Gwynneth. "He's taken very bad: sick headaches, agues, and a colicky kind of pain." She ticked the ailments off on her fingers. "Boils, shooting pains in his legs, and am I surprised? *No.*" Her little mouth shut tight as a trapdoor. "Mind you, most of his problems can be laid at the door of the Tavern Goch."

It was on the tip of Catherine's tongue to say "but you don't even know the man properly, and that old misery, Reverend Hughes, thinks that the soul of every man who isn't a regular worshipper is in imminent danger of hell." Instead, she asked, "So we won't be seeing you in the morning or in the afternoon? I plan to have a walk in the afternoon."

Nowadays, she told her aunt what she was going to do, before Gwynneth could get in first with a stream of requests.

"I shall do my sewing and some household tasks with Mair and Eliza in the morning."

"You must do what you like, Catherine," Gwynneth looked at her coldly. "Within sense and reason, of course."

At two-thirty the next day, on the beach at Whistling Sands, a young woman walked into the hut with the green door. Several minutes later, a young man walked out. The young woman, with her picnic basket, her parasol and pretty dress, her bright hair, her sketch pad, her pencils and rug, was designed for decoration and for idleness. The young man, with his coarse smock, his leather gaiters, and long socks coated with soap to avoid blisters, was dressed for hard work.

Once again, the clothes, with their faint smell of leather and animals, gave her a peculiar thrill as though, dressed like this, she could take on something of the power and the ruthlessness of a man. The mood did not last. By the time she reached the track leading down to Pantyporthman, she was feeling so sick with apprehension that she had to hide behind a hedge, her stomach heaving and her heart pounding. What right had she to change her world?

Feeling stiff and unreal, she walked down the path toward Deio's house. A brisk wind had got up from the west and was flattening the feathers of a group of Aylesbury ducks waddling across the yard. In a far yard, behind a fence made of slate and old bedsteads, some dust was rising, and she could see Rob Jones bobbing up and down on a horse. When Catherine peeped over the corral, a Corgi flew at her yapping furiously, and the bay horse—young, Catherine guessed, and newly broken—reared and spun.

"Geeedonwithityervarmint," growled Rob. When he stuck his heels into the horse's sides it leaped into the air like a pogo stick.

"Better, better . . . that's it bachey boy."

Although they were neighbors, Catherine hardly knew Rob—he was ten years older than Deio, part of the adult world. She saw him look at her and then ignore her as the horse, frightened by a sudden whoosh of wind rattling the fence, gave another leap. He gave the animal a sharp one with his stick, made it canter, and, when the bay saw it wouldn't move him, it grew quiet and started to concentrate again. Rob jumped down and led the horse toward her.

"Good-day boy," he said, with the hint of menace farming men reserved for strangers on their land. "What's up?"

"Boy from Abersoch," she said, in the gruffest voice she could manage. "For the job."

"Ah, boy from Abersoch," said Rob, his teeth bared in concentration. "You'd slipped my mind."

He unbuttoned one of his gaiters and when he straightened up, was alarmingly male with his black hair tossing against the sky, "Why so?"

She thought for a brief moment that he must have recognized her and said nervously, "Why what, sir?"

"Why do you want the job?"

"For money, your honor." She smiled with relief.

He laughed.

"Good. A lot of boys think droving is a great adventure. The last one of those we had ended up down the side of a cliff. Poor bastard. Can you ride, boy?"

"Yes, sir."

"Any good?"

"Good enough."

"Want to try this one?"

"If you like, your honor."

The young horse was still weaving and stamping its feet. She stepped forward and put her hand on its stirrups. "Stay where you are," said Rob. "You're no help to me with your back broken." He was thinking aloud. "If you did ride him to London, mind, we could sell him on and you could walk home." He appraised her as if she was no more than a lump of meat.

"I could do that," she said.

The wind was getting up so high, he told her to follow him into the tack room. They sat on either side of a table sagging with saddles and bits of tack and horse physics. "We're taking about two hundred Welsh Blacks to England," he said. "We'll start with about a hundred and pick up others at fairs and farms on the way. We'll need more men when we get to the mountains."

A collie dog walked in, sat, and moved his silver eye restlessly from Rob to Catherine. He looked like his master: hardworking, shrewd.

"Know anything about cattle?" Rob put his hand on the dog's head.

She shook her head.

"We buy 'em for between four and five pound each, sell 'em for about ten pound when we get to Smithfield. What with ferrying and shoeing and tollgates and boys like you, we earn every penny of what's over. You savvy, boy? If one of those stampedes or falls over a cliff or gets lost because you've been sleeping on the job, you will get a wanding you will never forget, and the price of the cow will come from your wages."

He told her the wage was one and six a day all found, rising to one and nine by Llangollen if she was worth it, and pulled a notebook and quill and ink from a drawer stuffed with mole traps.

"Your name, boy, before you leave? For my accounts."

"Joseph," she said, on the spur of the moment, "Joseph Morgan. Jo for short."

She had been taught never to tell a lie and her face flooded with color.

"From?"

"Abersoch." Damn, she'd chosen a town near enough for him to have relatives there. "Abersoch, Caernarfonshire."

"Great Britain, the World," he said, smiling properly for the first time.

He put out his hand to strike the bargain. Raised it and slapped it down against hers with a force that left it tingling for hours.

Chapter 12

*G*wynneth and Eliza were in the kitchen when Catherine got home, sitting on either side of the kitchen table spooning the late gooseberries into preserving jars. Father sat by the fire, drinking tea, and wolfing down some bread and cheese before going out into the fields again. The harvest was not done yet.

He barely looked up as she walked in. His natural reserve had deepened over the past few months into something more aggravating: a sulky, more-or-less permanent silence. The silence of a disappointed child who will not ask for what he wants. The silence that takes a great deal of energy to ignore and casts a long shadow. "Well, don't look at me then," she thought, disliking her own snappiness at a time like this, "and don't worry. I shall be gone soon."

She drew her eyes away from her father, who was wiping his mouth with the back of his hand, and looked toward the table where Gwynneth was bemoaning the slummocky ways of "Poor Mrs. Williams" whose house—there was no other word for it and they'd have to forgive her—"smelled." Writing, "Gooseberry 1853" in her very small writing on her own spotless labels, Gwynneth commented on what a sadness it was that so few people bothered to take proper pride in such matters nowadays. When she had finished her labels, Gwynneth lined them up carefully beside the jars and the liquid wax and said, without looking up, "And you, My Lady Catherine, have one of your headaches. I can tell by looking."

"How clever of you, Aunt," Catherine lied quickly, seeing an easy escape to her room.

"It's not very clever," said Gwynneth, bunching up her mouth and looking toward Father. "Sketching, riding, rushing about all over the place. An excess of anything is not good. Now where is my remedy?"

Quite worn out with her own importance, she rooted around the dresser drawer until the packet was found. "Do you need magic hand?"

"No thank you, Aunt," said Catherine quickly. Magic hand meant aunt's damp hand dragging seaweedlike across the temples while she murmured "poor child" and "dreadful business" or "it's all for the best whatever." It usually appeared when Father or some other worthy male was around.

"Well, tomorrow," her aunt decreed, "a nice lie-down in the afternoon and no sketching"—she made it sound like a disease— "and no rushing about all over the place mind. Don't you agree, Huw?"

He shrugged, and in that moment Catherine knew that he would not lift a finger to get her back. She looked at him miserably, wondering when they had lost each other. More than anything she wanted a sign from him. There was a clock on the wall above Father's head, with Davies of Caernarfon written on its face. It was five-thirty now. In a matter of hours she would be gone.

"Sit down by me," said Eliza. "Mair will bring you some tea."

Her sister's anxious face made tears rush to Catherine's eyes. Her dear, sweet sister deserved none of this.

"You mustn't worry about me, darling," she said. "I'm all right . . . a little tired maybe."

"Tired?" Auntie Gwynneth's face expressed the disbelief of one who had risen early, bottled ten pounds of black currants and four of gooseberries, and still found time to dispense advice and medicine to Blodwen Williams of Aberdaron. "Are you tired, Huw, with all that harvesting?" Father gave another sulky little shrug and walked stiffly toward the door.

"Go upstairs and lie down for a while," said Eliza. "I'll bring you up some of Aunt's splendid physic and some mint tea." Poor Eliza, always the peacemaker.

After supper, Catherine went upstairs to pack but, instead, threw herself on her bed. Then, remembering Rob's instruction that she should make a will before she left, she got up again and paced about. She looked at her three dresses, her cameo brooch, the bracelet of silver and coral her grandmother had given her. In the end, how laughably little she possessed. Her most precious possession? The lapwing that Deio had carved for her out of driftwood, which she wore around her neck.

Underneath her bed was a dark wooden box where she'd kept the five sovereigns her father had given her—it seemed like years ago—to buy the dress at Sarn. She was putting her money into a leather pouch when Eliza walked in with her tea and saw her on her hands and knees.

"What on earth—?"

"Eliza," Catherine straightened up, "put the tray down; sit beside me on the bed." Eliza sat down, hands folded like a child's on her soft cotton dress. Catherine could have wept.

"Eliza," she said in a low voice, "do you love me?"

"Of corth I do." Eliza, at seventeen, still had a slight but endearing lisp.

"Do you trust me?"

"Yes, oh yes. Catherine!" She grabbed her arm. "What is it?"

"Eliza, please don't be too upset, but I'm leaving home soon, very soon."

"What are you talking about?"

"I'm leaving because if I don't I'll go mad. I can't stand that woman and I can't stand my life. I have to find more to do than this."

She could see Eliza wanting to leap in with words of comfort, new ways of looking at Gwynneth, but knew she must finish in one rush.

"So I am going to London."

"To London!" Eliza's face was almost comically aghast. "Across Snowdon? To England?"

"Oh Eli," said Catherine, smiling through her tears, "you sound like Mair."

"And what if Black Fedu be there?"

They cried together for a while, Eliza's tears trickling down the neck of Catherine's bodice and her dear, pink and white face becoming hot and swollen against her sister's. After a while Eliza said, "Is it Mother still? I still think you blame yourself."

"Partly. I was hopeless."

"Catherine, it was not your fault. Please try to forgive yourself. I miss her so much, too," said Eliza, still sobbing, "but is there nothing I can say that would make you change your mind?"

"No, it's done now," replied Catherine quietly. "Try not to think of it as such a big thing. Men do it all the time, they travel, they study, and the world does not fall apart around them."

"But how will you get to Pwllheli?" asked Eliza, naming the town where the mail coach stopped.

"I'm not going that way," said Catherine. "I'm going with the drovers."

"The drovers! No Catherine, you can't! What will you tell Father? That you're running away with Deio? He'll murder you both when you get back."

"I'm not running away with Deio," said Catherine furiously. "I've wanted to do that journey all my life, and I'm tired of being ignorant. I'm tired of being bored. You must make Father see that."

"*I* must make Father see!" Eliza was as close to rage as she ever came. "Why me?"

"Because I can't reach him. He'll be harvesting until late tonight."

"What?" Horror dawned on Eliza's face. "What are you talking about?"

Catherine, with shaking hands, looked at the watch around her neck. The watch her mother had given her, which had marked off years of filling in the quiet periods of time between eating and dressing and going to bed. "Tonight. There's a party at Pantyporthman. We'll leave after that."

Her sister shook her head and wept.

Hours later, as she embraced her shivering sister on the stairs and saw again the fright on her face, she felt for the second time in her life like a murderess.

The moon was high that night. The drovers were careful to time their leaving to coincide with it, and it was almost as light as day. In its light the distant mountains shone pale blue and ghostly, and the sea broke like liquid silver. She stood in the shadows outside the kitchen door. Her father and the men were out there somewhere in the Nant Field, near the river. She could see the glow of their lanterns in the distance, bobbing up as the rows of corn lay down at their approach. They would finish soon, sit and have an ale together, and talk and laugh in a way she never heard Father laugh inside this house. She thought of him again, and how they had failed each other; how, in place of that warm love both had once felt, there was now a huge baffled blankness. Once she was gone he would not send for her; she would almost bet on it. He would let her slip through his fingers as he had allowed Mother to do, and a part of them both would die off, and he, too proud to acknowledge the hurt, would go on plowing and planting, and speaking in his secret silly voices to the animals that never let him down.

She stopped at the end of the drive where the two roads forked. She made herself feel the agony of turning around and looking at Carreg Plâs for what felt like the last time. The shadows of two large pine trees fell against the L-shaped house. The moonlight left reflections in the upstairs windows. "Good-bye, Mama," she whispered, imagining her still asleep behind the third window on the right. "Wish me luck."

Chapter 13

As Catherine passed the two massive stones at the end of the drive and took the lane leading toward Pantyporthman, she could hardly breathe. She tried to think only of Deio and of the journey ahead—the two fixed points in her world.

From the high hedge beside the road came a sudden scream, followed after an interval by another, then another, as some nighttime creature murdered one of its fellows by slow degrees. The sound made her pant with fear. She had never walked alone at night before, and did not know that time when the dark is alive with the sounds of animals mating, dying, and being born, and a human form becomes a blundering shadow.

She dashed along in a stumbling run for fifty yards or so and then stopped. From across the fields, bursts of music and laughter were coming from the drovers' house. She went down the track, past the pond and barns and fields of waiting cattle, toward the brightly lit house. Now she could hear the sounds of two men playing the fiddle together, trying to outdo each other in speed and dexterity. A flute joined in and there were shouts of "Come on there, Lewis!" and shrieks of laughter. She'd planned to test her disguise by wandering through the merrymakers, but her nerve failed her at the last minute and she stood, crouched, outside the kitchen window.

Raising her eyes above the cracked window frame, she saw several barrels of ale in the fireplace and a table crammed with food: raised pies, a joint of beef, fruit jellies, a big Cut-and-Come-Again cake. It was a little while before she could see Deio. The broad back of Ben Challoner, the local wheelwright, who was wolfing down a huge plate of meat as if it were the last he would see that year, was wedged in most of the window. In a tall chair beside the fire, bald head gleaming in the lamplight, was Mr. Roger Jones who ran the general store at Aberdaron.

It saddened Catherine to see how much jollier these people looked among their own. When Mr. Jones delivered to Carreg Plâs on Tuesdays, he backed from their door, almost incoherent with good manners and excuse-me-misses. Now, red and roaring, he was hollering for Lewis Jones, who was sitting on the settle, to get on and do his party piece. Lewis had a cat on his knee and its tail in his mouth. Lewis's eyes rolled soulfully. He squeezed the cat like a bagpipe, making it spit and yowl. Shrieks of "Stop it, you brute!" from the women, and fresh roars of laughter. The fiddlers, capering and making foolish faces, keeping pace. Meg Jones bent over and pretended to clout her husband upon the forehead and he pinched her on the bosom and said in a squeaky voice, "Oh Meg, my darling, my life," then pulled her on his knee and kissed her.

At the end of the kitchen, the dancers had rolled back a rush mat. Then Deio stood up, his shadow flying against the wall. He was dancing, a boy again, a beautiful heathen boy, lean and brown in the lamplight. He turned and looked straight toward her. She shrank back into the bushes, but he hadn't seen her. He looked again and, with no expression in his eyes that she could read, pulled a girl from the crowd—quite a pretty girl with dark hair and a round, good-natured face—who Catherine vaguely recognized as Mary Jones from Sunday school. Catherine watched her face light up, saw his hand around her waist tighten as he led her toward the dancers. When the music stopped, he swooped down upon the girl. He lightly kissed her and lightly let her go. Then she saw him lift Mary onto the windowsill, as if she were a feather, and kiss her again. Harder this time.

Catherine wanted to smack his smiling face, and the girl's. Then she began to shiver and wrapped her own arms around herself for comfort. This was nonsense, she told herself he was a childhood friend, her companion for the journey. He could play the young stag with whomever he liked. She had not lied to Eliza. That moment—the business in the fishing hut when she had let herself go (for so she thought of it, and even in the dark it made her face burn with shame)—had been nothing more than a regrettable, even wicked, weakness on her part.

He was walking across the kitchen now, another girl smiling like an idiot beside him. Her friend was gone. In his place, a handsome, shrewd young man, with a wary look in his eyes and his arms around any girl he liked. There was a kind of hardness now in those green eyes, a deliberate, even studied, coolness in his manner that both frightened her and set her free.

The rowdy blare of voices faded suddenly to a respectful hush. The Reverend Thomas Hughes stood up, threw a significant look at the clock above the dresser, which stood at a quarter past eleven, then fixed his gaze on the revelers, waiting for their smiles to fade.

"The time has come"—he steepled his fingers and lowered his voice—"for us to attend to the matter in hand. The drovers will soon be gone. Pray silence for these men, our neighbors, our friends, who face danger and hardship to relieve the hunger of the men of London." Admiring looks were shot through fingers at Lewis Jones, now stroking the cat; at Rob, draped around with the body of a sleeping child; and at Deio edging toward the door, determined to be first out.

"And pray God will keep them safe from the robbers, the evil men, the impostors, all that men are prey to on their journey."

Catherine, listening and trembling under the window, said a heartfelt "Amen."

"God speed," said the partygoers, patting the drovers' arms as they left the lighted room. "Come home in one piece." One woman asked Rob to bring her some of those new red currants from London so she could plant them next year, "and don't forget my marbled paper, mind." Rob's four-year-old son, a sturdy fellow with cheeks like ripe apples, held his arms out stiffly and started to bellow, "Don't go, Dadda," and was swooped up and kissed. Then the partygoers all moved to the window, jostling for a good position from which to watch the drovers leave.

Crouched in the shadows, waiting, Catherine heard the scrape of Deio's boots as he left the back door of the kitchen and strode on his slightly bandy legs across the yard toward her. She could see his form clearly in the moonlight, but was unable to read his expression. He was carrying a saddle and saddlebag and two bridles.

"Deio," she said softly.

"Good God, woman." He gazed at the small figure in front of him. The smock, the hat. "Jo from Abersoch." She stepped from the shadows.

"My God," he said with some distaste, "it's you."

The cattle were streaming down the moon-washed hills into the marshaling yard and the noise was deafening. He led her to a dark shed smelling sharply of urine. A bright bay horse stood saddled and tethered to the stable wall. She was wet with sweat and the whites of her eyes showed in the slatted light.

"Her name is Cariad," said Deio shortly. "Yours for the trip—then they will sell her in London. Rob is too heavy on her. You'll be all right." Her legs felt weak. She hoped he was right.

There was another roar outside and the crash of gates as more cattle came down the hill, then Rob's beard suddenly appeared over the stable door; his teeth gleamed in the moonlight.

"We'll leave at four-thirty sharp and you'll get your orders at Pistyll," he shouted. "Yes sir." She was thumped sharply on the shoulder by Cariad who was frightened by the noise.

"She's very green," Rob shouted, "watch her."

It took an hour to check supplies—the leathers, nails, hammers, food, guns, playing cards, sacks of flour, and smocks—then pack them neatly into rough saddlebags with tarpaulin covers. Toward morning, when streaks of yellow were showing in the dark hills above, Rob bellowed "Mount up," and Deio helped Catherine lead the mare into the yard. The mare was covered in a creamy foam of sweat and was dancing on the spot. She tightened the girths with a shaky, "Whoa there, Cariad." Then she leaped into the saddle as quickly as possible.

From behind, Rob gave a roar loud enough to splinter wood: "Heiptro Ho!" There was the clank of gates opening, and then a great rumbling sound as the last group of cattle came down the hill and all the dogs began barking at once as the three lots of cattle were merged into one group.

"Get back, get back," Rob shouted. Cariad had bounded into

the empty space, banging Catherine's knee on the gatepost as they passed.

"Now come out," yelled Lewis. The cattle surged up the moonlit track and Cariad, ears tensely pricked, leaped toward them. Turning to look back at the drovers' house, she could see the vague outlines of the few hardy souls who had stayed up all night to wave good-bye.

They were calling out, but no one could hear them, their voices drowned in the dark wave of thundering hooves heading toward the mountain.

Chapter 14

At the fork in the road, she hung back behind the cows and the shouting men, hoping to be on her own. It was the last view of Carreg Plâs. She thought this moment would pierce her heart but, turning, saw only a blur of trees, for Cariad, unused to saddlebags, was bucking and all she could think about was staying on.

For the next hour she concentrated on coming to a working understanding with her horse. She would treat her fairly, but she was in charge. The mare fought her for a while, tossing her head and snatching at the reins, but when Catherine talked to her and patted her neck and told her how clever she was, she settled to a steady trot—and part of Catherine settled, too.

The road widened as they left the peninsula moving from a narrow tributary into a much wider stream. Ahead of them, gauzy and indistinct, were the foothills of Snowdon. Mair had called it Eryi—The Place of Eagles—and when they were young, told them spine-chilling stories of the spirits who lived there: headless men and ravaged maidens left to die by the Romans. "If those peaks could speak," she'd said more than once, widening her currant eyes and holding up an admonishing finger, "they'd be struck dumb." Catherine pictured Mair's comforting bulk waddling through the kitchen in her red flannel petticoats. She was sad that there had been no time—and no words with which—to say good-bye. Poor Eliza, waking up and finding her really gone. Father would be on the rampage and probably with his gun.

She told herself she was part of the adventure now, not one of the ninnies waving good-bye from behind the kitchen curtains, so why did it feel so bad? They rode on for a couple of miles, and then she realized that all this excitement and Cariad's bouncing had left her with an overpowering need to go to what Gwynneth would call "the small room"—not exactly easy when you were surrounded by fields and open country. She told herself to wait. No lady, her aunt had once told her, ever needs to go to the Necessary more than three times a day.

When she stopped at the next gate, a shambled arrangement of old bedposts and rope, two ponies galloped up, stiff-necked with excitement, so that was impossible. Cariad was prancing again, panicked at the disappearance of the herd. Catherine dismounted quickly and, squatting behind a large clump of ferns, felt, for the first time in her life, like a savage. She buttoned the front of her breeches, and then dealt with another worry by flinging her head forward suddenly to see if her hat could fall off. It stayed firmly in place, her hair pinned and netted inside. She leaped back on her horse and, suddenly exhilarated, flung her arms around the animal's neck.

When she caught up with the drove again, they were beside a stream bordered with young willow trees. Deio was riding halfway up the herd, weaving loose-limbed and relaxed in and out of the cattle. Tegan, his collie, shadowed him. He turned and looked at her. No one ever looked better on a horse, thought Catherine. A troop of small boys appeared behind him like small woodland creatures creeping from the undergrowth. They had dirty bare feet and matted hair. One of them carried a tiny, pathetically cheeping, starling in a net in his hand.

"Where are you going, your honor?" the boy with the bird asked Deio. He was very thin.

"To London and back," replied Deio.

"To London!" The boy screwed up his face at this marvel beyond all comprehension. "Can we come, too, mister?"

Deio smiled down at the boy, the old sudden, wonderful smile, and Catherine felt herself light up. He made a move to gather him up on his horse, but the child shrank against the hedge, his hand tightening on the bird.

"What kept you?" said Deio, when the boys were waving dots on the track behind them and they were alone again. "Did you miss the turnoff?"

"No." She felt infuriatingly shy. "I was—" The bellow of a cow drowned her out.

"You were what?" he persisted. "I thought you'd turned tail and gone home."

Why must he scowl at her so, she thought, feeling tearful for the first time.

"Good Lord, no," she said, with as much volume as she could muster. "Cariad and I are getting on very well, thank you."

He smiled at her as suddenly as he had scowled, and lit a small pipe in a single elegant gesture. The smell of tobacco on the air reminded her of Father again, and to stop herself thinking, she asked what route they'd be taking. He leaned slightly out of his saddle and brought his face toward her so they did not have to shout. The gesture was intimate but his voice was cool and brisk.

"We'll get to Llangollen in nine or ten days' time. Two other droves will meet us there: one from Ffestinniog way, the other from Anglesea." He told her there was a bridge now from Anglesea but that they used to have to swim cows and horses over at high tide.

"Do you know what to do if you find yourself in deep water on a horse?" he asked.

"I am sure I do, but tell me again." She rather resented his schoolmasterish tone and suddenly wanted to tweak his nose and remind him they'd been playmates.

"Get off your horse immediately," he said, "and hang on for grim death by its tail. If you stay on you'll drown him."

"Well, thank you for the advice." She couldn't stop smiling. "And let's hope nothing like that happens."

He looked at her suspiciously, saying, "I'll move ahead of you now. I've told you all you need to know."

"Is everything all right?" she asked him suddenly.

"I expect so." He peered at her strangely. "Do you know you have dust all over your face?"

"I know."

"Don't you want a cloth?"

"Not really."

He scowled at her. "Perhaps I *will* borrow the cloth," she said meekly.

He told her to do what she liked, it made no difference to him. Then he broke off a long stick from a hazel tree above his head and swept it suddenly down on the rump of a cow ahead of him.

"A gadfly," he said shortly. "If he gets one of those under his tail he'll—"

"Gadabout?"

"Exactly." But he wouldn't smile. The path ahead of them seemed to go on for miles and miles. She suddenly felt very tired.

"Have we much farther to go before lunch?" she asked in as neutral a tone as possible.

A couple of hours, he told her, not long.

After a lunch of bread and some cheese washed down with some strong ale, Lewis, who ate with his eyes raking backwards and forwards across the cattle, split the drove into three lots.

"You boy," said Lewis, after an elaborate burp, "stay with Rob in the second drove. I need you fresh for tonight." What could he possibly mean? Another swarm of worries flew into her mind.

It got hot after lunch and she and Rob rode together in silence through a lovely valley to the north of Sarn. The sun blazed in the sky, and it was too hot for the birds to sing. A group of laborers eating lunch beside a hayrick had taken their smocks off. She could see their white, men's chests and their slackly buttoned trousers and was embarrassed. They leaped to their feet when they heard the rumble of cattle, waved hats and pitchforks at them as they passed, and looked at the cows and horses with keen competitive eyes.

"Those poor blighters aren't going nowhere." Rob lit his pipe and grinned.

They came to a short track and then a wood, where the noise of running water sounded like children laughing. Catherine, face scarlet from the heat and with her tight hat making her head ache, was glad of the shade. When Rob splashed his horse into the water, two dragonflies flew away, skimming across the surface of the stream. Cariad snorted and pawed at the water, wetting Rob's breeches and getting a slap on the nose for her troubles. Rob produced a silver flask from his pocket, took a short nip, and passed it to her without a word. It went down her throat like scorching flames, and it took all her strength not to violently expel it.

"See that clump of pines ahead?" said Rob ten minutes later, as they came out of the woods. He pointed toward three dots on the horizon. "Eight miles past them is Two Crosses. We'll get there in about three hours' time."

"Oh good," she said, hiding her dismay. Every bone in her body was beginning to ache with tiredness and she felt as crabby as a child. "Not far at all."

When they finally got to Three Crosses—a row of poor-looking houses beside a stinking open drain—it was dark enough for one or two stars to be out. The usual crowd of gawpers had gathered in the village and a halfwit shouted "Horse! Horse! Horse!"

Deio and Lewis, who'd arrived ahead of them, had driven their lot of cattle into a field. They were leaning against a barn, smoking short pipes and looking pleased with themselves.

"Journey's end," said Rob shortly, when she all but fell from her horse. "But still plenty to do." They tied up their horses and spent a maddening half hour trying to persuade the two lead cattle that there weren't ghosts in the field.

"Come on yer fuckin' shitbags," shouted Rob. "Bloody bastards."

Catherine saw Deio give her a sly, not altogether apologetic smile. She was too tired to care, swooningly, horribly tired, and felt a little sick. Then she had to stumble around in the half dark, watering and feeding horses, washing their bits and soaping their saddles. Then Rob, the perfectionist, slowly started to unpack from his saddlebags a series of little tins, each one marked—"nails," "soap," "accounts for trip," "orders in London," and so on—and each one, it seemed, containing a separate job to be completed.

"Don't want no girth galls, do we, lad?" said Rob as her bone-weary arm went up and down the straps.

They led the horses to a smaller paddock with a stream running through it, a gleam of silver now in the twilight. They set the horses free one by one, each one lying down and groaning with pleasure as it rolled, before galloping off to the stream and taking a long noisy drink. When she turned back, she saw Deio leaning on the gate looking at her, a shovel in one hand and a length of tarpaulin in the other.

She was unable to stop herself yawning hugely with tiredness—the kind of gesture that Aunt Gwynneth abhorred.

"Is there a farm nearby where we put up?" she asked him,

"No. There is a tavern nearby where the men sleep. You stay here." Stupid with tiredness, she watched him dig a hole, line it with straw and then stretch tarpaulin over the top. His muscles worked vigorously; he didn't seem at all tired.

"Is this a joke?" she asked, as he laid a bedroll on top of the straw. "I would prefer to stay in the tavern."

He gave her a funny look, a hard sad look, and she was immediately flustered. "Don't you all stay there?" she faltered.

"Lewis wants you here," he said, "that's the job you've been taken on for. They will take another boy on at Llangollen. You wanted this, Catherine," he said angrily, "don't look like that."

"Deio," she said, "you are not responsible for me." Her voice was more quavering than she would have chosen. "And thank you. I have had a most interesting day."

He touched his hand lightly on her back. Every vertebra of it now ached and twanged. She longed for something like a brotherly hug from him, a few words of encouragement, some acknowledgment of how much she had been through that day.

"Unless the cattle get out, which they won't," he said, with the same strange look, "don't come up to the tavern tonight. First night out . . . drinking and other things."

He lit a fire for her, and left her with the two collies, a safety lamp, and a box of matches. She heard him walk off into the darkness, and then he came back again.

"Catherine, this isn't right. It's too much for you. Please go home."

She wished she could give him clear reasons in a clear voice for this hunger inside, but out here in the dark all she felt was tired and all she longed for was a bath.

"Please, Deio, don't say anything." She put her head in her hands and maybe he touched her on the shoulder before he left, she couldn't be sure of anything.

When he was gone, she sat huddled in her blanket, her eyes traveling between the yellow moon and the fire, until a boy with dirty hands and excited eyes brought her down a plate of bread and cheese and some ale. He wanted to talk to her about the drovers. She stared at him, too tired to form words, and then cut him off. When she'd eaten, she lay down inside the shelter, her head poking out of the tarpaulin. The air was filled with the greatly magnified sound of animal teeth tearing and chewing. She meant to cry but, instead, slept as though she had been felled.

Chapter 15

They kept on riding, down wet green tracks, up gorse-covered hills, and to windy places where the silhouettes of primitive burial stones stood out against stupendous expanses of sky. Up there in the hills, the sense of slipping in and out of time was so strong, she could almost hear the clink of other horse's shoes and see the generations of drovers, of Romans, of Celts and Druids whose tracks they followed. And when the men bellowed "Heiptro Ho" she heard the same message: life, for all its brutality, was a journey, an adventure.

When she wasn't keeping watch, every third night, she fell asleep beside the drovers' dogs, their tired bodies jammed against hers beside the dying embers of a fire, and then she'd wake to the sensations of animal life around her: a dog licking her face, a dawn chorus, the sound of a stream of cattle, horses munching. Although the fear of sleeping on her own never quite left her, in time she became used to the constant changes of bed: to sagging pallets in farmers' houses, to heaps of straw in old barns with moonlight filtering through the rafters, to dry ditches covered by tarpaulin. After ten days on the road, she felt happy, really happy, for the first time in a long time.

Lewis's plan when they reached Bala was to take it easy over the Berwyn Mountains so the cattle would be fit and rested by the time they reached Llangollen, where some would be sold and others taken to Kent for summer pasturing. For the most part, they stuck to the wide-verged drovers' roads, through endless hills where, apart from the creak of a saddle or the cry of a bird, it was holy and silent. On other days, it was a clatter through small towns where she frankly gawped into upstairs windows at other people's lives—families eating, a man shaving, a woman brushing her hair—frozen into stage sets. Her body grew stronger; her senses became keen again, and her emotions were easily aroused. When a group of mourners passed them on a highway, pushing a coffin on a farm cart pathetically decorated with rowan leaves and scraps of cloth to keep bad luck away, she shed tears with the widow.

Her mother would have loved all this movement, this richness of life. She thought of her so often and of Eliza, even of Father, but she was not lonely. As long as she did her work well, and she made sure she did, the men treated her kindly. Lewis turned out to be a sheep in wolf's clothing. After they'd called in at some hillside farm or other, conducting a long wrangle over the price of this cow or that, he'd show her the workings of his mind. "I knew he'd take three pounds apiece." He'd give her his shrewd look. "Because his rent's due"; or, "I walked out on that one because even a blind man could see them runts is wormy."

Once or twice he slipped a toffee in her pocket or invited her to have a swig on his flask, and he liked to tease her, telling her she was a rum-looking creature for a boy and had she ever thought of becoming a jockey. One evening they were wading through a stream on their horses when he tried to flip her hat off and chuck her in the water, before she scrambled away.

"You and your firkin' hat," he shouted.

Deio was her only problem. He spoke to her and ate with her, rode within feet of her for mile after mile, but the old ease was gone. Sometimes a companionable silence turned dark and dangerous for no reason, and she wondered anxiously what she'd done to upset him so. At other times, he was quite different, seemed all lit up with a strange light. One evening, as they rode side by side through the Maid's Pass in the Berwyn Mountains, the setting sun brought a glow to their faces. Cariad was fit and strong by now and beautifully soft to her hand. They clattered together over an old stone bridge, and then rode to the top of the hill where they sat silently astride their horses like two savages on the rim of the world.

"Not a bad life," he said, watching a skylark fly away.

"It's heaven," she said.

"What is heaven?" She could feel him watching her.

"It's feeling free to be who you are."

"Is anybody?" The old note of impatience had come back in his voice.

"For a while maybe."

"For how long?"

She would have answered, but Cariad shied at a rock and banged into Deio's horse. The muscles of his leg lay against hers.

"We'll go down now," said Deio, as if nothing had happened, "there's cattle on the other side."

The path was too narrow to ride abreast so she rode behind him, feeling for a while very simple and secure, a pagan woman behind her mate. As they passed through a small copse of oak and sycamore trees, he turned in his saddle to tell her, "I saw six green woodpeckers here last trip."

"Oh Deio," she said when they were out of the trees and riding side by side again. "You are so lucky. You can spend your whole life like this."

"No, I can't, the trains will come. This will all be over soon."

"Then what?"

"I don't know. Home I suppose. Breed horses. Take them to London."

"On the train?" She tried to get him to smile.

He ignored this, asking, "So what are you going to do?" His eyes, when he looked at her, were startlingly green.

"I've told you . . . to London . . . London!" She closed her eyes, not wanting to think.

"To buy a fat pig."

When she opened her eyes, he was scowling. "No peasant, to live."

"Don't call me that." His eyes looked very black.

"I'm sorry. It was a joke once."

"Well it's not now." He pointed at a patch of bog cotton ringed with rushes. "Watch out."

"Thank you," she said meekly, but she was learning to use her eyes and had already noted the danger. "The bright green stuff will sink you, the rest is but a bog." She was quoting Lewis.

He smiled at her sourly. "You know everything now, don't you, clever girl? I expect you could get your certificate next week." His color was up and she recognized the set of his jaw.

"Deio, please!"

"A clever girl, riding away from home as if nothing mattered in the world except her own happiness. What about your father then? And Eliza? You haven't given them a thought."

"I have. I have!" Oh God blast and damn it, she was going to cry now. "I've been dreaming of my mother, for the first time since she died."

"Oh there's wonderful." He was quietly sarcastic. "That will be a great comfort to your father."

They bivouacked that night in a hollow of ground within earshot of the waterfalls near Pen Plaenau. When the horses were fed and the cattle settled, Rob, a massive shadow in the firelight, kneaded flour and water, set the damper in the fire, and took two rabbits from his saddlebag. He disemboweled the rabbits, slicing their bellies and leaving a steaming pile of entrails on the grass, then he cut off the feet and pushed the leg bones through the skin. He wrapped them in clay dampened in water, put them in the ashes of the fire, and pulled out a flask of brandy from his inside pocket. The fire and the small toenail of a moon hanging above a rim of dark hills were the only two points of light in the darkness.

"Hey ho, the diddle oh." He uncorked the brandy, threw it down his throat, then pulled a harmonica out of his pocket and blew a series of notes into the dark. The sound made her melancholy.

But not sad enough to spoil supper. When the men had put away several more brandies and smoked a few more pipes, smells of roasting meat filled the air.

"Well come on boyos, fork it into you," said Rob. He hauled the rabbits, black and smoking, from the fire, and when the skin was stripped off the meat fell from the bone.

"Eat or be eaten," Rob's teeth roared at her from the end of a fork. "Law of the jungle."

She ate with her hands off a tin plate, the fat dripping from her chin, and enjoyed every sweet and succulent and fire-tasting mouthful. When she looked up, Deio was watching her.

After supper, the local farmer, a redheaded man with damp red skin and an aggrieved expression, joined the men around the fire to collect the money for their grazing and to explain the sleeping accommodations. The three men, he said, could sleep at his house; the boy in the shearer's hut down by the river. There were a few bits of roof missing, but the hut was safe and gave good shelter. The man brought his boy, a pasty child of about nine, whose eyes glittered with excitement and who breathed noisily through his mouth. Lewis, mellow from the brandy, his face glowing in the firelight, said, "Ah, sit down y'ere and join us, man."

As the night wore on and the stars slowly multiplied above their heads, the men got a little drunker and the boy fell asleep in his father's arms. Then the men began one of those sleepy, interminable nonthinking yarns of the "do you remember so-and-so had that bay filly with the walleye" variety, which are not so much coherent thought as human animals taking comfort in the sounds and closeness of others.

She felt Deio watching her again. Through the dark like an animal. When a coolish wind got up she stood up, ready for sleep.

"Chuck a log on the fire, boy, before you leave us," said Lewis.

"I'll do it." Deio got to his feet in one powerful movement. "I'm leaving, too."

When they were out of the circle of light thrown by the fire, he took the saddlebag she carried. "Give me that."

"It's all right, I can carry it, really," she said stiffly.

"Give it to me." She handed it over without a word, and said, "I'm going down to check on the horses." She had been planning to go to bed but felt wary suddenly.

"I'll come with you."

It was dark down by the stream where the horses were tethered. As she walked among them with a lamp in her hand, they blinked at her out of dark long-lashed eyes and then plunged their heads again into the sweet grass at the water's edge. Only Cariad kept her head up and when she patted her, the mare licked her hand, liking the salt of human sweat.

Clambering up from the riverbank, she could see Deio's slightly bandy legs above her and his vague shape against the stars. He put out a hand to steady her and smiled. Then his mouth was on hers, so she could taste his brandy and smell wood smoke in his hair. It was a good smell, a man's smell, her body leaped toward him, then, panicked, she pushed him off. "Don't . . . oh please, don't Deio."

"Don't worry," he teased, as if it had all been a great joke, "you're miles from home." Then he held her head between his two hands and looked straight into her eyes.

"I don't understand, Catrin. What's all this about?"

"I don't know." She was trembling, half hoping to be in his arms again.

He let go of her and lit his pipe, and tried for a light tone. "You're quite a puzzle."

Her heart bled for him. And for herself.

"I don't know Deio," she said, "I wish I did."

Chapter 16

*T*he next morning she heard a splashing outside her hut. She poked her head around the door and saw Rob, less than ten yards away from her, pissing on the remains of last night's fire. Deio was behind him.

"Morning, lad." Rob's manhood swung like a turkey's neck from brown corduroy breeches. "Good sleep?"

"Yes, thank you," she muttered to the ground.

He buttoned up in a leisurely fashion and yawned several times, scratching himself under his privy parts. She had seen her father once, by mistake, undressed, and so was not completely taken by surprise. But when she looked up again and saw the expression on Deio's face, she stepped back and hugged herself.

When Rob had wandered off, Deio came into the hut and shut the door.

"Catrin," he said, "this is wrong. You must go home now."

"Surely that is for me to decide." She was shaking with nerves, and he looked fit to be tied.

"You know nothing about men," he said. "They are animals."

"*All* men? Animals? Oh Deio, please. You sound like the Reverend Hughes."

"Shut your mouth," he suddenly roared at her. "I don't need you to tell me what to think or how I feel." Then he clouted her on the shoulder—not a painful blow but a shocking one. The two dogs shot from the hut with their tails between their legs. She lost her temper.

"Don't you dare try to tell me what to do, you ignorant fool," she shouted. That was all, but the damage was done.

*   *   *

For a few days afterward, Deio kept a moody distance and would not speak. When he had to ride beside her, he sometimes muttered and swore at himself, and all her new feelings of independence seemed to disappear; she couldn't hang on to them. Although she had forbidden herself to speak to him, she found she missed him.

She was glad now that they had come to the end of the Berwyn Mountains and were within sight of the small town of Llangollen, on the banks of the River Dee. A town would give her the chance to review her options and, she hoped, cheer Deio up. The men had been talking about the place for days: its pretty women and good ale, and about the bareback race along the banks of the Dee that Deio had won.

"The local lads hold it every year on Fair Day," said Lewis, with that proud little curve of the lip he got when he spoke of his son. "One mile along the riverbank field with jumps, and bareback; last year he won it by a mile."

He gave some stew to Rob and Deio sprawled on the other side of the fire. "Eat up, lads."

"And that lad likes to win," Lewis continued, dunking his bread in the stew.

"Yes," she said.

"And I will." Deio's eyes gazed at her so steadily through the dark that she wondered why the others did not notice.

"Where do we put up in Llangollen?" She looked deliberately at Lewis.

"Well, that's a bit of a sore point, boy. Normally we stay at Slaw-sons, which is a common lodging house, but what with the fair to-morrow and the army in town drumming up men for the war, it was so full I had to dig into me pocket and get you into the Wynnstay, a proper hotel. So you behave yourself mind, no drinking, and keep your breeches on."

"Oh, I don't know," drawled Deio softly. He lay on his back and exhaled a plume of smoke into the stars. "It might do 'er good to get 'em off."

She flounced off to bed furious, slammed the door of the hut, and lay down with the dogs around her, too disturbed to sleep.

How dare he speak so rudely to her in public, how cruel to say "it might do her good," and deliberately put her disguise in jeopardy. All the men had sniggered as if it had been a great joke.

She thumped her pillow, pulled the blanket up tight, commanded herself to sleep. She hated him so much. But images of him kissing her, then striking her, went round and round in her head until she thought she was going mad. At three o'clock she woke with a start, determined on a course of action. The situation was impossible: she must strike out on her own for London, let her old life be severed from her as quickly and cleanly as a limb being amputated. The other alternative was to go home, and as soon as possible, and pretend none of this had ever happened. The dogs sighed and rewound themselves in tight balls. At length, she lay on her back, one arm flung across her face, thinking of all the stinging replies she should have made to him, how boldly she might have questioned his authority and with what clarity set down her future plans.

As the night wore on, her mind grew tired, and she accepted that her feelings toward Deio were so confused that she might have earned his anger. Led him on; bewildered him by craving the very protection that now unsettled her. Even now, there were moments when she saw him from a distance looking so fine that her heart swelled with such a warm regard, such a tenderness of shared associations, that she might under other circumstances have called it love. Deio was brave. He had helped to set her free, risking the anger of his family and his own reputation in the community to do so. For that alone, she would be forever grateful to him. Sometimes he felt so close to her she didn't know where he ended and she began. Then she saw that look in his eyes that scared her. It made her think of those horses who cry out in the darkness for their mate and wait with a desperate intensity for one reply. Then she wanted to push him off—she wasn't ready. It was too much.

And here was another bad thought: the next day they'd ride within a mile or so of her grandmother's house at Dyffryn Ceiriog on the borders of England and Wales. The idea of that house, with its pillows and pomanders, its excellent teas, its strict timetables, filled her with a most terrible homesickness. How wonderful to sink into that copper bath by the fire. To hear the housekeeper clink up the stairs laden with ginger cake and tea. All she had to do was ride there now and explain to her grandmother, an amiable and forgiving woman, what a goose she had been and how glad she was to be home, and all would be forgiven and forgotten. But then what?

Then home, and the blankness of knowing she hadn't done what she had set out to do. At last she slept, and when she woke, a gray light was filtering through the beams of the hut. She sat up with a quick panicky movement. A robin made the first note of the dawn chorus, then a chaffinch, then the tsk-task of the golden cret. Within seconds the riverbank was full of birdsong. White-faced, she took paper and pencil from her bag and, sitting cross-legged on her bed, surrounded by the sleeping dogs, did some sums.

One week later, they went to Llangollen to the fair. Deio, to her great relief, went on ahead with Rob and the twenty head of cattle they planned to sell. Deio, Lewis told her, had definitely decided to do the horse race. Lewis beamed at her. With his sons gone for the day and most of the cattle secure in a ha'penny field nearby, he seemed like a man released. He was wearing a suit she hadn't seen before of moss green cord, with the breeches tucked into a pair of beautiful old, cracked but highly polished, riding boots. His freshly shaved cheeks glowed like ripe apples and his mood, for reasons she did not fully understand, seemed positively frolicsome.

They rode for over an hour together, up to the top of Y Geriant, a foothill of the Berwyn Mountains that overlooked Llangollen. Lewis, who took a gloomy relish in such tales, told her that a local barber had been hanged near here for killing his wife. "You could 'ear terrrrrible terrrible cries, like a baby he crrried and his bones creakin' in the wind." They gazed down at the perfection of the town below: the scattered houses, the purple and brown hills, and the river that dashed through the valley in full flood, twirling ducks and trees in its wake.

"There's your view, boy," said Lewis with considerable satisfaction, as though the scene was one of his more successful negotiations. "All right is it?"

They came down from the hills to a road that curved beside the river into town. There was real heat in the sun now, which pierced the vapor of mist over the river and squeezed out drops of perspiration from under Lewis's hat. But Lewis, smart and garrulous on his jogging horse, seemed determined not to spoil the perfection of his dress by removing one detail. He received greetings now from the stream of carts and pedestrians that flowed along the picturesque road. He touched his hat to an old woman on a horse with two geese peeping from her saddlebags, promised a younger, prettier woman riding in a farm cart and squinting up from her knitting, that he would buy her some saucepans, some "prrroper saucepans mind from London," and agreed with her that you couldn't rely on the tinkers for nothing.

The road was curving in now toward the Dee, over a hump-backed bridge, around a sharp corner. On the corner stood a very fat man eating a meat pie, half of it dropping out of his mouth.

"I would not choose that spot if I was him," said Lewis, who liked disaster as much as scandal. "Twin brothers killed there last year. A horse doing the London to Holyhead Mail caught them, slap bang wallop. Took 'em both home to their mam in a bag. Worse than raspberry jam a friend of mine told me."

After registering appropriate shock, she asked Lewis, in a casual voice, how often the London to Holyhead Mail ran and whether it took passengers.

Twice a day he told her. *Twice a day!* No time at all for prevarication. "And if you ever go on it," he rattled on, "choose your driver well. The young drivers are always trying to beat their elders. There's one, Titus Johnson, who can do the journey in eighteen hours." *Eighteen hours.* The sky seemed to spin suddenly in front of her, and for a moment she felt quite sick. By this time tomorrow she could be gone, and everything in her life would be changed. . . .

Llangollen was crammed with marketgoers by the time they got there. After two weeks on horseback, living on plain fare in the depths of the countryside, the smells of fresh gingerbread, and faggots and peas affected her like a drug. Catherine couldn't wait to tether Cariad in a safe place and join this noisy surge of people, now jostling for a free sample from the strong-looking man selling Dr. Guber's Patent Medicine, now haggling for onions, or taking a gander at the poster of Hilda the Snake, showing the whites of her eyes and her rolls of flesh and the big grass snake around her neck.

But Lewis, to her disappointment, took her to the pens where the cattle and horses were kept. In a fenced-off corridor between the horses and the cattle was a gray line of men and women, some with placards around their necks: "Handy Boy," read one; "Strong Willing Girl," read another, worn by a wisp of a girl with a swelling beneath her apron. Every now and then, a farmer or his wife would step forward to inspect the teeth of one of these specimens, and the worm broke up into its human parts.

The desperate neighing of separated mares and foals, the moo-ings and trumpetings of cattle, the sound of humans baying for money, were deafening enough to shut Lewis up temporarily. But when they were out of the crush, he pointed toward two piebald horses with big heads tied to the railings in the forecourt of the market and told her he would teach her a thing or two about horse sales.

"Look at them, not worth their price and dear as a gift. You can bishop 'is teeth to make him look younger, dye the white bits on 'is face with Indian ink, puff out the hollows of his eyes. Those two boyos," he stared into the milky eyes of the guilty parties, "are ready for the pot."

Lewis's friendliness was starting to make her feel sad. "Save your breath," she felt like telling him, "you will have to find a new boy tomorrow." When Lewis suggested they go straightaway to the Hands Inn Hotel and leave the horses, she gratefully agreed.

At the Hands Inn, she understood the significance of Lewis's smart clothes when, standing with his hand on the neck of a horse dis-cussing business, he suddenly stopped dead. A good-looking, well-rouged blonde on the wrong side of thirty had stepped from the shadows. A vision in lavender silk with parasol to match.

"Lewis Jones!" the woman, walking with difficulty across the cobblestones, was grimacing and dimpling so enthusiastically that Catherine, under other circumstances, might have thought she was taking a fit.

"Well, Duw Duw Duw . . ." said Lewis. If she hadn't known him better, she would have thought he was blushing. "Now there is a sight for sore eyes."

The blonde pursed her lips and disdained to answer immediately. "And who is this handsome gee-gee fellow?" She fluttered her lace gloves on Cariad's neck.

"A new horse." Lewis couldn't take his eyes off the woman, or stop smiling. "He was as green as grass at the beginning of the trip, but the boy has bottomed him."

Catherine blushed with pleasure. It was the first compliment Lewis had ever paid her.

"That reminds me, I'd better pay the boy." Lewis seemed anxious suddenly to be rid of her. He pulled out an account book and pencil and made a quick calculation on the end page.

"Ten days work at two shillings a day," he said, "and here as a special favor is five pence to get into the races. Deio left a message with me that you were to go. Then you'll be sleeping at the Wynnstay, which is not a common lodging house—I couldn't get them into Slawson's," he explained to the blonde, "it is crammed, and that man with the bear is staying there. Behave yourself mind, keep your breeches on."

The woman shrieked and hit him with the handle of her parasol. Catherine tried a manly wink back, but only managed a terrified blink. The idea that she had earned this money—more than she had imagined—fairly and squarely by her own labor, excited her more she could have imagined. But now there was alarm. She was longing to see Deio at the horserace, but there was so much to organize: clean clothes, and a ticket on the stagecoach to London. And another nerve-racking thought: if the drovers were staying the night at the tavern, tonight she and Deio would be together for the first time under one roof.

Chapter 17

$\mathcal{W}$hen he got to the Wynnstay, Deio handed his horse over to the ostler with careful instructions as to when he should be fed. No horse ran well on too full, or too empty a stomach. Inside the hotel, he confirmed the bookings for the night with a maid. The maid, who was plump and comely, stood with one arm draped over the banisters. She raised her pretty mouth toward him, "Will there be a party tonight after the flappin?"

"Maybe," he said.

He carried on walking upstairs, with the maid following behind. Admiring his muscular thighs and the quality of his boots under the dust, she felt disappointed. He was so handsome but very out of sorts. She took him into a room that had a view of the street and the river beyond. He sat on the bed, his dark hair falling over his eyes. He gave the maid his boots to polish, and as the door closed, he put his head in his hands. It annoyed him to find that underneath his careful cool manner, he was almost shaking with excitement. Damn. He desperately needed to be calm. First for the race, then for Catrin. He saw the cup gleaming in his hands as he rode through a cheering crowd. Then thought of himself alone with her again, away from the men, and then, maybe, they could have a talk and a glass of wine together and a chance to see what was what.

It was so unlike him to feel out of control like this, and it drove him mad with frustration. He drew the curtains against the sound of the market and the distant plan, plan, plan, of a drum; the army was in town again, drumming up business. He'd thought of joining the army once: he sold plenty of good remounts to the cavalry in

London, and one of their men, a stuck-up arse but an officer, had watched him ride, had said he was the kind of man they needed. Now he daydreamed about himself in a scarlet cavalry uniform, with maybe a faint scar down his cheek. She was part of this dream, standing in a pretty dress, watching him on his plumed horse, her eyes bright with emotion.

Deio took off his dusty clothes and lay down on the bed. What a fool he was trying to impress her. An ignorant fool—she was right. Too nice he'd been to her up until now; too much the gentleman, too willing to give credence to her half-baked plans, too conscious that she was different from the others. Women were like horses, they could smell nervousness. Better in the old days when he took charge and told her what was what. Then they'd laughed and sung.

He lay down on his bed and closed his eyes. Feeling bristles as he stroked his face, he got up, poured water into a bowl, stripped to the waist and shaved with firm deliberate strokes. He wanted to look good at the flapping; he would smile at her as he passed the finishing line. When one half of the firm jaw was done, the maid came in with his now gleaming boots in her hand. She was completely unabashed to find him half undressed. He liked women like that. Straightforward. A pretty little thing, though not as pretty as the last one who worked here.

"Do you need anything, sir?" She went over to the window, a black silhouette, one hand stretched toward him. "I'd be happy to help you."

She was pretty enough. He let his eyes linger on her, then he thought of Catherine's eyes, opening like a seam of tortoiseshell, and again felt she was taking his power.

"Good luck with the race, sir." The girl closed the door behind her with a little wink. "Ride like you did last year and you'll learn them."

Catherine was walking toward the hotel, but stopped next door to a stall selling rabbits and eggs to listen to a man exhorting the crowd. A pair of handsome soldiers passed her, surrounded by gawping young men and children hiding behind their mother's skirts. They were walking toward the middle of the square where a tall man, wearing as much brass and oiled leather as a prize stallion at a show, stood on a carpet of cabbage leaves and cattle dung, shouting.

"Join the Twenty-third of foot, the Welch Fusiliers. A terrific regiment!" His jowls blew up like a puff adder. "The most glorrioouss, the grrrandest fighters. . . . Come on boyos, there's a queen's shilling for any man who steps up now and a field-marshal's baton in every knapsack."

Some jocular pushing and shoving broke out among the young men, one or two of whom had unconsciously stiffened their shoulders and thrown out their smocked chests, even those who pretended to mock the man's words. She saw a stoop-shouldered boy step forward, and then another after a whispered consultation with his mother.

"Grand lads, that's it. Step right up." The sergeant clamped his arm around the boys as though they were already gallant comrades. He steered their hands toward a large, leather register where they put a name or a mark.

How easy it is, she thought, for a man to change his life. A young woman had moved up beside her. She looked tired and had a baby on her hip and a frayed basket upon her head. She turned to Catherine suddenly and said as though she'd read her mind. "Men is lucky. They can go where they want to."

Catherine stared at her. They were about the same age, but the girl looked exhausted. "I am going myself to London," she heard herself say, "on the morrow."

"Well, a drover is always going somewhere," said the girl, who had already lost her front teeth, "and that's their good luck, too." With a practiced movement she took the basket down from her head, wiped the baby's mouth, sat it on the other hip, and placed her basket back on her head.

"Where would you go if you could?" Catherine asked impulsively.

"Any place but here," muttered the woman. She shot Catherine a suspicious look and prepared to move off.

"Tell me before you go," said Catherine, "where the Wynnstay Hotel is, and where I might pick up the coach?" But the woman's reply was drowned out in another volley of drums and more shouts from the prize stallion.

"They say the train to London is better now," said the woman wistfully. "It's twice as fast and 'alf the price, but I know you drovers aren't fussy on it."

"Of course, the *train*," said Catherine, as though she were in the habit of taking it several times a week. Her heart beat like a drum. A train tomorrow and to London. The girl placed her baby gently down in a spot between the cabbage stalks and a pile of swedes. She pointed out the post office and the general direction of the train and disappeared with a wincing smile into the crowd again.

Catherine watched her go, almost envious of the worn young mother, who had a certain home to go to, duties to perform. Decisions were horrible and she was so tired now and grandmother's house so close. Everything in life was turning out to be so unclear, so contradictory. In the distance she heard the shrill neighs of foals separated from their mothers, the calls of "Buy a penny potato yaaaah"—a blur of sound behind the ominous beating of the drums. She went to a stall, where the shopkeeper teased her about a sweetheart, and bought soap, a bristle hairbrush, a wash cloth, and a small bottle of lavender water. She took a short walk up a road that followed the line of the river. She had never in her life longed so completely and so suddenly for a bath. That at least would be like going home.

The hotel looked large and imposing; she ran up the front steps and through the door, then made her way swiftly toward the subdued roar of male voices coming from a taproom stinking of dogs and ale. The landlady, Mrs. Davies, appeared: a stout, highly colored woman with challenging eyes and quivery jowls.

"Have I had the pleasure of meeting you before, young sir?" said Mrs. Davies with a grand and distant expression.

"No, ma'am, you have not, but I am with the drovers, with Lewis Jones." Mrs. Davies's expression softened. Her jowls shook gently like a blancmange.

"Well, you should have said so straightaway. Mr. Lewis Jones is an old, old friend." She implied a depth of intimacy which few round that bar could ever have imagined. "My girl will see you up."

A short bark of "Bethan," and a maid appeared and led her upstairs and showed her into a dark, low-ceilinged room with a slanting floor and a low truckle bed. The bed had a rope mattress and a red eiderdown. The top two panes of the window were engraved in a yellow and red fleur-de-lys design that threw little jewels of light over the bedspread. Beside the bed was a deal table whose edges had been burned by a careless smoker, but the sheets looked clean, and the dish of potpourri near the window gave the room a clean scent of oranges and cinnamon. After ten days on the road it looked like heaven.

"Is it to your liking, sir?" asked the girl, turning down the coverlet.

"It will do very nicely," she said. "Thank you."

Catherine asked the maid to send up some bread and cheese, some ale, and some water for a bath. When she was gone, she put her saddlebag on the floor and flung herself on the bed, her body still swaying with Cariad's rocking rhythm. She could hear the murmur of the street and the river beyond.

"I'll have a bath, I'll sleep for no more than one hour, then I'll go to the races, and then I'll be gone," she told herself drowsily. And sleep she did, with the greedy hunger of a young animal, and would have kept on sleeping until the same time the next day had not the girl knocked on the door and cried, "Ready for your bath now, sir?"

A large copper bath, needing much pushing and pulling, appeared at the door, followed by the maid and a red-faced young lad. They filled the bath in relays with hot water from large jugs. The young man said resentfully that it was unusual for customers to require washing facilities during a fair day.

After they had gone, Catherine, now fully awake and almost swooning with impatience, dashed to the curtains, half closed them, peeled off gaiters stiff with horse sweat, breeches, grass-stained smock. She took off the hat she'd worn almost continuously for the last ten days and unwound the greasy rope of hair that was flat to her scalp. From a twist of brown paper in her pocket, she poured bath salts into the water and, groaning with pleasure, stepped naked into the bath, exclaiming out loud, "Ooh, wonderful!" She lay for a while, eyes closed, and surrendered her body to a state of infant bliss. She felt both more tired than she'd ever felt in her life and stronger. As she splashed and washed, the dying sun set through the red square of glass at the top of her window, flinging more jewels down across the water before snatching them away.

She washed her hair, awed and appalled at the dirt that flowed from it, and when the water grew cold, stood up, wrapped herself in a towel, and got out the blue-and-white dress she had brought from home and hidden at the bottom of her saddlebag. The dress was dusty and stank of the citronella the drovers used to keep flies from the horses. She dunked it in the bath and scrubbed it as well as she could, but the sight of it dripping, shrunken and pathetic on a hanger, brought a great wave of insecurity.

It was infuriating to care about clothes again so quickly, but now there was the terrifying thought of meeting Eleri's father, the famous surgeon at St. Thomas's Hospital. She imagined him immaculate, imperious, and herself in a creased dress, no petticoats, funny shoes, and no hat, in front of his desk.

"Oh Mama," she thought suddenly and with a horrible sense of loss, "I miss you so."

She tried to stop the voices now in her head, which never really went away and which reminded her how hopeless she'd been on that day, how she might have saved her mother. Why she had to go to London.

"My daughter Catherine," she would have said to him, her voice crackling with vivacity, "isn't she lovely?" And one could have floated through on her energy and her approval. She could have talked to her about Deio.

She looked at her watch; there was an hour to go before the race meeting. She felt sick. Everything in my life is going to change, she thought, and now the simple fact of leaving him, held back so carefully all day, overwhelmed her. She found a clean flannel shirt, slipped into it, and lay between the sheets, curled up like a baby.

The rumble of the voices from the bar downstairs grew less dense for a while and then swelled up again as the night began. She slept through the tinkling music of the barrel organ under her window, through the shouts of "get your faggots and peas yar," through a fistfight in which one of the protagonists kept yelling "a pox on your lyin' mouth Davies," and through another tub-thumping attempt by the Welch Fusiliers to pull in more recruits. And would have slept on until dawn, except that at two-thirty that morning there was a knock on her door, and Deio's voice sounding drunk and desperate saying, "Catherine, where are you? Let me in."

Chapter 18

She sat up suddenly, "Deio. I'm sorry!"

"Can I come in?" He hadn't heard her. "Chop. Chop. Open the door."

She lit a candle, put on a nightdress, and hurried to the door.

"You can't come in," she said in an urgent whisper.

"Why not?" His voice sounded very near.

The chain pulled away easily from its weak catch and he stumbled into the room bringing a breath of horses and ale with him.

"Where were you, Catrin? Or should I say Cath-er-rine," he said in his English voice.

"I wanted to come," she said, "but I fell fast asleep." He was swaying on his feet, glaring at her.

"I won, Catrin. I won!" His fist flared up like a giant's hand against the wall, and she saw how drunk he was—sober he would never have made such a naked gesture, not to her. "Thirty of us in the field," he said, "and a great field, too, big hunters, Rhys Harris's polo ponies, racehorses. He was nappy at the start, but then he went like a dream. I was flying, Catrin, flying." He smiled his beautiful smile.

"Oh Deio." She could not resist him in this mood. "I wish I'd seen you. Your father must be happy."

"Father happy," he repeated doggedly. "But *you* missed it. You miss things. There's time when you need people to be there an . . ." He sat down on the end of the bed and breathed out sharply as though once again she had let him down.

"I wish I'd seen you," she said again. "I have had a great deal to do here."

"What?" he said sharply.

She felt nervous of him suddenly, and evasive. His temper had been so uncertain lately.

"All manner of things. I'm going to London, Deio, I told you before. It's all arranged. Nothing's changed." She was twisting her hair up, trying to find a pin to make it more modest. He took the hair from her hands and his shadow shot against the wall and flattened.

"Leave it," he said in a low voice. "It's beautiful down, like silk." She was shaking, it was wrong to be here with him like this in her nightdress.

"Deio, please, I am tired. I must go back to sleep." She sat down on her bed.

"Catherine." He knelt down at her feet and held her face in his hands, and for that moment it almost felt like they were praying together. "Don't leave. Please don't leave. It's been difficult for me having you here, and maybe could, should, I don't know . . ."

"Deio please." *Dear God, please help me.*

"So much ahead, farm, and buy you things in London."

"You've had a lot to drink."

"I know what I'm say—" He put his head on the bed. She touched his hair, and he looked at her intensely. "I know what I'm saying. I want to be everything in the world to you."

"Dear God," she thought, "help me, help me." Then his left hand was pressed firmly against her ear, making a rushing sound like water in a cave. She thought of things she could say to him: we're too young; I'm frightened; I killed my mother.

"Deio . . . I must go. It's all arranged." He seemed to be breathing strangely.

"Why? Why? Why?"

"To study medicine or to nurse. I want to go. You saw my mother, what her life did to her." It hurt so much to say this.

"That won't happen to you," he said fiercely. "You have friends."

A bluish light from the window fell in slats across the bed. He got off his knees and sat down heavily on the bed with his head in his hands. His red rosette fell out of his breeches pocket. She picked it up and smoothed it carefully. "And you," she looked for words to salvage his pride, "I'll never forget you. You're in my heart forever."

"Oh bugger to that, don't want to be just in your heart." He looked at her so strangely she wondered if he'd heard a word. "I would rather be—"

"Deio! What? Don't! You are looking at me as though you hate me."

"I don't hate you." There were tears in his eyes. "Don't say that."

"Aren't you pleased at all that I know what I want to do?"

"I think you've gone mad woman," he said. "You know I . . . I . . . oh for God's sake."

He took her hair with one hand and her waist with another and put her down on the bed. He put his mouth on hers, and the full weight of his body on top of her. For a moment, her body seemed to take off in all directions as she kissed him and stroked his hair. And then she felt his hand over her body: under her nightdress, between her legs. The other, smelling of saddle soap went over her mouth. And then she was moving toward him, pushing herself toward him, toward his hand, which was moving deeper and harder. It was utterly strange and wicked. She froze for a moment closing her eyes.

"Deio." She could hardly breathe. "This is wrong, please stop."

Her head was jammed now between the bed and the wall.

"Feel it first, Catherine." His fingers were touching her; she felt a spiraling sweetness.

"No!" She was surprised at the strength she found to fling him off the bed. "Not like this, and don't you dare blame me."

With a crash, he fell from the bed. "What did you expect? We've been ten days together."

He was stumbling around now looking for a light for the candle.

She watched him in a stupor of misery, body still blazing and uncoiling, mind all tangled. "Try for once to understand me."

"I can't. I won't." He was on the bed beside her again and, suddenly, in one quick movement, lifted her skirts and entered her. They both cried out, and then her tears flowed through his hands.

Afterward, she lay rigid with shock and he staunched her bleeding.

"It's strange at first," he said. He was on his elbow looking at her. "But I'll make it wonderful."

Her voice seemed to come from miles away.

"I'm going to London." She sounded like a mechanical toy.

"Did I hurt you?"

"No. Yes. No. I'm all right." She was determined not to cry.

"Don't go to Lon— I'm sorry if I—" Now his voice was choked.

"I'm going, Deio. It's all arranged."

He got off the bed; put his shirttails back in his breeches. His eyes were dark in the candlelight. His red rosette on the floor.

"I didn't mean to hurt you."

"Please go."

She got up on her pillow and looked at the dark room. There were footsteps echoing in the streets outside as some revelers went home. Watching him walk toward the door, she felt an indescribable pain, a sense of loss never felt before. He turned around and looked at her before he left.

"I shall not give up on you," he said.

Part Two

London, 1854

Chapter 19

oom! Boom! Catherine, stepping off the train and into the dark cave of Euston Station, heard the drums immediately, and felt them in her skull. She had never seen so many people together in all her life, or been so scared.

For the last hour, she'd been watching blue sky become yellow smoke, green fields turn to smoke, and then row upon row of sooty houses, their washing lines hung with camisoles and shirts and combinations. "Kindly leave the train if this is your destination!" the guard was shouting. "All others change, please-uh! That's it, all change. Off you go."

She was pushed onto the platform, crowded with soldiers in new blue-and-green uniforms, and stood there with her saddlebag in one hand, her hat in the other. A boy, still young enough to have gosling fluff on his cheeks, was being kissed by a weeping mother. A man in civilian clothes with a huge leather suitcase shouted at her and bumped her painfully on the shins, half spinning her around.

"Excuse me," she said. "Where is Hyde Park?" but he'd gone, and left her shouting on her own.

Outside the station she clung to some railings and tried to make sense of the noise and the stream of people jostling one another and hurrying forward. "I'm in London," she thought in a blaze of surprise. "I am here at last." A man at the corner of the pavement shouted, "*Chronicle, Chronicle!* . . ." A horse swept by pulling a cart and airily depositing its dung, half on the harness and half on the street.

Driving in a cab toward the city, her face pressed against the window, she saw amazing shops crammed with costly goods; an old woman, filthy and in rags, holding a terrier in her arms; a man in a purple coach drawn by four grays, dressed in a gorgeous fur coat and smoking a cigar.

"How Mother would have loved this," she thought, "how she would have laughed."

Driving down Oxford Street in spite of everything, she thought of Deio. He'd talked about the mad rush at the end of every London drove to get the cattle down here and into the markets before the city woke up. He'd sung songs from the London theaters and told jokes that had the tears running down her face. And there he was again: on his knees in the moonlight, his face hungry and thwarted. *Look at me, Catrin,* he'd begged her before the end, *Look at me.* But no! Never! *I hate you, Deio, I can never love you again.*

"Tyburn," the coach driver shouted at the end of Oxford Street. "Where the criminals was once hexecuted. They used to watch them from the apartments up yonder." He pointed with his whip to some windows above a hat shop.

Green Street. A long narrow street with handsome sober houses and gay window boxes. Ferdinand Holdsworth's house was at number thirty. She stood at the corner with her head swimming from the strangeness of it all, realizing that thinking about a thing and actually doing it was so different. Soon she would have to bang on a perfect stranger's door and announce herself. She darted in the opposite direction, across a busy road, in the direction of an iron gate. "I'll count up to twenty and then I'll go," she said to herself.

On the other side of the road, at the park's entrance, a wizened old man was singing *I will gather this rose* to a monkey in a shawl. Oh, why must everything remind her of Deio; that was another of the songs he'd once sung in his Miss Pitkeathly voice to make her laugh. The old man doffed his cap, and she was so embarrassed that she went to the sign attached to the gate and read studiously, "The park keepers have orders to refuse admittance to the park to all beggars and any persons in rags, or those whose clothes are very dirty or who are not of decent appearance or bearing."

There was a spot of blood on the hem of her blue dress. Seeing it, she felt dirty again and touched with darkness. Plam! Plam!

Plam! Plam! The drumbeats again, coming from the park. She'd behaved like a creature gone mad. She stood on her own for a moment, shaking her head.

Two women walked by in silk dresses, both carrying small dogs. "Oh look," said one. "Them hosses again." Ten black horses from the Household Cavalry clattered by, their riders magnificent and impassive.

London! The thought kept breaking in on her. It was too sudden, too strange; she needed more time to think about it. *I will count up to thirty and then I'll go.* But instead, she spent a rootless, miserable hour wandering up and down Park Lane, looking into carriage shop windows and pretending from time to time to greet imaginary friends. London, she knew, was full of kidnappers and pickpockets.

And then she closed her eyes, breathed deeply, walked up the street, found the house, and banged on a brass door-knocker shaped like a fish.

A woman carrying a pile of clean sheets opened the door.

"My name," she said, "is Catherine Carreg."

"Is Mr. Holdsworth expecting you?" The woman looked put out.

"I hope so." Catherine tried not to sound too desperate. "I think his daughter, Miss Eleri Holdsworth, sent a note ahead of me."

"Ah, Miss Eleri." The woman rolled her eyes. "You had better come in."

Chapter 20

"My dear Miss Carreg." The tall, slightly stooped, gray-haired man stepped forward and took her hand. "What a delightful surprise. Eleri did tell me about you."

She shook his hand, warmed by his smile and the softened look of the housekeeper who had her dusty cloak in one hand and her saddlebag in the other.

"Margaret," he said, "would you be so kind as to make us tea? Cress sandwiches, I think, some walnut cake, and one or two of those scones if they are hanging about. Thank you."

Following Ferdinand Holdsworth up the mirrored hall, she caught a glimpse of her frightened face and crumpled clothes. She was in London but dressed for a hayride.

He led her into a large, light room, with windows opening onto a walled garden and what looked like stables behind. Its book-strewn tables, tapestry chairs, and general air of artistic untidiness struck her as a grander version of Eleri's home.

"What a lovely room," she said.

He thanked her and said his wife, Penelope, had set it up. This was her room—all the tapestries, the footstools, everything. He looked so resolutely cheerful when he said this that she knew his wife was dead.

"She was a wonderful needlewoman," he said. "She taught me to sew and knit. That one is mine." He pointed proudly at a green-and-purple footstool depicting deer and vine leaves.

"It's beautiful," she said.

"Oh yes," he said. "She was stern with me at the beginning.

'Shoddy work! Ferdinand,' she would say. 'Think of those Italian builders who used to teach their sons the rule of Cento Anni. One hundred years, not three, or five, so unpick it. Now!'"

They both laughed. He was a good mimic.

"I was telling Miss Carreg about that tartar Penelope Holdsworth," he said as Margaret appeared in the room with a laden tea tray.

"Oh sir!" The housekeeper set down a silver teapot and a walnut cake and some cress sandwiches. "The dearest lady who ever lived, as well you know. Now Miss Carreg, how do you like your tea?"

While Margaret bustled and poured, and replenished the pot, Ferdinand watched the girl. The surgeon in him noted the extreme pallor of her skin and the faint blue circles around her eyes. The poor child looked all done in.

His impulse was to offer her a bath and a bed for the night. He was ready to care in the way the lonely are, as an escape from loneliness, but he worried that this might compromise the girl and sound like an improper suggestion. On the other hand, Eleri had written to him, had asked him, perhaps as an envoy of her family. "Oh Penelope," he pleaded silently. "Tell me what to do."

"Another sandwich, my dear?" He was puzzled by this mysterious creature his daughter had sent. Her poise suggested a girl who had been well brought up, but her accent, now English and now with the singsong inflections of the Welsh, suggested a farmer's daughter; she ate like a refined young lady, but she was clearly starving.

"Do have some more cake, it's very good." No point in pressing her with questions until she had eaten and drunk. He talked for a while in his urbane and kindly way about the Lleyn Peninsula, and how he and his wife had discovered it on a walking holiday in Wales when they had been retracing the footsteps of the pilgrims, and how he had taken his children back there year after year, for there was something in the scenery that stirred the soul.

"Did you mind Eleri staying there?" Her eyes, very direct and intelligent, brought the general part of their conversation to an end.

"Penelope minded," he said. "She felt her desire to live alone in a more or less foreign country would attract a great deal of disapproval."

"Did you, do you . . . ?"

"No," he said. "I've seen quite a few clever women go mad for want of something to do. When Eleri was three years old she drew and painted as if time was running out. To have gifts like that and not to use them is a form of slow death. She was an absolute monster as a child."

They both laughed at that, and he held out the teapot toward her. "Now finish off that pot my dear, it's thirsty weather, and then you may refresh my memory about your London plans."

She put down her cup, her heart skipping with fear. She'd imagined having this conversation hours or days after meeting Mr. Holdsworth, but here he was, twinkling at her over the tea tray as if they'd been friends for years.

"I have come to London," she said, "to be a doctor, or if that is quite impossible, to get a professional nurse's training."

"I see," he said. "Have you had any nursing experience?"

"My mother died in childbirth a few months ago."

"Ah." Poor girl, he should have guessed, she had the fearful look of the recently bereaved. He did not answer her directly, but crossed his long legs and asked if she would mind his pipe. Then, wrapped inside a cloud of aromatic blue smoke, he disappeared for a bit.

"Impossible."

"Impossible?"

"Forgive me," he said, "but it is kinder to be blunt. You are too young, you are, if I may say so, a very attractive young woman. You would be like a lamb to the slaughter. Some of those medical students—I know, I teach them almost daily—have a strange reaction to all the death and suffering they see around them. I don't know quite how to put it, but it's almost an animal reaction. I'm being frank in order for you to truly understand. They make jokes about dead people who they call stiff 'uns. It's a way of dealing with fear. When we are not around they throw limbs at each other. Apart from that, you would be teased and tormented unmercifully from morning till night. I know what I talk of, my dear; there is one woman doctor now in the whole of London. I knew her quite well before her health collapsed and she was rendered a semi-invalid. My colleagues were, I'm afraid, very unhappy about a woman entering their profession, and they made her life a misery. It was very depressing to witness it."

She sat considering this, and then looked at him steadily. "What eyes," he thought, "the kind that make men want to perform great deeds."

"I am not afraid of the company of men," she told him. "I came to London with the cattle drovers, and worked beside them every day."

"No medical school would admit you," he continued doggedly. "Each one is as rule-bound as the next. There is another important question to consider: it takes about six years to become a doctor. You would have to apprentice yourself to a doctor and, in the unlikely event that he would agree to have you, it would cost your parents a great deal of money for your tuition, your instruments, your student's fees, and your lodgings. Is your father behind this?"

A dog sighed by the fire.

"I thought it better to find a situation before I asked him that question," she said guardedly, and then burst out, "Surely I can do something else. I am young. I'm keen to learn. Is the whole of the medical profession barred to me? Could I be a nurse?"

He signed again.

"Impossible. My students call them the band of angels because they have such a terrible reputation. Some are a step up from streetwalkers, some simply poor and desperate, some of course are magnificent—we don't often hear about them."

He replied that it was a scandalous situation and he was not proud of it. He put his fingers into steeples and rested his nose on top of them. She could see him looking puzzled as if some stray thought eluded him.

"So there's nothing else you can think of?" she persisted.

A silence, then he puffed a few more times on his pipe, making goldfish sounds. Perhaps one more thing, he said cautiously, but it might not appeal to her, or be easy to arrange.

She leaned forward eagerly.

"Yes?"

"Well, my old friend Dalrymple, who incidentally is one of the ablest surgeons in London, works once a week at the sanatoria for sick governesses in Harley Street. The full name of the place is The Institution for the Care of Sick Gentlewomen in Distressed Circumstances. The home is run by a remarkable lady, the daughter of aristocrats, who believes as you do that more women should be properly trained in medical matters. It is a very, how shall I say it, genteel place. The kind of place your father might approve of. The patients are mostly governesses, paid for by their relatives; there are no student surgeons, no improper patients. I have no idea if they need any help but it might be . . ."

"Mr. Holdsworth"—she jumped to her feet—"It's a capital idea. How can I ever thank you enough?"

"Please, please," he said nervously, "sit down, sit down. It's only the seed of a suggestion, of an idea. The lady in charge is formidable and fierce and will need to be handled quite carefully. I do, however, have one small card up my sleeve, which you will forgive me if I do not immediately reveal to you, but which might prove effective."

"What is the lady's name?"

"Her name," he said, "is Florence Nightingale."

She held both his hands. She thanked him from the bottom of her heart.

"Please don't," he said, "you may come to rue the day."

Chapter 21

efore their interview was over, Mr. Holdsworth agreed to approach Miss Nightingale on two conditions. The first: that Catherine immediately contact her family and inform them of her whereabouts and her plans. The second: that she stay at his home for a week in order to recover her health and strength. If she got the job, her life from then on would be hard and, in his professional opinion, she looked pale and run-down. Furthermore, he'd blushed at this and so had she, it might be helpful if Margaret could take her shopping and get her "um . . . kitted out."

The next day, after breakfast, she sat in a chair in the morning room, a sheet of writing paper on her knee, her tongue slightly protruding between her teeth, and wrote a letter to her father outlining her plans and enclosing a short note from Holdsworth. The second letter was more difficult. Remembering the look of stunned surprise on Eliza's face still brought tears to her eyes; she owed her sister such a profound apology.

By the end of the morning there were many crumpled pieces of paper in the wastepaper basket but the letter, with its entreaties of love and its desperate need for news from home, was finally done. She longed to tell Eliza about the drove and about Deio, but even to think about him brought her such mounting distress that she kept her counsel and, instead, asked her for practical things: "my brown portmanteau, if you please, my dark dress and bonnet, two pairs of woolen stockings, and as good a stock of underthings as you may find in my drawer. Also handkerchiefs, my dark leather boots with the side buttons, that sketch of mother and father from the top of the washstand, my book of poems, and one of Juno's shoes."

She enclosed some money to pay for the postage, telling Eliza to buy herself chocolates and scented soap with any that was left over.

"Please send these things quickly," she wrote, with more firmness than she felt, "for I hope to start work soon." Before she sealed the letter, she had a premonition that she might soon be very cold, an odd premonition, on that sunlit, bird-loud day, but strong enough for her to go back to her list and add, "and my blue cloak." That done, she felt a great release, like a tight hat coming off. She'd set it down, and was ready now.

She opened her eyes, took a deep breath and looked around the room. A clock ticked; she had to start now and was aware that for her this was a big moment. She picked up one of three books Mr. Holdsworth had left her that morning. He'd opened one, saying "Ferguson. It's the standard work on anatomy and physiology— he's a colleague of mine. Clerkwell C.F., although a bit of a quack in my opinion, is an astute observer of symptoms. Before the end of the day you will imagine yourself having every ailment invented by God—most students do."

She sat down in a leather chair near the window with Brook's theory of disease in her hands. It began with a section on typhus explaining a great controversy that now raged about the origins and spread of infectious diseases. The miasmic theorists said typhus was spread by the state of the atmosphere corrupted by terrestrial exhalations or vapors. The contagionists blamed poor sanitary conditions in the cities and the contamination of drinking water. A third group had clear evidence that the culprit was human fecal discharges in the water, or some agency resembling a living organism. As a child she'd had a vivid and recurring dream in which she'd suddenly discovered four new doors in Carreg Plâs, opening onto rooms never seen before. She'd moved through the rooms entranced, and now felt the same mix of curiosity and fear. What would she find? It was like lifting a stone and finding a keen, milling, new life of ideas and possibilities beneath the flat surface of things.

When she was finished with typhus, Margaret, who was being

very kind to her, put her head around the door and asked if she would like a tray of tea. When it came, she drank it down gratefully; after years of frittering her time, the effort of concentration was great. She turned the page and moved to the section on smallpox. There had once been a small outbreak of it at Aberdaron and her mother had gone to visit the sufferers. Everyone had blamed it on a long hot summer, but there might have been a thousand other explanations. By the time she'd finished with smallpox, the light was fading behind the French windows and she was stiff and yawning, but she wasn't done yet. She opened the section on childbirth, diseases of, and for the first time was disappointed. There was almost nothing here. "A condition," said the book curtly, "requiring the services of a trained midwife or accoucheur and not of interest to the general medical student." There were no pictures, and what information there was, was given in language too technical to understand.

Catherine could smell her mother's room again. Sick and sweet and dying. Felt her mother's hand in hers. "This is for you, Mother," she thought, "for you and for me."

And then she thought of Deio, how he'd suddenly arrived on the doorstep that day. He'd leaned down and put his face next to hers and absorbed her pain. Tender and strong, yet full of some deep understanding of her: she'd breathed him in, his strength, his smell of fresh air and smoke, his youth. These were the moments that were so hard to forget. She stood up and walked around in a fever, she had to get new thoughts in her head now, to learn to be alone. He'd changed everything on that night in Llangollen and she had, too, with her writhing body, her moans. The surge of feeling—unbelievable, like a wave breaking, and then the hurt and the blood. Dreadful and shameful.

Breathing heavily, she made herself sit down calmly. Beyond the darkening garden, London was a distant thrum. Somewhere out there was the Governesses' Home. She tried to picture it in her mind: a stately building with a library like Mr. Holdsworth's. Miss Nightingale at the blackboard teaching.

"Is there any news?" she asked Mr. Holdsworth a few hours later, as soon as he walked through the door.

"I only asked her this morning," he scolded her. "Be patient. And don't forget the second of my two conditions. I want some roses in those cheeks, before I even think of it."

Her father's letter came ten days later.

> *Dear Catherine,*
> *We are relieved to hear you are well, but your letter and your disappearance has shocked and upset us all.*
> *It seems you are quite set on spending your life away from home and I cannot feel glad about that, neither can Gwynneth, but in view of what has happened, and after taking advice from Rev. Hughes and Mr. Holdsworth about your reputation in this community, I say with regret that you should be given leave to try this new way of life for one year. After that time we shall have to review the situation as and when both parties see fit.*

The last bit hurt most. It sounded as if he were disposing of a field, or drawing up a loan agreement for a horse. But it was followed by an agreement that if she obtained a situation with Miss Nightingale he would pay her a small allowance quarterly and in advance. He had signed off:

> *I pray this will make you happy.*
> *With every best wish from your father.*

She folded the letter and put it back in its wrapper with a sudden longing for his tweedy smell, his strong arms, the safe feeling he'd once given her. She thought of the barley sugars he used to dole out from the tin in the little cupboard beside the fire. There seemed no way back, but she would miss him.

Eliza's letter smelled of violets. She wrote:

> *It was a wondrous relief to hear you are safe and well again. All we heard from Deio was that you were in London. Since then, Eleri has come down to the house to set our minds at rest*

and I feel I can breathe again, and whatever you decide to do will be all right because you are well.

The summer here has continued long and hot; we had too much grass and then suddenly, just on the week Father was to harvest, it looked like rain, so he and Alun and the Merediths worked day and night to get the harvest in, and Gwynneth and I spent those days in the kitchen, cooking up pies and ferrying them and lemonade to the fields. It was fortunate that we got it in before a big storm hit on Friday two weeks ago. A bolt of lightning got the Vaughans' barn near Pwhelli; Mr. V got hit by a brick on the forehead and knocked out.

Now, I have a secret for you, which is not really that anymore. You remember Gabriel Williams, don't you? He is tall, with dark curly hair and the sweetest smile you can imagine. He is a Gwynn Williams, the son of Ivor Williams who used to farm near Grandma's. He was, unexpectedly, at Grandma's party. I wish you had been there. It was a beautiful night—she had put up the Chinese lanterns and it was warm enough to open the windows and there was a full moon over the mountains. He marked five dances on my card, and then we sat in the garden and listened to the fat girl from Caernarfon singing "I Will Borrow This Rose." It was wonderful, Catherine. Yes, I am in love, definitely!!!! The next week, Gwynneth, who is delighted and already bursting with advice about gloves and dresses, escorted me over to his parents' house for lunch. His parents were so agreeable and kind. I think he might speak to Father soon. I wish I could speak to you about all of this. Please keep writing and tell me all the new things that are happening to you, I so want to know that you are well and happy,

With fondest, dearest, gladdest, love,

Eliza

As she folded the letter and put it back in its envelope, Catherine experienced what the Welsh call a *hiraeth* and there is no single word in English that so well describes a pang of love and longing and pride for a place and a person. She could see in her mind's eye Grandma's house in the moonlight: the veranda heavy-ringed with roses, the view of the iron-age fort on top of the hill, hear the tinkle of glasses, the laughter. How sweet Eliza must have been, lit up with love and surprise. How typical of her, too, not to utter one word of reproach. The letter also made more sense of father's, which, although stiff, was more prepared to see things her way. How proud he must be of Eliza: so steady and contented and feminine.

When she opened the parcel and took out the clothes, Eliza had embroidered her name in neat stitches on the collar of her cloak and two dresses. In the folds of the cloak were a lavender bag and a box of boiled lemon sweets. She put on her blue cloak and, slipping her hand in the pocket, found another of the wooden carvings Deio had done for her, years ago at Whistling Sands. An early version of the lapwing. He'd sat beside her muttering and whittling and making jokes. Seeing it again in the palm of her hand brought a new surge of longing and of pain, and before she knew what she'd done, she kissed it.

Chapter 22

One week passed, and then another. She ate and read and gained her strength, and grew impatient at asking Mr. Holdsworth the same question as he stepped through the door each night. And then one night he put a bottle of vintage champagne on the table and showed her a letter. Miss Nightingale had agreed to accept her for a three-month trial period as a probationer. She could start on Thursday the eighth of August, at eleven o'clock in the morning. She had a job!

And then the speed with which her life had changed seemed quite astounding. The following Thursday, after a quick wash, a check under the bed, a last nervous look at her portmanteau, packed and unpacked a dozen times, she was ready to leave, and in a high state of nerves. She felt in the strangest state of mind, as though none of this was quite real and she was watching everything from a distance.

Eliza had sent her a black dress to wear with shiny elbows and five jet buttons on each cuff. She said it had belonged to Mother, but Catherine, suspecting it was one of Gwynneth's cast-offs, hated its sour, sergy smell and the way it made her feel like a parlor maid or someone's maiden aunt. But at least for the time being it would save her the expense of having another made. When she went downstairs in it, Mr. Holdsworth, gallant to the last, pronounced her new look a tremendous success, and Margaret, who stood behind him, said it made her look very grown-up and responsible and that Mrs. Nightingale was lucky to have her.

"*Miss* Nightingale," Mr. Holdsworth reminded her, "a lady with many admirers but no husband."

Over breakfast, when Catherine said to him quietly, "I shall miss you," he put his *Morning Chronicle* down between the pats of butter and a silver toast rack.

"And I you." His endearingly large ears went pink with emotion.

"But I expect you will come to the Home to see Mr. Dalrymple," she said eagerly, "so I will see you."

"I hope so." To her surprise he looked longingly at his newspaper and sounded evasive.

"Will that be difficult?"

"I am not sure. It might be . . . I shall try and explain," he said. She topped up his teacup to fill an awkward pause. "Although," he continued, "I can't promise it will make any sense to you. But the nub of it is, Miss Nightingale might not like it."

"Not like what?"

"Our being friends."

"Why ever not?"

He looked at her, sighed, and decided to grasp the whole nettle at once. "Miss Nightingale," he said, "is the daughter of two aristocrats and, since she took over the home, the entire committee is comprised of society ladies who do good works: Lady Canning, and Lady Herbert, and Lady Bracebridge, and so on. They've made a fine job of it, too, compared to those other muddlers. But now . . . his is the difficult point to put across." He looked so uncomfortable she put her hand in his and squeezed it tight. "Very difficult. Miss Nightingale is adamant that ladies do not make good nurses, and nurses are a lower form of life than ladies. Miss Nightingale has . . ."

His ears went scarlet; he was a man who hated to be unpleasant about anyone. "Very firm convictions about class—like many women of her class and background. In order to get you your position, I had to emphasize the fact that you are a farmer's daughter—she has an *idée fixe* that farmer's daughters make good nurses—and so they may do, although I cannot for the life of me see why a sailor's daughter or a costermonger's daughter, or indeed a doctor's daughter, given a proper training and chance, should not be a nurse. Please never repeat what I'm saying to you. It was hard enough getting you in without spreading sedition among the ranks."

"So she has no idea that we're friends?" said Catherine.

"No," said Holdsworth unhappily. "In Miss Nightingale's book, there are surgeons and there are nurses, and any relationship between the two should be entirely professional. It pains me to be so blunt, but after a while she will see your worth and I daresay treat you with all the respect and affection you deserve."

She felt a cringe of shame then a flash of anger: first drover's clothes, now the parlor maid's dress. Why must a woman assume so many disguises in order to live an independent life? And now poor Mr. Holdsworth, who had tried so hard on her account, was almost stammering in his dismay.

"She is— You're— I'm sure she'll see what a fine young—"

"Is there anything else I should know about Miss Nightingale?" She tried to keep the hurt from her voice.

"Nothing that is unfavorable," he said firmly. "Indeed, I find her quite extraordinary. She has a first-class mind, and although one would hardly guess it under that gentle, hesitant manner, all the instincts of a born ruler—my friend Dalrymple is already wrapped round her finger." His eyes were sparkling. For politeness' sake she stayed at the table and drank a last cup of tea with him, but was suddenly anxious to be gone and to face the source of so many new misgivings. She glanced at her watch.

"I must go and get my things. The carriage will come for me in half an hour."

"Yes."

They both rose to their feet.

"Oh dear, I *shall* miss you." He put his hand out. "You have great spirit. I'm not surprised Eleri thinks so well of you."

"Thank you for everything." She put her hand in his. "I feel as if I have known you all my life—oh, I've brought you a present."

She drew from her pocket a marbled notebook and gave it to him. He took the book out of its wrappings of tissue paper. His gentle, precise hands made everything they touched look precious.

"It's beautiful," he said. "I shall treasure it and write all my most secret secrets in it. Now hold your horses for a second, don't run off. I have something for you, too."

He unlocked a cabinet and took out a small, tortoiseshell box about ten inches square with silver hinges at each corner and placed it in her hands. Inside it, cushioned in green velvet casings, were a pair of sharp scissors, a tiny thermometer like a bar of light, and a small probe with a tortoiseshell and silver handle and a hook on the end. The sight of them made her shiver with pleasure.

"Thomas Cushen, who made them, is an artist," he told her. "They were mine when I first became a medical student . . . Oh and take these, too, I have several copies around." He handed her *Gray's Anatomy* and Ferguson's book on physiology. "Read and read them again, my dear, until they are in your bones."

He thought of adding, "don't lose your dreams," but being a shy man, his ears went a shade pinker and he just shook her hand.

Chapter 23

They'd picked up another twenty Welsh Blacks from the Shrewsbury markets, and five rough-looking Welsh cobs with hips like coat hangers, presented by a young widow whose husband had died two months before of typhus. She patted each one and told Deio their names. She'd groomed the chief mare, Bonny, and tied a red ribbon in her mane and told him they'd bred her mother, too, and then she put a bag of lace into his hand and asked him to see if he could sell it at Barnet Market in London. A nuisance for him: there was so much pressing business to be done, the vellum book he kept in his pocket was stuffed with instructions: landlords' rents to be taken to London, twenty geese to be shod and delivered, some cattle to be dropped off at Kenilworth, twenty to be picked up. But he'd taken the lace, and patted Bonny, and said she was a tidy little mare, very well set up, and he'd find her the best home he could, and give her lots of green grass on the way. When he took them away, she hid her face in her apron and wailed. How they loved their horses. He couldn't bring himself to charge her for the shoeing.

That afternoon, he and Lewis and Rob helped Sion Fawr, a gentle giant of a man, famous for being one of the best blacksmiths in the area. He'd bent over the skittish cobs, lifting up their feet and talking silly nonsense to them to distract them, and when they were done, they helped with the cows, too. The sun was hot on their backs, and it was thirsty work seizing the muzzle of each cow, one hand gripping the horn and wrestling the beast into the dirt. Afterward, in the mild mosquitoey evening, they penned the beasts, jumped in the river naked, then dressed and sat on the banks under a willow tree, drinking beer and chewing the fat.

And he hadn't missed her at all; in fact, he told himself, he was glad to be shot of her. This was a man's world and she was better out of it.

Because Lewis was tight with a pound, they were working their way around the tollgates now from Shrewsbury to Gloucester, across the Berkshire Ridgeway, and then down to Padbury, Wendover, and Barnet Fair. He knew from experience that hard work blocked off the mind, and when they stopped to rest the cattle he began to handle the widow's cobs, to get them used to being brushed and touched and leaned against, and then, casually, as if it was the most natural thing in the world, he'd hop on. He'd taken to riding Cariad, Catherine's horse, too, although that brought the bruised feeling back. She was a talented mare, although moody and easily offended, and he was teaching her how to move away from his leg at the merest suggestion from him. He also tested her obedience by galloping her fast and making her stop at an adjustment of weight in his saddle. Lewis, who'd taught him this exercise from his days training polo ponies, would stop by and offer advice. Deio would listen, face impassive, head nodding, and go on with exactly what he was doing. He was too old for advice now. His father knew it, he knew it, and it angered them both.

"They think they know it all," Lewis told the blacksmith's father in the ale house. "Arrogant buggers," and carried on with his reminiscences of Waterloo where both had fought, and where both, if they were honest, had passed some of the most intensely enjoyable days of their lives.

The days were fine for Deio. His skin was darkening in the sun, the horses were growing harder and fitter and more biddable by the day. And being behind a herd of animals, all looking for ways of escape, didn't encourage dreaminess.

But the evenings hurt. When the sun dipped behind the hills and they built fires and lay smoking and listening to the sleepy sounds of late birds, then there was nothing left to think about but her. Then he'd lie in his variety of beds—the pile of blankets beside the fire on the Ridgeway, the truckle bed in The Plough at

Kenilworth, the four-poster in the Land Agent's house near Pad-bury—and feel some illness had struck him, a throbbing ache in some part of him that he hadn't known existed before, that came from a muddle, a confusion, a sense that he was being torn apart and had two selves. Lord Jesus Christ, he could kill her sometimes for bringing him to this. In the middle of what had felt like the best part of his life, she'd dragged him into a bog of confusion and made him feel a world away from knowing himself.

Normally a decisive man, what drove Deio mad was how his mind flipped back and forth like a weather vane depending on his mood and state of tiredness. With other women, when things went well they went well, and when they didn't, wallop, finished. He didn't have the patience or the time to patch things up; with her, nothing but confusion.

Once or twice he tried to think it through in the old, clear way. Reasons for loving her: many and various; reasons for being relieved she was gone: her recklessness, her desire to travel, lack of respect, and all the rest. Sometimes he felt indignant on behalf of her father. What kind of daughter would leave at a time like this? And then the look of her over the past few weeks: the hat, the breeches, the smudged face, had called up a feeling of hor-ror in him, and then the list would get all tangled again in his mind, and he'd see her in the moonlight in that hotel, remember the softness of her lips, the heat of her body; or times on the mountain laughing and adorable; that incredible look of gaiety, under her billycock hat; and her dancing in rhythm with Cariad's stride, looking every inch a drover's wife.

On the twenty-fourth day of the drove, he stood on a hill near Barnet looking down across the fields toward the smokestacks and the sooty sprawl of London. He told himself that if he could see her just one more time and set his mind at rest, he could be shot of her—of the feeling that somehow she was his responsibility—and all would be well, even better than before, because he would have faced down indecision and acted like a man.

With this thought in his head, he fell asleep that night in The

Horse and Jockey at Barnet happier than he'd felt for days. After a great day at the fair, his book was full. All that was left now was the last and trickiest bit through London and down to Smithfields.

The route planned was through Highgate to Holloway Road, then Upper Islington, Aldersgate Street, St. John's Street, and Clerkenwell. Other cattle would be coming down Oxford Street and the western part of the city. He woke at three-thirty next morning, dressed quickly, and then shaved by the light of a candle, just in case he saw her at the end of the day.

Four hours later, he and Rob and the two boys hired at Barnet collected the penned cattle and sleepy horses and started the tricky business of persuading them to walk through London. Lewis was in a foul mood, obsessively checking and rechecking the markings of the animals until they got the beasts to trot purposefully—down narrow streets thick with pig swill, up alleyways crisscrossed with rows of grimy washing, and, at last, into elegant thoroughfares with handsome Regency houses on either side. Lewis, still nervy and mean, hit one of the cobs who was snorting at a gas lamp, and made it shy into the crowd.

"That's good." Deio was beside him on Cariad. "That'll really settle him."

"You can fuck off," shouted Lewis. But they were doing well, until a carriage on John's Street held them up for half an hour. Lewis cursed, and waved his cudgels and prods at a man who shouted soundlessly inside the carriage like a lunatic in a box, while the cattle milled around him, depositing dung on his fine wheels. At the next corner, a woman selling pegs stepped blindly into the herd and had to be plucked out again by Rob, who doffed his cap to her and rode on. By the time they got to Marylebone, it was past eight and rush hour and Lewis did his party trick, shouting and singing in Welsh at another man sitting obstinately in his carriage, refusing to let them pass.

And then everyone joined in, roaring and bellowing, and the cattle were about to bolt when, at the corner of Marylebone Road near a church, as his horse wheeled around, he could have sworn he'd seen her in the back of a smart carriage, leaning forward, the straight line of her nose under a black bonnet. It *was* her. No, it couldn't be. Now, for sure, he'd gone mad and was hallucinating. He turned again, but his horse plunged to the side of the street. The carriage moved on, swallowed in a frenzy of activity.

Then Smithfields: a stinking cavern of noise and barking dogs and bellowing beasts, and men with red faces in bloodstained clothes, yelling and screaming. For the first time in three days, Lewis smiled, as they donned their drover's badges and penned and sorted cattle. He put his thumbs up. They'd made it in time for the butcher's eleven o'clock inspection. Of course he'd never doubted them.

By the end of the morning, hoarse from shouting, exhausted, and nearly a hundred and fifty guineas richer, Deio was about to join Lewis and Rob for an ale when a slight man in a smart uniform, stepped from the crowd. He cupped his hands and shouted, "horses" in his face. They went out the back so they could hear themselves speak, to the pens where the ten cobs were bunched together, showing the whites of their eyes. The man, said his name was Sergeant Dixon and he was a quartermaster for the Royal Dragoons.

"We need remounts for the Crimea, urgently," he said. "They have to be strong, uncomplicated, over fifteen point two, and preferably bay. I'll take this lot off your hands if you like."

"Nice of you to offer," said Deio, "but they'll sell themselves, they're nice types, and they're fit."

"Hop on then and show me," challenged the quartermaster.

As he slipped the bit between her lips Deio felt a niggle of excitement in the middle of him. He jumped on without stirrups, and swung her through a crowded alleyway toward a scruffy bit of open field out the back. He rode her quietly in small circles, taking his time, tuning her to him, making her block out the din, the fear, the smell, then he rode her full tilt toward a broken-down fence, stopping her dead three feet from it by rearranging the small of his back. To watch him, you'd think he'd done nothing.

"This war in the Crimea won't be over in a trice," the quartermaster told Lewis later, in The Bull over a jug of ale and a pork pie. "This is confidential but I know you've been a fighting man yourself and these things don't need to be spelled out. The sky is pretty much the limit at the moment, for good horses out there. I could get your son into a fine situation."

Lewis's face puckered with pride.

"He's a damn good rider," the soldier continued. "You simply would not believe half the autumn leaves we have to make horsemen of. We had the finest cavalry in the world, now they just chuck 'em on, give 'em a few lessons, then send 'em off to war, half of them shitting their breeches they're so windy."

"Same at Waterloo." Lewis was glowing with happiness. "Same thing altogether. The officers had some lovely horses, the others! Job lot would not cover it. Horrible sights I seen."

"He's a fine-looking young man, too. Nice uniform, plumes, parades—I think he'd take to it like a duck to water, Mr. Jones."

"Um." Lewis was half drunk and in a mood for confidences with a fellow soldier. "Awkward bugger mind. Sometimes, I can't tell him nothing."

"War's a fine academy for most young men," said the quartermaster. "It makes them grow up."

"What's this?" Deio had joined them, cleaned up and handsome in his London clothes. He sat down with his back to the fire.

"I was saying I could get you into the cavalry, smart young man like you."

"I don't want it." Deio lit a cheroot.

"Well . . . Oh hang about, let me get this young man's pot filled up."

"The question is"—had it been possible to whisper in such a noisy room, the quartermaster would have—"we *have* to get more horses out there one way or t'other. How long would it take you to find, say, twenty more like the ones you got, train 'em up, or bring them to the Barracks at Pimlico for us to sort out?"

"I'd sort them," said Deio, "then I'd know they were done. Three months."

"Fifteen pounds per horse guaranteed," said the man. "Do it right and it'll make your fortune. You could bring them yourself, or leave it to us, not everyone has a stomach for war."

He gave Deio a challenging look, and so did Lewis, and he felt a surge of anger; old farts thought they were the kings of the world just because they'd done it and you hadn't.

"I could go myself," he said. Excitement had flared up deep inside him. He could. He knew by the rapid way his father drank, and by the tense look in his eyes, that he'd be all for it. They both knew droving would be a mug's game once the train came through. He was already thinking of the horses he'd take, and decided to take Cariad. And now he felt a hunger to see Catherine again, to tell her, and see himself made new, not a whimpering boy pleading for a kiss, but a man going away to do a man's job, perhaps forever.

Chapter 24

hen she saw the drove making its way down Marylebone, she closed her eyes tight and breathed so hard that a line of sweat dripped under her hat. She didn't look up until the carriage had reached the Marylebone Road end of Harley Street, because if she did, it simply couldn't be borne. She had to do this now. The cabdriver swore and cursed as if there wasn't a lady in the back, and said that cows and carriages didn't go together. He told her a rambling story about a fellow he knew who'd been gored walking down Oxford Street and how he'd taken revenge. She barely heard him.

Not telling him to turn back took all her strength. After a series of stops and starts while the animals passed, they arrived an hour late, outside an elegant town house with a brass door plaque: The Institution for the Care of Sick Gentlewomen in Distressed Circumstances. She watched a flock of starlings take off into the blue skies, and a woman buy a bunch of violets from a street vendor, then she walked toward the solid oak door with her two suitcases in hand. She was so nervous she could hardly breathe.

A fat woman with a face like a cross red chicken opened the door.

"Yes?" she snapped.

"Good day to you, ma'am," said Catherine, "I've come to be a nurse."

The woman sighed. Her hands were flecked with flour.

"Round the back," she said.

At the back door, a young girl who had a heavy cold said, "Cub in." She took her through the kitchen where the stout woman was mashing potatoes in a cloud of steam.

"Cook's gone," whispered the girl to Catherine. "Mrs. Clark has to do everythid."

"Stop gassing, Millie," snapped Mrs. Clark, "take her up to her room and take the brush up with you. She'll have to turn it out herself now, there's another one coming at eleven-thirty." They made their way up the shadowy corridor where mops and pails were arranged with military precision. On the wall above them was a row of bells, each one connected to a number.

"They're new, them bells," the maid informed her. "Miss Nightingale's wineglass system. They went in last week."

Catherine smiled politely, not understanding, and followed her up a flight of stairs to the first landing. Everything was so neat: the wood on the backstairs gleamed, the blue-and-white curtains on the landings were starched and tied back crisply. On each landing, between the curtains, was a jug of cornflowers and white phlox, carefully arranged.

On the second floor, a white-haired woman in a nightgown burst from a row of identical doors, gave a girlish shriek and shot back into her room again.

"She's a silly old trout." The maid glared at the closed door and made a rude gesture. Catherine looked away shocked.

They were puffed by the time they'd reached the third landing, where Millie, between gasps, told her that some of the women who came here were as good as gold, and some were a pain in the neck, "very demanding and treats you like dirt."

"Why are most of them here?" asked Catherine.

"Tired," said Millie shortly, "some have conditions, some are fizzy and hysterical, others are bronchial. We have cancers, feminine conditions, most is just clapped out. This is you." She opened a scruffy door with her foot. "Make yourself at home."

The wretched room she walked into was so tiny that if you stretched out your arms from side to side you could touch the walls. In the corner was an iron bed, and above it a slanting garretlike ceiling with a crack in it that showed the lathes of the roof and, through them, white light. Someone had left a dirty, gray camisole on the piece of string that ran from one side of the room.

"She was a dirty girl." Millie's voice had fallen to a confidential whisper. "She drank, and didn't ever clean up after her. Mrs. Clark hates that, so now you must clean and after that come downstairs. The second sitting for lunch is in one hour. Wait for your bell."

When the door closed, Catherine took off her shoes and lay on the bed, trying not to mind that it was narrow and lumpy. It didn't matter, she told herself, she had arrived: a new job and a new life and it was bound to feel strange at first. She got up, hung her two dresses on the string and put her books and hairbrush on the windowsill. Then she took Deio's lapwing necklace out from her bodice and squeezed it till her knuckles went white. It was so annoying to miss him so much. Her mind was playing tricks with her. She unwrapped the watercolor Eleri had done of her mother and propped it on the washstand. Mother's slanting, tawny eyes looked back at her with a kind of wistful amusement.

There was three-quarters of an hour before lunch and she didn't know what to do, so she dozed until a broom banging against the wall woke her up. A voice was singing. She walked out into the dark corridor and knocked on the door.

"Yes?" A small woman opened it.

"My name is Catherine Carreg," she said. "I've just come. Do you have a dustpan I could borrow?"

"I do." The woman, who had a wild fuzz of brown hair and freckles, smiled brilliantly at her. "Come in. Isn't this grand?"

She held the door open, still smiling, on an identical room with the same kind of string for her clothes. On hers was a sad little gray woolen dress and a pair of much-darned stockings, pale at the heel from many washings.

"The room?" Catherine wondered for a second if she was being teased, but the woman's pleasure seemed genuine.

"Yes! I honestly can't bloody believe it."

"Where are you from?"

"Nurse Smart, St. Thomas's Hospital. Call me Lizzie. I'm relieving."

"Relieving?"

"Yeh." She patted the bed beside her. "Sit down. We've had a cholera epidemic at the hospital these past three months, a terrible do, then out of the blue my superintendent says there's a job with this Miss Nightingale, who's ever so posh and runs a sanitarium, and would I like to take it? Like to take it! What did she think?" Her eyes gleamed. "It's so nice here."

There were so many questions Catherine now longed to ask, but Lizzie, who seemed to brim with happiness, kept talking. She told Catherine how the word was that Miss Nightingale was a bit of a tartar with very high standards, that she had only just taken over here and had already dismissed four nurses, one surgeon, and a chaplain, so they'd have to look sharp, and where did she come from by the by?

From Wales, Catherine told her. She said she was relieving, too. Looking over her shoulder, she saw a tiny pair of well polished shoes already under the bed.

"Well . . . you can tell me the rest later," said her new companion kindly, after she'd fallen silent. "And don't mind me, I'm much too gabby."

"Oh no. I like to talk, it's just that I . . . well, there is so much to ask: Did you not have rooms of your own at St. Thomas's?"

"Oh Lor', no." Lizzie was attacking her hair with a comb. "I've been there for more than five years now, and I share a cupboard with three others. The new ones sleep in a kind of cage on the landing. I've never had a room of my own before."

"A cage! But—" A piercing bell rang. It came from the landing outside, where it seemed to leap up and down inside its glass house, shaking with rage.

"All right bossy boots." Lizzy went up to the bell and tapped the glass. "We're coming. . . . It's a clever thing though," she explained. "You press the switch downstairs and hear it up here. Millie downstairs was telling me about it. Miss Nightingale is very modern, she was telling me, very modern indeed. Goodness me, you're pretty, do you have a man friend? Oh don't mind me! I ask too many questions. Have you eaten? Well I have, but I'm not going to say no to another one."

Millie met them on the stairs on their way down to lunch and Lizzie, who seemed to deal with everyone with the same sort of straightforward friendliness, asked her straight out whether she thought Miss Nightingale would show her face at lunch, and Millie looked almost shocked, and said in a moist whisper that she was very important, and never ate with them but only did the announcements, and besides that a Lady Bracebridge and a Lady someone or other had come to see her earlier, with a pile of presents, and some lovely grub.

"What kind of lovely grub?" Lizzie's eyes were shining, she said she was a "porker when it came to food," which made Millie laugh, then cough, and Lizzie said that if she was Millie she'd take that cold home and give it a hot toddy of brandy and lemon.

"Quail's eggs, chocklick, Lapsang whatsomaflip tea, all from Fortnub and Masonds."

"Blimey oh riley," Lizzie said cheerfully, "it's as good as being at Buckingham Palace here." Millie said it was a good place to work if you could stick the governesses, and she wouldn't believe how many important people stopped by.

"Is she all right then, Miss Nightingale?" Lizzie asked Millie. Millie turned and looked at her, her red eyes scrunched up with the effort of thought.

"She's all right but a bit lah-di-dah and a bit frightening," she said. "You wouldn't want to cross her. She'll have you out of here as quick as ninepins if you don't behave." She was interrupted by a string of sneezes, and opened the door to the dining room. "Meet the customers."

On either side of a long wooden table were about thirteen or fourteen governesses, clattering away with their knives and forks. They were a somber group: two of them in wooden wheelchairs, and one, a depressed-looking woman in a dark wrapper with a black patch over her eye. Mrs. Clark, who was in the middle of telling a story when they walked in, left them standing awkwardly by the door. She was holding a steaming pile of mashed potatoes and ladling out stew into waiting white bowls. There were plates of stew, carrots, and cabbage and jugs of gravy on the table. Lizzie, behind Catherine, gave a low moan.

"No, that girl just walked out on me, just like that and without a word," Mrs. Clark was saying. "Miss Nightingale said she was very very sorry, but I was just going to have to carry on." A dollop of stew hit the plate. Mrs. Clark's eyes closed eloquently, "So!"

"Oh dear, oh dear," one or two of the governesses murmured.

"Oh goody!" said a small plump woman at the middle of the table who was watching the progress of the stewpot with gleaming eyes, and who appeared to be deaf. "Rabbit stew, a particular favorite."

"And I've got two new nurses to settle in." Mrs. Clark looked at them at last. "It takes time, my ladies, and that's my problem. Time."

The governesses glanced at them briefly and carried on eating, but the deaf one smiled, and said, "Halloo, well done! Well done!" in a general hearty way.

Catherine, who had had one or two very nice governesses when young, was surprised that no one had introduced them by name, but told herself that this was good for her; she was learning to be humble.

"Mrs. Clark," said Lizzie, who was smiling again. "Where do you want us?"

"Nurses at the end." Mrs. Clark, still appalled by her workload, pointed with her stew spoon toward the end of the table. "Millie will serve you. I only hope there's enough," she explained to the governesses. "I only heard they were coming at quarter to ten."

"Oh dear, dear, dear," the sympathetic little chorus started up again.

"Poor Mrs. Clark works so hard," said one.

Catherine and Lizzie had only just sat down and picked up their knives and forks and exchanged something like conspiratorial smiles with each other, when there was the noise of a door closing outside, and the squeak of a shoe in the corridor. Mrs. Clark's whole expression changed, she almost ran to the door, and then ran back.

"Sit up," she instructed the governesses. "Sit up straight! It's Miss Nightingale." She mouthed "*early*."

A scraping of chairs. Fourteen plates of rabbit stew and mixed vegetables left as the governesses got to their feet—even the crow-like figure in the wrapper did her best to rise.

And then Catherine felt the air in the room thrum with purpose, with tremendous excitement, as Florence Nightingale walked into the room. She was tall and slender with the kind of long and graceful neck designed for diamonds and well-cut evening dresses. Catherine, expecting someone older and worthier-looking, was much surprised by her youth and her beautiful smile.

Now she stood at the end of the table, amused but totally in control.

"Good-day to you all," she said gaily, "and sit down, please. Don't waste good food by letting it grow cold." The governesses began, flinchingly, to eat again, like dogs that are not sure the bone put down is for them.

"Two short announcements," she said in her low, musical voice. "Miss Anna Bowliss, having successfully completed a course of treatment with us, leaves tomorrow. She will be taking a last cup of tea with me tonight, you are all invited. Six o'clock sharp."

Her face was so expressionless that Catherine could not tell whether she looked forward to this. Miss Bowliss, small and plain, and strangely built like a pantomime horse with rather too much behind and not enough in front, stood up, went scarlet, and murmured, "Oh thank you! Thank you ever so much, Miss Nightingale." There was a smattering of applause and a few gasps of excitement.

Catherine learned later that the ceremony of the last cup addressed a problem at the Governesses' Home apparent since it had opened: many of the women who came to them wretchedly overworked and underpaid, soon discovered it was rather more fun being ill there than being well in the outside world. The sad but necessary task of shoehorning them back into the world of drafty attic bedrooms, awkward children, and employers belonged to Miss Nightingale. The little gathering (a party would be too fanfarish a word) was to soften the blow and mark their leave-taking

"Next," Miss Nightingale was getting impatient, "two new nurses have joined us today: Nurse Elizabeth Smart, from St. Thomas's Hospital, and Catherine Carreg, who"—she glanced briefly at her— "is to be a probationer. Mrs. Clark will have plenty for you to do this afternoon I'm quite sure, and I will see you at six, too.

"Last thing: Lady Herbert has sent up twelve pounds of raspberries from the country especially for you. Thank-you letters in that direction of course, and three volunteers to make jam in the kitchen this afternoon." Such was the zeal of the volunteers, some of whom pumped their arms in the air like children, that Miss Nightingale was forced to hold up a slender hand and make a firm decision. "Miss Poulter"—a stick-thin governess too timid to raise her hand—"Belinda Peterson, Thelma Sugg"—a sensible-looking woman who carried on eating and made no fuss.

"Oh and one last thing," said Miss Nightingale on her way out, "I should like to see you, Miss Carreg, for a private word, after the six o'clock gathering tonight. There are one or two matters we need to sort out."

"What on earth did she mean?" Catherine whispered anxiously, after she had gone. One or two of the governesses were craning to look at her.

"Have not the foggiest." Lizzie was tucking into her stew with abandon. "But I wouldn't worry about it," she whispered in a lower voice. "Women like that usually talk as if they've got a bun up their arse." Catherine didn't know whether to laugh or cry, Lizzie was so outspoken, and this was all so strange and new, and Miss Nightingale so sophisticated, so contained. She was every bit as alarming as Mr. Holdsworth had warned.

"She must be very clever to have so much influence so young."

Lizzie supposed so and said that if Catherine was not going to eat her potato she wouldn't mind it.

"The women here seem to worship her."

"'Course they do," came the reply. "It must be like staying at the Savoy for most of them. Stuck-up lot though, aren't they?"

"Have you met her before?" How grateful Catherine was already for her new confidante. "I don't know much about her."

"I have." Lizzie finished her potato and swallowed. "At St. Thomas, you wouldn't believe what it's been like, we've had all leave canceled, and the nurses have been dropping like flies. She came in from time to time with the superintendent."

"That was splendid of her. Did she nurse?"

"Of course not." Lizzie seemed quite surprised at the question. "I shouldn't think so. She's a lady, in't she? She looked at us, she talked to the bosses, and then she went. 'Ere pass me those carrots and have some yourself. You've got a long day ahead of you."

Chapter 25

*A*fter lunch, Catherine was sent down to the kitchen to get her orders from Mrs. Clark. It was bad luck that she arrived at the very moment Millie was out buying vegetables, a new governess was knocking timidly on the front door, and Mrs. C had decided she could sit down for five minutes with a glass of something in the kitchen.

Mrs. Clark, puffing and furious, ordered her out into the hall to tell whatever her name was to follow her upstairs.

Miss Widdicombe was a thin, high-shouldered, anxious young woman. Later, she was to tell Catherine all her woes: she was the daughter of a country parson from Somerset, and was a clever woman of thirty-two who knew Latin and Greek, and most of Wordsworth's "Prelude" by heart, but who could not stop crying. There was no money in her purse now after the expensive cab ride from the railway station, and nothing but anxiety in her heart. She was worried about the war in the Crimea, and about her brother, Simon, who was there with the 17th Lancers. She worried about herself and the flecks of blood she occasionally found in her handkerchief. She cared very much that the time for being loved and for being married had somehow sped by and left her high and dry, and she had come to dislike the children she taught, who, she suspected, neither liked nor respected her.

And Miss Widdicombe was tired, almost as tired as Nurse Smart but without any of the latter's native toughness. Now she cowered near the hall table, almost blubbering with nerves and exhaustion.

"My maid has gone out on an errand," Mrs. Clark told her grandly, "and we are very much at sixes and sevens today, but I shall show you up and Miss Carreg will help you with your bags."

Mrs. Clark's stout, bombazined back led the way upstairs, Catherine and the governess trailing behind her. The door, on the first floor, opened on a charming room with a comfortable bed, an embroidered chair, and high sash windows with a view of a laurel tree. Miss Widdicombe, however, who sat down immediately on the bed, seemed too tired to notice.

"It's a very nice room, isn't it," said Mrs. Clark pointedly. "That chair was brought up especially from Hertfordshire by Miss Nightingale."

"Oh." Miss Widdicombe was bewildered by this thought—a chair brought especially for her or for the home?

"Yes it was," said Mrs. Clark. "Put those cases in the cupboard Miss Carreg, and watch your boots, I think you have brought mud in with you." A small grain of dirt was lifted from the polished floorboards and inspected between red fingertips.

"Yes, that particular material," she continued, her voice taking on the upper-class drawl of her mistress, "came from the family home at Lea Hurst, which was small—only fifteen bedrooms." Mrs. Clark often slipped in a speech like this to new inmates when they arrived. Some of the governesses, she considered, had acquired airs and needed to be taken down an instant peg or two.

"It's a very nice chair," said Miss Widdicombe, feeling the air chill around her and searching for a reason. "I'm very sorry that I was late, but there was so much traffic on the roads, lots of cows and farmyard animals and things." She cleared her throat, a nervous habit much imitated by her pupils. "Hmmm . . . I meant to arrive at one-thirty sharp, but . . . hmmm . . . the coach driver got lost."

"Well, you've missed your lunch anyway," said Mrs. Clark. "There's nothing to be done about that. You'd better get into bed and wait until the doctor comes at five-thirty. Miss Carreg will bring a cup of tea and some bread and butter at four."

Catherine went scarlet; she was being treated like a chambermaid.

"Oh, thank you so much," said Miss Widdicombe, "this is . . ." but a slight trickle of blood had started in the back of her nose and would soon further annoy Mrs. Clark if she didn't get a handkerchief to it. "I'm so sorry," she said indistinctly, "and I am very much obliged to you, ma'am."

Mrs. Clark was slightly mollified, and after warning Miss Widdicombe not to put her suitcases on the chair, and informing her that her night for the bath was Wednesday, headed for the door.

Miss Widdicombe half lay on the bed as soon as Mrs. Clark was gone, and produced a small wad of cotton. "Can you? Would you frightfully mind?" she asked, and Catherine helped her pack her nose with it. Then they unpacked her two clean but ancient nightdresses, a few pieces of soap, and a gloomy-looking jet brooch. Miss Widdicombe looked so pale and tearful that Catherine caught a kind of panic from her. She hadn't a clue what she was doing here, or what she was supposed to be doing, and Miss Widdicombe seemed as embarrassed by her presence as she was.

After dithering around her room, Miss Widdicombe eventually went behind a screen and took off her dress, put on her nightgown and cap, and, helped by Catherine, got into bed with a little tearing cry of relief. Two minutes later, when she thought Miss Widdicombe was asleep, Catherine whispered, "Are you all right now?"

"No." Miss Widdicombe's red-rimmed eyes looked up from the bed. She shook her head; she seemed to be talking mostly to herself. "I'm so worried about everything."

"Is there anything in particular?" Catherine, unused to confidences from older women, hardly knew where to look.

"I'm worried about my brother, Simon," said Miss Widdicombe in a sad voice from the pillows. "He's a junior officer in Varna."

And now came an unexpected flood of talk. She explained he was her only brother, who had been a small asthmatic child with red hair that she wound around her fingers to make baby ringlets. He'd been in the Crimea six months now, and hated it. Father had insisted he go and won in the end by begging and borrowing enough to get Simon into a regiment, and off he'd gone, to Turkey, with two hunters borrowed from the family next door that he would not enjoy riding.

"He hates it," she said. "He spares me nothing in his letters home. The food is foul and everyone in the camp is getting ill. Poor Simon, he really is a fish out of water, he was terribly bullied at school—oh dear, I'm sorry." Blood and tears were mixing now in her handkerchief. "I haven't been able to talk to anyone about it for months. I'm so sorry."

"Here's a fresh handkerchief," said Catherine. She was terrified by the woman's tears; her own seemed so close to the surface and she had to stay strong. Poor Miss Widdicombe. She felt a little sorrier for her once she was safely asleep and a little more blood was trickling out of her nose. She found out later that Simon died while Miss Widdicombe was at the Home. The war across the world, soon to change all their lives, was escalating.

Chapter 26

While Catherine's first charge slept, she and Lizzie were taken in hand by Millie. She told them their official hours were from seven-thirty in the morning until seven-thirty at night, but because two other nurses had been so recently dismissed (one for cheeking Miss Nightingale, the other for getting pregnant and sicking up on pillowcases in the linen room) they were very short staffed and not to be surprised if their hours were longer. Millie, who had clearly taken a shine to Lizzie, also told them it was wise to watch your back at Number One Harley Street: there were spies everywhere and you could be turned out for anything from sloppiness in the kitchen to cheeking the governesses.

Lizzie listened to all this with her usual calm cheerfulness—nothing seemed to faze her—and when Millie asked her what her hours had been at St. Thomas's she said, "As many as you could put in without keeling over. No one was counting during the cholera epidemic. Everyone was wore out."

Millie furled her lip back. "Oh blimey oh riley, it's criminal. They don't let anyone infectious in here, thank goodness."

That afternoon, Millie showed Catherine how to empty and stack the chamber pots, which were left in the main lavatory on the first floor, rinsed, and then stored in a clove-and-ammonia-scented cupboard under the stairs. Bed-making was next, using hospital corners made with a sound like a pistol shot tight over hair mattresses. The white damask covers that came off the governesses' beds were folded and placed exactly in the middle on the backs of a chair, their ends lined up with the first horizontal spoke of the chair.

"Miss Highandmightingale is a tiger for neatness," Millie confided. "She tore me off a strip once for not doing a bed right."

Catherine's heart sank, and kept on sinking throughout the day. This wasn't what she'd come for, to fall straight back into the petty rigors of women's work, in a place where an inch either way in a folded bedspread spelled success or failure. And also—oh so horrible!—Father would have a fit: other people's chamber pots, and governess night soil, steaming and shameful, covered with a chintz tidy.

"Don't worry love, it'll be a doddle," Lizzie whispered when Millie's back was turned. "I'll show you what to do." She did a little shuffling dance on the floorboards and waggled her hands on either side of her starched cap. Catherine was amazed by her: this small, nondescript person, the kind of person she would normally pass in the street without a glance; amazed at her vitality, her practicality, her attitude to the work, so shamingly different from hers. Lizzie saw this new life as a holiday, a blinding stroke of good fortune, a real laugh; she even admired the chintz po covers and thought them "very ladylike."

In the late afternoon, Catherine ran upstairs with a cup of tea and a piece of bread and butter for Miss Widdicombe. She was fast asleep, her face buried in the pillow, her large, ringless left hand twitching on the bedspread.

"Don't dither by the door." Millie had come up behind her to check. "Close it, and let her be. Sometimes they sleep for twenty-four hours when they come."

Millie, who was less warm with her than with Lizzie and said she thought she was "quite lah-di-dah for here," took her into the linen room where bandages had to be rolled and stacked into neat rows, and where new nightdresses and sheets were cut out and readied for sewing. She gave her some needle and thread, hurled a few pieces of coal on the fire, and sat down beside it sewing and sniffing and sighing while the flames popped. At five o'clock, they ran up and down stairs again, putting on coverlets, taking food to bedbound patients, and returning clean chamber pots. Every bone in Catherine's body was aching and she was exhausted.

At six o'clock, Millie told her to run upstairs quickly, wash and fix her hair for the tea ceremony in Miss Nightingale's office at six-thirty to say good-bye to Miss Bowliss. Miss Nightingale hated any form of untidiness or lateness. She ran upstairs, splashed her face with rosewater and did her hair and, when she came downstairs again, all the governesses were standing under a chandelier in the hall near the front door, listening to the beautiful sound of their superintendent laughing inside her office with an unknown woman. The sight of them, so eager and yet so tentative, like large, sad, grown-up children accustomed to being left out, was desolating. Catherine stood apart from them and tried not to mind. And she tried not to think about Deio, who'd been at the back of her mind all day. This was what she had left him for; this was what she had come for.

"It is Lady Bracebridge, I'm sure it is." Miss Sugg tested the air knowledgeably. "She often comes on Thursdays and is a *particular* friend."

"It could be Elizabeth Herbert," said Millie, "she comes very regular. Her husband is prime minister." She gave Catherine a proud look.

"No no, quite wrong, Millie," said a fat governess. "He is the secretary of state for war. Have you not read a thing about the war in the Crimea?"

"Same diff." Millie, who couldn't read, and hated that fat bitch, made her tongue bulge through her cheek.

"It *is* Selina Bracebridge!" Sugg's fat cheeks wobbled, and because Catherine was her only audience, explained to her in an excited, mint-flavored whisper that this lady was a key member of the Home's committee, the wife of Sir Charles Bracebridge, a dashing statesman and an explorer, and a fine-looking woman herself.

"For goodness sake, shuussssh!" A small woman in a wooden wheelchair was eye-level with the keyhole. "Noise down! Are we eavesdroppers?"

"No we ain't, she told us six-thirty sharp," said Millie.

"Ssssh!!!" from three governesses.

"Thank you, darling, *bless* you for coming." The door suddenly opened on a cedar-paneled room and Miss Nightingale walked out arm-in-arm with Lady Selina, who was tall and blond and perfect in her coral silk hat, with a kind of ripeness to her looks that brought to mind bouncy thoroughbred horses, or corn-fed pedigree cows.

"Heavens above, you're all very early, aren't you?" A hint of irritation lurked behind Miss Nightingale's breezy greeting. "If I might just have time to show Lady Bracebridge to the door."

"Who is leaving today? Are we losing someone?" Selina's voice, cooing and slightly husky, was like a pigeon at dawn.

"Yes we are: Miss Bowliss," said Miss Nightingale. "Miss Bowliss from Yorkshire." They exchanged a secret smile, for Florence, a celebrated mimic, did a killing imitation of Miss Bowliss—her head on one side, her pantomime horsey bustle somehow elongated. "She's leaving tomorrow." Miss Nightingale opened the door. "So, farewell Selina, and thank you again for my *presents*, so many of them."

"Good evening, Lady Bracebridge," chorused the governesses, drab as pond life as she darted between them.

When the door opened, Catherine saw a carriage at the gate with two well-matched bays, ready to take their owner, almost skipping down the path now, home to her handsome husband. Her life. Beautiful horses. Father would have approved of the elegant barouche, the harness soft and supple as skin, the varnished doors, too. She would have liked to run out into the street and stroke their faces and admire them, but even that kind of movement was out of bounds now.

"Do come in all of you." Miss Nightingale returned and was kind enough to show them the contents of the two small packages she was carrying: tea, and some dark chocolate with knobs of crystallized violets on top. Selina had brought them from Fortnums.

The drawing room they filed into was large and well appointed, with a faint, reassuring odor of beeswax and potpourri. On a cedar table under the window someone had laid out a pile of Wedgwood plates, a large earthenware pot of tea, a jug of weak lemonade, and two plates of bread and butter and Madeira cake.

"Oh good-ey gumdrops," Miss Bowliss gasped.

Tea was poured, and drunk with fingers held just so, and the good china given its due deference. Once again Catherine felt nervous in the slender, even girlish, presence of Miss Nightingale, who looked well in an expensive, purple wool dress, very severely cut, and with a rim of white at the collar, and who handed out tea and encouraged cake-eating so kindly. Her clever, dark eyes seemed to miss nothing, and the intensity of their gaze and the intimidating neatness of her glossy chestnut-colored hair suggested high standards that might never be met.

"So," she said, after five minutes of chitchat with the governesses, "where is our guest of honor?"

Miss Bowliss, who'd come to the Home one month ago after a bout of pneumonia, was pushed toward the front, where she stood simpering and blushing. She wasn't born for the spotlight. She had worked for some minor aristocrats up north, had arrived at their house as a Yorkshire lass with a broad accent and straightforward views—often involving socks and the necessity for pulling them up—but long years of mingling with the gentry and with children had mixed in with her accent a widdle-tiddle way of talking that she'd used for so long in the schoolroom, that she could no longer remember to turn it off. And now, little finger crooked above a glass of lemonade, she stood up in the middle of the circle of governesses around Miss Nightingale and said, in her baby voice and with her head on one side, "I've had a lovelee, lovelee time here, Miss Nightingale. Thank you evsa mooch. It's been like paradise."

A small smattering of applause here, and Miss Nightingale stood up and took her hand. "I wish you all good luck, Miss Bowliss," she said in her low musical voice, "and I hope for your dear sake that you are now fully restored to health."

"Thank you, Miss Nightingale," replied Miss Bowliss. Her chin was wobbling and her eyes filling with tears. "I'll remember it my whole life long."

"Good," said Miss Nightingale briskly. Her lips made a smile.

Catherine noticed that all the governesses were gazing steadfastly at Miss Nightingale and not at Miss Bowliss. Miss Nightingale, with her fine face, her exquisite clothes, her air of breeding, inspired adoration, whereas Miss Bowliss—poor Miss Bowliss with her affectations and her strange figure—was like a Russian carriage: everything seemed ever so slightly wrong. Life was not fair to plain women.

Now Catherine sensed Miss Nightingale had grown bored with

the governesses: she wanted them to stop staring at her and go back to their rooms. She could see through the window that the lamps had been lit in the street outside and a swarm of gnats swam in the greenish light. It was time for prayers, and for baths for those on the Friday-night roster. Miss Nightingale made a special point of telling them that she would be at her desk, working on their behalf for most of this night. Her voice became a shade more distant as she agreed with Miss Sugg that, yes, there always was a great deal to do.

Five minutes later, she bade them good night, "With the exception of Miss Carreg, who I would like to stay."

When they were alone, she waited nervously while Miss Nightingale composed her desk again to pristine neatness, and covered the milk with a little mob-cap of net with beads hanging around it.

"Sit down," said Miss Nightingale. She stood against the large window and, giving her a long and penetrating look, said it had dawned on her over the last day that she knew very little about her, and that was a worry. She sat down behind her desk, got out a sheaf of papers, and confirmed that Catherine came from Wales and that she was a farmer's daughter, then wondered if Catherine had fully understood what was meant by the term "being on probation." She said that she was probably unaware that in a sense they were all probationers at this home, which had only been going for six months and was under continuous and close scrutiny by the authorities, for whom it was very much an experiment.

"I'm telling you this, Miss Carreg, for a particular reason." Miss Nightingale's voice was pure steel now, and her look frightening. "A young man came to the door last night asking for you in what I consider a very impertinent manner. He said your father had given him the address. If you are married, or in any other kind of trouble, you had better tell me right away."

Catherine bit her lip and felt herself blush as she told Miss Nightingale that she was not.

"Are you now going to tell me now that you have no idea who he was? If you are, save your breath."

Catherine, now feeling a strange mixture of exhilaration and mortification (so he had come for her after all!), asked if he was a young or an old man, and was told he was young and, as she had already been told, impertinent. Catherine then imagined how

Deio, who never cowed or excused himself, would enter this room, with a faintly swashbuckling air as though he carried a dagger in his boot. He would have looked Miss Nightingale in the eye and, amused and cautious, taken her on like another kind of wild beast whose secrets he would discover. Most women found this irresistible, Miss Nightingale clearly had not. Her heart jolted and for a mad moment she wanted to laugh. It was so naughty of him to have come here.

"I'm sorry. I think he may have been a friend from home. My neighbor."

"I know very little about you," Miss Nightingale repeated peevishly. "You're an unknown quantity. I had no idea for instance that you were so young, and am very out of sorts with myself for forgetting to ask Mr. Holdsworth such a fundamental question. We're all finding our feet here, Miss Carreg, and if there hadn't been such a rush to replace the two nurses . . ." Her clean little fingers clenched themselves in frustration and then spread on the gleaming desk.

"I'm sorry, ma'am."

"If he comes again, Miss Carreg, you leave. Is that absolutely crystal clear?"

It was. She looked at the stern set of her leader's mouth, and felt her spirits fall. Outside in the streets she could hear carriages moving through darkening streets; the sharp cries of someone selling something. Some curtains rattled above her, someone coughed, and she felt the night and the unfamiliar rooms close around her like clothes that didn't fit. When she'd been dismissed, Millie told her to go up to Miss Widdicombe's room and check she was all right. She'd just woken up and asked if she dared ask for a little tea again. Five minutes later, Catherine put a tray beside her bed. Miss Widdicombe thanked her shyly and said it was the best sleep she'd had in months. The two women looked each other in the eye and smiled and, as she left the room and went upstairs, she told herself that once she became a proper nurse things would change and improve and she wouldn't feel quite so far away from home.

Chapter 27

Then work began in earnest. In the mornings, prayers and breakfast, emptying chamber pots, making beds, taking up trays, running up and down stairs twenty, thirty times a day. She rolled bandages, stacking them in neat rows, darned, sewed, put on coverlets, took them off again, and helped to cook lunches. Then it was returning chamber pots, more sewing and, in between sweeping floors, chopping cabbage, and emptying slops, running errands for Mrs. Clark, whose head always seemed to be in a cloud of steam, and whose temper seemed set somewhere between simmering and boiling, depending on how many governesses they had in.

Catherine was prepared for some menial work, but after two weeks of this, she went to Nurse Smart, whom she now called Lizzie, and complained in some distress that she was nothing but a maid. Lizzie gave her a sideways look and said, "Well, what did you expect? That's what nursing is for most."

"I thought Miss Nightingale would teach me things," she said. "The things that you do: cupping and bleeding and bandaging."

Lizzie, who was sitting on her bed resting her legs, screwed up her face and squinted at her. "Catherine," she said, "sharpen up. How can she teach you what she don't know herself? And how many times do I have to tell you? She's a lady. She runs things, she don't do things. I doubt she's had more than three months experience in a hospital, and none of them at nursing."

Catherine sat down beside her and gave a soft howl of frustration. "Well, how did *you* learn?"

"Fifteen years hard labor" came the reply. "St. Thomas's, Doris Ward, Women's Foul Ward, Surgical, Midwifery, Magdalene, cholera, etcetera." She ticked them off on her small practical hands.

"Well, how can I learn?"

"I dunno."

"Oh, don't tease, help me. You teach me. I have an instrument case."

"Eeehh, an instrument case! Ain't she posh."

"I have some books."

Lizzie's face turned red. "You'll have to read them because I can't, and don't say anything else about that because I don't want to talk about it."

"Could you really teach me? Oh Lizzie, *please*, I'm feeling so hopeless, and maybe there's something I could teach you, too."

"Maybe. Now don't tug at that pretty hair, missie, it won't help you. 'Course I'll help you. When do you want to start?"

"Tomorrow?"

"Why not? But take a note Miss Carreg: I am strict. Oh, and another thing, don't shout it from the rooftops, in case Miss Nightingale and Mrs. Clark think . . . well, you know . . . they like the orders to come from them, and they've already got their eye on you."

"How do you know that?"

"Because I'm not daft. You're too young and you don't quite fit— and they'll have your guts for garters if you irk them."

"My what?"

"See Finemouth, you don't fit."

"Oh Lizzie." Catherine shook her friend and groaned. "Don't tease, I'm so grrrhhhh. I haven't even been outside the door for two and a half weeks."

"I know, love." Lizzie gave her an innocent look. "Welcome to working."

But Lizzie kept her word. The next day, she drew Catherine aside, and said, "A surgeon is coming today to take some blood from Miss Dwyer, room ten. They've asked me to help with the bandages, and if you want to come, too, I won't say nothing, only don't get me into trouble by keeling over."

"I won't. I'm tougher than you think, Lizzie."

"All right, all right, and if they ask you to go, don't make a hoity-toity fuss. Tell them you got confused, that you're a dim little Welsh girl."

"Don't tease. I will, I promise."

"All right then, follow me."

She followed Lizzie's practical little figure upstairs, feeling, as she had so often already, profoundly grateful for her calmness. They went up to the first-floor landing and through the door of room ten. Inside the room, Miss Dwyer, a faded but pretty woman in her forties, was sitting up in bed looking anxious. She'd arrived at the Home a week before, suffering from boils, poor circulation, and general debilitation. She wore a white mob-cap, had her sheets drawn up to her neck, and, as soon as she saw them, put her book aside and began to talk in a nervous, nonstop stream.

"Upon my soul, Nurse Smart, I am so happy to see you—all I've heard from Mrs. Clark today is that they will, repeat *will* take blood today, but"—her large eyes bulging—"*when* is the real question, which Mrs. Clark didn't address at all, and I've had no breakfast. I don't like the idea of it at all, the bleeding, they've done it so many times and it hurt the last time, and look—it did me no good before, so why should it this time?" She leaned forward and bent her head; on the back of her neck were three angry-looking sores.

"I can give you a powder for those," said Lizzie. "It will dry them out and stop the pain. Did they do the blistering here or somewhere else?"

"It was the doctor in Grantham, and he said it would positively do the trick. How much more blood do they need? I really am feeling so much better."

"Not much more, I shouldn't think, my love," said Lizzie in a kindly, neutral voice. "You can't go on and on, can you?"

While they were mixing up chalk powder in the dispensary room, Lizzie said that whoever had done the blisters on Miss Dwyer's neck should have their own neck wrung for letting them get so sore—what was the point? And that some of the more forward-looking doctors at St. Thomas's now forbade bloodletting for wounds and other lowering complaints, saying it cast a strain on the whole nervous system.

"That's it, a small spoonful of that chalk powder, and put the rest back with the top on tight. You must keep your working areas tidy."

"Are the other nurses allowed to mix medicine?" asked Catherine.

"Not all of them, no," said Lizzie, "but Miss Nightingale knows I done it for years at St. Thomas's, so without blowing my own trumpet, she knows she can trust me. I haven't lost anyone yet."

"You don't blow your own trumpet, Lizzie, nothing like enough."

While they waited for the doctor, Lizzie told Catherine what the medicines inside the bottles were for: "Opium for sedation. Senna. Castor oil for constipation and bringing babies on. Epsom salts: purging. Chalk and opium for diarrhea, quinine and antimony for reducing fever. To fortify patients doctors say brandy, port, and beef tea; to soothe them arrowroot and salep. Here." She shoved a piece of paper in Catherine's hand, and a pen. "If you can, write it down, never rely on your memory to carry you through."

Catherine wrote notes in her book, and looking up, saw Lizzie watching her in admiration. "Writing's nothing, Lizzie," she said, "I could so . . ."

"Don't talk about it." Lizzie's tone was distant. "One day maybe, not now. It doesn't matter."

The doctor arrived, a middle-aged man in a frock coat. His bursting face whiskers and clattery boots felt alarmingly male. His noisy boots made their way directly to Miss Dwyer's pillow, where she lay nervously twittering. He made her lean forward and had a look at her neck. He sent Lizzie off for some wadding, asked for a bowl, some string, and a cup, and with a sigh, strapped Miss Dwyer's arm to what looked like a broom handle. Catherine felt sorry for Miss Dwyer who now, silent and bound, waited with her green eyes open wide. The doctor tied a piece of string under her elbow. He looked out of the window, waited for a while, then prodded and pinched until he could find a vein. Catherine knew from her reading that the vein the doctor had selected on the thumb side of the arm was the larger vein, and the one most usually selected for bleeding.

The room lurched, and she tried to focus on a pair of battered shoes under the bed as she saw him tighten the string and then the blood leap as he plunged the knife, which he held like a pen, into

Miss Dwyer's arm. His sausagelike fingers, with their clumps of red hair above the knuckles, handed a lancet to Lizzie who gave him a bowl. He pinched the skin of the wound for a while, and then directed the flow of blood into the bowl.

"Don't move your arm," he warned Miss Dwyer, "I'm going to take several pints, and then Nurse Smart can bandage you." He handed Catherine a wad of bloody dressings without a word. She took them into the medicine room and threw them into a wastepaper basket, and then sat down heavily, feeling sick but pleased with herself—at least she hadn't fainted.

When she came back, Miss Dwyer, pale and relieved, had her eyes closed.

"That's the fourth time I've been bled in the past year," she told the doctor. "Two in one arm and two in the other—quite the old hand."

"You'll need to wash that arm nurse." The doctor had turned his back on her and spoke to Catherine. "And give me a pledget." He held the two flaps of skin together.

A pledget? She looked at Lizzie imploringly.

Lizzie handed her the bowl of water. "I'll get them," she said. She came back with a small, flattened mass of lint. The doctor pulled it in two and then, pressing the smaller one into the wound, put the larger one on top and told Lizzie to start bandaging, which she did, winding the material around the arm in a deft figure eight and then tying a bow.

"Well done, nurse," said the doctor pleasantly when she was finished. He yawned, and then winked at her. "Tell the night nurse she is to keep her arm still for twenty to thirty hours. No gadding about," he boomed at Miss Dwyer, who thanked him for his time and his patience.

Catherine's heart bounced with happiness. She had survived her first operation.

They looked like an odd pair, the slim, tawny-eyed, tallish girl and the small, plain, frizzy-haired woman with her square hands and her frank gaze, but from that time on they were inseparable.

Perhaps because there is nothing so gratifying to an expert as being able to hand on knowledge, painfully acquired, to an eager and admiring pupil. In this respect, Lizzie was as susceptible as the next, and from that day on began to train a willing slave. Whenever possible, they worked together, and if Mrs. Clark was about and there was an important procedure to be learned, Lizzie signaled it by a look or by saying out of the corner of her mouth, "Take a note, Miss Carreg."

By the time six weeks had passed, Catherine knew how to bandage efficiently; how to poultice, cup, and bleed; how to keep elementary notes on a patient's condition. She had helped Lizzie inject warm water up the back passage of a Miss Munroe, admitted for severe and chronic constipation, and helped get leeches out of a box—horrible gray, dead-looking things—and affix them to a pale woman from up north. Every day, she and Lizzie went to room six on the second floor and bandaged Miss Pond, whose arm had been badly burned trying to cook a Welsh rarebit on a schoolroom fire.

Sometimes it all seemed appallingly intimate: the dimpled white backs of Miss Munroe's legs; Miss Widdicombe's sobs and nightmares and all the rest. Without Lizzie, who was funny and kind and who seemed to know what to do, it would have been intolerable.

On duty, Lizzie wore a belt around her waist very like the ones the drovers had worn. Inside was her bandaging kit, wound powder, wadding, and sharp scissors. To watch her use the tools of her trade with quiet deft gestures and the neatness and precision of her cutting, was to see a craftswoman at work. Sometimes she handed the kit to Catherine and said, "Nurse Carreg, you do this," and Catherine's hand would tremble and her heart stir.

That first month she learned how a person could split themselves in two. She was haunted by the idea that Deio had come to the home and she hadn't seen him, and she was confused. Why, considering how badly he'd behaved, did his absence feel like an ache? Was she so very depraved? She longed to ask Lizzie's advice on this but thought she would shock her too much, and these thoughts wouldn't go away even at night, particularly at night, when her feet hurt and her head ached from studying too much by candlelight, and she forbade herself to think of home or anything connected with it.

She had a few rows with Lizzie, who could be a brusque and exacting teacher. And sometimes, a burst of laughter, or music from the street would make her prick up her ears like a stabled horse, and throw her into a kind of panic. What was she doing here?

Mrs. Clark was another sore point. She was starting to hate the woman's cross chicken face, her stout scurrying figure. As far as Clark was concerned nurses had only four things to recommend them: two arms and two legs, and if these were not permanently engaged in making beds, turning patients, washing, ironing, and sewing, she would not be responsible for the havoc that would ensue. As for book-learning, in Mrs. C's humble opinion—she'd never had the patience for it—it made a girl swollen-headed and rude to doctors.

Behind the scenes, Lizzie did a grand imitation of Mrs. C, and the legendary firings that were a staple of conversation in the dining room. "So, I says to her, pack up your things, and go!" In every institution she'd worked in, Lizzie told Catherine, there was one old and jealous animal like Mrs. C, "a bit too free with teeth and heels. Just keep your eye on her, that's all," she said, "and Miss Snootingale, too, for she is very watchful, and very very nervous."

"Nervous!" exclaimed Catherine. "I've never met any woman in my life who seemed less so."

"Catherine, oh Catherine, you are so wet behind the ears. She's never done this before, it's all new to her. Trust me on this."

"Urggh," said Catherine. "I'm tired of you knowing everything." Lizzie threw a pillow at her and the muttered lessons continued.

"Keep all your lights on when you're working," Lizzie scolded her one day. "You walked into that room like a child with a hoop. Train your mind not to wander. When a man or woman ails, they're like a frightened animal. Walk quiet, talk gentle, a heavy tread to a sick person is attached to a hand that might hurt him."

On the Tuesday of that week they went up together to room eleven to see Mrs. Thompkins, a widow, operated on the day before for a prolapsed womb. Together, they undressed the blushing governess; they put her into a sitz bath, changed her padding, dressed her in a clean nightgown, and put her back into bed again. When they had left her room again, Lizzie said, "You did all right in there." Her first compliment. "You seemed natural," she continued. "If you're doing sommat to them, like we did with Miss Philips for her piles or Mrs. Thompkins for her womb fall, don't go all grand on 'em like the doctors do, and don't whisper at 'em like their mother has just died, but look them in the eye, treat them in a friendly way, say 'how are you then?' 'How do you feel?' Show it's normal, and that's better than all the medicines in the world to some."

Sometimes they were joined by two other nurses—tired-looking middle-aged women with families, who came in on a daily basis and envied them the food. Then, when they didn't get the same shift, they would pass each other on the stairs. Lizzie, bleary-eyed from the nightwatch, almost limping with fatigue as she climbed the stairs; Catherine, bright-eyed on her way down.

"Take a note, Miss Carreg." She'd wag her finger solemnly. "Take a note." Or she'd give her her Mrs. Clark look and make her laugh.

On one such morning, in early September, they were crossing on the stairs when Lizzie handed over a small bundle of letters.

"Mrs. Clark said these came for you."

The top letter was in Eliza's careful hand with its round, rather childish o's and curling y's and g's. She'd written several times since Catherine had left; happy letters, full of details of dresses and furniture, and the only geraniums worth having. Her little sister, so grown-up and so clearly in love with Gabriel Williams, who had a farm close to Grandma's and thirty acres of rich land with a river running through it. How proud Father must have been of her. Catherine hoped it might mean he would mind less about her, but there was no sign of it in his letter, which held his check and his usual curt note. Underneath this letter was another, in Deio's handwriting. The sight of it communicated an almost physical fear and she let it lie in its string until she got to the third landing. He wrote, without preamble:

> *Dear Catherine,*
>   *My circumstances have changed and I come to London a great deal, to the Cavalry Riding School in Pimlico, who are starting to buy my horses to take to the Crimea. I am doing well*

from it. I shall call on you again soon when I come up, to see how
you are.

No mention of how he had got her address, no apology either to
her or to Miss Nightingale. She stuffed the letter in her pocket and
felt her mouth go dry. *How dare he do this to her?*

The door to Lizzie's room was half ajar when she walked in. Her
dress and pinafore were hanging on the string and she was lying
down, her eyes half closed.

"Are you all right?" Lizzie jumped to her feet. "You look as white
as a sheet."

"I don't know, Lizzie. I've never felt so—"

She gave Lizzie a strained look; how much could she tell without shocking her?

"Oh Lizzie, I'm . . . can I talk?"

"'Course you can," said Lizzie, "but sit down first before you fall
down and mess up my bed." She pushed Catherine down on the
bed and quickly loosened the top button of her dress.

"Hot in here, i'nt it?" she said quickly and casually, with her
usual lack of fuss. "Not quite enough windows. Now come on love,
let's have it. Chickenhead will be upstairs and after us soon if you
don't hurry."

"The thing is Lizzie," she said, "I've been very bad."

"Oh, this sounds good," said Lizzie. She'd been brushing her
hair and it stood out around her head like brown furze.

"The letters were from my family in Wales." To Catherine's humiliation, she had started to shake. Lizzie put the blanket around
her and pulled it up to her chin.

"Oh, bother," said Catherine, "this is all so silly."

"Oh for lawk's sake spit it out," said Lizzie, "it can't be that bad."

And then she told Lizzie as much as she could. She could not
speak about her mother, but she told her a bit about Deio, and how
she'd run away with him and the drove, and what a saint her sister
was, and how disgracefully she'd behaved, at least as far as Father
was concerned.

"Hold on, hold on." Lizzie's eyes were shining. "Blimey, I'm impressed. What a life you've led, and still very wet behind the ears."

"No, no, no, you don't understand about Deio." Catherine's eyes were wild. "He is the reason I'm here; I mean, without him I couldn't have come, and we've been friends our whole lives, and I worshipped him, and I . . . but then he, I . . . he . . . I don't know what to think about it."

"Come on, come on." Lizzie put her own black shawl around Catherine and gave her shoulders a brisk rub. "Nothing is that bad."

"Oh but it is. He tried to, well we did, and it was partly my fault. Maybe all my fault, he told me not to come here." And all the pent up tears, unshed in Llangollen, burst out. "And now he says he is coming to London, and he's already been and been rude to Miss Nightingale, and she says if he comes again, I have to go."

"Now, now, now, now." Lizzie held her for a while until the shaking and the tears stopped, and then calmly unloosed her hair and brushed it strand by strand as if to untangle all the snarls and distress in her head.

"I don't know what is the matter with me," said Catherine after a while. "I wanted this life, but I long for home. I'm so homesick, Lizzie, and so happy, too, sometimes. I wake up in the night, I think I must be mad, and then I go to work with you, and I'm so caught up in everything." Her face glared comically through her hair. "I got a letter from my sister today who is getting married and a letter from Deio who I could murder." She jerked her hair out of Lizzie's hand.

"Calm down, madam," said Lizzie, "have a little nip of this." She produced a small jam jar of brandy from under the bed and a glass, and poured Catherine half an inch "courtesy of old chicken head, who was so busy telling off Millie, she didn't see me. Don't look so shocked, love; take your comforts where you can. Now, let's talk about your young man first. How old is he? Twenty-three—oh the little lamb—all right, so he's not a little lamb, but he's a young man. A young man on a journey from Wales with a beautiful young lady, oh it's quite romantic this, i'nt it? How did you sleep?"

"In taverns, or under the stars."

"Oh, good God." Lizzie could scarcely believe her ears. "Right then, in taverns, under the stars." She sketched out a night sky with her sensible little hands. "Oh, it *is* romantic, Catherine, so what did you expect him to do? Sit up at night and darn with you? I'm sorry, dear, but men is men. Now then, do you have a problem down below, or a little one on the way?"

"No!" Catherine was mortified. "Nothing like that. So you're not shocked?" she said at last, raising her eyes above the blankets.

"Shocked!" Lizzie's look was boldly frank. "By that? Look, Catherine, if we are to be friends, I had better tell you a thing or two about myself and some of the other nurses you'll meet, otherwise you'll have a fit of the vapors." Lizzie poured herself a drink and sat down beside Catherine.

"I was born in the East End of London, Catherine, no more than six or seven miles from here, Stepney if you must know, and where I come from, London, not Wales, wherever that is—don't laugh, Catherine, because I really do not know—there are a lot worse fates for a woman than losing her virtue, whatever your bishops or your whatsanames may tell you."

Her face, as she calmly folded her hands over her apron, wore a new expression, mischievous and secretive. "A lot worse. In fact, I don't think I know one nurse, except those who work for the Sisterhoods, who have not you-know-whatted. That's why when they call us 'The Band of Angels,' they're having a laugh—we're real women not saints."

She told Catherine that in hospitals there were often men and women sleeping on the wards together, sometimes the men demanded it, sometimes not, and there was the human side to be considered, "a nurse giving out all the time and needing something back. A touch, a kiss, human affection, Catherine." It was nice, she told her, to find the right man and it's—Lizzie thought hard to find the right words—"well, it's all right really. Mind you some of them nurses are dreadfully low. I could tell you stories but I won't now. But as for falling once, which you haven't, but even if you had . . . it's nothing."

Catherine was astonished. Lizzie, so small and clean and self-possessed, drinking brandy and telling her these things. Her face burned and she developed an overpowering interest in the pattern of the bedspread.

"But you, Lizzie, surely . . ."

"'Course." Lizzie's eyes were full of rich memories. "Me too."

One day, she said, she might tell Catherine her whole life story, but not now, it was too long and not all very nice, but about this, "I'll tell you if you like, a little bit to help you feel better."

This was so embarrassing, but so wonderful, a stone lifting off her heart. Catherine sat more comfortably on the bed and tried not to grimace at the taste of the brandy. Lizzie, whose voice had dropped a tone, was telling her in a dreamy voice that, at St. Thomas's Hospital, there was a gentleman, "a mature gentleman, in his forties, a doctor if you must know, happily married and with three children of his own. He has a house in the country, and lodgings near the hospital where he stays for two days a week. Once a month on my day off," Lizzie was whispering now, "I go to see him—don't look so shocked, it's nothing—he smokes a small cigar in the downstairs room. I go upstairs, I have a bath. He buys me lemon oils that he gets for me specially, he comes upstairs and I lie down with him, and I'll tell you something else, Catherine, he makes me feel like a princess. He never says he loves me, but he says such nice things." She repeated them solemnly: " 'You've made me happier than I have ever been in my life, Lillibell,' and 'you're my little queen.' He works so hard that man, and his wife was took very poorly after her third confinement and can't have nothing more to do with him; he deserves some pleasure."

A flash of sunlight rippled through the room, illuminating the curtains. A shared tremor passed between the two women. Catherine smiled, glad that Lizzie had known love. And Lizzie, the sunlight making gauzy patterns across her small pale face, seemed quite transported.

"And let me tell you something else, Catherine Carreg," she said. "I'm proud to know him. He'll never marry me, but I don't mind."

"Why not?" Catherine touched her hand. "Why don't you mind?"

"Because I'm a nurse, madamoysal," said Lizzie. "There's plenty that hate the job and would do anything to go into service or get married to escape from it, but I like it. I like the people, I like the excitement. I like the stories you hear. My gentleman says his own wife can't think how to fill her days, and longs for evening to come. Why should I want to be like that? Blimey!" Lizzie leaped to her feet. "Look at the time!" It was quarter to eight. "You're late already."

She patted Catherine's hair and gave a tug to her skirt and said, "Tell her to boil her head."

She winked and, watching Catherine go downstairs, thought, "This is what it must feel like to have children of your own. She's got so much to learn it breaks my heart."

Chapter 28

Because she worried so continuously about her brother, Simon, and his regiment, and the fact that he was sure to fall off his borrowed horse and be bullied by his fellow officers, Amelia Widdicombe paid from her own slender purse for a copy of *The Times*, which was delivered to the Home each afternoon and from which she often read aloud in the evenings. She took a great interest in politics and often searched after supper for someone to explain her views to.

"Here is Turkey and here is Russia, and here," she explained to Miss Sugg one night, "are some of our more important trade routes."

"Yes, hang on a mo." Miss Sugg, who was knitting mufflers for the poor soldiers, held some blue wool up against the light then wound it around her needles. "Sorry, sorry, do go on." She put her glasses back on her nose and tried to look intelligent. Miss Widdicombe sighed. "You see the Russians are now rampant. They want to seize Sebastopol, which is in the Crimea, which is here."

Miss Sugg, who had to put her wool down to see Miss Widdicombe's quite complicated map, glared at her bent head.

"And once that's done," she drew another decisive line, "they'll block many of our trade routes to Turkey. I really should read you some of Simon's letters."

"Oh yes, I see." Miss Sugg's needles were clacking again and her voice trailing off; her powers of concentration had not been good after her illness. "Well, I expect we shall win anyway, shan't we?" she said.

"Oh heavens yes." Amelia gave an odd little snarl. "The war in the

Crimea will be another Waterloo." Miss Sugg's eyes went blank for a moment and she thought of how many sad sounds were embedded in the word "cry," "crime," "mea," "mea culpa." She was going to mention it to Amelia, but forgot and ate her biscuit instead.

But quite soon something strange happened that made them all sit up and take notice. It started in October, when large, wet leaves gathered outside the windows and there was a fire every day in the dining room, and the first sign was the number of important people who began calling to take tea with Miss Nightingale. This caused some private heartaches, too, among the governesses, who felt excluded from the excitement. Although sometimes they were allowed to finish up the half-eaten cakes and the transparently thin slices of bread and butter, mostly they hung about the banisters like large, wistful children and could only listen to the rat-tat-tat of committee meetings and the clink of the visitors' cups, and wonder who was there. Later, holding the special visitors' cups (blue Spode) like holy relics, they took them back to the pantry to wash and put away.

Then there came a week that put Mrs. Clark in the foulest of moods, for she was never out of the kitchen, and the blue cups were continuously in and out of the pantry, the doorbell never stopped, and the governesses all put on a pound or two from their extra teas.

Now came the wonderfully handsome Sidney Herbert, the Secretary at War, a particular friend of Miss Nightingale and one who made her laugh quite girlishly. He was so tall and blond and firm of jaw that all of them were half in love. Elizabeth, his spirited and beautiful wife, often came separately to drop off a new pamphlet on London's workhouses or some Belgian chocolates. Then Fanny, Miss Nightingale's mother arrived. She was wonderfully dressed and very popular with all of them because she brought peaches from the greenhouse and fresh eggs from the country, and sometimes game from local shoots.

"Her mother calls her Flo," Miss Sugg whispered reverently to Catherine. "Too sweet. And she brings her hampers from Fortnum and Mason's, and once, an owl in a cage."

When she came, Florence's voice reverted to the firm tones she used with the governesses. Her mother was often, they also noticed, shown the door within half an hour. And then, on a particularly wet Thursday, one of those dreary days when you don't expect anything to change, everything did. When Catherine looked back on it, what she remembered most was the rain that fell all morning, sheets of it, and the mud that had grown to six inches deep in the streets outside. And then her automatic fear that Deio would be out in this downpour, soaked to the skin on top of the mountains.

They were in the dining room when the news came. Nurses and governesses had finished their porridge and toast, wiped their mouths, put away their napkins, and were asking God to forgive them their trespasses when Miss Nightingale, breathless and pink and with a drop of rain on her cheeks, burst into morning prayers and stood by the door. She was fiddling with her gloves, almost stamping her foot with impatience. "Good morning, Miss Nightingale," they chorused.

"Good morning, ladies, nurses." She smiled, showing her perfect little teeth.

"Sit down, sit down. I have something extraordinary to tell you which affects us all. Try not to be too upset."

She seemed at a sudden loss for words, and sat with her head down, a rolled-up newspaper in her lap.

"Give me a second." She opened the paper. "It is about the war," she said at last. "Today, in *The Times,* there is the gravest news from Turkey, and the Crimea." Every eye was trained on Miss Nightingale's face and nobody noticed how pale Miss Widdicombe had become. "It comes from the paper's correspondent, William Howard Russell. I can do no better than to read the whole report."

Miss Tidy, a new inmate with bronchial pneumonia, began to cough, and Miss Nightingale drummed her fingers on the edge of the table. Catherine had never seen her more impatient.

"William Howard Russell," she repeated. "Miss Tidy, I wonder if you could do your coughing in the corridor, this is quite important. William Howard Russell is a war correspondent who has been traveling with the British army in the Crimea. He has inspected army hospitals there, traveled on sick transports, talked to men on guard duty, and this morning, dropped a bomb of his own in *The*

Times by revealing the frightful sufferings of our sick and wounded men in the Crimea. Listen." Mrs. Clark stood up and shut the door firmly on Miss Tidy's distant whoopings, and Miss Nightingale, her voice throbbing with anger, read:

> *It is with feelings of surprise and anger that the public will learn that no sufficient preparations have been made for the care of the wounded. Not only are there not sufficient surgeons, not only are there no dressers and nurses, there is not even linen to make bandages. Can it be said that the Battle of Alma has been an event to take the world by surprise? Yet, there is no preparation for the commonest surgical operations! Not only are men kept, in some cases for a week, without the hand of a medical man coming near their wounds, not only are they left to expire in agony, unheeded and shaken off, though catching desperately at the surgeon as he makes his rounds through the fetid ship, but now it is found that the commonest appliances of a workhouse sick ward are wanting, and that the men must die through the medical staff of the British Army having forgotten that old rags are necessary for the dressing of wounds.*

Even if the news had not been quite so terrible, Miss Nightingale had the gift of a great actress in being able to make a low and intimate voice reach every person in the room. You could have heard a pin drop, and when she finished, the look of stupefaction on the faces of her audience was total. How could this be? What about the bands? The parades of honor? The music in the streets? Their country was a great fighting nation and they'd all played their part: praying and knitting and writing letters.

There was the scraping of a chair. Miss Widdicombe got up.

"Well, it's all absolutely true," she enunciated carefully. "Simon, my brother, says so, too. It's a shambles." She waved quite belligerently at Miss Nightingale and then sat down, her head between the butter and the marmalade, and made a low moaning sound.

"Miss Widdicombe," cried Mrs. Clark. "Have a care!"

Lizzie was first to her. She loosened her collar and got her head down, talking to her softly until Miss Widdicombe, white-faced and already apologetic, was well enough to be led from the room. The atmosphere became tense and charged again.

"There is more." Miss Nightingale folded her hands and looked at them. "This morning, I received an extraordinary letter from Sidney Herbert, who some of you have met here. A number of ladies have immediately offered to go and nurse in Scutari and in the Crimea, but he says . . ." She took a letter from her pocket and began reading again, her voice almost inaudible with emotion.

" 'There is but one person in England that I know of who would be capable of organizing and superintending such a scheme and I have been several times on the point of asking you hypothetically, if supposing the attempt were made, you would attempt to direct it.' He *wants me* to go."

The governesses gasped. Miss Sugg burst into tears.

"And this morning—" Miss Nightingale's eyes were gleaming. She held her hand over her heart as though it were in danger of jumping out. "I have decided to accept. It will be hard for me to leave the superintendentship of this Home, but I must. I must."

Her face lost its customary control, and in the shocked silence that followed, more of the governesses started to cry. For all her fierceness, she had been wonderful to so many of them: lending them money, writing their letters, rubbing their feet when they were cold at night. So brave, so sure of things.

"When do you leave, Miss Nightingale?" Mrs. Pruitt sagged in her wheelchair.

"As soon as I can. There is no time to lose."

"How will you get there?"

"By boat to Boulogne as far as I know, and then on some military transport to Turkey. The details are by no means worked out. I only heard yesterday morning." She pressed both of her hands to her heart again. So young she looked, so beautiful and young and lit up.

There was only one question Catherine wanted to ask. Mrs. Clark beat her to it.

"How many nurses will you be taking, Miss Nightingale?"

Chapter 29

G od's teeth," said Lizzie when they talked about it later. "How many did you say she was taking?"

"About twenty-five, but she said she couldn't be sure."

"Do you want to go?"

"Yes, Lizzie, I do."

She had a vision of herself at the moment she said it, bending over a soldier in a hospital bed with Mr. Holdsworth's instrument case in her pocket.

"Are you soft in the head? Didn't you hear what they said about it?"

She had, and had felt a rising commotion within her. This was the waited-for moment, when everything changed and there was no turning back, when you committed yourself to a big jump.

"I want to save lives. I want to see the world. I want to be a proper nurse; I expect that all sounds very naive to you."

"It might do if I knew what it meant."

"Childish."

"Yes and no." Lizzie looked as stunned as she did. "Nobody knows. Nothing like this has ever happened before."

"Will you go?"

"I dunno." Lizzie looked puzzled and unhappy. "I really don't. Let's talk about you first," she said almost aggressively. "What about that young man who is going to come and see you? What will he think on it? Or your father, or your sister?"

She hated Lizzie for bringing up Deio at a time like this. She wanted to enjoy the clear feelings for a while longer.

"For the last time, Lizzie, he is not my sweetheart and I'm not here to run away from him. He was a childhood friend; I don't know what he is now."

Lizzie made a sarcastic lah-di-dah sound. She sat down on her bed with her head in her hands and her battered shoes turned inward. Catherine sat down beside her.

"Poor Lizzie, you'll miss someone won't you, if you go?"

"Yes, I will." She wiped a tear away with the back of her hand and looked about her. "And my room here and all." She looked tiny suddenly, and vulnerable. "But he's not going to leave his wife and I've got to go anyway, haven't I? I can't leave those soldiers like that and you cannot imagine how bad some of those nurses will be, handpicked by Miss Nightingale or no. She doesn't have a clue, Catherine." She cried a little more, her spare little frame tensed with misery, and said, "So now what are we going to do?"

"Oh Lizzie," said Catherine, "dear Lizzie, you are so good."

"Poppycock," said Lizzie, "but I still don't get you going."

So Catherine told her what she hadn't really explained to anyone in any detail before: all about market day, and Mother going into labor, the blood, the screams, her feelings of helplessness. "All I did was panic and run around. I really do think I could have saved her and this was the promise I made to her. I've got to try."

"But she didn't ask you to go to war." Lizzie was holding her hand tight.

"I know, but if I stay here and you go, all I'll be is a maid for the governesses and what's the point of that." Lizzie gave a deep sigh and let go of her hand.

"We don't have much time," said Catherine, "so we must go and see Miss Nightingale straightaway and tell her we want to go. If Mrs. Clark stops us on the stairs, we say that we have been asked to go."

"Oh lord," said Lizzie, "it's been so lovely here, I knew it wouldn't last."

Catherine looked sympathetic but in her heart of hearts she felt a huge release and a strong new emotion. "I'm really looking forward to it," she said suddenly.

"What are you brewing there, missie?" Lizzie was looking

at her with deep distrust. "Look, I understand what happened between you and your mother, but women die all the time in childbirth and there's nothing you can do, so are you really sure? You can be an awful silly girl sometimes, so talk it out loud, don't be nave or whatever the word is. Think before you jump. You have a bed here, three meals a day, an occupation, and your family and your young man to run home to if it all goes arse upwards."

"Language, Lizzie, and for the last time, he is *not* my young man. He disapproves of all of this. He hates it. That's why we shall never really ever get along."

"Well, my love, you can wave good-bye to him if you go to war— no man would want that." She felt sick and wanted to stop talking.

"Well, I'm going downstairs, Liz, even if you won't. Please come."

They went clattering downstairs together. Mrs. Clark was sitting on a chair outside Miss Nightingale's locked door. "I've had a morning and a half," she told them. "Ladies upstairs in hysterics, Sidney Herbert coming at three; Lord Lane for tea and dinner, and if I know her, she'll be up all night." Mrs. Clark's proud stare said she did indeed know her—better than any of them did.

Miss Nightingale did sit up for the entire night. She wrote thirty-seven letters.

She sat underneath a pretty green-grass lamp, working past the last sleepy chirp of the sparrow in the laurel tree, and the single rumble of the water cart in Harley Street, and the green light of dusk, and the blue light of morning, as if her whole life must be organized by the time dawn broke. She fired off tender, amusing, determined letters to her family. She finished a Sunday school sermon, promised long ago to local children, in which she asked them to consider humility and obedience to be the greatest of all virtues. She organized the future welfare of the governesses, and wrote to an ex-inmate in Kent, regretting that her navy blue merino cloak had not been left in the cupboard of room nineteen.

No detail was too small; no dark corner of her mind unswept.

She wrote to Messrs Wright and Cox, asking them to quote by

eleven o'clock the next morning for supplying one hundred yards of flannel and twenty-five of thick wool for the nurses' uniforms. She did the wages, wrote several checks, balanced the books, and finally, just as the first cret began to tinkle its dawn chorus in the lime trees that lined the avenue, drew a thin red line at the end of the accounts book and wrote: "On September 25th 1854, Miss Florence Nightingale resigned her position as Superintendent of the Governesses' Home."

Catherine and Lizzie stood outside her room the next morning. They knocked, and called out, "Miss Nightingale, may we come in please?"

"Come in," answered the clear voice, "come in."

Her room was perfectly neat. A spread fan of addressed envelopes lay on the desk ready for posting.

"We wish to volunteer for the Crimea." Better to say it quickly.

"Do you indeed!" Something glacial and remote in her expression suggested this was something you waited to be asked to do. "I have made no decisions yet," she said.

Catherine heard Lizzie, who was standing slightly behind her, give a sigh. She trod on Catherine's toe.

"Congratulations, ma'am, on your new appointment. Both of us feel sick to our stomicks about the sodgers, and if there is any small thing we can do to help we would like to."

"Thank you, Nurse Smart," she said, and smiled. "But as you can see"—she pointed toward the envelopes—"a busy night, and today will be busier still. Elizabeth Herbert and Lady Bracebridge will conduct the initial round of interviews. I think it only fair to warn that all of you must submit to the same process."

Perhaps she regretted her slight loss of control the day before. Today she seemed far less approachable.

"Yes, ma'am. Thank you very much, ma'am. We await your orders, ma'am." Lizzie curtsied but Catherine, who was not in the habit, couldn't. Miss Nightingale's glance swept over her before she addressed Lizzie.

"But I would be a fool not to recommend you, Nurse Smart," she said. "You've made a very favorable impression."

"Miss Carreg is a pretty fair nurse, too," said Lizzie in a rush. "I've been training her up and she's all right."

"Training her up?" Miss Nightingale frowned and straightened her paper knife. "I don't remember asking you to do that, Nurse Smart?"

The rebuke was lightly delivered, but Lizzie hung her head.

"No, ma'am, you didn't, ma'am."

"I didn't think I did, so can you not do that again unless expressly asked. Now, I'm afraid, I'm running out of time." Miss Nightingale stood up and looked at her watch. "The interviews take place tomorrow at the Herberts' house"—she scribbled on a piece of paper—"forty-nine Belgrave Square. From two-thirty onward. I won't be there for all of them, but will put in a good word for you." She looked at Lizzie.

"You, Miss Carreg," she delivered her *coup de main* swiftly, "are too young, and too inexperienced, and you will thank me one day for turning you down. Good-day to you, ladies."

Chapter 30

ell, that's that then," said Lizzie after the door closed behind them. "What a shame."

"It's not a shame," said Catherine. "I'm going and that's the end of it."

Lizzie bit her bottom lip and looked at her apprehensively.

"And how are you going to do that, madam?" she asked. Miss Tidy was peering at them through the banisters.

"Come upstairs," said Catherine, glaring at Miss Tidy quite rudely, "please, Lizzie."

They went up the back stairs into Lizzie's room and closed the door. "You said yourself," said Catherine, still whispering, "that most of the women who turn up will be unsuitable. Also, it has to be arranged so quickly that they may not come in the numbers Miss Nightingale expects."

"Fair comment, Catherine," said Lizzie, "fair comment. But what if Miss Nightingale sees you there after saying no?"

"She said herself that Lady Bracebridge will be there. If she chooses me and you put in another word for me, I surely have a chance."

"Me! She won't even recognize me," said Lizzie, "they live in a world of their own and, to be honest, Cath, I think you do, too, sometimes." She gave a deep sigh. "Look, it's no skin off my nose if you try, but next time, don't look so lah-di-dah and don't look 'em so much in the eye, you'll be marked down as an awkward customer."

"Like this then?" Catherine pulled a baby face and cast her eyes to the ground.

"Perfect," said Lizzie with a playful punch. "And put a cushion in your stays—you're not fat enough."

Torrential rain the next day—the day of the interviews. Three inches in two hours. It lashed against the windows and made the governesses shudder in their beds. Mrs. Clark, who'd been sent all over London on this and that urgent message, went off in a vast tarpaulin looking wild-eyed and important.

"Well, that's a bit of luck," said Lizzie, watching her go from the attic window. "I'll leave now and get back as quick as I can. You can go later. Oh I'm nervous. Now don't be upset, but I've told Miss Widdicombe your plan; she's going to help you find some wheels."

"Oh dear, was that sensible?"

Lizzie was swiping at her cloak with a clothes brush, and polishing her shoes. She plunged a hairbrush into the thick frizz of her hair. "Don't worry, she won't let us down. I'm going to look for her brother when we get there."

At two o'clock that afternoon Miss Widdicombe, quite lit up by the drama, hitched up her skirts, pelted out into the street, and five minutes later returned with a cab for Catherine. "Good luck," she mouthed as the cab pulled away, "good luck!"

The cab swished through the gunmetal gray light, swinging around Baker Street and then into Oxford Street, where there was such a downpour that she was temporarily plunged into darkness. She held on to a little leather strap on the side of the cab and felt quite strange at the thought of being out in the world on her own. All her life she'd had to tell people—Mother, Mair, Father, governesses—exactly where she was, and now all those ropes were being cut one by one. The carriage shushed around a corner, soaking a road sweeper; then, slowly, the shops came into focus and, on a corner near Hyde Park, two children jumped across a puddle laughing their heads off—and she thought of him. He could be in London, or Wales, or anywhere now, leading his own life as she was about to lead hers. Good for him and good for her, she decided: everybody, eventually, had to grow up. The wheels of the cab stormed beneath her. She felt slightly sick.

Ten minutes later, the cabbie pulled up behind two carriage horses tethered to a row of beech trees in front of a beautiful house.

"There you go, love," he said, "Forty-nine Belgrave Square." She stepped out into a puddle of muddy water, which soaked the hem of her dress.

A tall, imposing woman came to the door and took her umbrella. As she stepped into the hall, which was warm and light with mirrors on either side, her foot slipped into a soft carpet.

"This is Miss Carreg," the tall woman told a maid, "take her downstairs with the others."

She wondered if the maid could hear her heart thumping as she led the way. She was taken to a medium-sized pantry room where a row of wet and bedraggled women, some still steaming from the rain, sat on a row of benches. Above their heads was a shelf that another maid, in a spotless white apron, was rapidly emptying of jars of preserved fruit, flour, tea, and sugar. The room smelled of wet wool and bodies. Catherine sat on the furthermost edge of the bench near the door until a small woman, surrounded by packages, appeared and she was told to budge up. She wedged Catherine in beside a bulky woman with a damp shoulder who smelled of gin. She took out a gray rag and blew her nose.

"Don't you trust us not to nick it?" she said to the maid, her phlegmy laugh becoming a cough.

"I'm only following orders, ladies," said the maid in a huff, "sorry."

Catherine felt sick and panicky. To distract herself, she looked quickly from one face to another. This woman, whose split boots were making puddles on the floor, had dark circles etched under her eyes; the next, a yellowish complexion and filthy boots. Then there was a fat woman with swollen lips, leaning heavily on her knees and breathing through her mouth. Lizzie was right, she thought, there was the world as it was, and the world as you wanted it to be.

They sat there for nearly an hour.

Twice the maid came back and removed more provisions. "Don't touch anything that isn't yours," she said.

"They think we're thieves," the fat woman with the thick lips told Catherine, who looked away.

At last, the woman at the end of the row, who wore a green dress and a black net hat dirty enough to have been taken from a dustbin, stood up and said, "Bugger this. I've got a job to go to tonight and children to feed. Miss Thing will have to do without me."

"That's right" and "You tell 'em girl" were muttered from the bench, but nobody else moved and no one complained when the maid suddenly came in and told Miss Carreg she could go up since she was closest to the door.

Up she went again, across the hall, and up another staircase and through a high, curved double door into a warm, high-ceilinged room, where she could hear rain splattering against large square windows. This room had peach-colored walls and golden sofas, and some beautiful mirrors reflecting back a dancing fire, some important-looking relatives, and charming furniture.

At the end of the room she saw Selina Bracebridge, blond and bouncy as ever, sitting at her desk behind a pile of papers. Lady Bracebridge didn't remember they'd met before and introduced herself. She said she would be joined in the selection process by Lady Cranworth and Lady Canning for, as she might well imagine, Miss Nightingale had a great deal on her mind. Unlikely, her brief smile seemed to convey, that Catherine would understand the workings of Miss Nightingale's mind, but it was important to be polite. Her ladyship opened a large leather register.

"Your name?" she said.

"Catherine Carreg."

Carreg. Welsh word, from stone. She stood as straight as she could but remembered to keep her eyes down. *I want to go. I'm going to go.* The words kept coming in her head.

"From?"

"The Lleyn Peninsula in Wales, originally."

"How must I write that down? Or perhaps you don't know."

"I do. L-L-E-Y-N pronounced hleen. But I believe, ma'am, we may have met at the Home for Governesses where I work."

"We did? I don't remember that pleasure."

Oh blast it! Looking down, Catherine saw she had brought some mud in on the hem of her dress and could smell the wool as it dried. Wet sheep. Like home. It was awful, she thought, to have come so far and to want something this much.

"Your age?"

"Twenty-six, ma'am," she lied.

"You're young for this." Selina Bracebridge suddenly closed her eyes and stifled a yawn. Her diamond ring winked in the peach light.

"None of them are used to this kind of work," thought Catherine.

"Miss Nightingale has expressly asked for older women."

"I have had a great deal of experience, ma'am," she said, "and I have a reference from a surgeon, Mr. Holdsworth." She handed her the letter.

"I know Ferdinand Holdsworth; such a very nice man." Lady Bracebridge read the letter without expression and then laid it aside. Flames from the fire turned her face and hair into a glowing mass of pinks and golds. "So, does he support you in this venture?"

"Yes, my lady"—or at least he would when she asked him to.

"So I may write to him?"

"You may write to him."

"Good." The letter was put aside. "Tell me, why do you wish to go?" Lady B looked fiercer. "Do you have a religious motive? We are not sending women out to be chaplains you know."

This remark annoyed her greatly, but she kept her temper saying quietly, "No, your ladyship, I want to be a nurse." *Or a doctor if it could ever be allowed.*

"No doubt you are aware of the sisterhoods," said Lady Bracebridge, "religious orders that are beginning to train nurses. They have some fine qualities but some do tend to think of nursing as a road to salvation, or at least Rome."

"I nursed in Wales and at the Home with Nurse Smart."

"I don't think I know, Nurse Smart," Lady Bracebridge said vaguely, "there were three other people interviewing this morning apart from myself. Now . . ." She stood up, and Catherine, for a moment, thought the interview might be over, but after a short pause, Lady Bracebridge began to pepper her with questions.

"Do you have children? Don't bother to make me up a story if you have. In some ways we welcome them as a sign of maturity although, naturally, they would be left at home."

This woman. Her dander was rising. *She treats me like a servant, or a penitent.*

"No, your ladyship. No children."

"Any husbands or things?" she said carelessly.

"No."

"Any communicable diseases?"

"No." *Oh unbearable! Eyes down. Eyes down.*

"Any record that would make a speedy departure from England convenient for you?"

"No."

"Are you prepared to be sober, honest, punctual, quiet, orderly, and clean? Do you realize that failure to be these things could result in instant dismissal? Do you have a high sense of duty? Are you prepared to obey Miss Nightingale in every particular, or accept the consequences?"

"Yes." *She wants a band of angels, not nurses.*

And then, from the hallway outside, the sound of dogs yapping, doors slamming and a low musical voice crying "Selina, dearest, I'm back!" The door burst open and Miss Nightingale flew across the carpet and clasped Lady Bracebridge by the arms.

"What a morning! I've never had such a day. I've simply sped back and forth across London, from the War Office to the uniform makers and then to Mother's. How goes it here?"

"Oh Florence," Lady Bracebridge was gleaming with excitement, "*I must, I will* hear every word, so do stay please, just sit, *sit*, have tea by the fire with me. I have just about finished with Miss Carreg here."

"Miss Carreg?" Miss Nightingale hadn't noticed her, but now she was giving her a terrible look. "What on earth are you doing here?"

Catherine could hear her heart thumping, as Miss Nightingale took off her dark blue bonnet and placed it precisely on a low settle.

"I gave you no permission to come. In fact I told you not to."

"I want to go, Miss Nightingale." She looked her straight in the eye. "I want to go more than anything I've ever wanted in my life before."

"Why?" There was no softening of her expression.

"I want to help."

"Why?"

I killed my mother. "To help the poor soldiers, Miss Nightingale, and because I want to serve you absolutely."

Still frowning a little, Miss Nightingale walked across the length of carpet, a floating graceful walk, and asked to see Miss Carreg's particulars. Lady B passed her the sheaf of papers. A butler came in with a tea trolley. "Not yet Phillips," he was told, "put the crumpets near the fire and bring the pot back when we've finished with Miss Carreg."

Then Lady Bracebridge told Miss Nightingale, with a significant look, that they'd only had fifty-two applicants that morning. Both thought it wasn't as many as they'd expected and they would need to think about it.

"Our time is already running out," Catherine heard Miss Nightingale say, and then she was given another freezing look for being within earshot of such an important conversation.

"Go downstairs," said Miss Nightingale suddenly. "Right away! We need time to talk and have our tea."

Back in the basement again, she was led into a smaller, more airless room where she waited on her own surrounded by brooms and pails. She was shaking with shock at the anticipation of the rocket from Miss Nightingale that hadn't quite come, and angry, too: Lady Bracebridge had not asked her one single question about her nursing abilities but had treated her like a servant, and a dim one at that.

Half past three. Quarter to four. Half past four. She began to doze in a kind of dull agony of waiting. When she closed her eyes, she half dreamed she was with her mother. She saw the outline of her beautiful, straight nose as she'd held her hand when they'd stood together, looking over the water to Bardsey Island. *Oh we'll go a roaming, the two of us you and I.* The door opened again and she was instantly awake. They were taking her upstairs again. Lady Bracebridge stood in front of her and her heart almost stopped beating.

"Miss Carreg," she said. "We have sent a messenger this afternoon to Mr. Holdsworth asking him for a further reference. You are too young for us and, if someone better qualified and more suitable turns up, you will not come, but if they don't, can you sail with us on October 21?"

Good God! She felt her stomach fall away.

"I can," she said.

"Very well. A uniform and a draft letter of agreement awaits you at the door, just in case."

Chapter 31

$\mathcal{B}$ ack at the Home, the door flew open as soon as she touched it.

"Well?" Amelia Widdicombe and Lizzie said together.

"I am going," she said. "If nobody more suitable turns up."

"Oh blessings!" Miss W closed her eyes and nodded her head vigorously.

"Well done, you."

"What about you, Lizzie?" Catherine said anxiously. "What did they say to you?"

Lizzie looked at her, a strange expression on her face, both amused and terrified. She squeezed her hand very tight. "I'm going, too."

"Oh thank God, Lizzie," she said, flooded with relief.

"Oh, please, dear ladies, go soon, and go fast." Miss Widdicombe's red-rimmed eyes were filling up again. "There is so much work ahead of you."

"Well, give her a chance to get her cloak off first," said Lizzie in her usual practical voice. "She's dripping all over Mrs. Clark's floor."

"And I dripped mud all over Lady Bracebridge's carpets earlier." Catherine felt a sense of rising hysteria.

"You did what!" All the tensions of the day exploded into school-girlish chortles as she told them, Miss Widdicombe holding her long face in her hands and letting out strangled squeals, and Lizzie sitting on the stairs roaring.

"And they asked if I drank or had a criminal record," Catherine eventually gasped out, but as she said it, she felt the laughter become tears.

"They asked you what?" Miss Widdicombe stopped laughing, too. "Why should they assume that?"

"They always do," said Lizzie flatly. "They ask every nurse straight outright before she gets a situation, I can't see the harm in it."

"But it pains me to think of you or Nurse Smart being treated like a low person." Miss Widdicombe had suddenly become their friend and ally. "You are both," her eyes were filling up again, "so good, so kind."

"Oh nothing like that," Catherine assured her quickly. She wanted to hold this in her mind as a good day and not think about the questions she'd been asked, or the row of smelly fat women, or any of the other painful things—like telling Deio—that lay ahead.

"Well, let's talk about something else," said Miss W quickly. "Was Miss Nightingale there, and if so, what was she wearing? And what did she say?" Her protruding teeth gleamed as she waited for the fun bits.

"She was only there for a short while," Catherine heard herself say in a trembling voice. "She is remarkable, you know. If anybody can lead this expedition it is she."

She was remarkable Miss Widdicombe agreed, and a tear slid down her cheek.

Catherine felt tired suddenly, with the glassy, head-spinning tiredness of a child who has been shrieking and playacting for too long and who yearns suddenly to be normal and to go to bed. But their raised voices and laughter had drawn two of the governesses to the top of the stairs.

"What on earth is going on?" called Miss Tidy.

"They have been chosen," Miss Widdicombe called upstairs in a stricken voice. "They are going to war with Miss Nightingale, in four days' time! My brother's there you know."

And now there was no escape. Lizzie, who was on duty, went off to turn down the beds and mix the medicines, but Catherine was kidnapped by the governesses, who entreated her to come upstairs and then bundled her into Miss Tidy's room. She was still carrying the parcel that Lady Bracebridge had given her as she walked out the door, and they wanted to know what was inside it.

"It's her uniform," the governesses whispered to one another. They were treating her with such deference it made her feel awkward. Miss Tidy took scissors from her manicure case and was about to snip the string when the bell rang for evening prayers. Miss Tidy, not normally a rebellious person, went to her door and locked it.

"They won't miss us for a few moments"—she gave them a defiant look—"they've more or less forgotten us."

The string was snipped. Catherine lifted a lump of gray wool out of its rain-soaked wrappings and the eager smiles died on everybody's lips. When she shook it out, the dress, made from a dirty-looking tweed in a salt-and-pepper color, looked enormous. There was a short woolen cloak and a jacket in gray worsted, and folded inside the jacket a blue-checked apron and an ugly holland scarf with the words "Scutari" embroidered in red across the corner.

"Oh dear," said Miss Widdicombe, as Catherine held the dress up against herself, "What a very odd garment . . ."

Catherine snatched it back. Now that their smiles had changed from admiration to pity, she felt painfully exposed.

"It's not odd at all," she said. "I shall feel very proud to wear it."

But Miss W could not let it alone. "I don't understand why it's so horrid." She picked up the dress again and gazed at it minutely, as if its lumpy seams and crude embroidery held some secret message for her. "I mean it's not a thing of beauty." She thought with a pang of Simon's riding boots from Steiner's, and the mess kit, encased in tissue paper and in a beautiful box. "Not like the Horse Guards' feathers and plumes, or the Dragoons' scarlet jackets and spurs and so forth, but why should it be? They've never made a uniform for women going to war before, and I am quite sure that your wish is to do God's work, and in a way that does not draw attention to yourself. This will serve you very well," she ended bravely.

"I shall get my needle out tonight," thought Catherine, who was not listening, "and at least fit it at the sides, otherwise I shall look a fright."

"Just think how anxious those men must feel." Miss Widdicombe had resumed her shrewd look. "They've never in their lives worked side by side with women. Oh look! A note in the pocket."

The letter, written on officially headed notepaper, said she should take a stock of underthings, four cotton nightcaps, one cotton umbrella, and a carpetbag. No colored ribbons or flowers were allowed.

"I have only four days left," Catherine told Miss Widdicombe in alarm, "how on earth can I get a message home in time?"

"A message via the stagecoach will be better," said Miss W sensibly, "and you will be sure of getting it there, particularly if you mark it well. But don't worry if it doesn't, I have a bag you may have and a spare dress. Oh your poor mother and father, they will miss you."

"And I have some coins that I am prepared to give you." Miss Tidy was still in her defiant mood. "Four pounds, not a great deal, but it will keep you until you are paid. Don't trouble to return it, I do not believe in loans, and you may take my traveling rug." She pulled a rug knitted in blue and green squares from the washstand beside the bed. "It will be bitterly cold there."

What good women they suddenly seemed to her. For one absurd moment she wished they could all come. The bell for prayers was ringing in the hall again, this time with a more shrill and impatient note.

"Now ladies," said Miss Tidy, whom generosity had lent an air of sad majesty. "I think we are summoned to an even more important engagement."

They went downstairs to the refectory, where it was dark outside the windows and the leaves of the laurel tree rattled against the panes. Without Mrs. Clark and Miss Nightingale, the room already felt deserted. Catherine took her place at the long narrow table among the women, who seemed to nestle around her tonight. They bowed their heads over the scratch meal of bread and cheese and cold potato and said, "For these and all thy gifts may the Lord make us truly thankful." As darkness deepened, she prayed to God to make her brave about Deio and to help her one day understand all the confusion in her head about him. She asked to be kept safe and to have the courage to write the letters she had to write on the morrow. She must see Mr. Holdsworth, too, although she was sure he would support her. Then one of the governesses gave a little cough. They were waiting for her to stop praying so that they could begin eating.

Chapter 32

eio Jones knew enough about wild things to know that, if you wanted to catch them, the best thing was to turn your back on them and act unconcerned, and then they might, just might, come to you. So he wasn't all that surprised when the boy had run up to him with her letter. He'd been sitting on a wooden fence, watching his horses, and ripped the letter open with his heart pounding. She said she wanted to meet him that week with some important news.

He felt a spurt of triumph, a feeling of pride salvaged—in the end he'd known she'd come running. And he was glad, so glad that the sky and the horse had spun after reading her letter, and he'd had to get down from the fence. The truth was that he could have wept with relief to find she was safe—the sense that somehow he was responsible for her had never left him. There was so much news to tell her, too; so much had changed and he hated the thought of leaving the country without letting her know.

A week after she'd left for the governesses' home, and with his father's blessing, he'd taken out a three-months lease on a five-acre smallholding two miles northeast of Barnet. It was part of a livery stables that had gone broke, so there were twelve reasonable, though shabby, boxes for the horses, plus, and this was a great bonus, some gallops up the road that belonged to a racehorse trainer called Boy Robertson. Deio had fenced the three acres of scrubby grass at his own expense because he liked his horses to be turned out every day, to have the chance to live like horses; then he'd tidied up the grass, sorted out the pump and water containers, and with one hundred and twenty pounds left over from the last drove, had set himself up in business as a purveyor of high-class horses to the cavalry. After his first meeting with the quartermaster from the Royal Dragoons, he'd gone up to meet him at the Pimlico Barracks.

He'd been introduced as a decent horseman and, after a good meal, told again how desperate they were in the Crimea for remounts. Hundreds of horses had been shipped out from Ireland, but they were running low, and there'd even been talk of a commission, without the usual strings attached, if he could help. Most men, Dixon said, had to pay for their uniforms, and their horses, and their mess bills, but they were prepared to make exceptional conditions for exceptional times. He'd declined the offer: some of the men he'd seen lounging around the barracks in their furs and fluff, talking in that silly affected way—"I say old thing that's a veddy veddy fine hoss"—struck him as the most awful asses, not his type at all, but he had formed a plan for going as a free agent to the Crimea and selling his own horses there. Dixon had as good as said there was nothing to stop him doing it, and if Deio, wink wink, wanted a partner, he, Deio, knew where to look. Dixon would need "only a small donation, mind," but it might help oil a few wheels. Deio hadn't batted an eyelid—this kind of thing went on all the time in the droving world.

He moved into a nice little cottage on the edge of his fields. He'd crammed the kitchen with saddles and bridles, wormers, leather punches, drench. A woman came in every day to cook and clean for him. In between, he'd been roaming around on Moonshine. The nervous young gray he'd ridden across Wales was a different horse now: fit, muscled, confident, cocky, a real eye-catcher. Together they'd appeared at local livery yards and stables, taken tea with local farmers, made casual inquiries at ale houses, and now he had his work cut out for him, with fifteen cracking good sorts that he was fittening, fattening, and training. Too many really, but he'd hired a couple of the lads who worked part-time at the racing stables and who were better than average riders, and he kept them busy.

He woke each morning at five and went through the dew-soaked grass to the wooden shelter where Moonshine stuck her head out and nickered for him. She butted his hand with her head, demanding her hugs before breakfast, and then Cariad, now confident and jealous, sank her head in his hands. Always a groan somewhere inside him as the horse leaned against him and looked at him steadily through her thick lashes. He wanted Catherine to see the muscle he'd built on her and how beautiful she was now.

After he'd mixed the morning feeds, the boys arrived from the racing stables. They'd tack up, and riding one and leading one, go up into the hills. They worked the horses in rotation: sometimes he took them to the racetrack and gave them long steady gallops; at other times he made them supple by working them on a circle in the middle of a field. He taught them the verbal commands he'd heard at the barracks: "Charge. To line. Wheel back." He'd toughened them mentally, too, bit by bit, first by building their confidence and then, gradually, changing creatures whose natural state was startle and flight into disciplined servants who could cope with fires, loud bangs, sudden movements, and flag-waving.

If he hadn't been missing her, he would have been perfectly happy; this was what he loved doing best and what most fulfilled him. The pure sensuous joy, a sculptor's joy, of putting muscles on a horse, seeing a weedy neck develop topline, watching a stiff mover become a fluid athlete. There were constant frustrations, but the joy was in releasing these animals, finding their strengths and their weaknesses. Each horse was so different, the puzzle was never-ending, and it never bored him.

At home with his brothers, and with Lewis, there were a thousand interruptions, constant advice; here, he worked on his own instincts, open and listening, watching, and waiting. In only six short weeks, he'd transformed three rejects from the racetracks, seven part-breds from the sales, and five thoroughbreds from a local squire who'd gone broke into well-mannered, useful horses with a sense of pride in themselves.

At nights he'd smoke and watch them, rolling or drinking or standing in the fields, and feel a wave of anxiety about them. They were innocent. Within a matter of weeks they'd be tossing around in some ship, or in a camp somewhere in the Crimea. Some would have owners who rode well and respected them; some would love them as much as they loved their wives. For others, it would be the start of a nightmare.

He worried about Cariad. He'd decided she must go, too, it was almost a test he'd set himself. She was talented, but she was sensitive, the kind of horse that, if you bullied her, closed herself down and made herself vulnerable and only half alive and half smart. With Catherine, on the drove, she'd grown so confident she was now the boss mare of the herd. Her defenses had come down, and now when he approached her she was sweet as butter, and while he held her conker-colored head, she'd close her eyes in bliss. He'd rub her head and softly pull each ear, and sometimes she let out a deep sigh. But now he knew he must change his thoughts.

Every week, he sent a letter to the shipping agent in Portsmouth, asking when there would be places for him and his horses on the boat going east. And every time he made this inquiry something inside him blazed with surprise, he was going to war, and that felt good. A new world with new thoughts.

When she'd left him on the drove he'd felt as bad as he'd ever felt in his life, and it took him a long time to get over it, and the reason why he longed for new thoughts was that the old ones still kept bobbing up like a fish that refuses to die. Yesterday, for instance, he'd gone to a farm near Windsor to look at a few animals and seen this six-year-old gelding called Troy. He was almost jet-black and would need smartening up. His matted tail hung almost to the ground, but he had the presence of a seventeen-hand stallion, and huge violet and black eyes and suddenly—it had flashed into his mind before he could do anything about it—he'd pictured her hopping on, and crouched down low, and galloping in that reckless way she had, and then saying, "Oh Deio, he's beautiful." His whole body had blossomed with happiness in that moment and he'd felt the kind of shared joy you might feel when you had a baby, something secret and strong and sacred.

He was counting out the notes into the farmer's hand when a boy rushed out of the house, flung his arms around the horse's neck, and asked where he was taking him to. He was noncommittal. Some people lit up like candles when you told them their horses would soon be warriors; this boy, you only had to look at him, would be devastated. With a boy like that the bond with their horse was too deep to properly understand. And she'd be upset about Cariad, too, he knew it, which was why the mare was his test: it was his horse, his life. She'd lost the right to say where she went.

Deio wrote Catherine a brief reply, with the suggestion that they meet at the Pimlico Barracks in London. His plan was to take a few horses up, she could watch them work, see him ride the moves on Cariad and Moonshine. They'd have a laugh about the cavalry officers; she hated pompous twits as much as he did, but she would respond to the setting: the beautiful stables, the sand school, the undoubted brilliance of some of the riding. England had the finest cavalry and horses in the world, and it meant something that they now saw something in him that they wanted. He imagined her eyes widening when he told her, and how his news might change everything, and make her hand go around his waist or tears come to her eyes. They might even make a plan about what they could do when he got home, assuming always that he survived. It annoyed him how much he still needed her blessing before he took off into the blue yonder.

Chapter 33

For a few days after Miss Nightingale's astonishing news, everything at the Home felt chaotic and somehow illogical. Nobody, for instance, remembered to ask her if the reference from Ferdinand Holdsworth had arrived, which was lucky since he, appalled by the idea, had refused to write one. Then Mrs. Clark had appeared in her room, put two official-looking letters on her bed, and said, "Well, it looks like you're off, too," but in a flat way, as though she'd asked her to go to the pantry for a cup of sugar. She said that two older, better-qualified nurses had dropped out. Mrs. Clark was permanently in flight nowadays and far too grand to explain anything to nurses or governesses. When Catherine reported this conversation to Lizzie later on, she said, "That's a laugh—better qualified in what? Drinking gin and sleeping rough?"

But now she had two upsetting letters to write:

Dear Father,
October 17, 1854

   Trust me and try to love and forgive me. Sidney Herbert, the secretary at war, has asked our superintendent, Miss Nightingale, to take a party of nurses east and I have been chosen. We leave on October 21st from London Bridge. We will stop in France, Malta, and Egypt, and arrive in Constantinople two or three weeks hence.

   You do not have to send me money. We will receive twelve to fourteen shillings a week for board, lodgings, and uniform, and after three months good conduct this will go up to between sixteen and eighteen shillings.

It grieves me deeply to take this decision without being sure it is what you would want, but everything has happened so fast. Try to be proud of me. I long for your blessing.

Posts to London are much improved at the moment, pray God I may hear from you before I leave. After that, letters can be sent to me at The Barracks Hospital, Scutari.

I am ever your loving daughter.
Catherine

To her sister she wrote

Dear Eliza,
October 17, 1854

Do you remember Tramp, that old dog who loved to bring dead rabbits to the door and drop them there for us? He was always so sure that what pleased him would please us. Well, I know that my news may shock you and make you unhappy (I have resigned myself to the idea that Father may not write to me at all), but I beg you to try and understand at least some of my reasons for going to Scutari.

Your last letter made me so proud of you and made me bless again your good fortune. Gabriel Williams is the luckiest man on earth. I can so imagine you planting your orchard, laying up your chutneys and jams, and making your farm as neat and welcoming as a new pin. As for me—so few of Mother's domestic arts rubbed off onto me that even if I could come home and settle happily down (assuming any man would have me) I would not feel happy or settled.

There was a time when my restlessness made me unhappy, but that time is gone. Ever since Mother died I knew what I wanted to do in life, and although the nurses' training has been hard it has been what I needed. But why must every joy bring pain? I am already thinking of our separation, of your sadness, of the dear animals, and how much I will miss you all.

The posts to and from Constantinople are quite good, and

letters to us are free, so please lay in a good supply of pens and
wax and end papers and write to me, everything, and anything.
Thank you for your locket. Thank you for the woolen blanket.
Thank you for your love. You should see me in my uniform—it
was so enormous I had to take in the side seams.

> *Good-bye my love, I will write to you soon,*
> *Catherine*

And then time simply flew and it was only a few days before she left, then six, then three, and suddenly she had a day to pack and be gone from the Home to join the other nurses in temporary lodgings. When she was a child, her mother had once told her that some leave-takings felt like little deaths. An odd thing to tell a child and yet, on the night before she left the governesses' home, she knew what that meant. With Lizzie gone—she'd taken half a day off to say good-bye to her gentleman friend—she felt dreamlike and unreal, already half gone. She rolled up her dresses, straightened the counterpane on her bed for the last time, felt how quickly a life could be folded up and put away.

When Catherine was finished, she sat on a chair near the window. Outside, the branches of the ash tree were bare and the pale pinks and blues of the autumn sky were breaking up. She sat with the lapwing carving in her hand. She was meeting Deio in two days' time to say good-bye. She put the wooden bird aside and unwrapped the small portrait Eleri had done of her mother, which she'd tucked between the folds of a dress rolled and ready to go. She stared at it. She would never properly understand now how her mother had thought or felt, what her good memories had been. Mother was half smiling in the picture, but those tawny eyes looked watchful, wary. Once she had stood on the lawn at Clytha, laughing, in a white dress with pearl buttons. What had happened to all her hope and happiness, to Father's love for his stunning bride?

When did one stop believing?

Hold me, Mama. Tell me I am doing the right thing. She closed her eyes and smelled the faint sweetness of tea rose in her mother's hair.

And now the sound of horse's hooves passing in the street outside brought an extra surge of misery when she thought of Deio. A few nights ago she'd had a dream in which she'd put on her new uniform and stood in front of him. He'd looked at her disgusted. He'd said, "Good God, woman, this gets worse and worse and worse."

A few hours later, the hansom cab appeared, and she'd stood in the same strange disembodied mood on the steps with her bags around her and said farewell to Miss Poulter and Miss Sugg and the other governesses. The poor things had the mournful air of survivors on a sinking ship. They'd all have to move on soon, to new homes, new unsatisfactory jobs, new anxieties. They had been passed over for a more interesting idea.

Miss Nightingale and Mrs. Clark had gone already to their new headquarters—Sidney Herbert's house in Belgravia—to make last-minute arrangements for the journey.

When the cab arrived, Miss Widdicombe came out of the house, quite pink under her bonnet from the exertion of carrying Catherine's carpetbag in one hand, and a parcel and two pots of raspberry jam in the other.

"My dear," she said, "could I trouble you to take these few treats to Simon? It would ease my heart to think of him having something personal from home. If only I could afford more, but, alas, I can't."

The pots were bound to leak, but seeing Miss Widdicombe's long, sweet, horselike face work so desperately against tears, made it impossible to say no. "Of course I'll take them," she said, shaking her hand and finding herself hugged. "Oh, and give me the address of your employer. If I see your brother or hear of him I'll write to you immediately."

"It is not entirely clear to me yet whether or not I *have* an address or a situation," said Miss W with sad dignity. "I have not actually heard from that gentleman since my illness."

"So what will happen to you? Can you go home?"

"I think so," said Miss W. "Yes, I am sure Father will have me back. Oh Catherine," she suddenly burst out, "if I was braver and younger, I'd come, too—there's nothing for me here."

When the carriage drove off, Miss Widdicombe stood slightly apart from the other women; her high shoulders and her attempt at a jaunty wave was the last thing Catherine saw.

Chapter 34

While Catherine moved across a London that was lighting its lamps and fires and drawing the curtains on another evening, Elizabeth Herbert, Lizzie to her friend Florence Nightingale, and her doting husband, Sidney, put the finishing touches to an evening that promised to be memorable and extraordinary. All day long, the house had thrummed with excitement: feet running up and down stairs and sharp, excited voices, but now, in that lull between the end of the working day and the beginning of evening, she was able to walk about and see that everything was in place.

Forty chairs for forty nurses were laid out in Sidney's study; a small Chippendale desk, her place in history, had been carried to the hall. When the footman carrying the table had banged its leg on the door, she'd shouted at him, which was most unlike her. For a woman who regularly and skillfully organized soirees and dinner parties and complicated and subtle placements for prime ministers, foreign statesmen, poets, artists, and all kinds of extraordinary people, she was surprised at what a fever this whole evening had put her into.

The problem, bluntly stated, was that Elizabeth, though no snob, was not in the habit of entertaining servants in her sitting room. At Christmastime, it was true, in the servants' dining room next to the kitchen, she distributed (to a chorus of "God bless you, madams") punch and small presents to her own staff of fifteen. But forty nurses! Forty! And some of them quite, well, rough frankly. This was the problem that had vexed her all day and caused the darkening of her lovely eyes. The kitchen was out of the question—

too small and not suitable; the servants' dining room would have done for the nurses, but not under any circumstances for Sidney. A statesman talking on a matter of national importance could not do so against a background of cooking odors and wet mops. He needed, in her opinion and at the very least, his study, with its oak paneling and bound books and Persian carpet, to set him off and to make him look, as he so instinctively did, like the *beau idéal* of an English gentleman.

That decision made, she'd had another uncharacteristic dither over food. Earlier in the day she had told Mrs. Jennings, her house-keeper, to organize bread and cheese and ale for the forty nurses and to lay it out on the long mahogany table in the dining room for seven o'clock. Mrs. Jennings had told her, and rather heatedly at that, that they would need extra staff in each room to keep an eye on all the nurses, who, as everybody knew, had a reputation for being light-fingered.

The impertinent manner in which her housekeeper had gone on to suggest that they feed the nurses downstairs made Elizabeth Herbert wonder if her own servants had not in some way already become infected by the sudden elevation of these forty nurses into objects of national interest. An hour later she changed her mind again and decided all nurses should be fed at the boardinghouse in Victoria where they were to spend their last night. But her performance throughout the day had unsettled and displeased her—she did not care to look indecisive in front of Mrs. Jennings or, for that matter, Sidney, who had so much on his mind.

Walking through the hall, she saw Sidney's hat and whip had been flung on a chair. He'd come in late from his afternoon ride and now the door to his study was closed again. Last night he and Florence had worked until three in the morning, and the night before that until dawn. Flo's energy was ferocious, almost freakish; he, on the other hand, looked wrung out. Last night he'd come into her room and flopped on the bed beside her, too tired to get undressed. She'd said into the darkness, "Give *me* something to do, surely I can help."

She was surprised at how aggrieved she sounded.

"Be yourself, my love," he'd said, sleepily taking her hand. "Be your own sweet self." But the time when this reply might have pleased her had passed.

"I'd like to do more than that," she'd said tartly. "After all, one is oneself every day; tomorrow will be different."

Sidney had then suggested that she could, if she liked, greet each one of the women personally and then stay on to hear his speech.

"I could sit at the door with the register and tick off their names as they come," she'd said, making a conscious effort to soften her voice, "that would be useful."

"Capital idea, Chouchy," calling her by her pet name and sleepily stroking her breasts. "Excellent thought."

"Are you worried about Flo, darling?" She stroked his hair and marveled, as she had so many times, at how handsome he looked in profile.

"Dreadfully," he said, dropping his husband voice and speaking to her as a friend. "I don't think she has any idea yet of the job she has taken on. Think of the problems we have keeping the peace among our fifteen servants who have an easy situation in the middle of London. Think of taking them to the other side of the world to fight a war. But Flo is remarkable—she has no fear, thinks like a man."

"I never know what a man means when he says a woman thinks like a man," replied Elizabeth Herbert drowsily. She was enjoying holding her husband's hand and receiving these intimacies in the dark. "Is that a good thing or a bad thing?"

"What I mean I think," his voice beginning to trail into the realms of sleep, "is that, in spite of . . . charm . . . gentle ways, she is quite . . . terrifying . . . no—"

But he was asleep and then, so was she, worn out by her day. Up in the study Florence kept on working.

It was five forty-five p.m. on the twentieth of October, and lights blazed at every window of Sidney Herbert's house. There was a fire in all the main rooms; the day had been very cold and the air was raw. While Catherine waited with the nurses outside at the bottom of the steps to be let in, Elizabeth Herbert levered herself with difficulty behind the Chippendale desk in the hall. She was wearing what was for her a simple dress: a pale blue crinoline—a ravishing shade against her long olive throat—matched by the pale blue sapphires on her neck and ears. Her dress had thirty-six yards of watered silk in its shimmering folds and had taken her dress-maker and her three assistants four weeks to make it at a cost of two hundred pounds.

The nurses' uniforms (cost: two shillings per dress; time of making: one hour) looked, if anything, even uglier en masse. The pepper-and-salt color made them look dirty even before they were worn, and the tentlike cut made the tall look taller, the fat fatter, the small smaller. Three parlormaids, sneaking looks at them from behind the curtains, were laughing at them and call-ing them frights. When the footman in his white powder and white gloves instructed them to line up they looked like a long, gray, dismal worm. Each time the footman shouted "Next!" from the front door, the worm broke into bits, then joined up again and moved on.

Elizabeth Herbert sat behind her desk in the hall, her pen poised. Her dark eyes glowed—work suited her.

"Name?"

"Sarah Barnes, your ladyship," from a fat woman with large, red, chapped hands. "From Seven Dials. I've come for the nursing."

Tick went Mrs. Herbert's pen.

"Name?"

"Harriet Erskine from Miss Sellon's." A long, pointed face with cunning eyes.

"Jolly good." Tick, Tick. "Follow the others to my husband's study—he'll speak to you soon."

"Name?"

"Sister Etheldreda from the Norwood order."

"From the Norwood order? Hold on, oh yes, there you are," tick, tick, "follow the others please."

"Mary Bowmen, St. John's House."

Emma Fagg, Anne Higgins, Maria Huddon, Eliza Forbes, Sarah Terrot, Elizabeth Wheeler, Etheldreda Pillars, Georgiana Moore, Elinor O'Dwyer. Elizabeth Herbert's pen moved busily up and down the register, this really was rather fun, until all forty women were organized into neat marks on her page.

A huge fire had been lit in the sumptuously paneled study of the Secretary at War. It spread its light over a collection of good-looking ancestors in gilded frames, the Aubusson rugs, and an empty leather-tooled desk facing forty chairs, now filling up with nurses and nuns. Most of the small tables in the room had been emptied of their ornaments.

Catherine arrived before Lizzie and kept a seat for her. Even though Lizzie had left her in no doubt that she would come—the money, she said, was too good to miss and there would be no more work at the Governess Home—Catherine couldn't help nervously twisting in her seat, hoping she would not be too late. Lizzie had been flying around London, saying good-bye to various relatives and to her gentleman friend, and they hadn't seen each other all day.

"Lizzie!" Her friend stood by the door, looking pale. She was swamped by her uniform and tugged at it uncomfortably as she sat down.

"Are you all right?" asked Catherine in a low voice.

"I'm all right," said Lizzie with a wry little smile. "Not the best afternoon of me life, but I'm still here. Ugh, this is itchy. God bless my soul, what a beautiful room."

Some version of her amazement seemed to have taken hold of most of the nurses, who conversed, if they dared to at all, in whispers as though they were in a cathedral.

"Tell me later what happened," whispered Catherine.

"Shussh!" a nun to the right of Catherine frowned. She had a small mouth and broken veins on her cheeks, and a meek, superior expression. "I could never love that face no matter how hard I tried," Catherine thought, and then felt ashamed—she would have to learn now to curb pettiness and mean thoughts.

The whispers died out as Elizabeth Herbert, in a swish of blue silk, entered the room. When she put her index finger in the air, her sapphire winked. "Ooh," went a nurse in front of them, "ain't she beautiful."

"Ladies, nurses," she announced, a charming tremor in her voice. "Welcome to you all, welcome to our house. I am the wife of Sidney Herbert." She smiled as if this was the most marvelous thing in the world. Catherine heard Lizzie pull her breath in sharply and saw a tear roll down her cheek.

"My message is that my husband and Miss Nightingale have been held up for a few minutes. To fill in the time I shall pass out your agreements for you to peruse."

"Lizzie, what's up?" she whispered.

"I'm a fool, Catherine, don't look at me." Lizzie stared at her workmanlike hands.

"Read them very carefully," Mrs. Herbert advised.

"I can't read," said one of the nurses.

The nun beside Catherine said "shush!" again, but before there was time to hand out the agreements the paneled doors opened again and all talk stopped.

"Mr. Sidneyah Herbertah," announced a liveried footman, "the Secretary at War."

There was a low sigh, almost a moan, from the women as he walked across the room and stood behind his desk. He was so handsome. No more than thirty years old, tall and graceful with thick darkish blond curls, dark eyes, and a strong, clever, kind face. Miss Nightingale walked behind him. She was dressed simply in a black merino dress with a spotless linen collar and cuffs. Her grave and humble expression suited the ecclesiastical severity of the dress. She followed Sidney Herbert to his desk and, sitting down on one of two carved chairs, folded her hands in her lap and waited for him to begin. He rustled some papers, his hair, boyish and adorable, gleamed in the lamplight. But when he looked up it was a man who faced them, a man with a tremendous air of natural authority.

"Ladies," his dark eyes made each one feel he addressed her personally. "You have a date with history, so I shall not keep you long. My most important task tonight is to welcome you and then to hand you over to your very able administrator, Miss Florence Nightingale, from henceforth superintendent of the Female Nursing Establishment of the English General Hospitals in Turkey. No woman in England has ever been so distinguished or so honored before, and no woman in England was ever worthier of this high honor."

"Strewth," breathed Lizzie.

Miss Nightingale, sitting in the lamplight with her hands folded demurely in her lap, merely seemed to listen intently as though he were speaking of somebody else. But then she favored him with a quick glance, radiant and ardent.

"There will be forty of you in all." Herbert looked up and down the four rows of chairs.

"You come from many different backgrounds and persuasions. Ten of you are Roman Catholic nuns." The nuns bowed their heads slightly.

"Eight are Anglican sisters from Blandford Street." The eight nodded in unison.

"The rest of you come from hospitals and private homes throughout the land, and from a wide variety of situations, but if this mission is to succeed, and pray God it will, you must put your differences behind you and all pull together. The eyes of the nation, the eyes of the world, are on Scutari. If you succeed, an enormous amount of good will be done, a prejudice will have been broken through, and a precedent established that will multiply the good to all time."

The fat woman sitting in front of Catherine became restless. "What's a president?" she asked in a rude whisper. The nun beside Catherine inhaled sharply and rattled her beads, but Mr. Herbert showed no sign of having taken offense. He had a beautiful smile and was smiling now.

"And now," he said, "I have nothing more to say to you except to hand you your agreements and to ask, if you would, having read them, sign them."

Four servants walked up and down the rows handing out sheets of paper.

Catherine's read, "Memorandum of agreement made this October 1854 between Miss Florence Nightingale on the one part, and Miss Catherine Carreg on the other part:

"Whereas the said Miss Nightingale, Superintendent, has undertaken to provide female nurses for the sick and wounded of the

British Army serving in Turkey; and in carrying out this object, she has engaged to employ the said Miss Carreg in the capacity of nurse, at a weekly salary varying from ten to eighteen shillings according to merit; and also to provide board and lodging."

There was an excited murmuring when those nurses who could read saw this. The money was almost double what most of them were used to. The rest of the agreement stated that, were she to become sick or wounded, her return fare would be paid by the government, but that if she was returned for bad bahavior—neglect of duty, immoral conduct, or intoxication—she would pay her own fare home and forfeit all claims on Miss Nightingale, "the whole of whose orders she undertakes to obey until discharged by the said Superintendent."

One of the nurses burst out "No! I haven't, I never did!" when they reached the part about neglect of duty and immoral conduct. A brief burst of laughter, for the first time that evening.

"Sign your agreements when you have read them," said a footman. "Step this way!" And then the gray line of women began to form again and move toward Sidney Herbert's desk: the fat women, already straining at the seams of their new dresses; the thin, wan-looking ones; the nuns still in their dark habits. And then Catherine, looking at them ahead of her, felt a throb of excitement and alarm, wondering who would be made and who broken by the task ahead of them.

When it was her turn: Mr. Herbert pushed a copy of the agreement toward her and fixed his dark eyes upon her as she, too, curtsied and signed.

Chapter 35

*N*ow she was in a high state of anxiety about the meeting with Deio the next day, and about everything. After the Herberts had finished with the nurses, they were taken in a carriage to a cold, dreary house, several streets away, where they were met by a landlady who looked sour and put upon. She took no account of the unusual nature of their evening but told them they must have an early night and get up early the next day to turn their rooms out.

The dormitory she led them to showed signs of a hasty conversion. There were twenty beds arranged in straight lines, each with a label and a name pinned above it. Each bed was divided from the next by an unhemmed "modesty" sheet. At the end of the room a row of jugs and basins for their ablutions. When the wind blew outside, the modesty sheets puckered like old men's mouths.

"Gawd, it's cold in here, ain't it?" said one of the nurses, who looked small and crumpled and had filthy hands.

"Perhaps they're getting us into the spirit of Roosia before we go," said another. "It's powerful cold out there you know."

The bad-tempered landlady appeared again to tell them to hang their uniforms on the hooks provided above the beds, and to stow bags or valises neatly under them. A poor-looking collection of bags they were, too—some no more than stained rags cobbled together, others of frayed leather, and stinking carpetbags looking like battered old family pets.

They were made to walk in a single file down to the kitchen, where they sat around a large scrubbed table laid with a plate of bread and cheese and a jug of ale. In the greenish blue shudder of a gas light, Catherine examined her new companions. Most of them looked old and fat and frightened and not at all like heroines. She was glad she'd arranged to meet Deio at Green Street.

Grace was said, the bread and cheese wolfed down, and, after a few chews, the woman next to Catherine said, "I don't like the cheese—too salty." She had small, suspicious eyes and a chin of several wobbling terraces.

"Very, very cheesy," said another, with a shudder. The woman opposite, stout and with so little hair she looked bald, scowled and told her to "get it down you miss fine-mouth—it's the best meal you've had this week."

Although the bald woman was delighted with this sally, no one laughed, no one responded. They were hungry women at the trough. The woman who hadn't liked the cheese took a long swig of ale and belched loudly.

Catherine, buoyed still by the drama and the urgency of Sidney Herbert's words, was determined not to take against them from the start. She knew enough about nurses by now to be aware of what hard lives they led. As a group they were generally reviled and, knowing that, why should they not seem cynical and wary and quick to take offense? Yet still, a kind of horror leaked out as she watched them eating with their mouths open, slurping down their ale and grumbling and picking their teeth. She tried to catch Lizzie's eye but Lizzie, who was used to these women and who had, after all, tried to warn her, looked away. After a while, when she could stand the low murmur of complaints no longer, and because in her family it was rude to eat without some attempt at conversation, she plucked up the courage to say: "Excuse me, but I do not know anybody's names. Might it not be a good idea to say who we are?"

A couple of women voiced agreement, but most of them looked back at her like a herd of cows being asked to move against their wills.

"My name," she said in a firm voice, "is Catherine Carreg. I come from Wales."

"Well, bully for you," said the woman with the chins.

"And perhaps," Lizzie came to her rescue at last, "we could tell where we have been working, too. We'll be living very close from now on. My name is Elizabeth Smart. My friends call me Lizzie. I was born in London and have been a nurse at St. Thomas's Hospital for seven years. What about you then?"

She looked at a red-faced woman with large red hands and unhappy blue eyes, who said, in a strong cockney accent, her name was Sarah Barnes. This was followed by a long pause, during which she chewed the rest of her bread and cheese, before adding, "I'm a widder from Seven Dials. My husband died of typhus last year." She folded her arms and closed her mouth as if that was all that could be said about her.

"And may I ask why you are going?" Lizzie had lovely manners no matter who she spoke to.

"You may if you like," said the woman. "I'm going for the money." This brought the second good laugh of the evening, and murmurs of encouragement and assent.

"I have five children to support, two of them ill, and no settled occupation," continued Nurse Barnes. "I can get twice as much as a nurse with Miss Nightingale, and if I die out east the government will pay my children. If I snuff it here they get nothing."

The next woman, tall, thin, marble-pale, and with a long undershot jaw, told them her name was Harriet Erskine. She spoke in a whisper and was sharply told by the other nurses, who were beginning to enjoy the show, to "Spit it out! Get on with it!" which made her whisper worse.

"I was trained, at Miss Sellon's, a High Anglican Sisterhood. I am going east to do what Mr. Herbert says and to help the soldiers. I have not been able to eat or think since I read of their sufferings."

Another murmur of assent at this, but one woman, who was small and hard-eyed, and who obviously fancied herself a wag, said, "Well, if you can't eat your victuals love, I'll eat them, and you'll be a stiffy before we get there."

Hearty laughter broke out.

"Pardon me, ladies." The landlady, jailerlike, a bunch of keys on her waist, opened the door. "If you have finished your repast, you may go to bed directly. Quietly please!" It was all very confusing, thought Catherine, walking wearily upstairs again, worn out now

by the high drama of the day. One moment they were treated by Sidney Herbert like selfless heroines with a chance of doing real good in the world, the next like a group of escaped convicts.

After she'd hung her salt-and-pepper dress on the hook provided and put on her nightgown and cap, she stood shivering behind the curtain and hearing other women shiver and shudder, too. She turned to Lizzie, whose shadow billowed behind her curtain. She wanted to ask her advice about how to speak to Deio, and to ask how things had gone with her gentleman friend that afternoon. But Lizzie looked so low she kept her own mouth shut, and lay on the hard narrow bed wondering if Florence Nightingale had a sweetheart to whom she was now saying a tearful good-bye. It seemed unlikely. She thought of the widow Barnes's five children and this hateful night for them, and for their mother, too. She wanted to rise above these melancholy thoughts and hold on to the excitement of the day, but when she fell asleep she dreamed of Deio, a confused dream down by the hut at Whistling Sands. The horses were tied up. The sea was flapping. He was pouring sand in her ears.

Chapter 36

The following day, Deio came up to London early, left the horses in stables at the barracks, and rushed up to the corner of Green Street and Park Lane. She arrived ten minutes late, flushed, apologetic, beautiful and slightly thinner, in the blue dress he loved. They sat down on a bench together, and he smelled her smell of lavender and green grass and clean skin, and tried to stop grinning, and then tried not to look disappointed when she said she was too busy to go and see the horses working. She said she had to go back to the boardinghouse. "My time isn't my own anymore," she said. "I'm sorry."

She was grinning, too, as if she couldn't believe he was there, and buried her head in his chest crying, "Oh Deio!" and he had to hold himself in. It was just so shocking and sudden, dreamlike and odd, to see her there—her pale skin, her eyes, the scattering of freckles on her nose.

At first, she was nothing like as angry as he'd expected her to be after the night in Llangollen. She even let him take her arm as they walked down Park Lane, and it was wonderful to feel her there and to walk with her through the dazzling light of an early autumn day. He took her to a chophouse he knew called William's near Shepherd's Market. It was not a good choice—although it was early lunchtime it was crammed and the din made it hard to talk. She seemed happy enough though, and attracted a good deal of attention when she walked in. She was so irresistible when she was lit up. As she sat down, she took off her bonnet, and her eyes sparkled. She said it was fun to be out, and when he ordered a glass of ale, she looked a little shy then asked for a glass of porter, which for some reason shocked him very much.

"Deio!" she said. "I'm not a child, so don't give me your aunt Gwynneth look."

"There now, dear child," he said in his aunt Gwynneth voice, "no need for silliness at all, at all!" And then he realized he hadn't really laughed with anybody in a long time, and it felt so good, and then he wanted to take her in his arms and hold her tight. Instead, he ordered her some of William's famous grouse pie and a whole jug of wine. She ate with enjoyment just as she always had, and he watched her covetously, drinking her in. When they had finished, the wine, the warmth of the room, the magic of being with her again, felt so right that when he said he had something to tell her, and she said she had something to tell him, too, his heart swooped with joy, for he had a premonition that she was going to tell him that she had come to her senses and done with London now, and would go home and wait for him.

"You first," she said.

So, feeling serious and proud, he told her about the horses, the boat, how they'd dangled the idea of a commission in front of him. "Oh my God," she'd said softly. "Oh God." He said how short they were of horses out there, and how he'd make a lot of money but would be back soon.

"Oh Deio." She looked confused and said something odd about her having a friend out there. Not the response he'd expected. Then she'd asked if he would be going home to the Lleyn before he left, and produced two letters—one for her father, one for Eliza—and asked him to take them.

He'd stared stupidly at the letters, and been so caught up in his own version of how things would be that he'd said she could take them home herself now. He could find out coach times, or would she prefer the train? He felt protective again, glad to be looking after her.

The chophouse grew less busy and the waiter, thinking they looked a romantic couple, moved them to a quieter alcove near the fire. The noisy party near the bar had left. Deio felt an immense tenderness. His girl, and possibly in shock now and saying funny things.

Then she looked at him and said, "Deio, I'm not going home either. I'm going to Turkey. I've been asked to join a party of nurses at a military hospital at a place called Scutari. We're leaving later tonight."

"Catrin," his eyes went black. "Is this a joke?"

"I'm going with Miss Nightingale. She's been asked to take the first nurses ever to go to war."

He was staring at her, still not believing.

"Don't Catrin."

"I am going."

"Oh my God," he said, "this gets worse and worse."

"Would you like some more porter, sir?" The waiter had appeared.

"No," said Deio. "Leave us."

"I'll be there before you, but we're not going to where the fighting is, but to a hospital in Scutari . . ." her voice was faltering. "I hoped you'd take these letters home."

There was a surge of noise as some officers came into the restaurant and started to order drinks and call out to one another. The waiter came over again and asked if they'd been happy with their meal; the handsome young couple looked so pale and so strange.

"You don't understand, do you, Deio?" she said at last.

"No," he said, after a long moment in which the room seemed to spin and somewhere dimly inside him he was aware of a sickening disappointment and fear. "I don't. This is a horrible idea."

"Men are dying there," she said, "because conditions are so bad."

"I don't give a damn about that at the moment. I may later. Are you sure you've got this right? They've never sent women to war before?"

"Never before, Deio." Her turn to look proud, scared. "It's the first time ever."

"Nurses," he said stupidly, "but you're not a nurse. This is a joke."

Then she'd got riled, and had gathered her coat around her. "You're making me angry, Deio; you have no idea what I do now. I'm in training."

"Training! For what?"

A middle-aged man, drunk but harmless, came toward her from

the bar, made a cheers sign with his glass, and wavered toward the door. Deio stood up and was about to knock him senseless.

She stood up, too. "I'm going."

"Catrin, sit down. Please."

"I don't have very long now."

Then he let her have it. He shouldn't have but he was desperate. He pointed toward the men at the bar and said in a low furious voice, "Do you have any idea how men like that see nurses? They call them skirts, cracks, crumpets. Those are the polite words."

She didn't let him finish. She scraped her chair back, her face went white, and then red, then she smacked him across the face.

"You bastard."

"Nice language, Catrin. You're already beginning to sound like a nurse."

"You taught me first, you hypocrite."

A cheer from the men at the bar. He flung some coins down on the table and watched her slam through the door and zigzag through the thicket of carriages on Park Lane. He caught up with her running through a line of oak trees parallel to Rotten Row. He held her from behind, pinned her against a tree, practically sobbing into her hair.

"It can't be right. It can't be so. Please don't go."

"You are disgusting, Deio," she raged. "How dare you say things like that to me, they are some of the finest women I ever met. And don't you ever, ever, ever speak to me like that again." She tossed her hair back and glared at him. "Once again you have the mistaken idea that I come to you to seek permission to lead my own life. Well I don't. I simply asked you to take a letter home to Father and to Eliza."

"Well, I won't." He drew back from her, almost colliding with two women in silk habits, gossiping as they rode down Rotten Row. "I am not running a messenger service for stupid runaway girls."

As he drew his fob watch from his top pocket the sunlight winked on the case, just as it had all those years ago when they were soul mates and his grown-up ways had enchanted her. He said some more things that he regretted later, warned her that if she did this her reputation was gone forever and that she never ever would be able to go home again, and then, seeing the expression on her face, he stopped.

"I have an appointment at four," he said at last. "Shall I find a hansom for you, or do you ride in a cab?" Everything was slipping away and there was nothing he could do about it. "Do you have any money?"

"Do not trouble yourself," she said. "I am paid for my work."

The final indignity: there was nothing he could do for her.

They walked out of the park together, through the gates, then into the noise of London. A man with a billboard at the corner of the street was shouting about the war, something about Sebastopol. A fine row of horses, skittering sideways, held up the traffic as they clattered across the street. He found her a cab, insisted on paying. They parted in silence, not a sign, not a word. It was the most pain he'd ever felt. As the cab drew off, he stood on the corner of the pavement turned to stone, watching her face grow smaller and smaller and finally disappear.

They left that night. A miserable, cold, blank day; one of those days when the sky holds no mysteries.

They took them down to London Bridge. They bundled them through the bustling crowds. No bunting, no bands, no flags, no fuss. They weren't soldiers. They were women, and some who had come from outside London and never seen crowds before were terrified by them and the thought of the train.

The train was going down to Portsmouth. The women were bundled into the carriages and told to sit there quietly until further notice. Catherine sat near the window; next to her was Sarah Barnes, the widow from Seven Dials, miserable as a dumb animal being led to slaughter at the thought of what she had left behind. Her oldest, she told Catherine, was thirteen, so she'd be all right. She was the head of their family, steady as a rock.

"They'll be all right," she repeated several times. "I told them not to come to the station, it's dangerous going home alone, and the youngest has a bad cold."

The two nuns sitting beside her nodded and tutted and drew out their prayer books. How soft and unused their hands looked, and how gentle their faces.

The carriage was tiny, airless. Everyone was shy, conscious of where their knees ended and others began, but as soon as they were settled with reasonable comfort the glass door opened and a large, untidy-looking nurse who Catherine recognized from the night before as Emma Fagg, appeared, sniffed a great deal, and sat down, spreading her baggages around her.

Catherine cleared the window with her glove. She'd spent a miserable night, lost in Deio's pain and her own; and although he was there, like a throbbing tooth, she'd temporarily closed off that part of her mind because it was too much. Now, in spite of the crush of bodies, which she hated, and her poor night's sleep, she felt keyed up, even excited.

Outside on the platform, a man was playing a pennywhistle. A guard strolled by, his trolley piled high with suitcases and carpetbags, and on top of it she suddenly saw the family suitcase Eliza had sent. It was a good suitcase; Mother and Father had used it once for their honeymoon and never again, but now it was cracked as a riverbed, its middle lashed with rope. Seeing it roll by made her stomach churn. Through her circle of cleared glass she could see a gray-haired nurse saying good-bye to her old parents. They were clinging to her, their worn old faces collapsed with sorrow as she tried to board the train. A woman in a dark cloak stepped between them. Miss Nightingale, smiling, emphatically addressing the nurse, swooping down on her with a quick, fierce, oddly feline gesture, and then saying something to the old people that made them leave almost immediately.

Catherine pressed her face right against the window.

"My God, she's a cool one." Emma Fagg was watching, too. "She looks no more bothered than if she was going on a country walk."

Even the nuns stood up now—all of them wanting to see their new leader, who was now talking to a well-dressed woman in a fur-lined pelisse and muff.

"Lady Hornby." The Widow Barnes was authoritative. "She done my interview. She's a friend of Miss Nightingale's. She's already been to the Crimea to collect flowers from the battlefields. She's got lovely horkids from Alma."

"Orchids! Oooh, a very useful person to go to war with." Emma Fagg's sarcasm was interrupted by a mighty sneeze. Catherine felt the fine mist settle on her cheek. "She said Miss Nightingale was a miracle worker," said the Widow Barnes. "She done all her paperwork last week, every last bit of it right down to writing out her lessons for the children in her parish."

The word "children" stopped her flow and she sat down again and put her big red hands over her mouth. Catherine was sorry. With a new world, strange work, and a war ahead of her, she liked hearing the Widow Barnes say nice things about Miss Nightingale. All of them needed to trust, to admire, to ascribe to her almost supernatural powers of endurance and organization. The same bewildered mix of need and loyalty that leads children to support cruel and hopeless parents, not that Miss Nightingale was either of these things, but none of them really knew her well, and it was all so new.

At Portsmouth they caught the boat to France. A small crowd saw them off and a band played "Don't Go Johnny" and "Wave the Flag for England." The crowd threw confetti and jostled one another to get a view of them as they stood in their uniforms and waved back from the first deck. A woman held a baby up above the crowds, helping it clutch a paper Union Jack in its podgy, useless hands and wave it. And then Sarah Barnes broke down. Too big to cry with grace, she was like a big dumb animal in pain.

"Oh my God, oh my God," she sobbed, as the whistle blew and the gangway and the lines were cleared, "I shouldna come. I don't want to go."

One of the ladies, who had been keeping an eye on the nurses from an upper deck, swooped down, said something sharp to her about England and led her off downstairs, out of the public gaze. It was ungrateful, she was told, to cry in front of people good enough to turn out on a cold day to wave good-bye to them.

"I've got three little ones," said Sarah Barnes, bending over and clutching her stomach as though in physical pain. "I've left them in London with the two eldest."

"That *is* hard," agreed Lady Hornby, "but we're all making sacrifices." She felt sympathy for the woman, but was eager now to be back on the upper deck with Florence, who was behaving superbly.

The boat pulled out a little more and a few feet of water separated them now from England. The bands, the songs, grew fainter, the paper streamers began to snap, and one by one they saw the faces of the people on the shore rubbed out.

Deio arrived too late to see them go. His carriage had been held up in Ashford by a torrent of rain that had turned a pothole in the road into a temporary lake, and then by a herd of cows a boy was moving so ineptly he'd got out and helped him, couldn't stop himself. Now, he stood on the quay soaking wet, his hair plastered to his temples. The crowd had mostly gone, leaving sweet wrappers and soggy colored bunting in their wake. The steamer was a dot on the horizon.

"What time did that ship leave?" he asked an old sailor who stood next to a pile of sodden rope.

"No more than half an hour ago, less maybe," said the man.

"Goddamn," said Deio, facing the wilderness of the sea. His face was white with rage. He thumped one fist into the other and watched the steamer disappear. He was too late. She was gone.

Part Three

Scutari and the Crimea

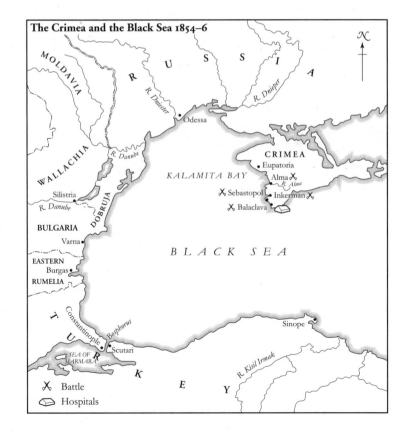

Chapter 37

Constantinople, November 2, 1854

They traveled east in an old mail boat called the *Vectis*, and as it drifted toward the shore, Catherine and Lizzie stood on the deck together watching the city's hills, trees, spires, and churches take shape.

It was snowing; a gauzy, sunlit snow like the inside of one of those children's toys that, when shaken, suggests magical Christmas scenes. The snow lay on the domes of the mosques, the points of minarets, and on the tips of trees. It sparkled and swirled in the air, making a soft drapery of light behind which the city trembled.

"Did you ever imagine it would be so beautiful?" said Catherine.

"Never." Lizzie gave a soft groan.

Catherine longed to know immediately where the Barrack Hospital was, but for the moment kept her mouth shut. Lizzie had been so seasick during the second of two big storms on the way out that Catherine thought she would lose her. Now, thin and pale and covered in bruises, she leaned her head on the rails and watched the shimmering city.

"We made it, Lizzie." Catherine put her arm around her and gave her a gentle hug. "You can put your shoes on again," she teased, for Lizzie had been barefoot for most of the voyage, frightened that seawater would spoil her one pair of boots.

"Boil your head, missie" came the mumbled reply.

* * *

They dropped anchor off Seraglio Point. The fishy smell, the screech of seagulls, and the slap of water against the boat reminded her of home, of Aberdaron. Then boats appeared out of the mist: brilliantly painted, gondola-shaped boats called caïques, which seemed to float above the sea and skim through the snow. A man in a fishing boat sang what sounded like *Behommmmen naaah, bee oommmeeen nah.* He was dressed in wide, baggy, blue trousers; his lips were blue with cold. *Beh ommmmmeen naaah.* A brave, free sound like a drover's cry. A man braced against the elements singing, and her soul singing, too. They were alive! After ten days of storms, of seasickness, of overflowing water closets and boredom and basket-making, and the listless circular conversations of fifteen women in a too-small cabin, they were alive and could leave the ship.

"Listen, Lizzie! Look! Isn't he wonderful?" The boat had drawn up below them and was bobbing in their wake. The man caught her glance and held it, and his cheerful expression changed to a look of deep disgust. She drew back quickly.

"Why did he look at me like that, Lizzie?" she cried.

"Eeerrrr." Lizzie lifted her head from the railings; the skin under her eyes was blue with cold and fatigue. "He don't like us much, does he? What a funny look."

A bell rang and men began shouting in foreign tongues. Then, one by one, ghostly apparitions against a white sky, the nurses and sisters appeared on deck. Their faces were pale, their eyes ringed with sea salt, their uniforms sodden and grimy. It was the first day of their new life and they looked worn out before they had begun.

"Poor bleeders," said Lizzie, looking at them. "Do we look as bad as they do, Catherine?"

"Yes, we do," said Catherine. They began to giggle weakly, and Lizzie slipped down the rails and had to wipe her eyes on her apron.

"You're a bad influence on me, Catherine," she said, giving her a weak punch, "a silly little sod."

Emma Fagg came up first, leaning heavily on the stair railings and gazing around her slowly like a stupefied animal. She'd been sent to bed for three days on the voyage for conversing with a sailor and was still angry about it. Next came Widow Barnes, shrunken and pale. Then one of the Norwood nuns, walking warily as if she still couldn't believe in a ground that did not give way, or a sky not waiting to drop things on her head. During the voyage, the nuns had exchanged becoming black habits for ugly dresses of coarse white serge with a linen headdress, which gave them a ghastly, spectral appearance.

Two nuns were embracing and thanking God for their survival when Lady Bracebridge, in a green crinoline with a huge sea stain on its hem, was suddenly hoisted up the flight of stairs by a French sailor. In her arms was a tiny poodle, hunched and shivering, a green jeweled collar around its neck.

"Good morning, everybody!" she sang out.

"Good morning, Lady Bracebridge!" they chorused back, one or two of them smiling foolishly. Lady Bracebridge had innocently become the butt of many jokes on board the *Vectis*. Prostrate with seasickness for most of the voyage—despite being given the highest, safest cabin—she'd made the mistake, even during bouts of illness, of trying to improve their minds, and appeared at intervals, staggering and green, to talk on a wide variety of subjects: the movement of tides, the exact Latin name for stars, sea birds, the best way to hem a skirt, French art.

Nurse Clara Sharpe, a wicked mimic, had her down to such a "T," that Emma Fagg had wet her drawers one night listening. "And another great theeng about Beetlegerst," Clara would say, screwing up her face and gazing intently at a star, "ees eet . . ." and then she would clap her hand over her mouth and rush downstairs retching.

But still, Catherine thought, Lady B at sea was nothing like as chilly or as snobbish as she'd been in London at Sidney Herbert's house. She'd sat with them several times on deck and told spellbinding stories of her extensive travels. Now she stood in the prow of the *Vectis*, her penetrating eyes trying to pierce the mist and find signals.

"Constantinople," she told them, "is quite one of my most favorite cities on earth." She explained that they were sailing down a stretch of water called the Bosphorus, and that the Bosphorus neatly divided Asia *so* (a jab of her parasol to the right of the boat) and Europe (a jab to her left). "Shut *it*," whispered Emma Fagg to Clara Sharpe, who was starting to wobble her head and purse her lips. "I'm listening and you listen, too, it's *important*." Lady B said that Constantinople had, for thousands of years, been a crucial part of British sea routes to India, which was one reason why the Russians had to be kept away from it.

"Lady Bracebridge," asked Catherine when she had finished, "on what side of the water is Scutari and the Barrack Hospital?"

"It used to be called the Sulemin Barrack Hospital," she said, "and as far as I can remember, it is over there, on the European side of the Bosphorus. Nothing to see yet, but all will be revealed as morning advances. We will have to check with Miss Nightingale."

She pointed her parasol over the port-side railings. The shapes of four blackbirds wheeled in the sky against the fog, and they could hear men's voices speaking what Fagg whispered to Sharpe was "gobshite and jabber jabber."

Lady B swiveled her parasol back toward Constantinople, then her poodle started to retch. She put it down, turning her back on it while it was being sick, and continued. "Over there is the Byzantine church of St. Sophia; the gates of Felicity, the walls of the Grand Seraglio where the sultan keeps his harem . . . ignore it! ignore it!" This to the nurses who wanted to watch the poodle. "No water, and nothing I can do. It's a marvellous city," she carried on, "quite one of my favorites."

"But where are the soldiers, my lady?" Sarah Barnes was gazing solidly into the white mist. "I want to go and nurse them."

Before Lady B could answer, the door was flung open. Miss Nightingale, conspicuous by her absence since Boulogne, now burst onto the deck looking pink and bustling and with no trace of the seasickness that had kept her confined to her cabin. She wore a black silk dress and a white goffered bonnet so well starched she must have kept it for this moment.

"May I ask what on earth you are all doing up here?" she said, with an exasperated look in Lady B's direction.

"I was showing them the sights." Lady Bracebridge had taken the poodle by the scruff of its neck and was trying to stuff it into the folds of her dress. It was unusual to hear her voice falter, but Miss Nightingale did seem on the verge of quite a bad temper.

"The sights!" Miss Nightingale glared at her. She stepped around the pile of yellow foam the poodle had spat up. "Have you quite taken leave of your senses? Lord Napier, the secretary to the British ambassador to Constantinople, will be coming aboard soon to welcome us. All of you"—her eyes traveled with a look of strained impatience over the nuns, Lady Bracebridge, Sarah Barnes, Lizzie, and the rest—"go downstairs at once, wash your faces, change your clothes, and do your hair."

"But there is no water, Miss Nightingale," said Emma Fagg in her irritating nasal whine.

"There is rainwater in the canvas on the deck." Miss Nightingale rapped out each word. "I shall have it brought down."

They went belowdecks as quickly as possible to their tiny cabin, where half a bucket of rainwater had been left for them all to share. Nobody said too much; they were still very much in a mind to love, even to worship, Miss Nightingale. But when they got down there, bumping into one another in the narrow, foul-smelling cabin, they did grumble about how they were expected to clean up in a cabin whose floors were still awash with vomit and slops from the water closet. Still, they spat on their hands and scrubbed with their hems and did the best they could. Everyone was so relieved to have survived the voyage and to know that their work would soon begin. They combed each other's matted hair, they straightened bonnets. Morale was high. Two of the Norwood nuns, Sister Agnes and Sister Etheldreda, began to sing beautifully in low voices, and in unison, a lovely skidding song with a refrain of *In Excelsis Gloria, Gloria, Gloria*. For once, nobody complained about the Latin. They were all so happy to be alive.

A while later, they heard a shrill sound coming from the decks and then feet thundering above their heads. A French deckhand knocked on the cabin door, half torn off its hinges during the last gale and, jerking his fingers upwards said, "Hup now, lady say." Spit had only just shifted the top layer of salt and dirt from their faces and there was nothing to be done about filthy, damp-smelling, uniforms. They clattered upstairs again, staying very close to one another in case Miss Nightingale was cross. She was standing alone on the deck, silhouetted against the white sky; a light sprinkling of snow delicately iced her bonnet. She ordered them to stand in a straight line, not to slouch, and to keep their mouths closed. Her eyes were very black and bright. They had never seen her so nervous before.

A shrill blast of whistles sent seagulls screeching away, then Lord Napier appeared out of the sky, brilliant as a tropical bird. He wore a bright scarlet uniform crisscrossed with gold braid and jangling medals, and high, shining boots; a high, plumed hat increased his considerable height by a foot or more. The splendid caïque he had arrived in, lined with red scarlet and carved with gold leaf, bobbed on the water like a jewelry box.

The nurses and nuns stood at one end of the deck; he at the other. He walked down the deck toward them, a veritable cockerel among muddy hens and, to judge by his first swift glance, not a happy cockerel. He put a monocle to his left eye and let it travel for a while up and down them. All around her, Catherine could feel women with their eyes down, but as Lord Napier passed her she looked at him directly, saw his gray careful eyes, his well-trimmed mustaches, his ludicrous hat.

Miss Nightingale had an instinct for how to make occasions out of unpromising moments—it was part of her brilliance. And now, looking small and suitably awed but determined, she placed her two hands together as if in prayer, touched her hands to her lips, let them fall in a humble supplicating gesture to her waist, and told Lord Napier she was quite certain she spoke for every one of them when she said how honored and grateful they were to be there. Napier allowed himself a wincing smile that he quickly shut off.

"My orders, Miss Nightingale," he said in a barking voice, "are to extend personal greetings to you from the ambassador, Lord Stratford de Redclyffe, and to ask you to proceed with me at once to the Barrack Hospital at Scutari."

In the same staccato voice, he told them that while they had been at sea an important battle had been fought at Balaclava and the wounded were expected within hours. They all looked nervously toward Scutari as he said this. The sky had lightened, the

mist lifted; now they could see the outlines of a huge square building with a tower in each corner.

"That is the Barrack Hospital," said Lord Napier, "where we
will soon find out if you can help us." He flexed his jaw under his
chin strap. "And if you cannot, I am quite sure you will not hinder
us in our quest for peace." He stopped and removed his monocle.
The feathers from his hat flared out in the stiff, smelly breeze from
the shore. Miss Nightingale waited patiently beside him until she
was quite sure his speech was over. She shook his hand. There was
a loud jangle of spurs, medals, sword, and his short and disappoint-
ing visit was over.

After he had gone, they looked at Miss Nightingale. Then one
of the nurses, the pale and intense Harriet Erskine, spoke up. "Oh,
Miss Nightingale," she pleaded, "when we anchor, don't let there be
any red-tape delays. Let us get straight to nursing the poor fellows."

But Miss Nightingale, watching Lord Napier's caïque thrusting
through the water like an exotic fish, shook her head and frowned
and said, "The strongest of you will be wanted at the washtub."

It crossed Catherine's mind briefly that this was an odd thing
to say, but there was no time to think. A few moments later, ten
caïques drew up alongside, and the sailors came and lowered the
nurses over the side, four to a craft. There were screams at this: the
caïques at close quarters looked frail as leaves, and the water that
swirled around them was dark and sinister and littered with rubbish. A Turkish family rowed as close as they could to the ship to
look at them. The women, dressed in ferigees and yashmaks, stared
at them from black eyes, jabbering and gesticulating; then some
boys in bright woolen hats rowed up to them, shrieking and dropping coins and pretending to juggle and dive. But the nurses felt
too anxious to indulge them. By now the mist had gone entirely; on
top of the hill the hospital had taken shape.

Chapter 38

As they grew closer to the shore, the fishy-smelling water grew more foul and their oarsman had to use all his skill to negotiate the piles of rubbish and broken crates flung into the sea. For a while they drifted on, trying not to breathe, then a ferocious barking and growling from the shore drew their attention to a pack of mangy dogs, fighting over what, from a distance, looked like a large, waterlogged rabbit. The boatman paddled as close as he could toward the thing washing backwards and forwards in the water.

"*At*," he repeated several times, "*olu at*."

Through a stretch of scarlet water, Catherine saw the remains of a gray horse, still in its bridle, its eyes pecked clean away. All chatter in the boat gave way to an appalled silence; some of the women put their faces into their handkerchiefs.

Now the mists had cleared, the scene of desolation was complete. Beyond the shoreline, sitting on a muddy beach, was a row of fat buzzards. On the top of the hill, the hospital—huge and dark and with faint lights shining dimly in its windows—looked both human and terrifying: like the skull of a skeleton lit from within, or the kind of monster's castle a child would draw.

For a while, Catherine's mind tried to hold off the idea that this really was the place, but when one of the nurses shouted "Is that it?" from their boat across to Miss Nightingale, she turned and silently nodded her head.

They were docking. The Turkish skipper threw stones at the dogs, then steered them between the dead horse and a sagging pier.

A small crowd of people in rags were watching them; one of them was barefoot, with bandages stuck over legs so badly ulcerated they looked chewed. Catherine thought at first they must be locals, but then she heard one of the men speaking English, and saw that under the grime he wore a cherry-colored tunic. A woman with bad teeth, wearing a dirty green dress, tottered around for a while like someone about to propose a toast, but raised her hand instead in a tired salute.

"Welcome to Scutari," she shouted.

Miss Nightingale went ashore first. She was spirited away by two high-ranking officers who appeared and scattered the small crowd away as if they were no more than stones. Then a young officer, with ginger muttonchops, came to deal with them. More people arrived to stare and marvel at them, while the drunken woman shook her head and called them "stupid buggers" for coming. Captain Muttonchop's mouth opened foolishly; he seemed to have no idea what to do with the nurses, but eventually he said to follow him, quick sticks and on foot, to the hospital.

"Halt! To the right face! Advance," he shouted. A freezing cold wind had got up and the ground was slippery underfoot, but they tried weakly to obey. Catherine, trembling and sweating, could still feel the pitch of the waves inside her head, and the wild lurching of her stomach. They were all seasick and worn out by sleepless nights and not enough food. Up the hill they went, some of the crowd following. She could hear someone playing "Cheer, Boys, Cheer" on a squeaky pennywhistle, and although nobody actually laughed out loud at them, there was suppressed mirth in the air, and when one man in the crowd called out that "them Amazons will need some drilling," she could see the young officer smirk.

At the end of a steep rutted track they came to a pair of large iron gates.

"My God," gasped Clara Sharpe, squinting through the gates. "In't it horrible?"

*   *   *

The Barrack was one of four British hospitals run by the British army in Turkey. The others were the Turkish Military Hospital—accommodation for a thousand patients—the General Hospital, half an hour's walk away, and the Palace Hospital, once the Sultan's summer palace. The Barrack Hospital was the worst of them.

The hospital consisted of miles of dilapidated corridors running around three sides of a quadrangle; the fourth side had been burned down by fire, so it was a building with no heart. In the empty spaces left by the quadrangle, where fountains, trees, even benches might have been, there was a sea of gray slime, stuck here and there with rubbish—broken beds, a chair, a drum, a line of washing broken down and caked with mud.

There was a sense of almost willful ugliness about the place. It came from the rotten basement, from the mudflats of the quadrangle, the long freezing corridors with their broken windows and filthy floors. Even the windows were designed for ugliness. They did not point, as they could have, toward the Bosphorus or Constantinople, or to the beautiful cypress-covered hills beyond, but inwards to the gray slime and the other dirty windows and everything that was wretched and ugly and broken and could not be mended.

The nurses walked through the main gates in appalled silence. There was a smell of eggs and drains and ingrained dirt that wafted up from the huge cellars underneath and hung about the place. Catherine wanted to clutch Lizzie's arm but feared it might look unmilitary.

"This is called the Sultan's Gate," said the young captain. "*To your right turn!* Your quarters are in the tower at the end of this corridor."

They pushed their feet through the dirty snow. The sky above looked milky and curdled; it would snow again before dark. The officer, anxious to be rid of them, bundled them through the door and up a short flight of narrow stairs. At the top of the stairs was a small semicircular room, a tower with three windows looking out onto a pale sky.

"Right!" he said. "Let's get *mobile*. Room allocation."

Her heart sank to her boots as he showed them around. The

tower was divided into six freezingly cold, damp, and smelly rooms. The room that the officer suggested as a kitchen had no fuel, no food, no tables, and no chairs. The bedrooms were tiny, no more than ten feet square, and as dank and moldy as underground cellars. But their main problem, it was obvious from the start, would be overcrowding. The officer told them that the three doctors who had lived here before had asked for a transfer because it was too small. Now it was to house forty nurses; you could barely fit a sheet of paper between the beds.

To everyone's relief, Miss Nightingale now reappeared on the scene. She'd taken off her bonnet, rolled up her sleeves, and seemed to be in remarkably high spirits as she looked at them and squinted at their quarters as if she had nothing more troubling on her mind than the placement for a dinner party.

"Silence please, ladies," she said. "I'm thinking." She pressed her gloved hand briefly against her temple. "I am trying to think how best to arrange this."

After a while she said, "I shall have my ten Norwood nuns to the right of me." One or two bridled at the "my," for they were still wary of accepting her authority.

"And my nurses to the left. Follow me, please."

They followed her into another freezing room, which had a curious forest of white fungus growing through a carpet of dust. In the corner of the room was a bed, sheets rumpled from its previous occupant, and a po filled to the brim with pee.

Sarah Barnes, the widow, looked at the room and said it was all right, she'd lived in much worse than that, and quite a few of the other women agreed, but one of the nuns, Sister Agnes, saw the expression on Catherine's face. She put her hand on her shoulder and said they must not mind the room but must keep their minds on how wet and weary the soldiers must be in their lines, and what an honor it would be to nurse them soon.

Miss Nightingale walked into the room during this brave speech, and with that fierce flash of temper that had so surprised Catherine when she had seen it on the railway station at London Bridge, asked Sister Agnes on whose authority had she told Miss Carreg when and where she would be working?

"The strongest of you," she repeated, "will be wanted at the washtub."

Sister Agnes, blinking like a child about to be struck, promised Miss Nightingale she would do whatever work she was asked to do. Miss Nightingale became serene and kindly again. But the warning was clear: two queen bees at Scutari would be one queen bee too many.

After Miss Nightingale left, a medical orderly—a lad of no more than seventeen with a cheeky smile—brought in two copper basins filled with weak tea, and some stale, sour-tasting bread. There was no milk, but a small paper twist with brown sugar in it.

"Thank you, handsome," Clara Sharpe's voice was tired, "your mum must love you."

"She do," he said, but now he seemed resentful.

They fell on the tea as though it were champagne—they'd had nothing since breakfast, and some, due to seasickness, had not eaten properly for nearly two weeks.

The boy brought mattresses and a small pile of thin, gray blankets marked with an arrow and with B.O. stitched in the corner. They counted the mattresses: only six for ten of them, so Lizzie politely asked if it would be a bother for him to get them some more, and maybe a few more blankets. Two panes of glass were broken in the window and snow was puffing through it. Their hands were blue with cold.

"Yes." The boy scratched underneath his filthy smock. "It would be too much trouble." He followed this with a long recitation about how the purveyor, "let's call him Mr. X," would "hang him up by the ears" if he gave them beds that had not been countersigned by Mr. Y, who would also need to get documentation from Mr. Z. If the thought of sleeping ten to a room with only six beds had not been so depressing they might have laughed, the list of names he had to consult was so droll.

"And I'm not supposed to talk to you lot without Miss Nightingale's permission neither," he scowled, "she just told me that."

"Well, you're a stuck up little bumwipe," said Emma Fagg.

"Miss *Fagg!*" One of the nuns clutched her rosary.

"Well he *is* stuck up," Fagg muttered. "I'd have him up by his ears, too, if he was mine."

The boy, who was young enough to be her son, set his jaw.

"That's my orders, old lady, and if you don't like it . . . go home," he said softly.

That first night, Catherine lay down on the floor with the other women around her, saw their breath puffing into the air, smelled them. Her whole body was still rocking with the motion of the boat, and she was drifting in and out of an uneasy dream about a horse, when she snapped to, instantly awake, her ears aching with cold, and had a painful moment of truth. This was going to be too much for her. She'd already crossed the line. Shocked and frightened by the dilapidated hospital, humiliated by her dreams, she felt half broken before her work began. But there was Lizzie, sleeping serenely no more than two feet to the left of her, and Widow Barnes (making sucking and bubbling noises) to the right. They could sleep; some of them even thought the room an improvement on the places they had left.

It's my fault. She sat up in the freezing air and thought of how Deio's arms had wrapped around her when she was cold. *He said this would happen and it has.*

At about three o'clock, rain fell hard against the windows and what shreds of curtains remained were sucked into the broken panes of glass. The whine of the wind rose to a howl and rain began to drip on the floor with a noisy plopping sound. She sat up again in bed, shivering with cold, and thought to herself almost calmly, "I am in hell and this is all my fault."

She got out of bed to look for buckets; they'd been given one for washing, and one for slops. The ground under her bare feet was furry with dust and freezing. She walked around the sleeping women toward the drip-drop sound and found the leak underneath a fireplace where a knifelike draft came down the chimney. She stood on a square of straw matting that, as she put her bucket down, tore away like paper. Feeling breath on her feet, she looked down and saw Emma Fagg's long jaw on a pillow, her head half in the fireplace. She disliked Emma Fagg: her irritating voice, her complaints, and for one irrational moment wanted to stamp on her. "What is it?" Emma sat up, a woolen hat half over her eyes.

"Nothing," she said crossly, "go back to sleep."

As Catherine raised her candle toward the ceiling, a loud rustling made her blood freeze with horror. "There's a Russian soldier up there," she thought. "He'll put a dagger through my heart." And then, a soft commotion above her head like stockinged feet running. She looked up into a pair of bright yellow eyes. Too scared to scream she blundered back to her bed, tripping over her nightdress.

"Lizzie, wake up!" she whispered. "There's someone on the roof watching us."

Lizzie sat up instantly. Long years of practice had taught her to wake up sensible.

"Are you sure?"

"Yes," she pleaded. "Please come and look with me."

"If this is nothing you've had it." Lizzie, shivering in her nightdress, looked green with fatigue. Catherine led her back toward the fireplace, a faint light from the window outlining the shape of her nightcap. A chilly wind from the fireplace swirled down its hole, ruffled their nightdresses, and blew out Lizzie's candle. She swore softly.

"It's all right," said Lizzie in a trembling voice, but before Catherine could find her tinderbox she shrieked out loud. Sarah Barnes sprang up in her bed saying "Wahiawa" under her nightcap like a great big terrified baby. Then they all shrieked together, until Lizzie said, "Be quiet, you soppy dates. It's only a rat."

They lit another candle and held it up and there it was: the size of a lapdog and blacker than any rat Catherine had seen in England, with a long shaggy coat and lemony-green eyes. Lizzie picked up a broom and banged the beam, and it lumbered off into some dark hole between the roof and the rafters.

It would have been all right, as Fagg kept saying, if it had been a normal-sized rat, the kind they were used to, but as dawn came over the windowsill, lighting their wan faces, all any of them could talk about was the size of that foreign rat. Fagg, her voice even more bunged up than usual first thing in the morning, told them of a rat "almost as big as a pussy cad" that had crept up on her mother as she lay abed in her house in Seven Dials, "in Lundudd. It bit her on her chind."

Loud sniff.

And then everybody else told their rat stories and seemed to cheer up, except Catherine, who didn't have one. In her world, rats lived in barns outside the house. She thought of her bedroom at Carreg Plâs: the pretty eiderdown with its cabbage-rose pattern, the faint smell of pomander and furniture polish. The muscles on her neck stood out like organ stops and at that moment she would have given everything in the world she had ever owned to leave this frightful place and go home.

Chapter 39

The next day they were moved to a new room in the same tower, and directly above Miss Nightingale's quarters.

Catherine was to share with Lizzie, Emma Fagg, Anne Higgins, Sarah Barnes, Georgiana Barry, a nurse from Bermondsey, and a Mrs. Wilson, a gray-faced woman who had suffered dreadfully from seasickness on the way out.

The room had three large windows, one overlooking the Sea of Marmora, the other the faint outlines of Constantinople, and from the third, if you stood on your tiptoes, a large graveyard and the General Hospital, with snowcapped mountains behind it.

Catherine, staring out, saw she was living on an isthmus again, and the memory of her mother, trapped and bleeding in her bedroom at Carreg Plâs, cut like a knife and brought an unpleasant swooping sensation in her body as though she were going to faint. She gripped the wood of the windowsill; it was soft and crumbled in her hands.

"All right, love?" Lizzie's face swam into view.

"Yes, thank you," she said, dazed and nauseous. "What's everyone doing?"

"Cleaning." Lizzie raised her eyebrows. "What else?"

The floor was sticky with dirt, and in the corner were piles of half-gnawed rags and some rat droppings. She was working up a sweat, when Emma Fagg came at her with a mattress in her hands.

"Out of my way," she said, "pip, pip. I want to put this down." She planted her feet in the middle of the small pile of dirt Catherine had swept.

"Bide your time," Catherine said sharply. "I haven't finished the floor yet."

"Bide your time yourself, you stuck-up madam," said Fagg, thrusting her jaw out. She had thick eyebrows that met in the middle and a weak smile.

Catherine felt her fists clench, she wanted to hit her very hard. "I must be careful," she thought. "I'm as angry as she is."

The redheaded orderly arrived with a tray of breakfast—a weak tea that was barely warm and had an unpleasant aftertaste, and sour black bread. They sat down on the floor to eat. The orderly had told them there wasn't a solitary table in the whole hospital, not even for operations, and no chairs either. After breakfast they put a box over a hole in the carpet, and sat down crossed-legged on their rolled up clothes.

Clara Sharpe said it felt as though they were in the sultan's harem, sitting like this. "Pass us a fig, Fatima," she said. Anne Higgins, a stout woman with a slow, hissing laugh like steam escaping, went "ssss . . . ssss . . . sss."

Catherine wanted to hit someone again. She was sick to death of inactivity, of stupid jokes, of being cold and confined. Let them work, for God's sake. But no. When their dirty cups had been washed up, Nurse Barnes, always greatly interested in her own health, unpacked her own medicine box and dwelt lovingly on the quantities of Carnation corn caps, Sloane's liniment, and Shaw's blood purifier, which she admitted, to general approval, she'd nicked from her last employer.

"In fact, I nicked them all." She goggled her eyes at her own cheek. "I wouldn't from you lot, mind, but they paid me so bad."

She told them about an attack of measles she'd had three years ago so severe that, "Me spots grew inwards. *Inwards.* I promise you. My son fetched me a bottle of Shaw's, and I was up that night cooking his dinner."

"You've told us that already," said Emma Fagg, "twice."

But Barnsie, as they now all called the widow, got away with it. Everybody liked her because she was so softhearted but, when the floor was swept, Catherine was horrified to see Barnsie put her mattress down next to hers and say with a smile, "I'll sleep here next to you." All of them smelled, after days without a proper wash, but the widow had a particularly odd and terrible smell, like old meat; she was also a snorer.

"All right then, my precious?" Barnsie squeezed her hand.

"Yes, thank you," said Catherine, determined not to cry; it was just that she felt so homesick.

That night, Barnsie turned toward Catherine in the dark and said she thought she was a bit of a "dark horse," and although the others talked about their fellows, she'd never said a word. "You've never even said if you've got a sweetheart, and I bet you have—lovely girl like you."

Catherine said, with a terrible sinking of her heart, that she hadn't, so there was nothing much to say about that. It hurt so much to say it that Barnsie must have noticed. She changed the subject abruptly, and said, "Right then," as though Catherine had been pestering her for days, "so I'd better tell you my story at last."

She got up on one elbow and came so close to her in the dark, that Catherine could see the outline of her teeth, which were childishly large and friendly. Her story took nearly an hour to tell; Catherine never could quite work out whether she told it out of tact, or to test, or out of a simpleminded desire to entertain. All she knew was that with Barnsie's puffing breath on her cheek and the occasional flash of her eye in the dark, she felt like the prey of some unstoppable wild beast come to tell her that its life was as important, as repulsive, as wonderful, as the next person's.

Her parents, Barnsie told her, were street people. Her father's principal occupation had been as a coachman on the London to Brighton run, but his "chief abiding place" was the taproom, and, since people hadn't taken kindly to being driven at an erratic pace, he "soon took up residence there, more or less permanent." After that, she said, they'd lived in Seven Dials, in a house that was "nothing better than a kind of tent, which is why I don't think this room is as bad as some of the other stuck-up arses I could mention."

"Barnsie!"

"I don't mean you. You're my silly little girl." Barnsie squeezed her hand in the dark, and, in spite of herself, Catherine smiled. When they'd first moved to Seven Dials, Barnsie went on, her mother had set up her own street stall, "although where she got the money for the combs and children's toys and such like was nobody's business." But then, one day a young thief, no more than thirteen or fourteen, had come, knocked her mother out cold, and took her stuff, and not long after that her mother was a stiff 'un. There was a long sigh in the dark, and Catherine, feeling a rising hysteria, put her hands over her eyes.

"Please stop talking," she wanted to beg her, but the harsh voice kept going.

"I'm ten years old, and I go out on the street to take over where my mother left off. *Come buy this lot. Penny the lot. Lovely knife, cut your butter wiv it.*"

There was a thump on the wall next to them.

"Firkin silly bitches."

"Barnsie! Barnsie!"

"I'm only talking. So, where was I? Well, that's it . . . then I find that selling things is another way of starving, so I'll put it in a nutshell for you: I had two younger brothers and sisters, and they're starving, too, so I goes up to the dolly shop I know in Seven Dials, and I buys myself a crinoline and a lovely little pork pie hat with a feather, and I'm not ashamed to tell you this, I put myself out on the street."

"Barnsie, please don't . . . you don't have to tell me . . ."

"I do, I have to, you're much too wet behind the ears. We won't stay like this forever, we'll be meeting soldiers soon, and you don't have a clue." And Barnsie went on to tell her in some detail of the gentlemen she had lain with, what she had done for them, and they for her.

"So what do you think to that?" she asked eventually. "You've gone eversa quiet."

She was thinking about Deio in the chophouse. *Do you know what most men call nurses? Skirts, cracks, crumpets.*

But Barnsie, dear Barnsie, so comfortable, so warm with a bosom any child would love to sink their head in. Not evil, not dirty, and now, her round blue eyes staring at her in the dark, waiting for an answer.

Catherine gave a shuddering sigh. "I think, well, I think . . . a great deal of evil has been done to you in your life."

"Evil be buggered." Barnsie sat up in bed. "I wasn't 'ticed. Nobody forced me. I like it—some of it anyway. It's only women like you that find it disgusting, women like me think it's all right. I had dresses, I had hats, me brothers and sisters had food in their mouths and I was my own master and mistress. What's so bloody evil about that?"

"Barnsie, shush, keep your voice down. So why did you stop?" She knew it was wrong of her but she was riveted.

"Ah well," she said, more calmly. "I met a bullyboy didn't I? His name was George. Gorge with George." Barnsie seemed to think this was funny and gave a rattling laugh that ended in a cough. "He wanted my money and when I didn't give it, he gives me a shiner and I can't work, and the next night he's waiting there with another one for me. So I stopped, and for the next few months I gets a respectable job working for an old man dying of tuberculosis."

She said she'd grown fond of this old gentleman, although nursing was not as well paid or as much fun as being on the streets, and she might have left had not a son entered the picture.

"The son took me upstairs one day, and a baby followed. I was eighteen."

"But did he not admit his guilt and support you?" Now Catherine sat up in bed, her eyes flashing.

A snort in the dark. "Oh my God, she's a caution! No, he did not support me. He broke off all communications with me; shortly afterward I'm dismissed with a bad character. And do you know something that will make you smile, Catherine"—she pronounced it Cafrin—"I fell for him. He was lovely looking, tall and dark, and I've got a lovely little baby who is up at the foundling hospital in Marylebone. The sisters know all about him, and they told me if I stay here and save me money and don't drink, I've got a better chance of getting him out."

"Oh Barnsie, how hard that must be."

"He is beautiful." Barnsie's voice broke. "Very beautiful." A long silence, and then more cheerfully, "Well, there's a lot more where that came from." A great yawn and then even breathing—that would be the last of her until the rising bell at five.

Catherine lay in the dark with her eyes wide open, horrified, yet obscurely thrilled. Could it really be true what she said about physical love? That some women lay with men and still loved them afterward, even if they weren't married, and why did poor women like it, and married women who were better off find it disgusting? And was what she'd done with Deio what it actually was? And then the thought of him came flooding back to her: his lips tasting of smoke, the easy way he sat on his horse and smiled at her, his shining black hair. She tried to shudder again—for surely the memory of the full-length of his body lying on hers was disturbing? Degrading. Only now, she remembered her excitement at seeing his outline in the dark; the feeling of liquid silver that had run through her veins when he'd kissed her; first tenderly, then as if to claim her, and then—Oh! Was this what Barnsie meant, the unexpected uproar in her own body at the brief taste of his mouth, before she threw him off?

Chapter 40

They stayed in their freezing room for two weeks, sewing bandages, stuffing stump pillows, and sorting piles of rotten linen. Then one morning Anne Higgins, who was staring out of the window, started to moan.

"Oh *God have Mercy!* Get over here and look at this."

They dashed to the window. Down at the pier, orderlies were unloading from boat after boat what at first glance looked like huge, dirty fish. Then they saw they were British soldiers, many of them almost naked and blue with cold. The women moaned to see how their bones stuck out, and the rough way some were thrown onto the stretchers.

"Good God almighty! Oh my God!" Most of the women were in tears it was so horrible.

It was snowing again outside; a dog on a short length of chain barked as the men were roped onto litters and hauled up the muddy hill. They watched one old pensioner holding the front end of a litter drop a man down the hill, and saw how he bounced pointlessly like a muddy snowball until he stopped screaming.

"Please God," breathed Lizzie, who had clutched Catherine's hand so hard her nails left marks, "when are they going to let us help?"

It was at that moment that Miss Nightingale burst into their room without knocking. "Nurses, please!" She clapped her hands. "Away from that window at once. I want to introduce you to Dr. Menzies, the senior medical officer at the Barrack Hospital, and a very important man indeed."

"Miss Nightingale," Catherine couldn't stop herself. "Those poor men . . . why can't we help them?"

"Be quiet at *once*, Miss Carreg," snapped Miss Nightingale coldly. She bowed her head and looked up at the doctor demurely through her eyelashes. "We are entirely at Dr. Menzies's disposal."

"Thank you, Miss Nightingale." Dr. Menzies's smile conveyed no warmth. "It is a distressing sight I grant you, but they will be well taken care of and the matter is in hand."

Miss Nightingale raised her head and gave him a steady look.

"That is all we care about," she said, and gave the nurses a warning glance. *I know what I'm doing. Don't you dare cross me.*

"It occurred to me, Dr. Menzies," she said in the same mild and supplicating voice, "that we might possibly have some small role to perform in the way of women's work: sewing, washing—whatever would suit you best."

"Possibly," replied Dr. Menzies reluctantly. "It would be a shame to have brought you all this way for nothing." He shifted his features now and crinkled his eyes. *They hate us,* Catherine thought, *they don't want us here.* That possibility had not occurred to her before.

Later in the day, an unusually subdued Lady Bracebridge appeared. "Miss Nightingale has drawn up a timetable for you all," she said. "Keep quiet while I read it."

"At eight o'clock precisely each morning," she began, "you will assemble downstairs, dressed in your full uniform ready for prayers. Prayers will be conducted in Miss Nightingale's room. After prayers, you must go back to your room and wait for the nine o'clock bell to ring. When the nine o'clock bell rings, you will be taken either to a ward, or a kitchen, or to the linen stores, or the washtub. When you go, you will be supervised either by myself or Miss Nightingale, or perhaps Mrs. Clark when she is well. You are not, and I shall repeat, *not,* ever to go *anywhere* without special permission from Miss Nightingale herself. Failure to obey will result in instant dismissal. At half past two, you will dine in your room. Your food will be brought to you. Eat it all: rations are scarce. Likewise, you are advised that water will be limited to one pint per person each day. At half past four, you will return to your room and stay there until prayers at nine, after which time you will go to bed."

Lady B went on to say that, if it could be arranged, they might, every now and then, be taken on a supervised walk, at which a certain amount of sarcasm and jeering broke out among the nurses, Clara Sharpe muttering that that was bloody generous of them.

"Your last instruction is that you do *nothing* and speak to *no one* without permission," Lady B had to raise her voice. Even she, Catherine noticed, had flea bites on her face now. "And be warned that any of you who feel inclined to drink, or to engage in any kind of coarse conduct, will be punished by instant dismissal. Is this clear?"

"Clear as firkin day," whispered Sharpe, then, in a louder voice, "Sorry to ask this, my ladyship, but when will we nurse the soldiers?"

"When we are asked to" came the firm reply.

"And when will that be?"

"Don't push me," Lady B's voice had risen almost to a scream. "It's not up to *me*." And then she left, her shoulders high, the back of her skirts rimmed with dirt. She wasn't quite a lady and they were certainly not nurses, but all that would change.

It was Higgins who, during the long hours shut in their room, read to them from books, or told them the plots of the penny dreadfuls she adored. One afternoon—they were sewing and it was snowing outside, a dreaming, drifting, muffling snow that seemed to emphasize their isolation—she told them about a book called *The Diary of an Idle Woman in Constantinople*. They jeered and laughed bitterly at the title. "Don't laugh," said Higgins, "it's about a real lady and the sights she saw there. Come here."

She took them to the window and pointed across the misty water.

"The palace of Topkapi is over there," she said in a mysterious voice, and to Barnsie, whose face was covered in flea bites, "stop scratching!" "Listen!" she went on. "The people who lived across there were once part of a very rich country." Sounds of derision from the floor where the nurses were sitting—the chairs still hadn't come.

"It's true," Lizzie chimed in, "Lady B told me. It's beautiful inside that palace, the walls are covered in mosaics, the cellars crammed with jewels. There are beautiful pavilions and hanging gardens and water splashing everywhere and horses with saddles encrusted with pearls, and sumptuous feasts with thirty courses."

It tugged at Catherine's heartstrings to see her friend's pale face so lit up by a silly story.

"Here," said Higgins, "who's telling this? The food was something wonderful," she went on in her important voice.

"I'll thump you if you talk about food," said Barnsie. "I'm so hungry I could cry."

But Barnsie was shouted down with cries of "What food?"

"There was sumptuous feasts, all night: roast pigeons, pastries dripping with honey, fresh fruits, sherbets."

"And the harem, Anne Higgins," said Clara with a nasty snigger, "tell us about that." They all knew about the two sailors.

"There were three hundred women locked up in the Sultan's harem, and if he liked them they slept on silk beds and had a bath in milk and then he stuck it in them!" Whoooo! from the women. "But if he got sick of them it was off to the dungeons with you, or they sent you to the Palace of Tears."

"How do you remember all this, Anne?" Catherine was impressed.

"I read it in a book."

Catherine saw Lizzie dip her head and wince, she so wanted to read. And Catherine wanted to teach her, but it was a delicate matter.

"Wonderful life, ain't it?" said Clara Sharpe, "being a fucking woman."

Then a discussion about whether they'd rather be a nurse or in the harem broke out, and the thought of Higgins or Barnsie being odalisques was so rich, they all started to laugh.

"Oh, the nuns wouldn't like this." Clara Sharpe wiped tears of laughter from her eyes. "Oh it's a bit too rich for them. I shouldn't like to see Sister Agnes in a . . ." she was gasping at her own wit, "in a . . . milk bath," she exploded.

Her shout of laughter got them all going, and soon, hooting and cackling, they were collapsing on the floor, holding their sides, giving way to that kind of wild laughter that feels so strangely close to tears.

It was a week later, after morning prayers, that their real work seemed to begin. First, Mr. Ware, the chief purveyor of the Barrack Hospital, a pompous man in his seventies, turned up puffing at their door to say he would take them on a walking tour of the hospital that morning. He had closed his eyes and pursed his lips when he said good morning to them, and when he opened his eyes again Catherine caught a look of immense weariness as if to say, "This lot are one more problem I have to face."

Then, at a surprisingly fast pace for such a stout man, he led them down the series of muddy tracks that crisscrossed the hospital square. First stop was the gate they had come through on the first day. "Hospital entrance!" he barked, and then pointed toward a honeycomb of dirty windows on his right, only just visible through the gloom. "Troop depot," he rattled out, quickly speeding up his pace. "Stables." He was almost running. Catherine found she could not bear to look at the horses, it hurt too much. "Accommodation for almost two hundred horses. Two-o-o horses. And the kitchens . . ." A blur of steamed-up windows, the silhouette of a huge pot, but Ware told them there was no time to look around.

When they got back, their heads were swimming, their skirts and boots covered in mud, and all of them had been startled by what a large and confusing place the hospital was. "It's more like a blooming town," commented Clara Sharpe, scarlet from her run in the snow.

Later they learned that, like all towns, the hospital had its dark secrets. Ware had not, for instance, taken them into the network of cellars under the hospital where close to two hundred prostitutes lived. They'd made their homes around the shadowy pipes and on top of the sewers and here they met their customers and had their children and, in many cases, starved to death unseen, like rats under the floorboards.

Clara Sharpe had pointed out another strange omission. "Mr. Ware," she said, "where are the patients?"

"My dear madam"—Mr. Ware clutched his head as if it was a precious box full of secrets—"If you expect to just walk into a ward and start work you are to be sadly disappointed. There are procedures to be followed."

"Which ones?" Sharpe was not impressed.

"Well," he said, "picture yourself in that ward over there." He pointed to the left. "A young infantryman is admitted. He is wearing the uniform he fell in. His leg has been shot off. You must procure for him a bed, a blanket, a meal, a nightshirt, and some medical attention. How, and in what order are you going to do all that?"

"I don't know," admitted Clara. She had her hands on her hips and was giving him a lemony look. "You'd better tell me."

"I will tell you." Mr. Ware was magnanimous. "For his bed, he needs a pink slip of paper, to be taken to the ward officer and countersigned by me. For his meal you go to the ground floor and stand in line for a spoon diet or, if meat, line up for a blue slip that must be countersigned by his ward officer and an orderly. If he needs a special diet, stand in line on the second floor. As for his nightshirt, knife, fork, and spoon, it is army regulations that he provides same for himself."

It was Catherine's turn to glare at Mr. Ware. All the men they'd watched land at the hospital had done so half naked, half starved, and with no possessions at all.

"What happens to men without full kits?" she asked clearly.

"And if he is without them," continued Ware glassily without bothering to look at her, "the man for him is Mr. Gumpney from stores, and only then with the correct paperwork. Stores have a habit of marching off and when they do, men like Mr. Gumpney from stores are held responsible and have to pay for any deficits from their wages."

An orderly came in holding up a fistful of papers for Ware to sign, which he did hurriedly, with one knee held up and used as a desk. While his pen was darting, Miss Nightingale came in and waited until the pen was wiped and put back in his pocket.

"Mr. Ware," she said at last, "thank you for interrupting a busy morning on our behalf. You have so many pressing things to do." She smiled at him. Ware was bowled over. He bowed jerkily and almost backed out of the door, promising more of his time at a later date.

Clara Sharpe was not charmed. "Well, that was all clear as mud, wasn't it?" she muttered when he was gone. A nun standing next to her frowned gently, but Clara was off.

"Miss Nightingale," she said, "I beg your pardon, but I do have one question: What are we going to do today?"

"Soon," said Miss Nightingale deliberately. Her smile had gone.

"Not today?"

"I have given you my answer, Miss Sharpe."

"But we see those soldiers landing, it's . . . horrible, terrible."

"Miss Sharpe"—an edge of steel in her voice—"when I give an order, you must trust it's the right one. And if you find this impossible, you will have to go home, and the sooner the better."

An old man with a sweet face and a gammy leg came through the door at this moment with a piece of paper in his hand. He gave them all a friendly smile and told them they'd surely be needed soon—all hell had broken loose outside, and an order had come through for them to move their bedrooms up one floor.

"They're landing a lot of men, and they want the ground floor for stores again."

Miss Nightingale gave him an icy look. "I am taking my orders from Dr. Menzies," she said. "I don't remember him mentioning you."

"Well, miss," he was completely unoffended, "Private Sam Parker is my name, and if you do want me I am at your service and very happy to see to you, and your gels, too."

She shut the door on him, blotting out his smile.

Chapter 41

On the third of November, they woke to find a dead woman among them. Poor Mrs. Wilson, a quiet type, had never recovered from the journey and had caught dysentery soon after her arrival. Now, pale and looking peaceful, she lay on the divan, her face covered in fleabites. Two orderlies took her away in a cloth bag and buried her in a graveyard they could see from their window. None of them were invited to her funeral.

And then fear arrived like a new inmate in their room. They could feel it in the air, a quiet beating like trapped wings below the normal surface of things; a strained look in other people's eyes. Sometimes it looked like anger and sudden shouts would erupt out of some trivial misunderstanding, and sometimes it felt like grief, and tears arrived as though they had stood waiting. At nights, Catherine couldn't stop herself brooding over her mother's death: the blood, the bed; herself at the window shrieking "Tell me what to do."

Realistically, they knew that their hospital would not be invaded—the fighting, the Crimea, was over a hundred miles away—but dying was now a real possibility and irrational fears sprang up: a Russian could climb through the window and murder them; or they'd die from a rat bite or some foreign disease. It hardly mattered. Once fear was in the blood it raced around the body like a contagion.

In this mood, all of them were morbidly sensitive to news of the war and aware that no two people ever said the same thing. When, for example, they'd asked Miss Nightingale what had happened at the Battle of Balaclava, she'd turned it into a sermon that they could learn from. She told them that during a charge by the Heavy Brigade, a few months ago, five hundred British men had fought against three to four thousand Russians. "That charge will go down as one of the great feats of cavalry against cavalry in the history of the world. Every man in that line," she said, "expected to be killed, but they obeyed instructions to the letter; they rode in perfect formation through flank after flank of Russian forces. Do you see how important it was for them to stay in line?"

She gazed at each one of them intently.

"Yes miss," a number of their ranks said meekly.

"And why, if I say to you 'stay back until it is time to move forward,' you must obey, as any good soldier must obey their commander?"

"Yes, Miss Nightingale," they practically shouted.

She had them, for that moment, in her hand, united in an ecstasy of pride and emotion. Shame that, a few moments later, Miss Nightingale was interrupted by Sam Parker, the ancient pensioner who had become their favorite orderly. He limped through the door with another roll of linen for them to hem, smiling his gummy smile, and Miss Nightingale, who often in some strange way seemed to be in flight from them, left abruptly. He might have followed, but they pulled him back into the room and begged him to finish the story she had started—they were so starved for news.

Sam, who had served in the Peninsular War as a regimental drummer, was indiscreet and amusing and liked nothing better than to gossip.

"I'm too old to be flogged," he said, "so I'll talk to you gels."

He held up a chilblained finger and closed the door. "A bit confidential this."

He told them that after this wonderful charge by the Heavy Brigade, there was another charge, this time by the Light Brigade.

"A shambles," he whispered. "A complete moog-up. Those men you see being lifted up the hills in the morning, you should hear what they say of it. Most of them, if they weren't so weak and low in spirits, would die of rage. They say if you were to search the length and breadth of England, you'd be hard put to find two greater muffs than Lord Lucan and Lord Cardigan."

The room went very quiet. Catherine saw Barnsie's knuckles turn white.

"What happened, Sam?" asked Lizzie.

"The whole thing was no better thought out than a barroom brawl; our horses and men were starving before they went into battle; the Rooskies were snug as bugs in their silk underwear."

Poor Sam, he was so cut up. They watched his mouth stiffening and swallowing.

"After Balaclava," he said when he had found his voice again, "Lord Cardibag goes back to his yacht; has a bath and a bottle of Champagne."

"Oh come on, Sam," they said, "now you are making up a story."

"I am not!" he said with heat. "You ask Miss Whatsit. He keeps a yacht in the bay, and the soldiers went home to dry biscuits and tents under a foot of water. Oh, don't let me start, ladies, I'll spit blood just to think of it."

She thought of Deio and felt a cold terror. If he'd decided to come, she would never forgive herself. Barnsie, who had a soft spot for Sam, patted his arm. He looked at her and tried to control himself.

"I should never have come out here," he told her. "I'm too old and I've been a silly old fool. I volunteered you know."

Barnsie put her arm around him. She sat and talked to him in a low, crooning voice, while Catherine sat and suffered. His story confirmed her worst fears. Nobody told the truth here; nobody could be trusted. Miss Nightingale, who they'd been invited to think of as a kind of saint, was in the end a government official, and if there was a choice between the government's line and the unvarnished truth, there *was* no choice. Then Sam gave them the bale of cotton that, like most of the linens in that hospital, was spotted with green damp in some places. He told them to cut it up into bandages and slings.

"There isn't enough bandages in the world to stem all the blood down there," he said quietly. "It's a knacker's yard, and if you want Sam Parker's opinion you'll be on the wards next week."

*   *   *

That afternoon a lump of gristle and a bare piece of bone came close to ruining Catherine's life. She was sitting sailor fashion on the floor next to Lizzie, who was sewing a length of canvas that she was stuffing with damp straw. Their hands were so cold they took turns warming them under the blanket. Catherine had finished three mattresses and Lizzie, with her quick neat gestures, was putting the final row of stitches at the end of the fourth, when the entire seam came apart in her hands in a moldy hopeless little puff of air, and then she exploded.

"I'm sick to death of sewing," she shouted. "I'm going downstairs."

"Watch out!" Lizzie saw the accident coming before she did. Catherine's hand came down on the point of a sharp canvas knife, blood surged and a flap of skin below the ring finger of her left hand dangled.

They were always short of water, but Lizzie immediately poured half of her pint-ration into a bowl and put some iodine in it. And then everybody was very kind: Clara Sharpe helped Lizzie staunch the blood and bandage the wound; Barnsie hauled herself up from the floor and patted her shoulder.

Freezing cold and unable to sew, she passed the afternoon waiting and watching, trying not to hear the cries of a new crop of wounded men being unloaded outside their window. The sky outside looked perfectly blank and she felt as pointless as the snowflakes drifting down. At four o'clock, the redheaded orderly arrived with lunch.

Catherine looked into the dirty pail of food he'd left on the floor, and something snapped. The dish of the day was a dark gray stew, shiny with globules of fat, and composed mostly of bone and gristle. With a spoon in her good hand, she poked through the bones and the fat and found at the bottom of the burned pan a piece of blue rag tied to a chunk of raw meat. She shrieked with rage, speared the piece of meat with a fork, quit the room, marched down the stairs, and knocked with her foot on Miss Nightingale's door.

She could hear voices inside, then a silence, and then shadows underneath the door rearranged themselves. When the door opened, Miss Nightingale stood in the light, a sheaf of papers in her hand. Behind her was a middle-aged man sitting at the desk in a frock coat.

"Miss Carreg?" Miss Nightingale said coldly, "what are *you* doing here?"

"Miss Nightingale," she said, "we can't work and now it seems we can't eat either." The piece of meat hung in her hand, dripping its gravy on the floor.

"What are you doing? What is that?" Miss Nightingale was livid.

She heard herself say, "We have had enough."

"Enough!" Miss Nightingale was one of those people who grew quieter as they grew angrier. "How dare you stand there and say that."

"Miss Nightingale," she said, "we cannot work on food like this?" There was a lamp on the desk. She held the raw meat under it.

"I warn you, Miss Carreg, if that drips on my papers I shall be very angry indeed." She walked across the room and found a plate, a knife and a fork, apologizing to the doctor, who was smiling, for holding him up; she cleared some papers from her desk, put the meat on a plate under the circle of lamplight. She sliced the meat in half, exposing a red tangle of uncooked veins and yellow fat.

"Delicious!" The doctor's whiskers twitched, he was enjoying this scene like a man at a cockfight. "This is the way we feed our men." Then he looked at Catherine, a full look that seemed to sweep from the top of her head to her toes.

"Perhaps she does have a point here," he said, "it is a bit of a dog's dinner."

"She has no right to say so," said Miss Nightingale in a confidential aside. "If the meat is good enough for the men it is good enough for us."

Catherine knew there was no question of Miss Nightingale and Lady Bracebridge's eating the same food as they. Theirs was cooked separately by Mrs. Clark. But now Miss Nightingale was cutting a flap of meat from the edge of the gristle. She put it in her mouth and chewed it neatly until it was swallowed up.

"Perfectly edible, Miss Carreg," she said when she was finished, "take it up to the other nurses and tell them it's that or nothing."

Chapter 42

$\mathcal{T}$he doctor stood up.

"Before you leave," he said, "show me your hand. It looks sore."

"It's nothing," she said shortly, "it's just a cut."

"Miss Carreg, if Dr. Cavendish wishes to see it, *show it to him.* He knows what the risks are."

Miss Nightingale smiled at him, one professional to another, and Catherine held out her hand. When the doctor leaned over her, she saw the stained rim of his collar, the full damp mouth above the bristling whiskers.

"I can't see well in this light." He squinted at the bandage. "She'd better come into my dispensary, Miss Nightingale—I'll send her back upstairs afterward."

"Oh, would he indeed," Catherine thought, "like a child to be sent packing."

"Thank you so much, Dr. Cavendish, for all your help this morning. We are of course entirely in your hands."

The doctor was taller than she had expected and strongly built. His dark frock coat had a greenish mold growing on top and was stained with rusty spots of blood. He gestured toward the door and she had no choice but to follow him.

A gray day outside, the hospital looked gloomy in the later afternoon light. They passed three soldiers in the corridor wearing a strange collection of clothes—a tattered fur hat, a dressing, a flapping blanket. She held her breath as they passed; their smell was frightful and they knew it; they looked the other way as though ashamed. Farther up the corridor, where a gust of snow blew through an open window, a group of orderlies, almost as ragged as the soldiers, were washing dishes in an incongruously beautiful marble basin set in the wall. They stopped and stared at her in amazement.

"Yes, it's a woman, and she is injured," Dr. Cavendish snapped. "Let us pass."

He opened a door to the left of the fountain and ushered her in. "My consulting rooms." He bowed.

The room was small, dark, and showed signs of a hasty conversion. A shirt hung from a rusty nail and a divan, which ran Turkish style around the room, was covered in an untidy tangle of bandages, papers, and medical implements. There was no table and no chairs.

"Sit down." He took a bundle of papers from the divan. "Not very grand is it?"

He put a match to the wick of a brass oil lamp and light flared up over both of them. He had peculiar eyes, she noticed: they were large and veiny, slightly protruding, and curiously blank. You thought of eyeballs rather than eyes when you looked in them. He was looking at her now.

"Sit down, sit down," he said impatiently, "let me take a look at you. I wish our orderlies could dress a wound this well," he murmured, as he untied Lizzie's expert bandaging. His fingernails were thick with dirt.

Catherine was shaking. She didn't like this. Her finger, blood-stained and grimy, lay in his hand.

"Does it hurt?"

"A little, but it's nothing."

"Things that hurt"—he moved his hand down the pad of hers, and made a little circle with his thumb—"are not good for you."

"I feel," her voice sounded strange to her, "like a perfect fool. You must be so busy here and I am wasting your time with a silly cut."

He drew his forefinger down the lifeline of her palm.

"Cuts like this are always to be treated seriously, especially in a pisshole like this."

"Sir!"

"Forgive me. I've been living with men too long."

He kept her hand in his; she could see a muscle throbbing in his jaw.

"What's this?" He touched her breast. "Nothing!" Her face was flaming. Looking down she saw stains from the meat she had carried had dropped on her bodice and looked like watery blood.

"So, no wound there?" He was teasing her and she couldn't bear it. "Look," his voice was quiet again, gentle. "Don't look so startled. I'm not the enemy, I'm a doctor, and you'll be on the wards soon. We need you fighting fit."

"Why do you say that?" For the first time their eyes properly engaged.

"Well, you cannot sit up there forever like the Princesses in the Tower."

"That's not what we want! We want to work."

"It was a joke, heavens! What a *spirited* girl. A dirty girl, too."

She pulled away from him saying fiercely, "I hate being dirty."

"Do you want a bath then? I could arrange it."

"No!"

"Why not?"

"I don't want to."

"She doesn't want to." He looked at her again.

"Oh dear." She saw that his shirt was now splattered with her blood. "I'm sorry, but can I go back now?"

"Not before I've dressed your finger."

She let him wash her finger with the sticky, tarlike substance that passed for soap in Scutari. He shook white powder on it and while he was tying the bandage he gave a huge yawn, his tongue rearing up in his mouth, his eyes squeezed shut. "He's completely exhausted," she thought.

"We'll need you soon," he murmured. "But they'll wait for a catastrophe."

"But we could have been helping these past few weeks, it seems so silly."

"My dear Nurse," he yawned again, "do you have any idea how terrified the hospital administrators are by you and by your Miss Nightingale? Half of them are convinced you are government spies, the rest are embarrassed by the very idea of women in a men's hospital. I'm quite"—he showed her the tip of his tongue—"excited."

She blushed scarlet to the roots of her hair.

"I'm not surprised they're frightened of your leader," he continued in a more neutral tone. "She is very efficient."

Here was her chance to leave. "I must go." She looked longingly toward the door. "Please, Miss Nightingale is very strict on knowing where we go at all times,"

"I'm not finished yet"—his blank eyes glared at her—"and by the way, I don't criticize the woman, although I'm not quite sure of the point of a woman who thinks like a man." He sounded annoyed. He took his coat down from a hook.

"I have one last thing to tell you," he said, "and I'd like you to think about it. Quite the worst wounds we treat here are to men shot or stabbed in the back as they run away. Injuries to the chest are nothing like as bad. What does that suggest to you, Catherine?"

"I don't know." She wished he wouldn't call her by her first name.

"Life belongs to the brave. You're a good-looking girl and I could make life a lot easier for you." He took a step toward her but she sprang away. "Think about it, Catherine."

She was conscious of his eyeballs again—flicking between her and the door.

"I don't wish to die with a wound in the back or the front." She felt dreamlike, not sure what she was saying.

"No," he said, as she backed toward the door, "I don't think you should either."

Barnsie and the old orderly, Sam Parker, were out in the corridor when she left Dr. Cavendish's room. He was helping Barnsie fill her pail from the dribble of brown water coming from the fountain.

"Catherine." Barnsie's eyes were full of concern. "Where on earth have you been? We was told you was at the doctor's then you didn't come back."

"I'm all right, Barnsie," she said, shaking still.

"Well, you won't be for long. Miss Nightingale wants to see you in her room as soon as you get back. And she's hopping mad."

"How did you know I was here?"

"Sam told me." Her fond smile was returned by Sam sweeping off his fur cap and showing her his gums. "He's my mine of information. She's our baby," she told him, "and Miss Nightingale is ever so strict."

They escorted her to Miss Nightingale's door and, as she watched them hobble back to the tower with their water pails, she felt an odd kind of need for both of them. They felt stable and secure, almost like parents, and, for better or for worse, she felt she could confide in Barnsie now and tell her about the doctor and how uncomfortable their meeting made her feel. But now she swallowed nervously and looked at Miss Nightingale's closed door—she was in trouble again.

Miss Nightingale was nothing if not mercurial. "How is your poor hand?" she asked as soon as Catherine walked into the room.

"Better thank you, ma'am, Dr. Cavendish bandaged it."

"Good." She smiled at her fondly. "Something exciting has happened in your absence. *Food* has arrived, and a *stove*—come and see."

Food was such a worry and obsession with all of them that they both couldn't help smiling, and Miss Nightingale was almost dancing as she took Catherine down into a small room filled with sacks of flour and sugar. On the windowsill were two charcoal burners with two saucepans steaming on top of them, clouding up the windows.

"Broth in one, jelly in the other." Miss Nightingale was beaming.

Saliva shot into Catherine's mouth. Perhaps she would give her something to eat.

Miss Nightingale lifted the lids on both saucepans and stirred them, filling the air with the smell of warm jelly and good broth, then replaced the lids and led her upstairs again. She could have howled.

"There isn't a moment to lose," said Miss N. "Tell me, are you right- or left-handed?"

"Right."

"Good, so you won't be able to sew this afternoon, but you can still write. I need an acting purveyor, do you accept the job? Mrs. Clark is too ill to do it today."

Her eyes were gleaming; she was irresistible in this mood.

In the study, Miss Nightingale poked the charcoal and explained the job: two days previously, she said, she'd been given permission for the first time to make a thorough inspection of the hospital kitchens, which, theoretically, supplied upwards of three thousand patients and staff with food.

"I shall not go into details, but I felt . . . I knew some improvements could be made. Now can you keep a secret that is not really a secret?"

"Of course, Miss Nightingale."

"Next week I plan to set up a properly working extra-diet kitchen. I have five more portable stoves in store as well as a quantity of wine, beef essences, arrowroot, and sago. I bought it in Marseilles on my way out."

There was a tremor of self-satisfaction in her voice, as if Miss Nightingale enjoyed her own clever, logical mind.

"I have been given permission to visit the Purveyor's stores this afternoon, for we lack pots and pans, but first I need you to make an inventory so there's no confusion between the things we have bought and paid for and those lent to us by the hospital."

She handed her a quill and a sheet of paper and said quietly, "But there is one thing I must say to you before we start. If you ever speak to me again as you did earlier you will be on the next boat home. Dr. Cavendish is a respected surgeon and it was mortifying. Now don't say another word about it—we don't have time. Oh, another thing. I hope it is clearly understood between us that you do not discuss *any* detail of what you write down today, however trivial it may seem. Do you understand that?"

"I do."

"Good. Head your first sheet Requirements. Draw a line under it, then on separate lines note the following:

"Socks: one hundred pairs.

"Slippers: two thousand pairs.

"Flannel: one hundred yards. Query flannel shirts—am I going too fast for you?"

"No."

"Good. Continue . . .

"Drawers and mitts, soap ad libitum, the soap here is bad . . . knives, forks, spoons. Coconut matting—the kind used in workhouses is best. Air cushions a hundred—fifty round with a hole in the middle for bedsores. Then put three hundred brushes, combs, and a razor for every man.

"No." She caught Catherine's surprised look. "None. Up until now," she said, "washing has been considered a minor detail. Surprising isn't it, how easy it is to forget the simplest things in a war." She was looking bland and official again. "Bye the bye, what did Dr. Cavendish say about your hand?"

"He said it was not serious at all," she lied. "I'm sure I don't need to see him again."

"Let us hope it heals well."

"Let's hope so, ma'am."

Miss Nightingale was concentrating with her eyes closed when Catherine saw steam rising through the floorboards.

"Soaps . . . flannels . . . tin basins . . . sponges."

"Miss Nightingale."

"Hush, I'm trying to think. Sugar . . . linen—not the coarse kind . . ."

"Miss Nightingale! There's something burning in the kitchen."

When Miss Nightingale saw the brown trail of arrowroot pouring under the kitchen door she flew into a rage. "Why can't people *think*? Why are they so *sloppy*? I expressly told an orderly to watch that."

Two tears gathered in the corners of her eyes, and as she fiercely drove them away Catherine caught a glimpse of an angry little girl beneath that fiercely controlled exterior. Miss Nightingale said it was her last good saucepan and if they wanted another they'd have to go to the hospital kitchen now. The idea of a walk after such a claustrophobic day was irresistible.

"No, of course *you* can't go. You don't even know where the kitchens are."

"I do. Mr. Ware showed us."

Miss Nightingale looked at her intensely. She was still upset and breathing heavily. "It must be done today—it has to be," she muttered, thinking hard. At last she said, "Well, perhaps I will send you. For reasons I don't want to discuss, I'd rather send you with the message than involve other people."

Then she told her to sit down and have a bowl of broth. This was astonishing: a bowl of lamb broth carefully flavored and with fat gleaming pearls of barley, some diced potatoes, a few carrots and even onions in the bottom of it. It was so much more delicious than anything she had eaten for weeks that she longed to take it away like an animal, to groan over it, to lick the bowl, but it was gone so fast, and then she had to wash the bowl.

Miss N said it would be better if she didn't mention the food to the other nurses, there wasn't enough, yet, to go around. Then she lent her a black cloak, drew a map, and told her to keep her eyes down and under no circumstances to speak to anyone even if she was spoken to.

Miss Nightingale arranged for an escort to take her out of the tower and into the quadrangle. When she stepped out a mizzling rain was falling and it was already growing dark. In the greenish light that shone through the ward windows, she saw the dark humps of the patients with one or two upright silhouettes moving among them, flickering figures that frightened her.

The orderly walked ahead of her, his feet crunching through the snow. As they turned up a muddy path leading across the square, a group of young men came toward them, shouting and throwing snowballs at one another and making strange wild noises as they passed her. One of them stepped toward her with a silly smile and pointed at her bandaged hand. "Alma?" he said, and made the others laugh.

Their sounds grew fainter. She was passing a broken bench and a ditch half full of rubbish when she saw a tall man, covered in a tarpaulin, sloshing through the mud toward her. He lifted his hat.

"Ah what a surprise—it's Nurse Carreg again."

"Dr. Cavendish." His sopping whiskers under the tarpaulin made him look old and otterlike.

"So you told me a naughty fib, they do allow you out occasionally."

"No, this is an absolute exception."

"But a fortunate one: there was one more question I forgot to ask you this morning, and I need it for my notes," he said in a serious voice.

"Yes, Doctor?"

"Do you have a sweetheart back home?"

"I do." The lie flew out of her mouth. "Thank you," she added preposterously.

"He is a very lucky man, Nurse Carreg." He lifted the tarpaulin as if it was a hat. She stepped away from him.

"So, good evening, until the next time."

Chapter 43

The capital nerve of Dr. Cavendish's question and the foolish civility with which she had answered it, made her blood boil as she splashed on through the mud, thinking of the many stinging replies she could, and should, have given. The sight of him had added to her growing sense of vulnerability. Behind the ward windows she could see the figures of patients, like shadow puppets that could be summoned or banished at will, and again she was frightened. What if, when the time came, she simply wasn't up to it?

There was a time when her nerve had failed, when she almost automatically remembered the tests and Deio. Soaring through the air off the rocks above Whistling Sands, galloping down the beach so fast it felt like flying. All the brave things they'd done together were stamped indelibly on her mind, but this was harder, so much harder, and now her dreams . . . of what? Of being independent? Of thinking for herself even if she thought wrongly? Of making up for Mother's death? They confused and humiliated her almost as much as they had confused him. What a long time ago it seemed now since they'd boasted to each other in that chophouse in Park Lane. What babies, and what a fool she'd been—so prissily sure of her rights, and ready to tell him what was important in life.

The orderly carried on ahead of her, his head down against the rain.

"Catherine! Nurse Carreg." Sam walked up beside her.

"Sam, what are *you* doing here?" Sam's fur hat was soaked and pathetic as if some old tired animal had climbed on his head and died there. His sweet smile lit up the gloom.

"Hang on a mo—I'm going to see a man about a dog."

He said a few words to the orderly and came back again.

"I told him to get lost. His duty officer wants him back on the wards."

"Sam," she said, "is that really true?"

"Middling," he said, waggling his fingers, "but they were Barnsie's orders and I dursn't disobey."

His face went so soppy when he spoke of Sarah Barnes that she knew they were falling in love.

"She worries about you, miss, and you were gone a long time."

"Well, there was an emergency," she said nervously. "There was nobody else around so—" She looked at him carefully. "The only person who stopped me was Dr. Cavendish."

"Oh!" Sam's reaction was swift. "Don't talk to him."

"Why not?"

"I don't know, but try not to . . . I think he's a tosser—"

"Sam, you're so naughty," she said when they'd stopped laughing. She felt so much better walking with him but then they passed the stables and a horse, a miserable thin creature with no blankets. It was tethered to a palm tree heavy with snow.

"Those are the poor buggers I feel sorry for," said Sam following her gaze. "They didn't ask to come here, I'd give anything in the world to have a carrot or a bowl of warm gruel to give him."

"Oh Sam," she said, "so would I."

"Oh dear." he winced. "I shouldn't have said that. I've made you sad. I'll tell you a better thing. Talking to a fellow last night who's just come from Sebastopol and he saw a fine lot of horses come off the boat. He reckoned close on five hundred were killed in the Light Brigade charge and these were their replacements."

She let the news sink in for a moment, watching her feet, trying not to panic.

"Sam!" she said at last, "do you have any idea . . ."

"What?" Sam shouted. They'd reached the kitchen and a noisy crowd of waiting men were clattering their pails.

"Who he was?"

"Can't hear," bellowed Sam, who was slightly deaf anyway. "This is the kitchen," he said, pointing toward two huge charred doors. "We stop here until it opens."

She was being pushed toward the doors by the crowd of desperate-looking men. Their hair was matted, their faces filthy. They held lumps of meat in their hands, tied with string or torn strips of uniform.

"Are they soldiers, Sam?" She was trying not to meet anyone's eye.

"Orderlies," he said shortly.

"They look so ill themselves." *Don't let it be him. Not him.*

"They are; they spend each morning freezing to death in line waiting for patients' victuals to get cooked, and each afternoon fighting over whose meat is whose—it's a terrible system. The cooks, poor bastards, are trying to feed over two thousand men here."

"Who's your lady friend, Sam?" One of the men made a chirruping, mocking sound.

"Shut your gob up," said Sam good-naturedly, "a lovely gel—too good for the likes o' you."

The roar this brought from the others—the bellowing and caterwauling—reminded her of penned animals at the cattle market, but then the noise stopped abruptly as the two kitchen doors were pushed open by a man in a filthy apron.

"DINNA! MEATA!" He shouted, "SOUP! STAY IN LINE! STAY IN LINE."

As the line surged forward, a man with a rusty pail banged her painfully on the shins. A few were admitted; the kitchen door was slammed again.

"Why did they close the door?" she shouted.

"Riots." Sam's lips were blue with cold. "There's not enough to go round and tempers get very high."

She was shoved inside the kitchen, a huge black hole with five cauldrons in the middle and walls black with grease, where snow fluttered down through the rafters of a broken roof. You could see stars above the pall of noxious smoke. Four cooks stood beside the pots, shouting and swearing, hands purple with cold. They were ladling a horrible-looking gray stew into weighing scales, then into the men's pails, shouting, "Next! Get on with it, and hurry up! Hurry up!"

One of the cooks, with a large suppurating burn on his hand, threw some tea into the greasy water that the meat had come out of, and then stirred it with a huge wooden spoon. He looked white with fatigue and was shrieking like a madman.

A gust of wind cleared the kitchen of smoke for a moment. "Saucepan!" she shrieked, "I need a saucepan." But the man shook his head before the words were out. All she could see was a pile of greenish-looking meat on the floor and one or two scrawny chickens waiting to be killed.

Sloshing back across the quadrangle she had a sick feeling in the pit of her stomach. Sam had gone before she could ask the question she dreaded, but if it was true that an army marched on its stomach, all of them were doomed. There were too many men here and not enough food, and not enough places to land it. Some things in the end were very simple.

Part Four

Balaclava, November 1854

Chapter 44

$\int$ creaming, the black horse fell down through the sky. Strapped in a canvas surcingle, he was flung from the ship, carried through the frozen air like a giant insect and dropped into a small boat in the harbor below. While snow turned to ice on his eye-lashes, his mane, his tail, he stared, stupefied, at the men above him, and at the sea. He tried to brace his legs, and then fell on his knees, banging the side of his head on the boat. His stomach was rioting; voices jabbered at him, poked him in the sides with a sharp stick, then threw him overboard again into the sea, where he tasted saltwater and sewage and human remains. Then, a tall, dark man rushed into the water and stood beside him. "Good boy," he said, listening to the sobbing breaths, "Good lad. You're all right." He kissed the horse on the neck. He told him what a clever boy he'd been. They stood absolutely still for a moment while the man put his face close to the horse, absorbing its shock and distress. Deio was so relieved he was smiling. Midnight had landed, stunned but without a scratch.

He was three hundred miles north of where Catherine was. If he'd wanted it, he could have sold his horses quickly and been in Scutari within weeks. His ship, the *Robert Lowe*, was even going there after Balaclava. But he didn't want it, not yet. She was there of course, always, practically part of his body and blood. He'd felt a kind of pure pain, almost as if he could die of her after she'd left, and a bitter taste, too. Over and over again he'd thought about the night in Llangollen: his clumsiness, his drunkenness, his hunger; but then he would remember how she'd turned to him in the dark and how she'd looked at him. He'd seen it, felt it, and that was what confused him and made him angry with her.

She'd so confused him: so much the lady sometimes, and at others the wild girl blaming him for her wildness. She'd not played fair, and other people had got hurt, too. Her sister was pale as a ghost at her own wedding—the rumor was she'd only married that dull plodder Gabriel to comfort the father who'd lost a wife and a daughter in one year.

"Whoooa! Whoooa! Hold it! Hold it! Hold it!" Bonny fell with a wallop into the waves and let out a terrible groan. Poor bloody bastards, here was a trip they'd never forget. The cob showered him with freezing water as she hauled herself up. He rubbed her head, crooned nonsense, "You're here now, silly girl, swimming girl, brave girl." The horse relaxed a little, but he didn't. To watch his horses falling through space like this, one by one, was slow torture, and yet everything felt so speeded up now: the landing, being here at last after so many days at sea. From the hills above them he could already hear the crump of firearms, the whirr and hiss of shells. So quick!

It was startlingly cold. His hands, blue and useless, fumbled with the horse's head collar and his eyes and nose stung as though they'd been slapped. But it felt good to be outside—he'd hated being shut up almost as much as the horses did. The beach he led Bonny along was full of sewage and smelled of rotten eggs. A small crowd standing on the pier gaped at him: the man who plucked horses out of the sky. Bonny sniffed the freezing air. She was a tough mare and she was coming around, but he had to hand her to a stranger, a thing he'd normally never do, while he ran back to the ship where another horse was falling.

Magic this time, an Irish draft, flying down like a huge dark bat through the sky.

"Jesus Christ, Magic, keep your head up!" Deio called. The horse looked numb with shock, its nose covered now in the yellow froth of the harbor.

"Nice hossis, mister," called a man on the pier. "Many more to come?"

Only now he noticed how odd these people looked in their fezzes and forage caps and long greatcoats, parts of uniforms teamed with baggy Turkish trousers. Lots of foreigners, too—French, Turkish, English—babbling away, staring at him. He hated them seeing his horses, look so wretched and undone.

"Three down, seventeen to go," he said shortly. "Watch that mare!"

He could never understand why people were so switched off around horses: they had so many ways in which to hurt you—a stamp on the foot that could leave you hobbling for weeks, an agonizing bite, a kick that could be to kingdom come. You had to learn to think before they did.

"I'll feel calmer when Moonshine's down," he thought, watching her fall with a clump into the boat. The knock-kneed gray he'd ridden beside Catherine on the drove was his favorite now. Companion and soul mate. She was in her sling now; he saw her looking for him. She seemed to stay in the sky forever, screaming and falling. When he saw her get up, he could have cried like a baby in gratitude.

The seven and a half hours it took to unload the rest of his horses taught him one fundamental lesson of war: everything took longer than expected.

After the fifth horse had landed, a furious official told him he was holding up four other ships in the harbor that had been due to land supplies before him. Deio told him the horses would panic and bolt if they left them much longer in tiny stables on board without their companions. The man said that was his problem. He left him in no doubt at all about how unimportant a civilian was. Deio raced down to the hold again.

Tom Pymn, the tiny lad who'd been helping him with the horses, was there. He was one of sixty hastily assembled recruits going to plug up some hole in a regiment in Balaclava. Seventeen years old, his one passion in life was horses, although he'd never owned one. With some training, he'd been useful in the mornings, his skinny shoulders straining as he hurled heaps of droppings over the deck rails into the sea. During several bad storms on the way out, when the floors got wet and slippery and the horses fell, and sometimes fought and screamed, the boy had moved among them, surprisingly bold, crooning at them, patting them with the entranced absorption of a lover.

When he got down Tom had changed into his new uniform. His forage cap still had creases in it where it had been folded; his new boots were streaked with horse manure.

"Silly buggers outside," said Deio. "They think horses are the same as sacks of coal." The boy said a horse wasn't a sack of coal, and a tremor of feeling seemed to go through him. He put his arms around Honeypot, his favorite. He buried his head in her mane.

Deio told him to watch out, that he'd have plenty of time to mess up his uniform when they landed.

"Funny thought, in't it?" said the boy, trying to look brave and unconcerned. "I could be in the trenches tonight. Where will you be?"

"Not far from Sebastopol," said Deio, as if he were in the habit of riding toward enemy lines quite regularly. "The Fifth Dragoons have some stables up there." He pictured proper sheds and beds of straw. And then, he finished to himself silently, I'll see some action and then go and see Lady Catherine and tell her what's what. He often addressed her more sternly in his thoughts than he really felt.

"I don't know where I'll be, do I, Honeypot?" The boy put his face next to the horse and closed his eyes. "I expect we'll get our orders when we land."

Deio wanted to put a hand on his shoulder but he didn't.

"Have you ever fired a musket in your life?" Deio asked.

"Not yet."

"I could give you a quick lesson."

"I would like that."

"Have you been on a march?"

"No." The boy suddenly creased his face up and beamed as if this was a good joke.

"Well, Honey will cry her little eyes out tonight. She says you're the only one who's ever understood what a top horse she is."

The boy could not joke about this. "I'll miss her," he said. "It's been the best two weeks of my life."

*   *   *

When they landed the rest of the horses in the late afternoon, two soldiers from the Fifth Dragoons were waiting to meet them. Deio tried not to feel shocked at their scruffy appearance: the mangy greatcoats, the tattered fez one wore, and his truly wretched horse. He wanted to find his earlier mood of excitement again, to start strong and stay that way.

The officer pleased him by admiring the horses. He'd have no trouble selling them, he said, money was just about the only thing they weren't short of. He asked if any had been seasick on the way out. Deio told him horses couldn't be sick, which was why the sea was so dangerous for them, they were either dead or alive and there was not much in between.

The adjutant frowned, annoyed he hadn't known this himself.

"Well, I hope you've brought plenty of supplies with you, young man—this place is on the bones of its arse."

Deio pointed toward the two packhorses weighed down with barley and oats. He was trained to provision, to imagine the worst.

"I won't be here long," he said.

The officer gave a hollow laugh. "Oh, won't you indeed." He looked down at the jumble of ships in the harbor.

They tied the horses one behind the other and rode through the main road of Balaclava toward the hills behind, dodging a stream of dirty brown water that ran down the street. The rocky hills, the robed men, the strangeness of it all, it was like something out of those Bible books his mother had read him, but it smelled more. When they came to a hovel with a few loaves of bread in the window, the Turkish shopkeeper rushed out at them yelling, "Yes plis Johnny bonno. Come inside! Come inside!"

Swaying and weary, the horses had no energy to shy at him, but made funny faces as their acutely sensitive noses examined the sick, sweet smell of Balaclava, that combination of badly buried corpses and rivers of sewage. Deio tried to close his mind to it, too, and to the emaciated men they passed on their way. He would do it all in stages. Get the horses up the hill. Make them dry and comfortable.

As they climbed, the duty officer, Captain Charles, made breathless conversation.

"Hard to believe this place was once a beauty spot, roses, grapes, so forth. Shit hole now."

The dark hills in front of them suddenly boomed with a sound like thunder, and then there was a shrill whistling sound, sheweeeeeeeee.

"They're shelling up there, a place called Sandbag Hill that the Cossacks want. Seen any action yet?"

Deio's reply was interrupted by the appearance of two young cavalry officers, who admired the horses and then began a lengthy conversation with Captain Charles about some tavern they'd been to the night before.

"Sorry not to introduce you, Jones," said Charles in an offhand voice as they rode away. "Now, where were we? Oh yes, action— have you seen any?"

The question annoyed Deio. No, you bastard, he thought, but I'll be up to it if that's what you're wondering.

"Not yet."

"Quite exciting really." The officer's pale eyes flickered. "It gets quite hot up there."

"I'd like to help in any way I can," said Deio.

"Help?" the man said, as if that was the last thing on anybody's mind. "Well, action can be arranged if that's what you mean," he said smoothly, and stroked Bandit's mane. "Give me a good price for that horse and I'll arrange anything you like."

Deio felt a hot surge of triumph. New boy he might be, but the first part of his plan was working.

At the top of the hill, the wind veered around from the north, cutting like steel.

"We're lucky to have made it," said the adjutant. "This road is often impassable." Now Deio was on top and could see the whole harbor, he saw all the traps: the clogged muddy streets, steep hills, a tiny harbor already jammed with ships, the bottleneck entrance into the Black Sea beyond.

"What's the population of Balaclava?" he asked casually.

The adjutant drew in his lips.

"Whew! You've got me on the spot there—fifty, seventy thousand? I do know that around Balaclava the allies have two hundred thousand men living within the space of twenty square miles."

"And the Russian army. How big?"

"Oh, twice, three, four, five times that amount. It doesn't bear thinking about, so on the whole we don't."

His deliberately vague and patronizing reply annoyed Deio.

"I bet you don't," he thought, "because if you did, you would never sleep again."

Two hours later, Deio looked around him and, through the gloom, saw row upon row of pointed tents pitched on a river of mud. They had arrived at the camp. In a clearing at the end of one row he saw a wooden triangle against the sky.

"There have been so many floggings lately," the adjutant told him, "they don't bother to take it down."

"Why?"

"Drink mostly, or desertion."

The flaps of one or two tents parted as they rode by. Gaunt men, blue with cold in their underwear, or in filthy uniforms, stared at them. It was shocking to see how ill some looked. Another group stood in a ragged line holding muskets. Most of them had no shoes.

"They're fell in for trench duty," said the adjutant. He rebuked one sharply for not saluting him.

"They'll be over there tonight."

He pointed toward the westerly horizon, where, as if on cue, a line of flames crossed the sky, followed by a whirling and a hissing sound as if a dozen snakes had been let out of the bag at once.

He asked the adjutant if they did that all night. With the same infuriatingly bland smile he told him not to worry about it. "You'll get used to it—unless of course you die from it."

Chapter 45

*N*ovember 1854, and real winter had arrived, more bitter than anything they had ever known. They had been at the hospital for less than a month but already it felt like a lifetime.

Every day from their window they could hear, above the whine of the wind and the screech of birds, the sound of the Dead March being played by a military band, twenty, thirty, forty times a day. The British had been defeated at Sebastopol, and now the army had more casualties than the whole of the rest of the war put together. And each day, the music sounded flatter and more wound down as, one by one, the musicians went down with dysentery, Crimean fever, chest infections, and other illnesses, and were replaced by less able men. Then, because the groanings and scrapings of the band were said to lower the men's spirits, the music stopped altogether; but the new silence felt worse, said the nurses, and full of bad omens.

One morning, the redheaded orderly woke them early and told them to go to Miss Nightingale's study, Mrs. Clark had letters for them. Yawning and scratching, they went downstairs. A charcoal fire was lit in the study and the nuns were waiting beside it. It was the first time since they'd arrived that they'd seen the full complement of nurses and sisters together and it was a shock to see how ill and ragged the others looked. Mrs. Clark, who had been ill for months with pneumonia, came into the room. All her old bounce had gone and she looked dazed and shrunken. When the nurses saw that the basket she was carrying had letters in it, there was a roar like animals at feeding time.

She passed Catherine two letters, which she opened hungrily.

The first, from her father, enclosed a sovereign wrapped up in cloth so it wouldn't show through the envelope. He told her that the horses were well and hoped she was, too. She tried to feel happy that he had at least sent her some money, surely that showed he cared, but the contents of his letter, and the sight of her own red fleabitten hand holding it, pierced her. He felt like a stranger and so did she to herself.

The letter from Eliza was all about her wedding. How strange to think of her own sister married without her being there, and, even more strange and exciting news: she was with child. She and Gabriel would move soon into a new farmhouse, Ty Nwyyd, and were happily planning their first Christmas there. No other news and no mention of Deio. She'd so hoped for some.

"All right, my love?" Barnsie appeared at her side. "You've gone very pale."

"Yes, thank you. My sister has been married. What about you? Did you get a letter?"

"Not really," said Barnsie with a brave and unconcerned look.

"Do your children know your address here?"

Barnsie's china-doll eyes opened a fraction wider. "No," she said carefully, "they can't—" She couldn't finish.

"You should have asked me." Catherine put her arm around her. "I would have written for you."

"I didn't think." Barnsie folded her arms over her stomach and bent over as though in pain. "I never imagined for a solitary moment that a letter would get here, and now I haven't got one. Stupid cow."

Catherine had her arm around Barnsie and was trying to think of something she could say when the room went quiet.

Miss Nightingale walked in, radiating purpose and energy and wearing her important dress: the black merino wool with the spotless linen collar.

She walked to the window, folded her hands, and waited. When they were absolutely silent, she spoke in a low voice.

"Sisters and nurses, I have an important announcement to make. Listen very carefully, everything we have worked for depends on it. I have in my hand the order we have all been patiently waiting for. It comes from Dr. Andrew Smith, the director of hospitals in

Turkey, and from the British government itself." She held up the letter, but did not need to read from it.

"What it says is that the situation at this hospital has reached a point of utmost seriousness. There are two thousand gravely ill men here, and only a handful of orderlies and doctors to look after them."

Some of the nurses began to cry; the nuns crossed themselves.

"Hush! Listen! This is *so* important."

She looked them over, she smiled.

"Ladies, our work can begin."

She lifted up her hand to silence the small commotion that followed.

"Now listen *all of you* and listen well." Mrs. Clark started coughing and hurried from the room with her handkerchief over her mouth.

"When you are on your wards in about one hour from now, never forget you are under the absolute authority of the doctor in charge of that ward. *Do nothing on your own initiative.*

"None of you," she gave the nuns her famous stare, "have been brought here to save souls, or"—this to the nurses—"to find husbands or friends. If there is the slightest hint of a suggestion of any impropriety, I shall have no hesitation in sending you home." Her face was hard as steel when she said this and Barnsie dug her fingers so hard into Catherine's hand she almost shrieked.

Then the smile again. Dazzling. Delicious. She looked at each and every one of them as if they were precious to her, and all was forgiven in that moment—the waiting, the bullying, and the hunger. They would have died for her.

After this, she read out the lists of who was to go where. Lizzie was assigned to ward five, a mixed ward where Miss Nightingale explained that men with war wounds would be mixed in with men with diseases such as cholera and typhoid. Catherine prayed she would be sent to the same place.

"Ward four," announced Miss Nightingale, "Sister Ignatius, Emma Fagg, Catherine Carreg, and Clara Sharpe. You'll be working with Dr. Perrett, Dr. Stephenson, and Dr. Cavendish. Get your bonnets and cloaks and go down immediately. May God be with you."

Chapter 46

Ten minutes later, as she and Lizzie put on their cloaks in the nurse's tower, she caught their reflection in the glass. They were white as ghosts.

"So Lizzie," she said, "it's come."

"Are you scared?"

"Yes—are you?"

"Yes."

While Lizzie helped her tie the bow on her bonnet, she knew she'd never had a friend like this. Someone who was so clear about themselves that they seemed to reflect you back honestly, who saw all your best, and your worst, sides and loved you still.

"Catherine," she said, "may I speak honestly? I am more frightened for you than I am for myself."

"Why?"

"Because you've not been in a proper hospital and this will be worse. Are you braced for it?"

"Yes . . . no . . . I don't know. How can I know? I've tried to learn as much as I can but—"

"You have, you have. You've done splendid," Lizzie interrupted. "But there are some things you can't know about because you haven't seen them, and this will be beyond imagining. Try to keep breathing. I know it sounds silly, but if you stop breathing you may faint. Breathe and say to yourself, 'This, too, will pass.' Oh love . . . !"

It was unusual for Lizzie to be physically demonstrative, but she put her arms around Catherine and hugged her.

And then the orderly came. He took Catherine's party downstairs, and marched them along the corridors to a door marked Ward 4. The nurses and the nuns smiled at each other grimly. Here was the point of no turning back, what they had longed for during the past dreary weeks and what they now most feared.

They stepped through the door. Clara Sharpe immediately put her hand over her nose and called out a muffled "Oh *God*" for the smell was so atrocious: sickly sweet and rotten, a combination of living and dying flesh, of bodies unwashed for weeks, of fetid wounds, and of the night soil that lay in four huge tubs in the middle of the room.

It was fortunate at first that they could barely see. The smoke from the stove and the men's tobacco was so thick that a ray of sunlight coming through the windows seemed to be cutting through fog. When the smoke cleared they were more careful to step around the heaps of rags that lay in puddles on the floor. Then they saw that the rags were men, lying there and staring at them, their hair matted, their chins grimy and unshaven. Now they heard them moaning and calling out.

Frozen like a stone, Catherine walked with the other nurses, through the smoke, to the far end of the room. When a sudden blast of icy wind cleared the smoke she saw that the ward was actually part of a crudely converted corridor. Above them, part of the ceiling had broken and you could see the sky, and now they felt flakes of snow falling on their faces. At the far end, in one of several ramshackle beds crammed together, was a boy no more than eighteen. Poking out from the end of the bed they saw his boots with the toes cut out, showing a foot half eaten by frostbite. Some of the others lay half naked in the remnants of army uniforms.

The nurses looked at the men, then looked away as though ashamed. Clara Sharpe moaned again.

After they had hung their coats up they were taken to another smoky room and introduced to the duty officer, Dr. Perrett, who was sorting in a feverish way through a pile of medical implements soaking in a bowl of rusty water.

They curtsied, and Sister Ignatius gave him their names.

"Emma Fagg, sir, and Clara Sharpe. Catherine Carreg."

"Nurses, good day." He sighed. He had deeply hooded eyes and looked foreign. He introduced them to the two ward orderlies: Private Wilkes, a rough-looking man with a dark stubby beard, and a boy called Nobby who was too shy to meet their eyes. Dr. Perrett had a bad cold and, between bursts of coughing, told them there were close to sixty men in the ward and that soon the number would swell—dramatically. Almost all of them, he said, were suffering from noncombat injuries: cholera, dysentery, frostbite, exposure. Most of the operations at Scutari were being done for sepsis and removal of bullets, or secondary amputations due to sepsis.

He told them there was no time for him to show them around properly, but that the best way for them to understand the place would be for them to listen to the orderlies' report, which took place each morning when the men on night watch left their posts and the day shift took over.

He did not smile or look at them while he talked, but the impression was not of an unfriendly man but of a man who had become a kind of machine.

The night orderlies came into the smoky room, an exhausted-looking old man and a younger man whose arm was missing below the elbow. They closed the door, put down two empty unwashed food pails, and saluted Dr. Perrett.

"Twenty-four new men admitted last night, sah! All of them in need of mattresses, spoons, forks, and a nightshirt, but we have run out of dockets. Sir, can you supply same?"

"No." Perrett had a strange habit of feeling his head and face carefully, as though for a tumor, before he spoke. "Nothing here. Ask stores."

"Died in the night," continued the old man, "Bevan, Carstairs, Dannerly, and Smythe. In the corridor outside awaiting tags."

Sister Ignatius crossed herself and murmured. The boy shot her a strange, almost gleeful look, as if to say, *Just you wait—worse where this came from.*

"On the operation list today," he went on, "Flannery, amputation; Jones, amputation from frostbite; Wilson, a bleeding; Bendon, the same. We are short on leeches and wadding. Mr. Ware says there are none in store, and they are waiting for some to come from Constantinople."

Then a list of those suffering with cholera, typhoid or dysentery, frostbite or pneumonia, some with a combination of these.

"Await your orders, sir." said the old man at last.

"None." Perrett fingered his head. "Let's do the rounds." He seemed to remember the nurses were there and tried for a smile that didn't come.

"Don't forget, none of these men are used to seeing women in a hospital and some of them will find your presence disturbing. Stay behind me in a line and try not to look directly at them. We are all going to have to get used to you."

He carried on rubbing his head.

Back in the ward, the smell hit them like a wave again. One of the orderlies was lowering a scrawny-looking chicken into some boiling water on the stove. Catherine's head swam and a sick-tasting saliva filled her mouth.

"Please God," she prayed, "don't let me faint." *This, too, will pass.*

They walked in a line down the narrow corridor between the beds; one or two of the men turned their faces to the wall and groaned as if the sight of them was the last straw. One young lad with a dazed expression sat up in bed, smiled, and waved.

"Begin at bed one," said Dr. Perrett when they'd reached the end of the ward. "Name," he consulted a tag at the end of a nest of gray rags on a wooden pallet bed, "Jenkins, Scots Hussars."

A middle-aged man, mustache caked with blood and mud, hauled himself up on his elbow and gave them the polite, eager smile they would see on the faces of so many of the desperately ill. The orderly said the man had come in the day before. He'd spent two weeks on one of the transports from Sebastopol. During this talk, the patient looked from one face to another like a quarried animal. Perrett told him to stick his tongue out. He felt it, said it was freezing, and confirmed he had cholera.

"Show me your feet, Jenkins," Perrett said in the same flat

voice. The man's feet jerked feebly under the bedclothes as if he was embarrassed. The orderly told him sharply to do as he was told, took the soiled blanket from his feet, and revealed a pair of boots that looked as if they'd been soaked in water for some weeks.

They took the boots off, releasing another cloud of noxious fumes into the air. Jenkins' feet were gray and rotten, and looked as if some animal had made its dinner out of them. Catherine's mouth filled again; she was going to be sick.

"Frostbite," said Perrett. "Let them dry out for the day—that left one may have to come off old chap."

The soldier's eyes registered no change of expression at this, he seemed beyond caring. Catherine saw the young orderly give them that strange challenging look again. *This is it; can you bear this?*

"How do you register the instructions for each case?" she heard Sister Ignatius ask.

"Those of you who can write, should write them in a notebook. Provide your own of course, there are none in store." Perrett had the same bright and bitter way of repeating the three favorite words in the hospital.

The man in the first bed started to retch and cough as they moved on, then he was sick. Catherine closed her eyes again. *Breathe, breathe.* It was upsetting to hear him mumble that he was sorry.

"Shall I—?" Sister Ignatius, who had worked as a missionary in Africa, was quite happy to help.

"No," said Perrett, "Wilkes will do that later."

The next bed. "Forrester."

Forrester, a waxen-faced man of about forty, was suffering from frostbite and exposure, Perrett told them, the after-effects of having lain in a ditch for over a fortnight. The man's teeth looked large and ghastly, like tombstones. His arms were gray and hugely swollen. He tried to turn his face to his pillow when he saw them, but after Perrett told him to stay at attention until his examination was over he stared at the ceiling where you could see the curdled sky through the broken rafters and the beginnings of a snowstorm.

He was asked if he thought he was getting better.

"What I need," he said, "is a bullet through the skull."

His eyes flickered briefly toward Perrett.

"You see, this is what worries me most about having you women here," Perrett said to the nurses. "That you will start to mollycoddle the men and put up with that sort of thing. The best thing that can happen to people like"—he checked the label again—"like Forrester here, is to rejoin their regiments."

Forrester listened carefully as if Perrett was talking about somebody else.

Catherine already knew that this was a cruel remark. Sam had told her that for most men the bitterest of all pills was being taken ill before they had a chance to fight.

"Fucking women. Wonderful," the man said clearly as they left, and everyone ignored him.

Their last patient was a young boy with very blond hair and a thin face. The doctor, who was starting to cough again and to yawn, told them he'd been wounded in action during a Charge by the Heavy Brigade and had taken a lance at the base of his spine; he'd lost the use of his legs and sometimes wandered in his mind at night, thinking he was back in battle.

When the boy saw women looking down at him, his face broke into a beautiful, hopeful smile and he muttered, "Bless their faces."

"Turn over," said Perrett.

He was examining the wound, which smelled rusty like old blood, when a tall young man appeared. He had tied his bootlaces together and wore his boots around his neck. His feet were blue with cold on the muddy floor. He was crying and said he didn't have a bed. The young orderly led him off, very gently Catherine noticed, and helped him onto an empty bed, where he lay with snow fluttering down on his face.

"There you are, old man." He patted him on the shoulder. "You need a bit of shut-eye don't you?"

After the rounds, Dr. Perrett gave them a list of jobs to do. Sister Ignatius and Catherine were to clean the floor at the end of the ward and straighten any empty beds. Emma Fagg and Clara were to go with him and copy down the list of special diets for the men.

Before the doctor left, Sister Ignatius took a small black book from her habit and asked if she might say some prayers with the men. She gave the nurses a slightly defiant look as she did so— Miss Nightingale had expressly forbidden any such overtures.

The doctor sighed and said no. He said they should give the men time to get used to them and she would be in their way.

"Save your prayers, Sister," he said. "This is only the beginning."

Chapter 47

*A*round three o'clock, Nobby took plugs of tobacco around for the cholera patients, who were ordered to smoke to stop the spread of airborne infections. Some of them were too ill to smoke and she saw one boy try to hide his ration. Others tried manfully to obey, and the sight of these obedient half skeletons trying to "smoke up, lads" was strange and sad. After this, the nurses were told that a dish of tea had arrived for them and was waiting in the orderlies' room. There had been no time for lunch and, after inhaling so much smoke, they were thirsty and they hurried back as fast as they could. But when they got to the room, they found no tea had been left for them, and there were cries of disappointment.

Clara Sharpe collapsed like a puppet on the floor.

"I want my tea. I need it," she moaned. "Go to the kitchen and see where it is, Cathy—you've got the youngest legs."

She agreed, because she had a splitting headache and was longing for some fresh air. She left by the side door, crossed the quadrangle and walked down the track toward the kitchen door. It was shut with a large bolt across it. A soldier walking by told her it was closed for the day.

Running back to the hospital building through the late-afternoon gloom, she felt stiff and bruised as though shock had made her suddenly old. A knifelike wind tossed her hair and skirts around and made eerie sounds in the flagpoles at the hospital gates. At the end of the path, she took a deep breath: this was it, ward four. From now on it would be her test. She opened the door and went into the orderlies' room again, but the nurses had gone, leaving their empty cups behind them.

She went into the corridor to look for them. A door halfway up the hall was open, spilling a greenish light into the hall. She looked inside in case they were there. A tall man in a dark frock coat was sitting there. It was Dr. Cavendish.

"Nurse Carreg, how are you?" He smiled broadly when he recognized her. "How's that hand?"

"Very much better." She tried to avoid looking at those damp whiskers, those blank eyes. "Is Dr. Perrett here?" she said.

"Do you see him here?" he asked sarcastically, and then in a softer voice, "He stood in for me this morning. I had three operations to do." She saw blood still under his fingernails.

To her relief there was a timid knock on the door. It was Sister Ignatius.

"Oh good, there you are Catherine," she said. "We were worried about you. Forgive me doctor but she is our youngest and we thought she was lost."

"No, she is not lost." He kept his eyes on her and carried on intently as if they were alone.

"Yes, I do work here and in wards five to ten, too."

Sister Ignatius, with the air of one who has blundered into a private conversation, took out a prayer book and began to read.

"There's no need for that, Sister," he said, "I can hear the men's breakfasts arriving. Only seven hours late of course, but to a starving man it will taste better than nothing. Won't it, Catherine?"

He smiled again, making her feel trapped and uneasy.

"Yes sir."

"So do I see you tomorrow?"

"I don't know, sir."

"No, we do know, Catherine, with respect," interrupted Sister Ignatius, anxious to be of help. "The new lists have just gone up—we're here for three weeks."

"Well, that's awfully good news, isn't it?" he said blandly after the door had closed.

She hated how he looked at her, it made her flesh crawl.

"Sit down for a second."

"Sir I—"

"All right, all right, leave me, go back to work," he cried face-tiously. "But I must say everything about you confuses me. You're not fat, and you don't look like a drunk and you have very good teeth. How did you slip through the net?"

He thought this a splendid joke. She wanted to strike him.

"I can only repeat my offer." He swiveled his eyes, he looked her up and down. "I can be your friend here. Don't turn me down."

That night Lady Bracebridge took them on a chaperoned walk through the tombs and the willow trees and the quarter of a mile or so of rubbish that lay beyond the hospital gates. A high sea was running beyond the cliffs and the ground underneath them shook from the boom of the waves. It was a strange night to choose for an outing: most of them were dead on their feet after their first day on the wards, but this lack of logic was beginning to feel normal now.

Lizzie and Catherine linked arms, too tired at first to talk much.

Then Lizzie said, "Did you get a letter from him today?"

"Who?"

"You know! Him. That boy you rode across Wales with. Your sweetheart."

"He is not my—"

"Oops, sorry I spoke."

"No, I'm sorry, I didn't mean to snap. I heard from my sister, happy and married and with child; thank heavens there is only one black sheep in our family."

"Why did you leave him, Cath? I still don't understand." Lizzie was remorseless and Catherine was half glad of the forbidden lux-ury of talking about him.

"I didn't leave him, Lizzie, I let my family separate us. That was my first mistake, except now I can see that. I loved him too much and would always have been his child. Does that make any sense at all."

"I'm sorry, I didn't realize." Lizzie held her hand and the tears held back all day spilled over.

"No, no. Thank you for asking, I think about him so much. The torture is to have loved like that and made such a mess of it and still to feel that I needed to do things like this, to prove to myself in a way that I could be strong on my own. Oh, it sounds quite stupid now, because now I don't know if I *am* strong enough."

Lizzie put her arm around her and gave her a look full of warm understanding.

"Falling in love too young is one of the most dangerous things that can happen to you. Nobody would choose it like that. You're unformed, like a baby's head before the two halves of your skull have joined, and then they get their head stuck in yours and you don't know where you end and they begin. Learning to think for yourself is one of the most important things in life, even if you think wrongly sometimes. That way you can't blame people later for all the things you haven't done."

Then Catherine heard herself commit a great disloyalty. "My mother blamed my father all her life." She'd never said anything like that before.

Their group came to a sudden halt. Lady Bracebridge had taken a wrong path and they were passing a bar and the sound of distant music. A group of soldiers came to the windows and made yelping sounds as they went by.

"Do you have any feelings for him now?" Lizzie said, after Lady B had told the men off. "Does it feel like a strong attachment?"

"I would hate anything bad to happen to him." She was exhausted at having said so much and wanted to draw back.

"Well, naturally." Lizzie was brisk. "I haven't even met him and I wouldn't want that."

"Well, I do feel I know more about men now," she said cautiously, "and that must be a good thing." This amused Lizzie, who gave her a pinch.

"Did you hear from your gentleman, Lizzie?"

"No." Her face was shut. "I told you, I didn't expect to, but I know what you mean about your life feeling separate."

As they turned to face the harbor, a gust of wind dragged Catherine's hair from her bonnet and flung it against her face. White caps were breaking and boats skimmed about at what looked like immense speed. She remembered the Water Horse and all the stories Deio had told her about it: how beautiful it was coming out of the water, gleaming and magical, and how badly you wanted it, to ride it, to own it, to take on all its power and beauty. Sometimes it let you; sometimes it took you as far out as it possibly could and drowned you.

Turning back toward the hospital again, she shivered with fear. Many of the men she'd seen today were young. They had imagined war and life to be a splendid adventure and look what had happened to them. The soldiers were no longer shadows behind the windows. They were human beings: they had names, faces, feelings; some had already tried to talk to her about their sweethearts and mothers. They would show her in the weeks to come what she was made of.

Chapter 48

*D*ecember 1854. The system was falling apart—any fool could see that. As the days went by there was less food, less water, smaller and smaller buckets of fuel for the fire. Little problems loomed large: no rags, for instance, for your monthlies, so you had to keep washing them if you could and wear them damp, which made your thighs chafe. The big things were worse, and after three weeks on the ward without a break, they were all beginning to feel strange and slightly mad. Sometimes at night, when they weren't too tired to talk, Clara Sharpe, painfully thin now and covered in fleabites, would start the game.

They'd pretend to get all dressed up and go to their favorite chophouse; they'd order pea and ham soup for starters, hot rolls, fried fish, potatoes, treacle pudding and custard, roasts of beef, jugs of porter, steak and kidney pudding, spotted dick . . . Although they were tired beyond anything they had ever known, they could go on like this for hours and sometimes, if they had the energy, they'd go on to the music hall and sing, *I had a dream, a happy dream,* or a dirty song with the chorus of *I gave him what he didn't like and sold his silver spoons,* which still made her blush.

At Scutari there was no bath at all for the nurses and her skin was driving her mad. At nights, particularly, it felt like armies of ants, stinging and hot, crawled over her and settled in odd places, like the webs of her fingers or behind her knees. Once a week when the modesty curtain went up, the nurses shrank behind it trying to wash bodies, hair, and clothes in the quarter of an hour allotted to them, and in half a bucket of water, but that didn't help and now everything—skin, hair, dresses—felt sticky and smelled of mold.

Her fantasy was of Mair, lighting the fire in the upstairs bedroom at Carreg Plâs. She was taking off her bloodstained apron, her dress, the gray liberty bodice, pantaloons. Adding a dash of lime essence to hot steaming water, lying in it up to her chin, watching the fire and listening to the rooks outside and, if she could bear it, she'd think of him and feel the ache in her thighs from galloping the ponies.

She *had* to cling on. Now, waking in the dark mornings, the sight of her uniform made her heart thump. Gray with dirt, its cuffs mottled with mud, it hung on a hook next to Lizzie's and Barnsie's, above a row of neatly polished shoes (shoe polish mysteriously, was one thing they had boxes and boxes of).

Blood was the hardest thing of all to wash out; all of them wore it like a permanent stain. They spent most of their time on the wards trying to take it from tangled hair and old bandages, from faces and dolls and pictures and handkerchiefs; strange what the men carried closest to their hearts.

Blood and fear were with them all the time. Now that the patients in the hospital had swelled to three thousand, even getting to your ward was a kind of torture. You had to close your ears, eyes, and nose and push your way through four miles of men in the corridors, crammed bed to bed, with no more than a foot or two between them.

Each morning after breakfast, Miss Nightingale, neat as ever but paler than before, said prayers with them, and tried to tell them only cheerful things: that they had managed to feed two hundred men the day before with beef tea or with jellies, or that she'd given lice combs to sixty men in the main ward, or that a new lady helper had been sent by the ambassador to help with the soldier's wives. But now they had to comfort the two thousand men who may not have been fed. They could see it, everyone could: the hospital was like a large and icy pond where soon all the faults and the weaknesses would join up and with one almighty crack drag them all under.

They all broke rules now, cut corners. *Never work on a ward without being supervised by a doctor. Don't address the men directly.* Ridiculous. The wounded poured in like an avalanche and all of them rushed about doing what they could. Sometimes she and a nun, or a young orderly, would be left in sole charge of upwards of fifty men, all gravely ill. No time to ask Lizzie "Is this right?" or, "Shall I do that?" Mostly you just did it and faced the possibility of being an instrument of torture, or ending a man's life when a better-trained person might have saved it.

Dr. Cavendish frightened her, too; he was around so much. She tried to put herself down for duty on wards where she didn't think he'd appear, but, in the end, she went where she was sent.

One morning she was told to go with two of the nuns, Sister Patricia and Sister Maria, to ward four. Lizzie was supposed to go, too, but had caught a bad chest infection and been sent to bed by Miss Nightingale. Approaching the door, Catherine could see Sister Maria's lips moving, steeling herself for the moment of reentering hell. They tried to block out the cries of suffering as they joined the unending stream of bodies, dead and alive, orderlies, medicine and stretchers, passing through the beds.

Only a few could be saved.

That morning, rain had fallen heavily in the night so there was a large puddle, almost a lake, they had to step around. Some of the men had abandoned their beds and lay in a lifeless pile by the door. At the bottom of this tangle, Catherine saw a young man staring at her, willing her to look at him. His eyes were gooseberry colored and his beard so matted it looked like the back end of a sheep.

She knelt down to talk to him.

"Where are you from?"

"Off a transport from Balaclava last night," he whispered. "Thank God we're safe." The other men stared up at them, and when some tried to get to their feet, the smell of blood and diarrhea moved toward them. Then the calling out began, and this was the moment most dreaded because the men thought they had a chance now.

"Nurse, HELP ME! HELP ME!" from a boy with one arm hanging in a filthy bandage.

"A drink, for the love of God, miss" from inside a beard caked with frost and blood.

"I hate to trouble you, missus." Heartbreaking when they were so polite and there was still nothing the nurses could do.

"Good-day to you all, you bootiful angels, could I trouble you for a chamber pot?" This man's eyes glittered with delirium. "I don't want to fire over me friend here."

Sister Maria's eyes rolled in terror like a horse about to bolt. They smiled, they nodded, they rushed by.

"Good-day . . . good morning."

"Welcome . . . yes, yes, don't worry we'll see you comfortable."

"We'll be back in a moment."

Lies. Perhaps the men knew already. They must have seen how many of them there were and the state of the wards.

First job: tidy up the beds. There were two kinds: wooden trestles with planks laid over them, and ordinary straw pallets on the floor for emergency bedding. Sometimes the straw pallets were so impregnated with blood and mess from the diarrhea patients that they had to be taken out the back and burned, but mostly they stayed—with no beds in store, no time to make new ones, and a flood of new customers coming in, you couldn't afford to throw anything away. Most of the beds swarmed with lice—when a man died they simply jumped from his cold body to a warmer one next door.

Once the beds were done they did the floor. The orderlies were supposed to, but with women around they resented it and usually left it to them. It was a hopeless business anyway. The tiles broke away as you swept them, and on rainy days mud squelched halfway up your boots.

An orderly watched them while they swept. He had his arm around a young boy whose hair was full of twigs and dirt. When they were finished, he helped them put the boy on a mattress in the corner of the room next to a tub of night soil that, as usual, was brimming.

"There you are, lad." The orderly's big rough hands smoothed down the blanket. "Right as rain."

The boy began to jabber in a bright, demented way. "My arm," he implored Catherine and Sister Patricia, "it's poorly. I'd like to get it off you see."

The orderly went off shaking his head. He told them they may as well help the boy because Dr. Perrett and Dr. Cavendish were operating and the other duty doctor was ill. "D'you know what I tink about Dr. Perrett," Sister Patricia whispered when they were alone. "I tink he's as mad as a hatter."

Catherine agreed. In the last week Perrett had stopped talking and now rubbed his head in that strange way of his almost all the time.

The boy gave a groan. Her hands were already shaking.

"If we leave him, he'll die," whispered Catherine.

"Will she mind?" Sister P was terrified of Miss Nightingale.

"No," said Catherine wearily, "because she won't know."

"There now you poor ting, it's not nice, not nice at all," Sister P told him without looking. "Take that bandage off, Catherine, let's have a look at it." A flash of anger. *You do it*, she wanted to say. Sister Patricia looked ashy white, her lips were moving. Catherine glanced quickly at the swollen bandage and hated her fear of it.

Breathe in, block the mind off. Take the bandage off as gently as you can without prolonging the agony. Oh, how it stank. Parts of it were embedded into the skin and he shouted out twice.

"Tell me if you want me to stop," she said.

"Go on," he panted, "get it done."

Slowly his hand appeared—bright red and hot to the touch. Then the elbow, swollen with water, and near the shoulder the upper arm blue and black like a monstrous sausage that needed pricking. The look, the smell, the sheer weight of the limb told her it must have been immersed in water for several days. She almost had the bandage off when a large part of the arm broke away from the socket and a crowd of maggots swarmed out.

The boy passed out. Sister Patricia clasped Catherine's hand.

"Oh dear," she softly moaned, "poor ting. Horrible. Horrible. Go and get the doctor. Quick."

She raced down the corridor, and through another heap of

wounded men. Nobody in the duty doctor's room, but next door in the dispensary, Dr. Perrett was sitting with his back to her, round-shouldered, smoking. He turned around in an eager, jerky way.

"Ah! Nurse, nurse, nurse, come in, come in," he said. "I've been thinking about God. Do you believe in him?"

"I do, sir, but please could—"

"I think he's a shitarse."

He put his head on one side and gave her a sneaky infant's grin as though he expected mama to be cross. There was a tear in his overall and she could smell brandy.

"He's gone," she thought, surprised at how little she cared. Sam had already told her two other surgeons had blown their brains out.

"I won't be a second, Dr. Perrett," she told him smoothly. She reached for a tincture of iodine on the shelf above his head and a small bag of wadding. "I'm on my way to pick up some bandages, won't be long." More lies, more rushing.

Was there a choice, she wondered as she made her way back to the ward? A small part of your mind that helped you choose between going mad and going on? She thought it might be like the cliff over the sea at Whistling Sands, on one side grass and sunlight and very close by on the other side, black rocks, black sea.

"Let me help you with those?" She hadn't even noticed Cavendish coming up behind her.

"No, no thank you, no. I'm fine."

He was wearing an operating gown, and his boots glistened with blood. He asked if her finger was all right now and she said it was fine.

"Hang on, hang on," he said as she tried to walk away, "are you all right, Catherine?" She hated him using her first name and felt preposterously shy. He told her he'd come to relieve Perrett. "He's had enough, poor fellow." He seemed gentler, more respectful than before. "Here give me those." He took half the bandages from her pile. Two orderlies went by them carrying an empty stretcher and they were pushed together. She could feel his hand against her back.

"I'm taking this medicine to a boy near the tubs," she babbled. "We took his bandage off, his arm is very bad."

"I've seen it," he said. "Sister Patricia called me over on my way here. You'd better come with me to the dispensary; I've got something better for it."

They walked back down to the doctors' room together. The medicine bottles were scattered in a sticky pile, the chair on its side. Dr. Perrett had gone. She could hear herself breathing strangely. He closed the door behind them.

"Do you know what Perrett's problem is?" He was sorting through the bottles with his back to her.

"No, I would not presume to."

"He's been up to his neck in blood for the past year and now he's drowning in it. He can't stop work, he never sleeps, and he's as stricken as his patients."

"But how can you turn your back on this?" She was longing for the door to open.

"You must," he looked at her. "It's like coming up for air. Does Miss Nightingale give you time off?"

"Chaperoned walks, prayer meetings, but it's the last thing on our minds."

"Silly," he said quietly. "A day away refreshes the mind, helps you work better. What's that scratch on your neck, Catherine?" He pointed to where she'd attacked last night's fleas with her nails, and drew back her hair.

"It's nothing, we're all itchy," she said.

"I had a day off in Constantinople only last week," he spoke as if he wasn't holding her hair and looking in a professional way at her neck. "A caïque first thing in the morning across the Golden Horn, breakfast at Mimars, hot rolls, coffee. A carriage down to Sultanamet for . . . I'm not sure if this is fleas or scabies, Catherine, but there is something I can do about it."

"I'm all right." She stood still as a statue.

He drew back the hair on the other side of her neck.

"Supper that night with the ambassador, yes, a very nice day, and no I'm sorry but it's not all right. If I can cure it, I will." He locked the door.

With a light touch on her shoulder he led her toward the cupboard and opened its door. She could see their distorted reflections in the black bottles, his black and gray hair over her cap, his eyes protruding, and the light gleaming back at them from purple-colored medicines.

"I've got some stuff in here for scabies," he said. "It's called Poonga oil, I heard about it in India and it works a treat. Now draw your wrapper down to your waist, Catherine."

"Sir, please, for the love of God."

His friendly smile died, and his big carved face grew severe.

"Draw your wrapper down to your waist. Do as I tell you. They use it for lamp oil as well as for scabies over there."

She unbuttoned her woolen wrapper, and then her bodice, then his big hands moved swiftly around her breasts, and she could feel the wet of the ointment. It was shockingly intimate and she hated it.

"Yes," he said casually, as if the rubbing of her breasts was the last thing on his mind. "Don't for goodness sake make the mistake Perrett's making. The human heart can only take so much and you are every bit as important as every one of those poor wretches lying out there. Fight for your life, break rules if you must. There. Does that feel better? I would guess you'll need about three or four treatments. You should also have baths, lots of baths, a thorough soaping, lots of scrubbing."

"Please." She was unable to bear it. "Please, I want to go back now."

"Of course." His eyes when he looked as her seemed as blank as pebbles. "I'm operating this morning. We're all busy, Catherine. Do your dress up now, there's a good girl."

There was a knock on the door, then the muffled voice of an orderly through the door saying he wanted that day's operation list. "Dr. Menzies says that Captain Perrett will not be back on duty today, so if you please, sir, would you do his—he will send a written order to that effect."

"Oh, how they do love their written orders," Cavendish whispered impishly to Catherine, making her a colleague in the know.

She stared at him, bewildered and ashamed: had he been kind

or funny with her, it was so hard to tell? The itching did feel better.

"And Powell," Cavendish shouted through the door, "could you check with Ware we have a supply of chloroform, the last batch we had was bad."

"Damn," he said when the orderly was gone. "I meant to ask for more Poonga oil for your scabies. But don't worry dear, we'll get you well."

Chapter 49

The day after Deio arrived, he was put in the care of two soldiers: Private Arkwright, a tall sour-looking man who the
men called The Silent Friend, and a man called Chalk who, although bent and prematurely aged, had a cheerful, confiding manner.

They took him down to "the stables," a large ramshackle shed
on the edge of a sea of mud. Two sides of the shed were broken
and almost entirely exposed to wind, rain, and snow, of which there
seemed to be a lot in Balaclava. Inside this miserable dwelling fifty
or so horses were huddled together, some the same handsome char-
gers who had pranced through London a year or so before. Their
bones stood out like coat hangers, their coats and eyes were dull
and, where there was room, they stood with their heads close to
the ground.

"What happened to their tails?" he asked.

Chalk said they'd been eating them because they were hungry.

"How many have you lost?"

"Hundreds," said Chalk, "thousands if you count the ones left to
starve at Varna; there were five hundred alone killed in the Light
Brigade's charge."

"Listen to that one coughing," said Deio. His dander was up. "A
flu would sweep through this lot like a fire. I tell you something,
man, I won't leave mine here."

It was a calculated risk. He already knew how much they needed
him.

"Now look here!" Chalk's confiding manner was an ordeal—he

was in the early stages of scurvy and his breath stank. "You're a free agent here, so you're not bound by army regulations. What do you need?"

Deio thought for a while, made a quick sketch on the back of an envelope.

"A drier site than this; some straw. Eight or ten thick upright poles, a hammer, some solid timber."

Arkwright's gray face collapsed in despair. "Not possible. Wood is only to be used for firewood now."

"Shut up you big, pregnant gel," said Chalk, who seemed to enjoy sparring with Arkwright, "and use your head. As I said, he's a free agent. Have you got your own nails? Any rope?"

"Both."

"A hammer?"

"Yes, and a saw."

"Capital, capital," said Chalk. "We could ride out this morning and see what we can find."

He asked if Chalk could leave the camp without permission, and Chalk said he had it.

"They've told us to keep you happy, if you see what I mean." Chalk's yellowing eyes winked, his breath was almost unbearable.

Pride flared up inside Deio. He had lots of cards in his hand and was confident that he could make it work here.

They ate breakfast in Arkwright and Chalk's foul and drafty little tent. It was just about big enough to lie down in if you lay on the diagonal. There were no chairs, and two muskets had to be put outside in the mud so they could sit down. They ate stale eggs, hard biscuits tasting of tar, and a poisonous cup of coffee that took Arkwright a good half hour to make, first roasting the green beans over a sulky fire that filled the tent with smoke. Hungry as he was, Deio wanted to shout with impatience, he was longing to see his horses settled, and decided that from now on he'd eat with them.

"My pleasure," said Chalk, when he thanked him for the coffee. His gums were bright scarlet and spongy when he smiled. Chalk said that Arkwright could do with a decent meal himself. He said they were lads together and had grown up in the same small village in Kent, and that Arkwright had been very talkative himself then.

After breakfast Deio got out his grooming kit and, whistling softly through his teeth, gave Midnight, his best-looking horse, a proper grooming. The horse enjoyed the attention, standing in a trance while his handsome head was brushed. All the sweat and rain marks were at last brushed away, and finally his mane was damped and combed to one side. When he was done, Deio sweated, the horse gleamed, and Chalk and Akrwright's eyes stood out on stalks. You didn't see horses like that in the Crimea nowadays.

Then Deio polished up his good saddle with some saddle soap and neat's-foot oil. He cleaned his bridle, slipped a bit through Midnight's mouth, and swung up into the saddle. Chalk, thrilled by this unexpected diversion, followed behind him on Magic, and with two pack animals behind them, they left the camp.

A bitter wind blew down from the hills. The freezing rain, which had fallen earlier, had not drained away but left the track they rode on rock solid in some places and treacherous. Deio was prepared. Under waxed chaps he wore a thick pair of breeches and the long greased stockings Meg knitted, which kept him dry on the Welsh hills. Two wool shirts, a coat, a black wide-awake hat, and, in front of him, rolled up like a cigar and tied to the D rings of his saddle, a large tarpaulin with a hole in it for his head.

Chalk was impressed: "Compare yourself to those poor blighters," he said, and pointed at a group of men coming toward them, shoeless and dressed in damp rags; they looked like whipped animals. They'd been up all night on trench duty.

"What do you reckon on this then?" said Chalk to the bedraggled soldiers, preening on his horse.

"Sight for sore eyes," mumbled one man, "beautiful."

Deio could hardly bear to look: he wasn't ready yet. This was his first day in the Crimea. His biggest test yet. He felt excited, released, anxious to feel on top of the new world he had entered.

Halfway through the morning he realized he hadn't thought of Catherine once, and he was glad.

*   *   *

The first blow to his confidence came as they rode toward the village of Kadikoi, which Chalk thought had been recently ransacked, and where he thought they might find themselves a big pile of wood. They were crossing a bridge on the outskirts of the village when a group of twenty or so British soldiers, uniformed and on horseback, appeared from the other side.

Their officer asked them who they were and what they thought they were doing. Chalk had looked guilty, fumbled for his papers, made them both look like arses.

"I've brought some horses here to sell," Deio sat calmly on his horse. "Private Chalk has been assigned to show me around."

"Oh, indeed?" Midnight was cantering on the spot, delighted to be free again after being confined on the ship.

"How long are you here for?" Compared to Midnight, the man's horse was a joke—skin and bone and swan-necked, so maybe it rankled. He snatched the papers from Chalk's hand and addressed Deio like a servant.

Deio said he would stay as long as he had to. There was a pause while the officer waited for him to say "sir," but he didn't.

"A week? A month?"

"However long it takes."

"So what is the going rate for a thing like that?" The officer pointed at Midnight with his whip.

"A hundred pounds." He named the highest price he could get away with. "Bred to race and trained at the cavalry school in Pimlico."

The other men were clattering across the bridge, eyes lighting on his horses like flies on fresh meat.

"The man's a horse dealer from Wales," the officer told them, "reckons he'll get a hundred pounds for that one."

They muttered among themselves and rode away without a word, except he heard one say, "He just might." But that didn't please him.

"Who were they?" he asked Chalk. He felt ruffled by the encounter, as though he'd been tested and failed.

"They're from the Eleventh, they've been on an outlying piquet," said Chalk, who was saluting and grinning.

"What's that?" Deio didn't like not knowing the language, it made him feel small.

"Well"—Chalk rode up beside him—"a piquet is a group of men who go out four or five miles in advance, or in the rear of the army, to keep watch on any approach of the enemy. It's a sod of a job— they're often gone for twenty-four hours at a time."

Deio felt a little envious. He could do that. He could do it well.

"And your vidette," Chalk said, lighting a furtive pipe, "is the lot who detach from the piquet to give notice of any Cossack bother."

He asked how often they met a Cossack.

"Oh every day, once or twice at least," said Chalk, blowing out smoke. "We could meet them now, round the next corner."

Without thinking, Deio tightened his hand on his shotgun. So it could happen at any time. He felt a quickening in himself, as though all his nerve endings were closer to his skin, and he was almost disappointed when Chalk pointed around the next corner at the small village where he said they should stop.

Through a small vineyard, across a river, and then they were in the center of a small village near Kadikoi. Chalk said he didn't know its name and couldn't care less. Some of the houses had been boarded up, and outside in the few acres surrounding them, the skeletons of vines lay on the ground, their supports stripped away.

In the main street, cannon balls were strewn about, and halfway down it the decomposed body of a donkey, still in its shafts, which for some reason made Chalk laugh. The wheels had gone from the cart and someone had cut a neat hunk from its quarters. Vultures circled above them in the sky.

Although Midnight was a bold horse, Deio had to give him a couple of sharp ones to get him past the donkey—he did not like it at all. They trotted down the street, and at the next crossroads Chalk stopped outside a dismal little house, where he dismounted and went through the front door.

The dwelling was tiny and low-ceilinged. In the primitive kitchen was a fire blackened picture of a Russian Christ on the wall, above a small cooking fire. A spilled bottle of olive oil lay on the floor, and a loaf of bread with a muddy footprint in it.

Chalk already had his ax in his hand. His spongy red gums were smiling.

"Help yourself, boyo," he said.

Deio, surprised and confused but determined not to show it, wandered through the house for a while. In the kitchen—presumably the main room, where the family had eaten and drunk and cooked—Chalk was already making a fearful din, banging and ripping.

"How do you know we can do this?" Deio asked.

"I just know," said Chalk mysteriously, "you hear about these places."

In the bedroom there was a cupboard near the window. Deio looked inside it—everything had been taken except an embroidered blouse on a hook at the back, half wrapped in a newspaper with strange foreign-looking print on it. Underneath he saw a pair of thick leather boots well preserved, carefully polished. Poor people, he guessed, who learned to look after what they'd got. He laid the boots and blouse on the bed. For a second he thought of keeping the blouse for Catherine—she needn't know. Then the idea struck him as disgusting, degrading, and he felt a flash of anger. He must stop thinking like this. Stop thinking, full stop. Taking the ax, he ripped the door from its hinges.

Chapter 50

She was learning, slowly, to control her fear, to think of life as being a series of actions not feelings, and to learn that sleep and black jokes (there were lots of these; they laughed until they cried at the craziest things) were the best cures for the jitters. She was getting good at it until something happened that broke through all her defenses.

It happened on a night when the wind had got up early outside the nurses' tower and built to a deafening roar. They could see from their window the tossing boats, the rough black sea, and the blur of lights from Constantinople.

A pane of glass had broken in Miss Nightingale's extra-diet kitchen and part of the floor had flooded. Catherine and Emma Fagg had been sent down to help clear up and were humping around sacks of sago and arrowroot when a stricken-looking Barnsie burst into the room and clutched Catherine's arm.

"Cafrin!"

"What's the matter, Barnsie?" she said, "you look awful."

"Come up quickly my love. Lizzie's calling for you—she's not very well."

Lizzie had been off-color all month with a bad cough that had hung around, followed by a bout of dysentery, but apart from a day in bed she'd insisted she was well enough to work.

Catherine flew out of the kitchen and up the winding staircase that led to the top of the tower and the damp room reserved for sick nurses, praying all the way: *Please let her be saved. Don't let anything happen to her.*

She found Lizzie lying on a straw pallet with a torn curtain around it. The wind this high in the tower thumped and screamed like a mad person outside, and it was so cold inside the room that a layer of ice had formed on the inside of the window. Catherine, half running into the room, saw immediately the dark mulberry spots, the half-closed eyes.

"Lizzie." She knelt by her bed and held her boiling hand. Lizzie closed her eyes tightly—the lids were speckled with the same dark spots, her hair was damp.

"Catherine." A tear trickled out. "Never *run* into a room, Nurse Carreg," she said suddenly in a dry, faraway voice. "It alarms the patients."

"Oh Lizzie." She drew closer. "Tell me what you need. A drink? A foot rub? We'll get you on your feet again."

Lizzie moved her head slightly on the pillow. She gave her one of those level looks she'd so depended on, and the truth passed between them.

"No, we won't," she said.

There was a wooden bucket beside her bed with half an inch of brackish-looking water inside it. Catherine poured it into a tin cup and held it to Lizzie's lips.

"Drink Lizzie, please."

She opened her mouth and took a painful sip; when half the water dribbled down her chin, she opened her mouth convulsively again like a baby cuckoo. When Catherine saw her tongue she turned to stone.

"Take a note, Nurse Carreg," Lizzie had told her one day when they'd been nursing a soldier on the wards. "A tongue with white fur on it is typical of typhus."

She stayed for a while, rearranging the bedclothes, sponging her friend's head, holding her hand, and occasionally they conversed in low murmurs. Lizzie told her not to fret when she was gone, that nobody could have had a dearer friend. "I'm proud of you, Catherine. You've really grown up." And even now, she tried to tease. "You were quite a little madam when I met you." Then she started gasping and trying to throw the bedclothes off.

"Dear Catherine," Lizzie clutched her hand and kissed it, "what a pickle."

Two hours later she was dead.

Two orderlies arrived with a canvas stretcher to take her away.

"Bugger me, it's cold in here," one of them said.

When they put the stretcher down beside Lizzie's bed, one of the poles broke, so they had to take out a huge needle and sew her in it. Catherine looked away, she couldn't bear it.

"We're rushed off our feet," he told her. "We had sixty go in the night and nowhere to put them anymore. Stacked up outside like you wouldn't believe."

He was a young man with a chirpy manner, he meant her no distress.

She smiled back at him, at first feeling nothing more than a large and not disagreeable blankness.

"Poor Lizzie's gone," she told Emma Fagg and Clara later, when they walked into the nurses' room. "It happened very quickly. Try not to cry too much. She had a hard life. She's gone to a better place."

"Oooohhhh," Emma Fagg sat down heavily on her own bed, and annoyed her very much by moaning and wringing her hands. She stood up and put her arms around Catherine.

"Oh God! Oooooh! Where's it all going to end?" she cried.

"I don't know. I don't know." Catherine shook her head and smiled at them again. She really didn't feel too bad.

"A better place," she repeated again. Emma Fagg stank. She wished she would stop holding her.

Waking the next day, she tried to hold on to her blankness. After breakfast, the hospital vicar said prayers and she wished the other nurses wouldn't cry so. She went down to work on ward four and got through her duties like a sleepwalker. She smiled at people, she fetched things, gave answers, but, as the day progressed, she grew heavier and heavier as pain began to seep into her like water in a leaky ship.

As usual at two o'clock, the two special orderlies the nurses called the Black Boys went through the wards to collect that day's crop of dead. They wore no special clothes, observed no ceremonies, and were now such a familiar sight that no one even stopped talking as they passed. Or if they did, it was only to make grim jokes: "Business brisk, governor?" or "Good haul today, lads?"

As she watched them leave the ward and close the doors behind them, she felt the full impact of the blow. Soon they'd throw Lizzie, like a useless bag of bones, onto a bullock cart with a heap of others. It was unbearable that Lizzie, who was so singular, so fine, who had been born with nothing and loved by nobody as a child, should leave the world like this after having been so brave. She'd miss everything about her: the way her eyes crinkled when she laughed, how she told you things that mattered, and listened when you spoke to her. Lizzie was so much fun to tell your stories to. She'd been like a mother to her and her dearest friend.

They'd trundle her across the plain to the makeshift graveyard where they'd dug the big pits, and the Black Boys would whistle and sing as they slung her out with the others. No gentleness, no prayers, no ceremony; nothing but a body being tumbled into the frozen earth.

"Miss? Nurse? Are you all right?" She was sitting on the bed of a patient who'd been half blinded by a bayonet wound. A nasty scar from his lip to his nose, gave him the appearance of having a harelip.

"I'm all right. Are you all right? Do you need anything?" Her voice sounded choked and shivery.

"Miss, if you please, I would like you to read the newspaper to me."

The men loved these accounts; they seemed to set them alight.

"I don't have a paper," she answered in the same strange voice.

"I've got one here, miss," he said. "I've heard it before, but I wouldn't mind hearing it again." From under his mattress he took a filthy newspaper, still warm and curved from the contours of his body.

"Which part do you want?" she asked.

Now part of her was split off, she was walking beside Lizzie, her pallbearer across the plain. *Thank you Lizzie. Thank you, for being my friend.*

"That bit there." A shy grin like a boy asking for a wicked treat. "I was in the Ninety-third you know. I played the bugle."

"I know."

The brown paper had been ripped a bit under the mattress and the date was rubbed out, but she'd read it so many times before she almost knew it off by heart. The Battle of Alma.

"The story is torn," she told him through stiff lips, "I can't read the beginning."

"I know the beginning: the river, the battle, and the horses. Will you start there?"

"Then the Russians," she began, "wavered, steadied, advanced and a second volley was fired."

"Miss, could you give it out a little louder, if you don't mind"— he wagged his head up and down encouragingly—"I can't hardly hear a word."

"A second volley was fired, the men wished to run out and take on the cavalry hand-to-hand, then Sir Colin cried, 'Ninety-third! Ninety-third. Damn all that eagerness.'"

"Damn all that eagerness." He was loving this.

Damn all that eagerness. She could have howled like a wolf. How could he lie there, his one good eye gleaming? *Damn you and damn the government for bringing you here and neglecting you and for killing Lizzie.*

"That's the good bit," he told her with satisfaction, "*that's* the good bit."

She shook her head and wrung her hands.

"A bit louder, miss. It's nearly over."

"I'm sorry," she said, "but I can't . . . I'm very sorry."

He was so caught up he didn't notice. She looked down at him, lying on his pillow. His face, with its ugly lip and slack expression, was not a very nice or a very bright face. But he did not deserve her moment of hatred, or to be seen in that short, terrifying moment as the natural enemy of woman, the enemy of life itself.

*   *   *

She'd hardly slept for five nights because her skin itched so badly, but oddly enough she did sleep that night, a deep, deep, dreamless sleep that knocked her out as soon as her head hit the pillow. But when she woke the next morning she could not get out of bed. She saw, as though through an immense pane of glass, the other nurses bending over her, moving their lips, buttoning their boots and putting on their aprons. Barnsie's china doll eyes swooped down on her for a second.

"Come on, Cafrin, bell's gone twice."

Ding dong bell, pussy's in the well. Then Emma Fagg saying, "Everybody knows that," to Clara Sharpe who said she wasn't born yesterday.

If she kept her eyes closed, she thought it might not have happened and Lizzie might come. But it was Sister Ignatius, swooping down like a white seagull to tell her Miss Nightingale had said she was to go to the room in the tower to rest for a day or two. She didn't want to go, but had felt herself being moved up and then put down. She hated that room with its torn curtain and the sound of the howling wind outside. She wanted to stay with her herd.

She heard Sister Ignatius sigh. Above her head, she could see blank sky.

"Poor Catherine," the nun said. "Of all the people to go."

Catherine shook her head. *Go away! Go away, if you start telling me about God on his white cloud I'm going to scream.*

"You know I loved her, too." Sister's eyes gleamed through her wire spectacles. "She was one of the best people I ever met," she said quietly.

Catherine moaned softly. *Don't talk to me about it. Don't talk, don't.*

"Where are her things?" she asked as the tears poured down her face. "I don't even know who to send them to."

"We'll look for them together." Sister Ignatius helped her out of bed, but to her dismay, she felt too dizzy to stand.

"Here they are." Lizzie's green cloth bag still had a large seawater stain on it. There was a pair of glasses inside it, a piece of bread wrapped in a handkerchief, some writing paper with a few squiggles on, and a penny dreadful called *Emmalina's Secret*, which broke her heart. There had been no time to teach her to read.

"I'd like to keep them for a while," she said.

"I wouldn't do that if I were you," said Sister Ignatius, "it might look . . . people could think."

"What?" She was almost shouting. "Scavenger? Thief?"

She thought of the vultures, fat and revolting, who sat on the rim of the hill near Scutari.

"My dear, please." She felt herself being led quite firmly back to bed. "Lie down."

"I don't want to stay here."

"Miss Nightingale says you need to rest and I agree. I know about these things. In Africa, where I was a missionary, one saw it all the time. It's not a crime, there is no shame. The body and the mind simply shuts down for a day or two and will not admit any more horror or pain. Lie down, try and pray."

She lay back for a moment, shocked at how exhausted she felt, but no prayers came, only memories of the day her mother died, of Deio at the door, and then pain flooded into her and she heard herself gasping and crying.

Sister Ignatius came back mid-morning with a sheaf of prayers for her to read.

"There," she said, as if the whole matter could now be settled, "put yourself in God's hands."

The prayers stuck like a bone in her throat. Guilt, renunciation, suffering, paying back. Only words, nothing but words.

Sister Ignatius produced a letter from the folds of her habit. "This is for you. Is it from home?"

But the sight of the letter only brought another wave of sick panic—what pain she had brought them all, dragging them down into the darkness.

"There, there, there," soothed the nun, helping her hold it up. "Come along, read it."

She tried to take in the dancing letters, to fix Eliza's face in her mind.

"My sister has a baby," she said. The nun was looking at her curiously, waiting. "A new baby. I can't remember how many months old, or if it's been born at all."

The room lurched. Surely she could, should. But something held in tight was coming undone, and if it came undone she would not be able to work at all, and if she couldn't work she was done for.

Now she knew that Deio would not come to her door again to look after her. She was done for and he'd been right to mistrust all this. This tower, with its unlit fire, its damp walls, the howling wind outside, was her prison now, and Lizzie's tomb. She got up and looked through the window; the lights in Constantinople looked so far away. For the first time she thought it might be better to die soon.

Chapter 51

$\mathscr{E}$verybody was out at work when Dr. Cavendish dropped by the next day. He said he was the duty officer and had heard about her illness and Nurse Smart's death and naturally been concerned.

He talked to her gently for a while and asked her if she would like an extra blanket, or perhaps some soup for lunch. She felt so breakable that she almost found herself responding to his new kindness and for the first time thought she might really have misjudged him.

"Show me your tongue." She didn't like the sight of his big carved face so close to her, but he'd murmured something about typhus and she had poked out her tongue. She breathed a sigh of relief when he said, "I can see no sign of that illness," his hands feeling the glands under her chin.

His big fingers touched the edge of her wrapper. "So how is your skin after our treatment?" he said easily. "Much better." She shied away from him and pulled the blanket as high as she could.

"Nurse Carreg," he said, "you *must* stop this silly and hysterical behavior, I am trying to get you well again." Although he looked offended, he produced a bottle of his famous Poonga oil from his bag. He told her it was expensive and when she put it on herself she should rub it in well. "And please, Catherine," he said with an uncle-ish, forgiving smile, "do stop acting like a ninny, otherwise we could lose you, too. Have you suffered with nerves before? I don't think there is a soul here who hasn't felt themselves at some point to be mad or going mad."

"No, I have never suffered with nerves." She looked him straight in the eyes. "What I most want now is to go back to work."

"It was only a suggestion," he said mildly. "You see it is my job as duty officer to decide whether you go back to work or stay here, and I do worry as much about your state of mind as I do about your scabies." His eyes as expressionless as pebbles.

She looked at him again, trying to imagine what this would mean to her; she couldn't bear more sessions with him and the Poonga oil.

"I do feel better." She forced herself to sit up and smile.

"What I'm thinking is this," he said, "I have two urgent cases to attend to in Constantinople tomorrow and I need an assistant. There's a hammam near the Pera Palace hotel where they treat scabies very successfully."

"That is a very kind suggestion," she said, "but I don't think Miss Nightingale would allow it, or at least if she did, permission would not be granted so swiftly."

"I still don't think you have quite understood the situation," he said, still in the same mild voice. "You are my patient, I give the orders; besides, I can't change my appointments to suit her. There are other sick people who need me, too."

The thought of a whole day with him was indeed alarming, but the idea of a bath—and in Constantinople—was tempting. Lady Bracebridge had excited them all with her descriptions of the town's mosques and palaces, the covered markets full of spices and gold, figs and fresh eggs, and wonderful silks, and she and Lizzie had dreamed about going there when the war was over.

Her heart tussled with her head for a brief moment.

"*Will* you make sure you ask Miss Nightingale?" she said. "We are not even allowed to talk to a man without her permission."

"I am not a man." He pursed his lips and attempted to tease her. "I am a doctor, and I'm quite sure she'll only want what is best for you."

She slept badly that night: the scabies ants were on the march again and her skin seethed with thousands of tiny pinpricks. Waking on her own in the freezing room, she could hear the sea booming on the rocks below and she felt so alone she cried her heart out. Now Lizzie's death felt like a physical blow that had left every part of her feeling bruised and fearful, and everything about the arrangement she had made with Cavendish felt wrong.

When morning came he appeared again, his face gray in the early-morning light. "I've got some good news for you," he told her. "Miss Nightingale is in total agreement about you receiving treatment. We'll leave in three hours time."

"Are you sure?"

"Quite sure," he said firmly. He handed her a long black woolen cloak and a veil smelling faintly of sandalwood.

"Wear these for traveling and in Constantinople," he said. "A sizable portion of the population there would rather put themselves to the sword than gaze on an unveiled woman. No doubt the rules will change one day, as all unnatural rules do."

She took the cloak and held it; she did not like the thought of him dressing her. She wanted to ask him again whether Miss Nightingale had really given her permission, but was wary of testing his authority.

"May I ask what your urgent cases are in Constantinople?" she asked instead.

"You may. One is rather an interesting case actually. One of the officers there has a fragment of shell-shot embedded in his ear. I'm going to see if I can move it with this."

He took a small, trumpet shaped speculum out of his instrument case. "Sit down. I'll show you how it works."

She sat down very reluctantly on the bed.

"I'll put it in his ear so, and then I'll do this." He gave her a curious smile as he rotated the speculum inside her ear.

"There are other ways, of course," he said, withdrawing it. "A colleague of mine in Varna had a man with a small ivory ball stuck in his ear, it had detached from a pen of all things. He hit on the brilliant idea of dipping a small brush dipped in glue into the patient's ear, allowing the glue to harden and then removing brush and ball together." She liked him better when he spoke to her like this. He was said to be one of the best surgeons in the hospital and she felt there was much she could learn from him.

"Good lord," he said suddenly, looking at his watch. "Is that the time? I have some patients to see here, but I shall come back for you in three hours' time. I have ordered an Araba to take us down to the pier; the driver is Turkish. Put your veil on before you leave. Speak to no one on the way out. If you're stopped, pretend to be the wife of the driver."

Some part of her must have sensed this was wrong, for when he said this, her stomach spiraled with panic and she saw in miniature: her capture, her humiliation, the ship home.

"Forgive me, sir," she said, "but what time does Miss Nightingale want me back?"

"You are going to start annoying me, Catherine, if you continually second-guess me," he said, his expression darkening. "Miss Nightingale is fully conversant with the chain of command. You'll return when we're finished."

It wasn't the right answer but it felt too late to turn back.

Three hours later they drove in silence down the muddy track toward the pier. Across the Bosphorus, shimmering like a dream, she could see the mosques of Constantinople and couldn't help but feel excited. The storms of the night before had cleared and for once it was a beautiful day, brilliantly clear, cold and sunny. Down at the waterfront, a frisky green sea was making life difficult for the boatman, who was smiling and waving at them and trying to land.

"This is all a dream," she thought as she stepped into the caïque and they cast off and watched the shore recede. She'd hardly slept for six nights, and the itching beneath her cloak gave some sort of comfort—at least that felt real, and provided the reason for being here.

The caïque slogged through the belt of rubbish and foul water that ringed the shore, then, suddenly, they were free of it and in the middle of the harbor where the sea was blue as a baby's eyes and the wind cold and exhilarating. She pulled her shawl around her and shivered. How Lizzie would have loved this, the adventure, the change of scene; she could practically hear her at her elbow saying "Strewth, Catherine, look at that!" as the mosques and the buildings took shape.

After about half an hour, Dr. Cavendish, who to her relief had been silent for most of the journey, turned to her and said. "We're almost there. There's the jetty where we land and after that we're free as air."

"Free as air?" She was anxious again.

"Don't look so worried," he said irritably. "The day is all planned."

They docked near the Galata Bridge. A group of men at the end of the pier, who were drinking coffee and playing dice, gazed at them curiously. "Take no notice of them," he said, "they all gawp."

He bought her a cup of coffee, sweet and delicious and poured from a small copper pan. He asked her if she was hungry and she shook her head. It was all too strange. He said she must eat and that, later, he would bring her some food, or send her out to lunch to a place where she would be safe and where he was known.

So he might not be there at all, she thought. Good.

They went to the hammam in a carriage drawn by a skinny chestnut with bells around its bridle. Their driver sang as he took them up a high cobbled street, and as they lurched from side to side, she stared at a man with gold teeth selling snow-covered oranges and at a stream of curious carts dragged by donkeys and bullocks and the occasional fine-looking horse. It was all so fascinating and so new that she forgot to be so worried about Cavendish. On one street corner, when she was thrown awkwardly into his lap, they both laughed as they sprang apart and again she wondered if she hadn't exaggerated her fears about him.

At the top of the hill, the carriage plunged into a series of side streets and then it stopped.

"We're here." He helped her down from the carriage and led her into the cobbled street and through a high wooden door that was open. She was surprised to find her legs still felt weak and wobbly.

"Here we are," he said, "the hammam. What will happen to you behind these doors might feel strange to you, but the women here will treat you with respect. They are Muslims and to show hospitality to a stranger is part of their religion."

Now she was grateful for her veil—the idea of a man arranging to have her bathed filled her with a shyness.

He said she could wash her clothes here if she liked, and she was not to feel ashamed; the circumstances they all found themselves in were unusual to say the least. He handed her a cloth bag with something soft inside it.

"Change into this afterward," he said. "It's a dress."

"You've thought of everything," she said, alarmed.

"Yes," he said, "I have. I'm like that."

Inside the hammam, a fat, barefooted woman with a big smile led her into a high, light room where the walls were lined with wooden cabins that looked like bathing huts. She was given a towel and a large brass key and shown how to lock her hut and where to hang her clothes. It was cold in the hut, so she kept on her chemise and stockings and wrapped herself carefully in her own towel, terrified at her own daring, but so longing for a bath that she was trembling.

The woman returned and, holding her hand, took her into a steamy room with a high roof and a glass dome set in it. Inside it were twenty or so Turkish women, partly naked and washing either themselves or each other. She looked away, horrified, and was relieved when the fat woman gestured toward a dark corner of the room away from the others.

"Bonno, bonno." She pointed toward the slatted bench. "Is very good, very nice, sit down!"

Catherine obeyed, still shivering. In front of her a large tap protruded from the wall and underneath it were two buckets, one filled with hot water, the other with cold. The woman gave her a copper scoop and showed her with elaborate gestures how to cover her head, first in hot water then in cold. Laughing, she tugged at Catherine's chemise and petticoats, and off they came.

She felt a spasm of shame but then nothing but pure animal pleasure at the sensation of warm water pouring down her back and over her head. After months of damp wool and itching skin, it felt so wonderful.

The woman's eyes were half closed; her movements had a hypnotic slowness and she took no notice at all of Catherine's nakedness. As she poured the warm water again and again, nothing was rushed or awkward. At last she took a loofah from her apron pocket and gently, methodically, scrubbed her from head to toe.

Black worms of old skin began to stand up on her arms and legs. "Oh dear," she said, "I'm sorry I'm so dirty," and blushed.

The woman laughed at her. She sang a song in a sweeping, guttural voice. She took Catherine's head between her fingers and began with firm, rhythmic gestures, to knead in a sticky-looking soap. As she sang and scrubbed, bit by bit Catherine felt herself let go. She bowed her head and when her tears came, the woman dried them as if this was normal, too.

When she was clean again, they began to alternate hotter and hotter water with icy blasts from a cold bucket, then they brought her a fresh towel, rubbed her in some sweet-scented lotion and dried her.

"Is good?" A cup of coffee and a glass of water had appeared on a tray beside her. "Is finish now." She flashed her gold teeth and patted her on the arm.

Her skin was tingling, her blood sang, and she could have wept again with relief. The itching had gone.

When she'd finished her coffee she washed her clothes. As instructed, she'd brought her Scutari wrapper and aprons, and a chemise, in a cloth bag. It took her over half an hour, scrubbing and dunking the filthy wool felt like a kind of exorcism.

When she was finished, they took her clothes away to dry them and she changed into the tunic that Dr. Cavendish had brought for her. It was a soft cotton tunic, a pretty blue, and she liked the feel of it. The water and the heat had made her feel calmer than she had in months, and the physical ache of sadness about Lizzie felt more bearable. The ceiling of the bathhouse had stained glass set in it. Now she saw how beautiful it was to see the snow fluttering by, blurring and playing with the colors.

After she was dressed, she combed her hair luxuriously with her fingers and allowed it to hang loose until it was dry, then covered it with her veil. The woman came for her. She gestured toward the street outside and said, "He is waiting."

Chapter 52

Her body felt so fine now, so clean and new, her spirits so much lighter, that she couldn't help but enjoy the sensation of their carriage moving through crowded streets; the smells of spice and roasting meat from the street vendors, the marvelous variety of people walking through the streets: beggars and acrobats, street musicians, ordinary people looking as though they'd stepped from a Bible story. She stared hungrily at the wonderful city from behind her veil. Dr. Cavendish said they would have lunch at a hotel and that he might see another patient that afternoon. Now he had lapsed into silence beside her. He had shaved and his hair was damp.

After a short drive, they reached the Hotel Ambassadeurs, a pretty pink stucco building whose balconies overlooked a cobbled street. He told her to walk behind him into the hotel.

He seemed nervous, and she was, too. If she hadn't felt so hungry now she would have wanted, not exactly to go home soon—how could anyone think of Scutari as home?—but to be out of his presence, which was oppressive.

They went through a brass swing door and when he got to the reception desk, he frowned at her as if she should pay attention. He spoke to the English receptionist, she heard a braying laugh and another English voice calling from the bar, "But must you say that, Amelia?"

"Of *course* I must," said a young woman in a charming gray hat, "it's absolutely the thing."

A cloak trimmed with silver fox slipped from her shoulders and both Dr. Cavendish and the young officer at her side swooped to retrieve it and they all laughed in a rather artificial way. As he passed her he took off his hat and bowed. "Dr. Cavendish?" The woman recognized him. "What brings you again to this side of the waters? Surely not on duty?"

"Oh, I'm over to see patients quite often." He took her hand in his. "I'll go back to Scutari tonight, and you?"

"Well, I might be there myself soon." She sounded excited. "I got the ambassador to speak to Miss Nightingale about a special project for me."

Catherine felt she had stopped breathing, and felt him stiffen beside her.

"Come on, Amelia," said the lounging officer rudely. "I want to get to Smithson's before it closes."

"They are rude, aren't they?" She made a little frown in his direction. "Such babies."

Cavendish bowed at the company again and, when they'd gone, muttered about the madness of sending women like that to Scutari. He seemed very put out by the encounter.

"She knows the ambassador," he said to Catherine angrily, as if this was somehow her fault, and then asked, "Did she see you?"

"I don't think so." She was starting to feel heavyhearted and afraid again.

"Look, don't hang around here, go upstairs in front of me and wait at the top."

She disliked his tone and shot him a blazing look from above her veil, but she had no alternative. She walked up a short flight of stairs to a landing that had a row of solid doors on either side. He took a key, unlocked the second door along, and they stepped together into a small sitting room, furnished attractively in the English style with good furniture and Persian rugs. There was a small fire burning in a tiled hearth.

"What time is your patient coming?" she asked.

"Not sure, don't know," he said. He still seemed flustered and cross. "I can't think before eating. Are you hungry?"

"Yes." How horrible it felt to want food so much; as strong as the urge to breathe or to pass water, it seemed to override everything.

Hungry and humiliated, she sat in the half dark while he went downstairs to order food. A few moments later he was back with a waiter, who carried a tray covered with a blue and white napkin that he set down on a table near the window. When he whisked the napkin off, a fragrant spicy steam rose up and she could have cried. Here were soft pastries, piping hot and filled with meat, tomatoes, brilliantly red and sprinkled with coriander and olive oil, the taste of fat green and black olives, some small fishes, some small spicy sausages with a delicious-smell. The unleavened bread was wrapped up in a cloth and also steaming.

"It's called a mezze." He handed her a long-handled fork without looking at her.

"I can't eat it all so you'd better have some. And here." He held out a bottle of red wine. "Allow me."

She hesitated. The sight of so much food had brought a strange pang of sorrow. This was the meal she and Lizzie had dreamed about but now it felt so awkward and sad.

She closed her eyes and the tears ran down, and then she dried them, and ate and ate and ate. He kept piling food on her plate in a haphazard, thoughtless way, almost as if he was feeding coal to a fire.

The waiter returned with a lamb stew, steaming hot, and a pile of pale yellow rice scattered with herbs. He took a great deal of it, and then went to a chair in the corner of the room, where he ate in such an intent and secretive way she almost thought he had forgotten her and was relieved. But then, when he'd finished, he came back, sat down opposite her, and, sucking the last lamb bone, raised his eyes to look at her.

"There, you see." His lips were gleaming with oil. "You're enjoying yourself now, aren't you?"

She told him politely that the food was delicious. She wanted to ask him if she could take the bread back to Scutari, as a treat for . . . for . . . And then felt a great hole in her chest and wanted to howl. What a story all this would have made for Lizzie, how could she not be here?

"And now you're clean." A pause. "And *I'm* clean." He smiled at her for the first time since they'd arrived at the hotel.

"What time will we get back to Scutari?" she said nervously. "We have evening prayers at nine."

"Pipe down," he said to her suddenly, "a man could get very tired of your impertinence."

"It's just that Miss Nightingale . . ."

"I'll tell you something about Miss Nightingale," he said. "If it hadn't been for my intervention on the morning we met, she would have sent you home then and there." He said this in a flat voice, as if it were half a joke. "Don't look so serious," he went on, "my bark's worse than my bite." The remains of a mashed-up bit of fish from the mezze hung on his whiskers, he licked it away with his tongue.

"But *you* said you were on duty tonight."

"Oh, did I?" He was teasing her now. "So I did."

"Sir, please, I don't . . . I want to keep my job."

"Hush, hush, hush, hush. You are too fond of trying to make the rules."

He picked up another lamb bone and chewed on it. He looked at her and she was instantly afraid.

When he said, in the same level voice, that she should now go through into the next room and change back into her Scutari uniform; she was flooded with relief.

"Go, go," he said, "we don't have much time."

The new room had a blue rug and a white bed. White curtains were drawn back to reveal a sky full of snow again.

"Why do you think you are such a jittery young woman?" she heard him ask from the room beyond.

Her hands were trembling as she unpacked her uniform and put it on the chair. The sight of it, unlovely and never looking quite clean, filled her with a wave of revulsion and fear.

As she was slipping the tunic over her head, she felt his hand clamped over her breasts, and smelled his breath—a blast of alcohol and spices.

"No," she said. "No! Please . . . I don't want."

"A good clean girl now." He held her hair in one of his hands and kept mashing at her breasts with the other. "Drop your bodice. Drop it! I need to see how things are progressing."

She said she didn't want to show him, that she wanted to go home now.

"You've been a very naughty girl before." He told her she had very nearly got him into a frightfully awkward situation with Lady Amelia, who was, of course, a close friend of Miss Nightingale.

His big wet lips were against her ear now, one of his hands was fumbling between her legs, the other was over her mouth.

"Stop it— Don't—" she mumbled into the palm of his hand.

But his hand was inside the edge of her drawers and now it was . . .

"Don't!" She whirled around and tried to push him away. He grabbed her hair and put his fist against her cheek. She could smell the greasy fat from it. He told her if she was going to have to make a noise, he was going to have to stop her. His big carved face seemed all broken up, and his lips were stiff. She was instantly cold and still.

"Lie down on that bed," he said, "and keep your mouth shut."

While he held her down with one hand and undressed her with the other she smelled blasts of garlic from his mouth. "You're a very pretty girl," he told her, running his eyes up and down her body. He did not bother to take off his trousers, but unbuttoned the front and held his thing—stiff and purple—out.

He rubbed it while he talked to her in a gentle voice for a while.

"I wonder if I've been silly to trust you," he said. "You've led me on a bit, coming here and accepting a fine meal and a bath at my expense, and now you're trying to pretend you don't like having fun at all." His eyes popped out at the unfairness of this, his hand grew more and more frenzied. Sometimes he gasped, particularly with young women, it didn't do to be too nice to them . . . lessons to be learned. He smiled at her, almost sympathetically, then smacked her twice, hard, around the face, and then he went wild. And when he had finished, and she was covered in him, he turned out the lamp, and she heard, as if from a great distance, the clamoring streets outside, and a snatch of wild Turkish music. She could taste her own blood.

Chapter 53

"Oh, good God Almighty," said Barnsie when she got back to Scutari. "You're for it now. Mrs. Clark came in here two hours ago, shouting 'Where is Nurse Carreg?' She was doing a roll call and she went down to the ward to look for you. . . . Catherine, are you all right? You look dreadful."

"I'm all right." She sat, empty as a puppet, while Barnsie wiped her face and straightened her gown.

"Your lip's bleeding, Catherine, whatever's the matter with you?"

"I'm all right. I must go down to work."

"Ouch!" Barnsie bared her blackened teeth and started scrabbling under Emma Fagg's bed. "Here, have a drop of brandy—it's an emergency. The Fagg won't mind."

"No, I can't. I'm on duty."

"No, you're not my love." It was Barnsie's turn to look stricken. "Mrs. Clark said you were to be sure to stay here. We've got to tell the orderly as soon as you come in, and he'll take you down to see her."

Catherine lay down on the bed and closed her eyes.

"Don't go to sleep, love." Barnsie gazed down at her anxiously. "It'll only make things worse. You'd better take your dose of medicine. But where were you?"

"I'll tell you later." It seemed important to stay in this stonelike state.

"Oh Catherine, something's very wrong. I know it is. Please try to tell me if you can."

"I can't. I can't. I will."

"Bullies, fucking bullies." Barnsie took a brush from under the mattress and brushed Catherine's hair with it. "Is it them that's done this? They're always so bloody sure they're in the right. But where *were* you? I was out of my mind with worry."

"Please Barnsie, I can't. Don't make me."

"I'm sorry. Tell me when you can, but don't you ever forget you've got a good friend here. You can always count on her."

"I know. Put your arms around me, Barnsie. I'm so horrible."

"Oh no! Oh no no, no no." Barnsie held her tight. "You're the sweetest, prettiest, oh Catherine, for God's sake, what's happened? Please try and tell me."

But Catherine had fallen blankly into her arms and only looked at her.

The day was getting dark, and a loose pane was clattering in the window. Barnsie hauled her to her feet again and pointed her toward the stairs and the orderlies' room. An orderly took her on foot up a path that led from the hospital without saying a single word to her. She didn't mind, she was shatteringly tired, and she felt her body move in an odd, jerky way and she kept thinking of her name: Carreg—from stone.

"This is it," said the orderly. "Mrs. Clark's quarters. You are to go inside. I'll wait for you here."

Mrs. Clark rose to her feet when she walked in.

"You'd better sit down there"—she pointed toward a wooden chair with no arms—"and tell me where you've been."

A pause, like a sigh at all the unpleasantness to come. A clock ticked.

"I know you weren't on ward four, so don't bother lying to me."

"I was ill. I was in my room." She felt sweat break out on her forehead as she said this and she wondered if she was telling the truth.

Mrs. Clark advanced toward Catherine, her stout, bombazined waist at eye level with her, her corsets creaking. She was shouting now.

"Where were you? And who were you with? Don't waste my time with lies."

"I can't tell you. I don't know."

Mrs. Clark looked at her, a temper rash creeping up her throat and mannish chin.

"Do you know, this is quite horrifying to me," she said at last in a different voice—the refined one she used when she was trying to be Miss Nightingale. "Do you have no memory at all of that evening, sixteen months ago, when we all sat in Sidney Herbert's house, and he told us that the eyes of the world were upon us?"

"I do, ma'am."

"Did that not mean anything to you? And sit up straight and open your eyes when you talk to me."

"It meant a great deal." A terrible burning sense of shame— childlike, absolute, red-faced shame—was creeping over her. She was dirty and bad.

"So it meant a lot to you?"

Some sensations: a throb, a bruising ache between her legs making her feel nauseous.

"It meant a lot to me," she repeated.

"Oh rubbish! How could it?" There was gathering contempt in Mrs. Clark's expression. "You're making no sense to me now. You see, missy, I will speak to you plainly. I warned Miss Nightingale right from the start that you were too young and too inexperienced for work like this, and now you've proved me right. You've been flitting around, doing whatever you wanted to do, and I could have been in a great deal of trouble myself. I could have lost my job."

Dimly it came to Catherine that there was a smidgen of self-interest in Clark's fury: she'd been careless with the roll call for weeks and was in danger now of being found out.

"So now, you'd better tell me where you were."

For one mad moment she tried to imagine herself explaining the events that had led up to this catastrophe to Mrs. Clark—the day she'd taken her cut finger into Cavendish's room; his behavior with her on the wards, his promise that Miss Nightingale knew all about the trip to Constantinople. And knew at once that Mrs. Clark (who had an awe, it bordered on the simpering, for anybody in trousers and in power) would never believe her. She would be the one sent home and publicly branded a whore and a liar. And what pleasure the Mrs. Clarks of this world, tutting and shaking their heads, would get from saying *too young and too inexperienced. We told you so.*

A coldness rose up in her. If she were to survive this, she must tell some lies of her own.

"I was in my room, Mrs. Clark; I cannot think how you missed me."

"Carreg, you are starting to make me very angry." Mrs. Clark clenched her fists. "I'm going to smack you one if you don't stop this impertinence. I can easily get you sent home on the next boat without pay and without a letter."

"That you can. But, you know, all of us have been confused lately by the lack of roll calls."

"I don't know what you're talking to me about."

"Don't you?"

"All right. I'd better tell you something that was reported to me about *you* only a few days ago." Mrs. Clark's face grew foxy and vindictive.

"One of the medical staff, very senior and well respected, told me that, in his opinion, you were a fantasist; in case you don't know what that means, it means *you make things up.* He also said you were overfamiliar with the men."

Catherine put her head in her hands. So Cavendish had covered his tracks: how typical and how cunning.

"So what do you make of that?"

"Whoever said that is a liar himself."

"Don't you dare raise your voice to me, missy." Mrs. Clark was herself again, shrill and judgmental. "And don't you dare say that of him. D'you know you are wonderfully lucky not to be a man, for you should be flogged for this, and no, I'm not finished with you yet. None of us can afford a scandal now. *None of us.* And from now on you must present your monthly rags to me for my inspection; else you *will* be on that boat home."

Catherine looked at her for a moment, appalled.

"I can if you like," she said, "but I haven't come on for months." How disgusting it was having to talk to Mrs. Clark like this. "It's been too cold."

"Oooh! I've had enough." Mrs. Clark sat down again breathing heavily. "Quite enough. She's got an answer for everything and thinks I have nothing more to do with my time today than to bandy words with someone who tells lies, and quite a lot of them."

"I'm very tired," said Catherine suddenly. The pain was too sharp and she could feel her body leaking. "And I'm on duty, tonight. Can I please go back to the hospital now?"

"I still haven't decided what to do with you yet," said Mrs. Clark grandly, "and won't for a day or two—it might be the detention center, it might be the nurses' tower, or it might be the first boat home, but in the meantime, there must be one little word you wish to say to me?"

"I don't know which word you are talking about."

"Aren't you sorry?"

Not sorry at all you wretched bully, you fraud.

"I've done nothing wrong," she mumbled. She felt a kind of bright heat surge through her body, a corkscrewing sensation in her skull.

"Well, if you're not sorry, you can stand up now, you chit," Mrs. Clark's bulldog face was scarlet, "and go straight to that door and call the orderly. He will take you to the detention center."

She woke up in a small, drafty hut close to the hospital. A pale young woman, wearing a pair of men's boots and with a bad cough of her own, told her she was a soldier's wife and that she had been sent to look after her.

"You've been coughing summat fierce," she told her, "and crying out. You've kept us all awake for two nights."

She wanted to ask what was wrong with her, but her tongue felt too big and woolly and her mind slipped its moorings again. All night she'd been half dreaming and half hallucinating that she and Deio were in the stables feeding a starving pony. They had a big copper pan on a fire outside and they filled it with oats and bits of apple and rose petals and odd things like toffees and glasses of wine, filled with a tenderness that felt so sweet. *Poor horse. Darling little horse. We'll look after you.*

Then Cavendish appeared, his face old and baggy under a candle. He was doing some operation—a trepanning perhaps—holding the head of a woman, his drill creaking and groaning as it ground through the scalp making first a little hole, then one the size of a penny. Blood was trickling down the side of the woman's face; the veins stood out on his forehead. "Nice and steady," he kept telling her, "nice and steady. I'm making a space in the skull for the fluid to drain into. It's one of the oldest operations known to man."

It was horribly vivid: the way he put his finger in the hole; the geyser of blood spurting, him covering the bleeding hole with a wad of cotton and bandaging it tightly against her skull. Then he lifted the girl's chemise. He put his hand around her girlish bosom.

"Heartbeat quite strong." His hands kneading and separating the breasts. "Heartbeat quite strong."

When she woke up, she had the absurd hope that everything had been a bad dream. She opened her eyes and felt a stabbing headache, and then, shuffling toward the half-boarded window, saw nothing had changed: mud and puddles, gray sea, mist. A dirty curtain gusted toward her and covered her face. The effort of moving it made her cough then gasp with pain.

She heard a door creak and turned round slowly. *Oh no.* Cavendish was standing at the door. He was holding a tray. "I've brought you some junket and a glass of brandy," he said pleasantly. "One of your friends was on their way over, but I've saved her the trouble. We've all been quite worried about you."

"Worried about me!" He was fussing with the tray now, finding a chair by the bed to put it on, while she tried pathetically to cover herself.

"Yes, you've got what I believe the men call a Crimean Corker—bronchial pneumonia—it's an awful thing, it really drags you down."

Just like that: no hint of awkwardness, or remorse, nothing. Just his soft, slightly sarcastic voice saying, "Well, this is a nice spot isn't it, Nurse Carreg?" while he unpacked scissors, a jar of leeches, and some wadding and put them on the chair beside her bed.

She got back into bed as fast as she could.

"Who sent you here?" she said at last.

"Mrs. Clark—she's as worried as I am."

A shrilling in her brain like silent screaming.

"I'm much better"—she turned her face to the wall—"I just want to go back to work."

She could feel him gently move the bedclothes. He sat on the chair beside her bed. He opened his bag, rolled up his sleeves. From the distance she could hear a murmur of voices, and the sound of a boy crying.

"I'm going to scream this place down if you do anything else to me," she said.

"Catherine!"

"Don't call me by my first name," she said through clenched teeth. "It's Nurse Carreg."

"Good God!" He shook his head at the trivial pointlessness of her. "What a thing to worry about at a time like this." And ill as she was, she could see this would always be his trump card: that war made its own rules, and within these rules, what he did was of epic importance and what wounded her was petty and inappropriately narrow-minded.

He looked at her for a moment, and put his hand on her forehead. There was a long silence.

"Catherine," he said at last in a gentle voice, "I am not trying to hurt or harm you, I merely want you to listen to me and try and understand an unhappy man."

He tried to hold her hand but she put it under the blanket. "I did like taking you to Constantinople, I thought we had a lovely day together, and it made me think you could change me as I could change everything for you."

"Change what? For whom?" She shook her head in disbelief.

"For you. For *you* of course, and for me, too."

He stopped and sighed. "You see for a long time now, due perhaps to the pressure of my work, the world has felt dead to me—pointless and dead and stale. I've been unable to enjoy even the simplest things."

He was half mad, she saw it clearly now. The question was how to deal with him. She closed her eyes to give herself time.

"I do feel weak and confused," she said at last. Her lips were stiff with the effort of not shrieking, "What I think I most need is some time to get better."

"Of course, of course"—he leaned forward with a creaking of the chair—"you've been ill and delirious and your mind is bound to play tricks on you." His hands came down again on her forehead. "I'm glad you're seeing it more sensibly now," he said, "and don't forget to eat your junket dear, you're going to need all your strength." The chummy little smile he gave her made her writhe with shame and loathing. She closed her eyes to cut him off.

Chapter 54

It took Deio ten tedious days to build his horse shelter. While he worked, the wind from the plains cut like steel and there were constant snowstorms; every day his horses seemed to lose a little more weight and he saw how quickly his livelihood could slip away. He got some poles from a burned-down barn near Tchorgoun, a door from an abandoned village school, and when he found he lacked a strut for his last piece of canvas, Arkwright offered him two stripped skeletons. "Excuse me, dear, may I have this dance?" Chalk had joked as they hauled one to its feet. Its face wore a look of sneering surprise; there were scraps of flesh still clinging to its bones, too deep for the vultures to have picked at.

He worked with Chalk and Arkwright like a man possessed. He longed to get his horses dry again, to brush them and air the sodden rugs they stood in, to help them forget the horrors of the voyage and the hard and violent life that would soon be theirs.

They knew. He could tell by the way they watched him all day, their ears tensely pricked, as if he alone held the key to their existence. They knew their life was changing and would change again.

When the shelter was finished, its ingenious design and sturdy posts were much admired, as was his tent. His father, whose reverence for good equipment bordered on the fanatical, had bought it for him on his sixteenth birthday and driven him almost mad with impatience fussing about the stoutness of the guy ropes, the exact thickness of tarpaulin, the exact amount of wax he'd need for extra protection. Now he was humbly grateful for it and felt ashamed when the soldiers eyed it so hungrily. Their army tents leaked like colanders; they went to bed wet, slept wet, woke wet.

So he was kept busy and the horses helped, but now that the field shelter was finished he found himself in a more or less permanent, though concealed, state of panic. He worried about Chalk and Arkwright, who seemed almost to hero-worship him and want him to be their leader at a time when he'd never felt less sure of anything. He worried about the weather and the abysmal food and the horses, in particular about Catherine's horse, Cariad.

He'd known all along he should never have brought her—she was too young, too sensitive for war, and she played on his mind. He cringed to remember how he'd showed her off to the quartermaster at Smithfield's. What a young prat he now seemed to himself at this distance, impatient with the two old men and their wars, disdaining a commission for himself. He'd jump at one now if it meant more food for the horses.

Nothing felt stable about his life or his character anymore, and then one day, in early November, the whole map of his world was redrawn.

It began when Captain Gosford, a handsome, competitive cavalry officer with the 13th Hussars, came down to see him, or rather to see Cariad again. He'd taken a shine to her. "Quite a nice little mare," he'd said several times, running his hands over her bright chestnut neck and legs. "I could manage thirty pounds for her," he said in an offhand way.

"No," said Deio.

"All right, forty, but that's damned exorbitant."

"No."

Deio had no words to explain why Cariad still felt sacred and why selling her would be the biggest test of all.

Gosford had stomped off, annoyed, but returned later that day offering to take Deio to a camp, about seven miles away, where the French horsemen, the Chasseurs D'Afrique, lived and trained.

"It'll be a useful little recce for you Jones," he said, "to find out how much horses are making over there." He'd told Deio some girls as well as horses had landed in the Kamiesch, which was near the French camp. If they made good time, they could meet them in the tavern on the way home.

Gosford couldn't possibly know that even the possibility of lying with another woman made him feel light-headed with sorrow and confusion.

Later, he tried to wrestle with the problem: How in God's name was he supposed to think about her now and what did she expect of him? Part of him had never felt as sure about anything as he did about his love for her, and then, at other times, he felt he was totally deluded. If she loved him how could she have left like that? Even worse, left and made herself not quite a woman by becoming part of this horrible war.

Gosford had added a postscript, a kind of a bribe. "I've got a good idea," he said. "You and I could put on a bit of a display with the horses while we're there, a bit of jumping, a charge, show the Frenchies a thing or two. You're practically one of us now."

Deio's mind had leaped ahead at this. *You're practically one of us now* meant Gosford might help him ride in a real assault with the cavalry and do something magnificent and noteworthy. He saw himself flat out on Moonshine, sword in hand, blood high, all his training, all his courage put to the test. He saw Catherine's face lit up with pride. And then his own face crumpled into a kind of self-disgust; he was still daydreaming like a boy.

He'd agreed to go, but early in the morning on the day they were to leave, he was anxious again. The rain was pattering quite firmly now on the canvas of his tent, and walking the several yards of sucking mud that separated his tent from the field, it bothered him that his best and stoutest pair of leather boots were now so caked with mud that they looked like muddy boulders, and that there was never enough spare water or heat to clean them and oil them and dry them correctly. Details like this made him increasingly jumpy.

The horses pricked their ears when he saw them. Cariad, quick and jealous as always, stretched out her neck over the railings and watched him pour the chaff and barley into eight nosebags. He played with her ears, told her to move her great big bum and let her nip him. While the horses ate, he felt their ribs and squeezed their necks, and did complicated sums in his head. Cariad, like the rest of them, still looked well: her eyes shone, she had food in her belly, but it wasn't enough and it wouldn't last and the food could get stolen. He must sell soon.

Now the rain was coming down harder than before. The tarpaulin flapped with a muscular sound like a ship's sail.

"Want a hand?" Arkwright was sloshing through the mud toward him in his miserable boots. "This lot looks set in for the day."

Deio cursed. He hated to leave the horses in damp rugs and wanted a clear day to get them off. It still wasn't too late to cry off.

"I'll fill the hay nets," he yelled back. A surge of wind took his hat off and it was gone, with a sound like fire sucked up a chimney, over a puddle and into a ditch. Clambering over the straw to retrieve it, he felt for a moment a ridiculous figure. He was sick of the mud and the cold. He pictured the tavern the captain had described, saw it rosily lit with a big fire, and a bowl of soup served by a girl.

"Any chance you could keep an eye on the horses this morning for an hour or so?" he asked Arkwright. "I'm going to the French camp with Gosford. I'll bring back some meat and some eggs and some grain, if I can find it."

It took a lot to thrill Arkwright, but now his gray lips were twisted into almost a smile.

"I'm detailed for tomorrow night," he said. "Can you get back before then?"

"Oh God man," Deio replied confidently, "I'll be back before feed time. I don't like to leave them long."

Arkwright said it was a wise move to get more food before theirs ran out, but in the end he went because he wanted to.

Gosford was a tall young man, well-muscled and with a pouty, aggrieved-looking mouth. He had dressed himself in full military uniform for this expedition, but the cherry coat was already sodden and a large wet curl was plastered to his forehead below his hat.

"I shan't be able to stay out long," Deio warned Gosford as soon as he saw him. The thrumming wind, the condition of Gosford's horse, was making him nervous. "I want to be back by four or five to feed my horses."

"So, let's get mobile." Captain Gosford leaned down from his horse. "It's a fair hack over there."

Much to Gosford's amusement, before they left camp, Deio spread squares of padded tarpaulin under Moonshine and Troy's saddles to protect their backs and packed nosebags and towels to dry them off. Gosford asked if he had packed them a clean hand-kerchief and some sweeties, too. Deio was tempted to ask what his secret of success with horses was, but that would have been too cruel—his poor beast was standing wretchedly outside the com-pound, almost too tired to eat the hay he'd given it. In the end, he'd lent him Troy to ride, and the horse was dancing on the spot even before they left the camp. Gosford was thrilled by him. He bounded up the track out of the camp, up a high stony hill down from which water gushed like a stream.

From the distance came the occasional crackle of gunfire, fol-lowed by a slow, deep thumping sound. Gosford took no notice of this at all and they were silent for an hour, which Deio liked. It felt so good to be riding out again, but then Gosford started to talk, without drawing breath, about the promotion system in the cavalry, which he said was rotten to the core.

"First-class men get overlooked all the time because they can't afford to pay."

"Is that the only way?" said Deio.

"Not the only way." Gosford's small, pouty mouth shuddered unpleasantly.

"You can meet a senior officer's wife and give her a damn good you know whatting. I'm not joking." Rain had plastered another of Gosford's curls to his forehead. His pale eyes bulged.

"Well, well, well,' said Deio.

"You have to learn to work the system otherwise all the spoils go to old and greedy men."

"Ah."

"And if you've got something to offer, something out of the ordinary, it's a question of how you offer it best."

And you're palling up with me in the hopes of another kind of commission. The pieces of the puzzle slotted gently into place in Deio's mind. Gosford wanted to act as his agent. He was not in the least surprised or offended. For this was the world as his own father saw it: every man for himself. Dog eat dog, and a bargain always to be struck.

After a few hours ride, they arrived at the stables of the Chasseurs D'Afrique, half a mile on the other side of Kamiesch, a pleasant harbor town with a main street running steeply down to the harbor.

Deio knew that the Chasseurs had a reputation for being among the finest horsemen in the world, and was immediately impressed by their setup. Their stables, freshly painted and sturdy, had been built to last, not flung up overnight. At their approach, two black boys in woolly hats stopped adding dung to an immaculate heap and came to hold their horses.

Their contact, Captain Joel Tournier, clicked his heels when he met them. An urbane man with a charming smile, he ushered them into the tack room and offered them a cup of coffee that, after the foul green coffee of the camp, tasted heavenly.

He took them on a tour of the stables and boasted discreetly about the system of care and exercise that he had implemented.

"On this side," he said, "we put our fit horses that have been in the war but are happy to go again. This one, César, is very brave, pat him, he expects to be treated like a hero." A Selle François, large and dignified with a deep scar on his neck, accepted their caresses then turned away.

"Here are the invalids. They get complete box rest and treatments for cannonball wounds, simple strains, and bayonet holes. Here is our coward—we call him White Feather." He patted a dun gelding. "He went out twice and fainted with fear both times, now he is only used for the reconnaissance."

In the last row of stables was a group of some twenty horses who, he told them, had arrived the week before from North Africa. Deio didn't reckon much on them, thinking them weedy, Arab-looking types, but Tournier said they were tough. They were training them to charge.

After a while, Gosford's look of polite delight in all this was beginning to slip a little. "Oh come off it, Tournier," he said in the awkward, bluff manner that so offended some of the Frenchmen, "let's put an end to all this hot air and see them in action. We've got some decent new horses ourselves you know."

So the Frenchman told Deio he could choose any horse he wanted from the noninvalided group and Tournier would ride him. Deio chose a gray with clever-looking eyes that he guessed would be three-quarters Arab. When their horses were tacked up, they went out to a large and partially waterlogged field behind the stables. In the middle of it were several stuffed sacks suspended from a hangman's pole.

With a graceful shrug indicating "this was your idea," the captain turned his horse in a few sinuous circles, demonstrated a rein-back, took the mount from a standstill to a canter, then came back to a halt without any obvious aid. It was beautiful and impressive: a dance in which neither partner needed to dominate or to yield. For his finale, Tournier picked up a bayonet, galloped at full tilt toward the sack, and, with a bloodcurdling cry, sliced it in two.

"Nice horse, nice horse, not bad at all. Bit small and weedy neck," Gosford said out of the corner of his mouth to Deio. "You'd better show him your horse now."

Deio got on Moonshine and as soon as he began to circle him, he knew the horse's two weeks off had done him no favors—he felt stiff and lumpen beneath his fingers. He rode him around for a while, trying to gather him up, to inject some energy. He didn't feel right. Finally, Tournier asked him if he'd like to try what he called Le Sharge. The going was soggy beneath the horse's feet, mud was gathering in large, sticky lumps. The sky was dark. "Go on Jones, have a go," shouted Gosford.

He shortened his reins, spoke softly to Moonshine; as the horse gathered speed he felt the old exhilaration.

Too late, he saw the hole in the ground that Moonshine swerved to avoid.

"Ooh la, la!" the Frenchman called as the horse hit a patch of mud, crossed its back legs and came down heavily on its side. Deio's fall was neither painful nor serious—he leaped back into the saddle as if it hadn't happened—but it was a shock. He rarely fell off, and he hated the kind way the Frenchman dabbed at the mud on the side of his jacket, and Gosford's politely distant, "Bad luck, Jones."

For one awful moment as he sat, winded and muddier than ever, on his horse, he could have cried like a child. He was coming undone.

Chapter 55

A fter the riding fiasco, Tournier took them down to the tavern, which overlooked the harbor and was called, for a joke, La Caprice. From the dismal street it seemed, with its bright curtains, colored lights, and occasional bursts of music as the door opened, to be a disembodied thing, like a pleasure boat pursuing its own course through a wet and windy world.

"I can't stay late," said Deio as they walked in.

Gosford said Tournier's men would take care of the horses, and they'd be back before nightfall. "Stop looking so worried, man," he said, almost contemptuously.

This time it sounded like an order.

Inside, there was a tub of wet umbrellas and a pleasant fug of pipe and cigar smoke. Some off-duty officers lounged in comfortable chairs in front of a roaring fire.

If Gosford had been a horse he'd have been prancing, for the huge, dimpled mirror behind the bar gave back the reflection of four young women. They were brilliantly dressed in red and orange satin, their waists tightly girdled with wide purple belts shaped like corsets, their blouses half unlaced to show breasts like generous mounds of cream on top of some exotic dessert. When Deio and Gosford came into the room they pulled silly pleading faces to make them laugh.

Now, Gosford couldn't wait to get rid of him. He ran his hands through his hair and sneaked a glance at himself in the mirror before disappearing into the crowd. Deio stood on his own, feeling like a country bumpkin, surrounded by people speaking to each other in French. Then one of the whores reached the punch line of a story she was telling to a small man who sat at the bar with an empty sleeve. She looked at Deio above the man's bald head, she smiled at him.

And the map inside his head changed again. It was months now since he'd been with a woman, and suddenly the urge to have one was overwhelming.

And he wanted it straightforward again, not to think, but to feel the melting peace, the sense of triumph, the loss of consciousness. It needn't take long.

Behind the bar was a younger girl with a thin, pale, interesting face, pouring a measure of amber liquid into four small glasses. She had a cloud of blond hair and a flouncy way of putting down the glasses as if to say "I deserve better than this."

He knew she would come to him and she did. She took his arm and led him to a table on his own near the kitchen door, speaking to him in French, which made him shake his head and scowl at her. He was sick of feeling stupid and helpless and out of place.

"Have a drink," she said in English, and put down a glass of wine. He drank it swiftly and then another, still half looking for Gosford. Tournier appeared. His smoothly handsome, toffee-colored face was glowing. He insisted Deio drink a glass of whiskey. They talked a little more about the horses and then the Frenchman leaned back gracefully in his chair and looking over his shoulder, asked him which girl he wanted.

Duty and desire clashed briefly in Deio's head. He told Tournier he'd left his horses with inexperienced men and was worried.

Tournier said he understood, his own horses tormented him, but sometimes you had to let up. There was too much dying and madness going on for you not to allow yourself a little fun.

"I will run through the menu, you decide," he said. "That one," he indicated the blonde, "is called Candide and she is quite naughty but perfectly rideable, and happy to do anything you ask within a certain reason. That one," pointing to a redhead with short legs and a sway-backed walk, "is kind and very obliging. On that one, *elle s'appelle* Emmeline, you may use this." Tournier made the end of his crop quiver. "It's your choice."

Ten minutes later, Emmeline, holding an oil lamp in front of her, led him upstairs to her room. Underneath her bed was a chamber pot and a pair of discarded stockings. A parrot-colored dress hung from a hook on the wall.

She placed the lamp beside the bed, and he could see a pipe in an ashtray and smell its stale smell. Up close and away from the blur of smoke, she was nothing special—older than he'd thought, with a deep furrow running down the side of her mouth. Apart from the fact that he liked her hair and she was younger than some of the others, he had no idea why he'd chosen her; he'd never wanted to hit a woman.

"They don't like Englishmen," Arkwright had told him knowledgeably, "they think we're animals."

Now she stood with one leg up on a wooden stool, her skirt concertina'd out like a multicolored fan. She licked her lips and began slowly to undo her stockings. Suddenly he heard the wind again, bashing and screeling outside the window. Everything seemed to be taking too long. Now, she separated her suspenders from her stocking tops. Her hands looked chapped and clumsy. He didn't bother to get undressed, took off his boots only and his muddy breeches. He smelled, even to himself.

Her bed sagged and creaked as he pushed her down on it. The wind howled, a gush of rainwater ran down the windowpane.

He took her nipples between his fingertips. He was used to thinking about the creatures he rode and he thought about her briefly. She would be used to all sorts: those who lay on her sobbing about comrades killed in battle, those who used her with no more ceremony than a *pissoir*, those who craved her love and sympathy. And then, as she sighed and moaned and simulated ecstasy and terror and capture, he forgot to think about her, and then the wind simply flung itself on the window and the whole house shook and he was on his feet.

He had to get home.

But she was excited now. She tried to drag him back to bed, to kiss him, her breath faintly tinged with garlic.

She got nasty with him while he dressed and there was a muddle about money. The woman, smacking the side of her head with impatience, indicating she was not happy to be paid in English coin, which meant he had to find Tournier. He had had to hold out his hand like a child while Tournier picked through the coins in his hand. When the girl had gone, Tournier said he thought he should stay the night. He said the weather outside was terrible.

"No, I have to go back now." Deio almost said home, but the thought of the camp gave him a pain like a kick in the stomach. It was the first time he realized how homesick he was.

"I don't think it's possible," said Tournier, "it's the worst one I've seen out there—even I can't get back."

They went to the window together. There was a loud bang, a clattering sound from the street outside. They saw a man in a fur coat being blown like a giant fur moth from one side of the street to the other, chasing his tent.

The French soldiers had their noses pressed to the window, the girls were ooohing and aahing at the size of the waves. They reared up over the harbor wall and hurled themselves down with a cracking sound like walls falling.

"It's bigger than a storm, it's an *ouragan*—a hurricane," Tournier told him. "If you try and ride back across that plain you're a dead man. Go back to what you were doing." He winked, but Deio shook his head. He could have screamed.

They were forced to stay the night and, because the roads were blocked, until early afternoon of the following day, when there was a sudden exodus of very drunk people from the tavern. Gosford appeared, irritatingly pleased with himself and unconcerned. They walked back to the stables together through streets strewn with rubbish and broken tree branches and fallen masonry, Gosford, who had a hollow, emphatic way of making announcements, as if his was the final word on any subject, was sure the storm, though severe, would not have hit Balaclava.

"They get it full in the face here from the Black Sea," he insisted, "we're farther back, more protected."

"That's not what Tournier said." Deio had given up any pretense of being polite.

By the time the horses had been collected from the stables and saddled up, the light was already fading from the day. The harbor was quiet after the storm, covered in a glowing silvery light, but the hills in front of them were darkening and full of massing shadows.

The horses were jumpy, shying at the fallen trees in their path. When Moonshine refused to jump a ditch, Deio, who could never remember feeling more anxious in his life, gave him a sharp crack with his whip. The only thing that mattered in the world now was getting back.

Neither man spoke during the ride home. At the edge of the plain, they met four English soldiers crammed together in a hole in the ground underneath a stone ledge. They were soaked to the skin and shivering. They looked at Gosford with blank eyes as they saluted him.

"What's going on here?" he asked them sharply, "why aren't you all back at camp?"

"We'd like to be," said one who had no shoes. His toes were so blue they looked like ripe plums, "but we've no quarters to go to—it blew away, sir."

"Rubbish." Gosford rode on.

Now Deio's fear was so great he could only hear himself and his horse breathing.

They came down from the plain, threading their way through the clumps of trees; then up the muddy escarpment that led to the tented city. But when he saw the shattered huts and the fallen trees, and most of the tents gone, his mind simply shut down.

They'll be all right when I find them, he told himself, *they are strong and sensible and used to Welsh storms.*

But then he saw Arkwright. He stood next to Deio's tent, his eyes large and appalled. The canvas was shredded, the central pole bent at a strange angle. His cookery pots, his bedroll, his table, gone.

"Where are they?" shouted Deio. He ran over to the shelter. The two skeletons sat side by side as if they were having a quiet conversation, and that was all.

"Where are the horses, man?" he screamed at Arkwright.

"I don't know," said Arkwright. "I don't know." And then he burst into tears. "The wind blew them away."

Chapter 56

When Catherine woke up at the Detention Center and saw Barnsie, she thought she was having another hallucination. She was holding a piece of soap and a tiny bowl of sago.

"How on earth did you get here?" she said.

"Sam." Barnsie looked awfully pale and had bags under her eyes. She knelt down beside Catherine and embraced her.

"Oh, I've been so worried about you girl, it's been horrible. And I can't stay long, only about ten minutes, but I'm not leaving until you tell me what's happened, so spit it out quickly. I have to know."

So Catherine told her: about Cavendish and her cut finger, and being taken to his room, and (stammering and blushing) about the strange episodes when he rubbed himself and seemed to have a fit (Barnsie had snorted at this) and about going with him to Constantinople. While she talked, Barnsie's eyes had grown rounder and bluer and she'd even started to smile and ask all kind of irrelevant questions about Constantinople and Dr. Cavendish. She seemed, to Catherine's chagrin, generally more excited than upset.

"Well, that's men the world over for you" was her first reaction.

"But Barnsie, I feel like his prisoner. He can come and go here as he pleases, don't you understand that? There's nothing I can do about it. Look, I think I should just go back to Mrs. Clark and tell her everything."

"Tell her what, love?" Barnsie's face was discouraging.

"About him, and how he is with me, and about that day and how he tricked me into going."

"You didn't have to go, love, did you? You could have screamed or shouted or told someone." And anyway, she went on, they would never listen to her—it would be her word against his and his would win. That was the way of the world and that was what happened between gentlemen and servants the length and breadth of England.

Catherine had a sudden clear memory of a morning when a maid had been dismissed at her grandmother's house in the Lleyn. The red-eyed girl had been allowed to help grandmother with her last job—the taking down of the damask winter curtains and the putting up of the white muslin summer ones—and was then sent packing. She and Eliza had watched her small figure carrying its few possessions disappear like a dot down the drive. They'd been confused about why the girl had had to go so quickly, but trusted their grandmother, who was always thrillingly right about such things.

"Mrs. Clark says I'm to show my rags to her every month," she said blushing.

"Oh, now that *is* rubbish!" Finally Barnsie was indignant. "As if we haven't got enough blood around here for thousands of jam rags—but it's no more than many a servant girl back home has to do every month, my pet."

"I dream about killing him, Barnsie. He was so disgusting and it hurt so much and he kept telling me I really wanted him."

"Oh, they all say that, and yes, it does take a bit of time to start liking it" was Barnsie's unsatisfactory reply. Catherine simply couldn't believe how calmly she was taking this.

Barnsie then asked her if she thought she was pregnant, and if she thought she was, to come to her and she would tell her what to do.

"If I am, I will kill him, Barnsie. I hate him so much—he's always snooping and waiting."

And then she'd started coughing and couldn't talk anymore, and Barnsie had made her bed around her and squeezed her hand and advised her to try not to think too much, and that she would talk to Sam who might think of a solution for her.

*   *   *

Sam came to see her the next day. He was wearing his funny old fur hat, and he looked so angry and embarrassed that she knew at once that he knew.

"Barnsie told you, didn't she?" she said.

"I've heard one or two rumors on the grapevine." He took off his cap and grimaced sadly, as though she'd just announced a death.

"Sam," she said after a silence, "what would you do if you were me?"

"Go home," he said instantly, "sham sick. Well, you are that already, so get sicker and go home. Please go home."

"I can't do that," she said softly. "Not that."

"Plenty of men do it, Catherine, and I can't say as I blame them now. They shoot their hands or their feet off, some—beg your pardon, miss—put sand in their todgers, so it looks like they've got whatsaname."

"What do you mean?"

"You know." It was Sam's turn to look embarrassed. "Problems down there."

"Do you have any other ideas, Sam?"

"None really," he said. "You could stay here and let him ruin your life, it makes my blood boil to think of that, or I suppose," he smiled bleakly, "you could always get a transfer to the Crimea— they're gasping for doctors and nurses out there."

"They are?" She sat up so quickly in bed it made her cough again.

"It was a joke, Catherine," he said when she'd finished, "a silly joke. It's the worst place in the world out there."

"Who do you ask to go?"

"Oh my God!" he moaned, "Barnsie will kill me for this. I'd rather die than see a nice girl like you out there, even this place is better, trust me."

"But you don't understand, Sam, it's where I want to be."

"Look," he said desperately, "if you're doing it to try and get away from him, you won't. He's been there before—he was at the front line there for weeks, which is probably part of the reason why he's half cracked, and he could go again any time he liked—they're even more desperate for doctors than they are for nurses, and a man like him doesn't easily give up."

"Who do you think I should approach first: Mrs. Clark or Miss Nightingale?"

"Catherine, did you listen to a word I said?"

"Yes. But I'm not just doing it to get away from him." She looked at him to see if Barnsie had told him about Deio, too, but he just looked old and scared.

She glanced around her to see where they'd put her shoes and her dress. "Sam," she said, "can you help me stand up? I really do feel so much better."

"No," he said, putting on his cap, "you're not going anywhere until you've got rid of that cough," he said. "Oh, I wish I'd never come here."

"Don't be sorry, Sam," she said. "You've saved my life."

She went to Mrs. Clark a week later and put in her request.

"Well, yes, as it so happens, they are dreadfully short of nurses out there," said Mrs. Clark, unable to conceal the look of relief in her eyes, "and Lord Raglan has asked Miss Nightingale for volunteers. A girl like you might do very well there."

And perhaps some of Cavendish's rumors had flown in Miss Nightingale's direction, too, for later that day she was summoned to her office. She had expected an explosion of rage, but Miss Nightingale had opened the door with a small, almost sly, smile.

They sat down together beside her small charcoal fire.

"Is there any truth in this rumor that you wish to volunteer for the Balaclava Hospital?" she said in the gentlest of voices.

"There is, ma'am."

"Are you well enough?"

"Quite well now, thank you, Miss Nightingale."

"Do you realize how dangerous and how hard it is over there?" Miss Nightingale gave her one of her penetrating looks. "I shan't be there to look after you."

"I've been told, ma'am." Silence fell between them. All they could hear was the wind outside and the soft sighing of the fire. Miss Nightingale looked at her.

"I don't know what to say about this, Catherine. You are so young, and yet I suppose you have proved yourself here." She couldn't help it, she glowed at this. "I am very torn." Unusually, she seemed to be vacillating. "Do you care about the good reputation of our nurses here?" she asked suddenly.

"I do, Miss Nightingale."

"Because it's important for you to remember that you have been part of one big and happy family here. And families do not talk to other people about what goes wrong in them, or when we have done wrong."

"I have done nothing wrong," Catherine said. She was prepared to explain that Cavendish had said she had her permission, but Miss Nightingale graciously swept this aside.

"I was making a general point," she said. "Even when we do wrong things, our families don't lightly let us down." She'd said this in a low, tremulous, sincere voice. "And besides, I admire you for volunteering—it will show them my nurses have pluck as well as usefulness on their side."

How confusing it all was. Everything done with mirrors and so much unspoken, unexplained. But then Miss N fiddled with some papers on her desk, and said, "If you go to the Crimea, you'll go with a group of new nurses under the leadership of a Miss Mary Stanley. I shall be frank with you Miss Carreg," and here a note of steel in the flowing honey of Miss N's voice, "had I been consulted about Miss Stanley and her nurses, which I wasn't, they would all have been sent home: they are not properly trained and quite unsuitable."

She'd said that, without in any way wanting to make a spy of her, she thought it would be helpful if Catherine kept an eye on them. She'd be coming to Balaclava in early spring, and "perhaps you and I could have a walk and talk then." She added that she was anxious that all they had struggled and fought for should not be undone by a group of bleeding hearts and amateurs. Had she made herself clear? She had, quite surprisingly so, and Mrs. Clark, fearful of her position, must have kept her mouth shut. Cavendish's name had not been mentioned at all.

"It's going to be . . ." Miss Nightingale had hesitated and chosen her words carefully, "more testing than you can possibly imagine in Balaclava. You may want a day or two to make up your mind."

"I have made up my mind, ma'am. I want to go."

"Take this then, it's your wages." She had given her an envelope with thirty-six pounds of back pay in it and smiled at her so warmly that, for one strange and awkward moment, Catherine thought she might even kiss her.

"Good-bye, Miss Nightingale"—she bent her head, surprised to find her own eyes filled with tears—"I have so much to thank you for." And this was true, for she knew that whatever harsh thoughts she had had about her, nobody could deny she was extraordinary, and that without her ruthless efficiency, this world felt far more dangerous.

Before she left, the nurses had a party for her. Nancy Porter turned her cap back to front, and sang *I had a dream, a happy dream*, and Barnsie, who'd been tearful all day, gave her a lucky button for a present. Emma Fagg laid out a few scraps of cheese and some brandy on a towel on an upturned packing case.

Later in the evening, when they were in their beds, Barnsie, her voice muffled by the towel she wore over her face to keep the rats away, said she hoped that lightning would come and strike the bald head of that bastard Cavendish for sending her away.

"It's not just him, Barnsie. I must go now—you know my other reasons, please try not to cry."

She was only slightly comforted when Catherine had promised that, if she got back to England before Barnsie, she would look for her children.

"If I find them, I'm going to tell them what a fine mother they have."

"I'd come with you, Catherine, if it wasn't for them." Barnsie tore off her rat-towel; her face in that half light was full of pain.

"And Sam. Don't forget Sam."

But Barnsie was squeaking and sniffing, and finally blew her nose. Then, in a moist whisper, she said, "Here! Take a goosey at this," and pulled from her gown a piece of string with a cheap tin ring on it.

"It's a puzzle ring. It stands for the puzzle of life. Sam gave it to me."

Even with her red eyes, Barnsie looked coy, and suddenly much younger. "Silly old things at our age, but why not?"

"Barnsie," she said, "he is a prize; I'm so happy for you."

Barnsie told her not to laugh, but he'd found a cupboard under the stairs where they could meet; it was very snug, with rags in it for a bed. She said she'd never been so happy before and that Sam had said when they got back to London he'd look after her and the children and they could get the little one out of hospital.

"It's a beautiful ring, Barnsie. You deserve something beautiful."

"I don't think deserve comes into it," Barnsie had said with a naughty look. "He can be ever so imperious you know."

Then they hugged each other, and Barnsie said, "I hope you find your young man there; you love him don't you," and she hadn't been able to speak for hearing it put so nakedly.

Barnsie gave her a new handkerchief and a Christmas pudding (heaven knows where she'd got that from), which Catherine promised to eat when she got to Balaclava. Barnsie was convinced there was no food there.

She went out to the Crimea on a transport ship called the *Melbourne* with three other nurses and a Sellonite nun recently arrived from England. Three thousand men were boarded that morning, most dressed in rags and looking half dead. Sam told her they'd been declared well and were being sent back to their regiments to be shot at again.

Down belowdecks she could hear music, the clear sorrowing notes of a flute, and occasional gruff shouts. The ship was preparing to pull out, bells and foghorns were sounding. The two new nurses, Elsa Pruitt and Jane Hibbert, joined her on deck. They had recently arrived from England and their pale faces, poking like terrified field mice from beneath gray bonnets, made her feel as if she was very much older than she had been when she arrived.

The ship was ready to leave; gray water slapped against the prow and a brisk, fruity wind got up. She turned her back to her new companions, too full of emotion to speak.

This had been the most bizarre and mournful period of her life. So many miles traveled, so many tears shed, such passionate friendships, so much loss. (The thought of leaving Lizzie, up on the hill in her unmarked grave, had been almost unbearable.) She turned and looked for the last time at the Barrack Hospital, gaunt and terrifying in its skein of mist. *I shall never forget you* she promised Lizzie and Barnsie and all the rest. They'd all met in a situation of utmost horror and pain—the brave young men, and the hopeless cases—and yet they'd laughed and told stories, and forgiven one another their small transgressions. So much of what it meant to be human had survived against all odds. She had to believe this: to try every day to put the darkness behind her. What happened with Cavendish must not win, but stay buried, like a room that, for sanity's sake, must stay locked, but it would take constant vigilance.

Barnsie was on the shore, propped up by Sam, waving her handkerchief. He'd taken her aside before she left and made one last, impassioned plea for her to stop this madness. He'd told her that, whatever she might have heard to the contrary, this war was proving one of the worst cock-ups in England's history. He said she would see sights in Balaclava that would make Scutari look like a Sunday picnic; that the whole place was a powder keg waiting for a match.

When she'd asked him whether the allies could possibly win, he'd said, in his opinion, no—the big hope was that the allies would rise up one more time and storm Sebastopol, but they had a snowball's chance in hell of that working.

"You're not listening to me, Catherine, are you?" he'd said at last. "I can see it in your eyes."

"Sam," she'd said, "you have been such a good friend to all of us. I could never thank you—"

"Look." His face went scarlet with the effort of getting through. "If you're running away from that horse's arse Cavendish, it won't work you know. He could just as easily be on the next ship, and then you'll be with him and have none of your friends around you."

But her heart's needle had turned, she was past the point of taking advice: not from Sam, not even from Miss Nightingale.

Later that night, when the ship had left the harbor and was sailing through the Black Sea, she went out on deck again and saw the vastness and coldness of the sky around her and felt almost unbearably keyed up and excited, as though she were about to sit one of the greatest tests of her life. And this time there was no indecision. She was going—and now that she was going, she felt as though love had filled her with its own energy and daring, and she had to believe that Deio might be there, too. And if he was there, how much better it was to go to him, to suffer if she had to, cleanly and honestly, than to stay in the half-world of not knowing and regret.

Chapter 57

Deio was calling out but no one could hear him. There were miles and miles of dark plain around him. He was trying to run but his legs were working badly and the sucking mud meant he could only waddle. It felt like a bad dream, the worst dream ever. He was stumbling around in the dark making the sounds that usually fetched the horses in, but they were gone, and he was treading on faces in the mud, tripping over uprooted trees, watching a man flounder like a rabbit inside a tarpaulin collapsed on his head.

The snow had stopped but the wind was full in his face. "*Coooom onnnn cooome on inn.*" That cry was usually followed by thundering hooves, but tonight it sounded like mouse squeaks. He bawled their names out until his throat ached. When his lungs gave out, he sat on a stone, hanging his head in despair. Ahead of him, he could just about make out the faint hog's back of the Woronzoff road and the hills behind. He pictured the horses, their eyes bulging with terror galloping. A terrified horse had no plan but escape, and in the hours since they'd gone, they could be anywhere: down the hill toward Balaclava, across the plain, huddling for safety in the north or south valleys. He tried to think straight but his mind was careering about as fast as theirs were.

Wading through the mud he felt a new sensation: a total dislike of himself. He was a fool. He had broken all his own rules in order to show off and have a change of scene, and maybe a girl who he hadn't wanted anyway, and now all his precious beasts were racing around in the dark.

While he walked, his father seemed to appear beside him, jeering and furious. He'd been at Waterloo he knew about paying attention.

Now Deio felt the wisdom of the obsessive checking, the angry warnings, the way Lewis would listen to his animals, eyes bulging with apprehension, to what seemed like nothing. Behind closed doors, he and Rob used to fall around laughing, imitating him.

He was climbing up a narrow gorge, water poured out of it, crimped and black, under a moon half covered by wreaths of cloud. When the ground was level again, he put a cheroot in his mouth and tried four times to light it, but the matches and the cheroots were damp. Nothing was going to work for him tonight, and with the clouds now almost covering the moon, it would soon be impossible to see. *"Coooom oooonnn, cooooooooon!"* his voice had almost gone. For a few moments, out there on his own he swore and shouted and pleaded like a madman.

When he reached the camp three hours later, he was soaked again. While he'd been gone, Arkwright and some of the other men had made a pretty good job of putting the shelter up again with a length of tarpaulin and the skeletons.

Exhausted, he put his arms around Arkwright, who was crying again and saying he was sorry. He told him to stop being a silly bugger, it was not his fault. And mostly he meant it. Everything was changing, and would change again, and more than ever now he needed them to stay.

Arkwright helped him take off his mud-caked boots. When he took off his breeches water ran out of them and he thought of his mother's kitchen: the smell of stew coming from the range, the pulley above it where they dried wet clothes. Then he lay down on the floor, next to Chalk who was asleep. Halfway through the night Chalk, who stank of wet clothes and the bad-egg smell of powder from his musket, whimpered and put his arm around him. Deio didn't move or mind. He was so far down that, for the first time ever, he understood those fellows who simply lay down in the mud to die.

*   *   *

Gosford appeared under the flap of the tarpaulin the next morning, shaken and pale and offering to help. He could not bring himself to apologize, but he had at least dropped his air of elegant boredom, which was lucky because Deio's inclination was to strangle him with his bare hands.

He told them that the hurricane had blocked parts of the road to Balaclava, which meant that supplies and equipment couldn't get through. He cursed their lack of mules and ordinary pack animals, especially when the shores of Asia Minor were teeming with these animals. "But it's no good wringing one's hand now," he said. "What we desperately need is your horses back."

Deio looked at him warily. What he did with his own horses was his affair.

"Lend me Troy and we'll ride around the plains together," Gosford added. "You'll get more access with an officer present."

He hated being dependent on him more than ever, but he had no choice. Arkwright helped them tack up and put the empty halters in their saddlebags, and they rode out together through the camp. Darkness and snow had protected Deio on the night before, but this morning, in the weak winter sunlight, they saw what the hurricane had done. Every tent in the regiment, except for about five, was down, or lay in the mud at a crazy angle, and the ground between them was covered in dead horses and dead men, scattered randomly among all the other pointless objects: broken carts and shakos, harnesses, cooking pots, huts. A couple of troop horses with tattooed numbers on their shoulders were cantering about aimlessly, one with the remains of a tent's guy rope hanging from its mane.

The animals tried, pathetically, to join them, and although Deio was seething with impatience to find his own, he caught them and led them back to Arkwright and told him to give them some hay. Gosford said they would return them later to their owners and he would personally make it plain that Deio had rescued rather than stolen them.

Fuck you thought Deio, but then Gosford surprised him by saying he would never forgive himself if the horses were lost. He had given Deio bad advice and he was sorry.

Then Gosford told him what, amazingly for such a boastful man, hadn't been mentioned before: that he'd been one of the seven hundred horsemen in the Light Brigade Charge. His regiment, the 13th Hussars, had started out with one hundred and eight horses and come home with thirty-seven. These numbers flew about Deio's heads like bats. He couldn't talk. He was like an animal now, listening, desperate, his eyes trained like pistols on the far hills.

Gosford talked on. He told Deio that he'd had to pay a fortune for his own horse and equipment to come out to the Crimea, and that it had been the worst decision of his life.

"Lend me your eyeglass." Deio would have to shut him up somehow. Gosford gave it to him and he tilted it toward the hills, seeing nothing but grass and mud and sky, but Gosford was unstoppable. He wanted to tell him about the wonderful horse he'd brought out, his color, his little ways.

"He trusted me, you see. His name was Verdi. I'd helped to back him as a boy, and he was naturally brave."

Shut up, shut up, you bastard.

"Very light in the hand. It's a gift to have a horse like that to teach you things."

Gosford was telling him about how Verdi died.

"Up there, near the Causeway Heights."

Deio didn't even bother to follow his companion's eyes up to the hills, but he was half listening. A group of Russian troopers on reconnaissance had jumped on them, and Verdi had staggered and sat down. One of them had blown the back legs off him. Gosford had sat for hours, covered in blood, beside his dead horse and then walked home with the saddle on his head. He still hadn't dared tell his father. Deio shot him a brief look, but said nothing. A great blankness had settled over him.

"I won't leave you till we've found them," Gosford said suddenly.

He kept to his word. They searched all day, crisscrossing the wide plain and scrambling up hills and across gushing streams, until they were black with mud and both speechless with exhaustion. From time to time Troy and Moonshine gave piercing neighs, stopped, and listened with heartbreaking intensity for a reply.

They were on their way home when Deio saw the shape of two horses near a patch of scrubby trees and thought he was so far gone he was hallucinating. Then Troy stopped and gave a sound like a bellow of pain.

"Oh, Jesus Christ!" Deio flung himself off Moonshine and ran toward them. "Thank God."

They were so covered in mud they looked like prehistoric creatures, but it was Bessie and Jewel. He could tell Bessie from the long lugubrious head, the shape of her ears. A couple of vultures rose in the sky. He waded knee deep in mud toward her. "Bessie! Bessie! Bessie! My girl." He had his face against hers now and she was butting his hand and splattering him in mud and ravenously wolfing down the barley he held out in his hands. The other horse, Jewel, started clacking her teeth to show how helpless she was. The birds had already picked at a flap of raw flesh on her neck. He wiped her face and stood with her for a while absorbing her shock.

"How in the hell are we going to get her out?" shouted Gosford.

"Like this." Deio ran to his saddlebag, got a length of rope, and tied it around the croup, the very top of Moonshine's tail.

"It's the strongest part of their body," he told Gosford. He tied the other end to Jewel's tail and with an enormous sucking sound pulled her out of the bog backwards.

"Oh capital! Great stuff! Never seen that before!" Gosford clenched his fists and flung them in the air. They looked at each other for the first time without looking away.

Riding home with Gosford, and the two muddy horses following behind, he almost felt optimistic, but then Gosford volunteered it would be a miracle if they found all the others.

"Someone will find them and eat them, or sell them on the black market."

"Is it that bad?' Deio said angrily.

"It is," said Gosford. "I'm sorry."

Then he spelled out in detail what he had not liked to say earlier. There had never been a campaign like the Crimea for any of them: the rain, the mud, the complete lack of organization. The harbor was now choked with ships, and with winter approaching and no new supplies, all of them should expect the worst.

"What is the worst?" asked Deio.

"Don't ask," answered Gosford, "but consider your options well. I could probably get you a commission in the Thirteenth. Fellows are selling theirs and resigning all over the shop."

"What would I do?"

"Mostly intelligence gathering, riding out to the piquets; you could be part of the reconnaissance patrols."

"What I don't understand," said Deio playing for time, "is if we know the Russians are in Sebastopol, why we don't just attack them?"

"It's too late. Three weeks ago it might have worked, now we don't have enough men or enough food."

Deio looked at Gosford again.

"Is the situation this bad at Scutari?"

"Not yet, but it will be."

He could hear a kind of ringing in his ears.

Gosford said he should talk to Lieutenant-Colonel Hanbury of the 13th. If he liked, they could go and see him tomorrow.

Chapter 58

Catherine had waved good-bye to Barnsie and Sam and the rest of them until her arm ached, then stayed on deck until the ship had left the harbor and was well on its way. The ship had begun to roll and tilt almost as soon as they reached the Black Sea. High winds were expected and sailors were tying down any portable furniture. At last she went down to the cabin she'd been allocated to share with two nurses, two nuns, and Nancy Porter, the wife of the ship's carpenter.

There was barely an inch between the bunks and the cabin was tiny—no more than fourteen feet by twenty. Sister Clara had her eyes closed, her darned stockinged feet hanging over the edge of the bunk, her face already a pale gray. "I'm not asleep dear, I'm seasick," she said in a soft voice as Catherine walked in. "I'm afraid I am a very poor sailor. I shall probably be up all night."

"Oh, we'll look forward to that," said Porter, the brisk little woman who slept in the bunk below. She smiled at Catherine, who was having to brace herself against the walls, and carried on writing a letter, quite oblivious to the rough weather. "I'm writing to my mother," she told Catherine. "I'm telling her we'll be in Balaclava about the middle of February—that would be about it, wouldn't it?" she said after a few scratchings.

Catherine tried to hide a note of panic in her voice. "That long? I was told a week, ten days at the most. I even hoped we might be there before Christmas."

Porter pushed back her hair and snorted. "This is my fourth trip to Balaclava with my husband," she said with some grandeur, "and I don't think they've ever told us the truth about it once. At this time of year, there are always storms in the Black Sea, and the harbor at Balaclava isn't a proper harbor—more like an inland lake—and usually jammed to the eyeballs with ships. When you do get there it's normal to be stuck there a week or more."

Hearing this, she'd experienced such a terrible, seething impatience that she had to go up and stand on the deck, where she'd stayed for close to an hour, soaked and desperate and clinging to the rails while the sea bucked and rolled around her in a wilderness of waves. Down below, she could hear glass shattering and the sound of heavy objects skidding across a wooden floor. At the very bottom of the ship there were three hundred men stuffed in the hold, in quarters that Porter had said were designed for farm animals. How much longer could they all hold out?

She looked down at the waves again, gleaming coils of copper and green, roaring and groaning. She and Deio used to rush into the sea with their wooden swords, frightened and excited by the Water Horse. Advancing, retreating, screaming, they'd prance through the waves. He liked them, they said; he wouldn't kill them.

But tonight she couldn't even bear to think about Deio, it was too frightening; everything was at stake now, and the idea of an early death for both of them was appalling. But later, when the wind had died down and the night was immense and starry, she went down to the stuffy cabin again, put on her nightgown, brushed her hair, and, on the borderlines of sleep where everything was allowed, he came to her. He flopped beside her on the grass; he took her face between his hands and smiled at her; such a smile, it seemed to come flaming up from deep within him. She ran her fingers through his hair, she kissed him—a kiss that started at her toes and worked its way up to a blaze of happiness in her head.

And while she slept, black waves sped past the portholes and the dangerous world outside carried on with its business.

Beneath her Nancy Porter, who was missing her carpenter husband, rubbed herself until she groaned, and above her, in a cabin near the poop, the captain of the ship, Captain Gambon—a frail man in his early sixties who'd spent eleven of the worst months of his life ferrying the wounded across the Black Sea—drank another glass of whiskey and prayed to every god he could think of to get him home to Bournemouth before he did something drastic to himself. Down in the hold, those men who weren't too seasick, drank. They knew what they were going back to.

Splash! Splash! Splash! Splash! Only four days out, but everybody recognized the sound now, as each morning the night's catch of dead bodies was dropped over the side along with the night soil, the old food, and the rubbish. They were three hundred miles short of Balaclava and twenty-seven men had gone over the side already.

On the fifteenth of December there was a freak storm. The wind howled like an animal, the water sped, inky and vicious, past their porthole and a huge wave, which struck at about a quarter past three in the morning, flung them all from their bunks.

"Don't let me die here, God" was her first thought. She was lying on the floor, her cheek burning and bruised against Porter's buttoned boots. "Let me see him one more time." Waking and sleeping she felt him all the time now, like a quickening in her blood.

The storm died away as quickly as it had got up, but Nancy Porter, who got all the gossip from her husband, told her later that Captain Gambon, befuddled by sleep, made a poor decision: by cutting away the ship's masts, they lost two sheet anchors and could only ride on a stream anchor.

At five-thirty that morning, the ship limped ashore in the Bulgarian harbor of Varna, where a local shipwright estimated it would take three or four days to repair. The news, although bad, could have been worse, but Gambon had lost all sense of proportion. When he heard this, he took a bottle of rum, went down to his cabin, changed into his nightshirt and cap, and drank himself into a stupor.

By Christmas Eve, they were six miles from Balaclava—they could see the distant blur of hills and the masts of ships taking shape.

During their waiting days, Sister Clara, a Sellonite nun who had been sent to Scutari to recover from a bout of typhus, was given permission to hold a concert on Christmas Eve. On the day before the concert, she dispatched Catherine throughout the ship to borrow as many lanterns as she could.

In the end, so many people wanted to come that it was decided to have it on deck. As the light faded, a trail of lights, ghostly in the mist, was lit and the temperature fell. The men who were playing had to hold their fingers under their armpits, or get their friends to rub them because it was so cold outside. By seven o'clock, the band, looking poor and ragged in their scraps of uniforms and oddly assorted clothes, stood attentive and proud against a backdrop of dazzling stars waiting for a signal from Sister Clara, who stood on a wooden crate with the moon behind her.

"Gentlemen, officers, members of the crew, ladies," announced Sister Clara, "we present for you, a ceremony of carols."

During rehearsals, she'd been strict with them all about singing out. She'd told them that all truly bad choirs had one thing in common—*they were feeble*—and that they must have the courage to make great big mistakes. Big mistakes, she said, were always correctable, but what couldn't be corrected was *"mmmnnewww"*—Sister Clara's mewings had made the men laugh.

But tonight was their night, and gray-faced in the moonlight, exhausted and half starved, they sang as if nothing bad had ever happened to any of them, or ever would. They sang of silent nights and crackling fires, and merry gentlemen and figgy puddings. And they were good. One had to leave because of diarrhea, but the rest stayed and sang their hearts out.

After the interval Thomas Clancy, a regimental musician with the 8th Hussars, whose band had been wiped out by the war, played on a borrowed Russian trumpet (his own, his most precious possession, had been trampled on in a cavalry charge). As the clear notes of "Hark the Herald Angels" peeled out into the night, Clancy's eyes were tightly shut as if in pain. He was himself again and playing like an angel.

The nurses sighed as they listened and one or two of the men wept. The singing ship, the beautiful night, the sense that sorrow could be put off for a little while longer, filled them all with a longing for happier days, for peace.

When the last note sounded, it was hard to see the hopeful smiles on the faces of the men as their ship bore on. There was a storm of applause, playful shouts of bravo, and calls for an encore from Clancy. A good thing had happened, everybody felt it.

Perhaps in the end it was too much for Clancy to bear. The day after the concert—again the story was relayed by Nancy Porter—the quartermaster asked for the Russian trumpet back. They showed Clancy the docket he had signed which said that he understood it was only on loan. And some time in the early morning, Clancy, who did not know how to ask for things for himself, went downstairs and tried to hang himself from the rail of the stairs leading to the poop deck. A midshipman coming back from his night watch found him just in time, white and sweating, with the rope around his neck. Under other circumstances, Captain Gambon, still in a state of high agitation about not getting home for Christmas, might have flogged him to set an example, but in the end, he let the matter drop. Bigger things had overtaken them; and as the light grew, and the *Melbourne* sailed on, the cry went up that they had arrived in Balaclava.

Chapter 59

It was New Year's Eve, and Deio was in a dugout some seven and a half miles northeast of Balaclava, with Arkwright, Chalk, a gawky young trooper called Pennyworth, and Isaacs, a pale Yorkshireman with yellow eyes whose smell was almost unbearable.

They'd seen each other every day for weeks now, and though none of them would have said the words, they were now a gang, a herd who would, if necessary, fight and die for each other. Deio was their leader, although no one had actually said that either.

They were sitting in a circle around a sullen fire made of tree roots and some planks saved from the original horse shelter. The sixth member of the group was another skeleton from Arkwright's seemingly inexhaustible supply. A candle had been found and put inside the skull, lighting up for a moment its eye sockets and temples and ear holes before the wind put it out again.

It was all so bad by now: the daily rations of moldy and wet food, the mud, the heaps of wounded men, the hospital tents. Deio's horses had started to gnaw at each other's tails and manes to get something in their bellies.

He had five left now—Moonshine and Troy, Bessie, Jewel, and Midnight, who'd been found in the next camp. They stood for hours under the dripping tarpaulin, listless and depressed. None of the others had miraculously reappeared (how daft it seemed now to have thought they would). He missed them all, but it was the thought of Cariad that really undid him. She was the kind of horse whose nerves, even at the best of times, ate into her stamina; now he pictured her bewildered and starving, or smashed against a rock or with a broken leg, or found and roasted by hungry men. Many of the normal human decencies had been temporarily suspended. For the first time in his life he drank to forget and felt his mind learning to drift and slip its moorings. His usual state of alertness was too painful.

"*For auld lang syne my deara . . . for auld lang syne,*" he bellowed. "*We'll tak a cup o' kindness . . . yet, for the sake of auld lang syne.*"

"*It's all a'feared and gone.*" Pennyworth was singing another song, too drunk to remember the words. After a while the wind got up and the clash of tunes got on Deio's nerves. When he went back to check on the horses he saw a figure standing in the shadows near the corral. He was wearing a fur hat and filthy mess kit and was clearly a little drunk.

"Happy New Year," said Gosford warily, "and sorry, sorry, sorry, I've been so slow to get back to you about the other business."

"What other business?"

"Come on!" Gosford was offended and a little truculent. "We talked about it the other day. It's a great honor you know."

"What's an honor?" Deio was swaying himself. "I don't know what you're talking about man."

"A commission," Gosford's pouty little mouth was whispering now, "with the Thirteenth. Very urgent situation, say yes and by tomorrow you'll be out of this shit hole and a member of the cavalry. I can't ever remember it happening like this before."

"What's the rush?" Deio looked at Gosford and lit a cheroot. "What's happened?"

Gosford grabbed him by the arm. "Don't play games—you don't understand—it's bad now but going to get much, much worse. The harbor is jammed, nothing can move, and when your forage runs out you will die here."

Deio threw his cheroot away and ground it under his boot. From the corner of his eye he could see his horses watching him; they were sensitive to changes in human voices. Gosford was squawking with fear.

Deio sighed and looked around him. At the hopeless mud, and at his dwindling stock of hay.

"How do I get this *commission*?" He felt he was being tricked into something and that he wouldn't be able to resist.

"You won't regret it," said Gosford relieved. "There is no more exciting life, I promise you that. I'll take you to meet the CO in the morning."

Deio looked at him suspiciously.

"What do you want from this, Gosford?"

"Nothing but the loan of a horse—you'll understand better tomorrow. Are you a decent shot?"

"Yes," said Deio calmly. He felt a surging excitement in his blood. "I brought my own rifle. So what's the next move? A New Year's Eve tot with your leader?"

"Not tonight man, you're drunk," said Gosford, swaying and smiling. "Go to bed, go to sleep, trim your beard in the morning. I'll be back first thing and I promise you one thing"—he wagged his finger solemnly—"your life will change."

And so Deio became a cavalry officer, or as he put it to himself later, a killer with a license. The next morning Gosford had taken him to the hut of Lieutenant-Colonel Hanbury, temporarily in command of the 13th Hussars, a gaunt, exhausted-looking man, who sat at a walnut desk occasionally eating dried apricots.

Hanbury began by saying he had heard Deio was a first-class horseman with some fairly decent horses. "Correct?"

"Correct."

Hanbury waited for the "sir" that didn't come, and then got straight down to business by saying in a low voice that they were going to offer him a "most unusual arrangement." Unusual in the sense that joining the 13th was usually a privilege to be earned and paid for. (Later Deio found out that a few days before a large number of officers had sent in their papers and gone home, a source of great shame to the regiment.)

"Do you have any basic training?"

"No, but I can shoot, hunt, break horses—"

"He really is a first-class horseman," Gosford broke in anxiously.

"Well, sniping is rather like hunting only the game shoot back."

"I'm not worried about it. I can do it." He was conscious as he said it of that surge of happiness again. War had already stirred up lots of forbidden impulses, and he had been practicing, it seemed, forever.

"Good man."

Hanbury mopped his face with his handkerchief, sweat was pouring off it. He left the hut suddenly and when he came back shut the door.

"I shall have to be franker than I normally would be. We're in a desperate state. The harbor is jammed and it is almost impossible to land supplies. In the matter of horses . . . we've lost four hundred and seventy-five in this regiment alone since the war began; not just troopers, but pack horses, too. And it is lack of transport that could kill us all.

"Our only hope now is to gather as much intelligence about the Russian positions near Sebastopol as we can for one last big push in that direction. The work is dangerous and the need for swift horses and good riders paramount."

Deio felt his heart quicken again. "I can do that," he said quietly.

Hanbury got two fine-looking cups out of a hamper under his desk and a soldier brewed them a cup of strong coffee, the best he had had in months, and gave him some rum and a ham sandwich. Deio couldn't help himself, he walloped it down, and while he was eating, Hanbury told him more about the reconnaissance patrols. Because Deio was still quiet, he said they would provide him with a full uniform, a sword, and a revolver, and that he could forget the two pounds and eightpence a week officers normally paid to the mess.

"I have my own rifle, sir. A Minie."

"Ah, yes indeed, lovely little job that, far superior to the army issue."

Hanbury mopped his face again. He hadn't touched his cup of coffee.

"So," he said, "welcome to the Thirteenth. Delighted to have you aboard. Any questions?"

Deio asked if Arkwright and Chalk could be part of his team. He said they were first-class men and good with the horses. In truth, he knew he would feel strange without them now; they felt closer to him than family.

Gosford came back and put a large package of clothes in his arms. He offered Deio one of the huts that had been left behind. "You see, I told you your life would change." Deio wanted to wipe the triumphant smirk off his face; he said his tent was still up, and that he wanted to stay near his horses.

"Here, Jones, take this back to your tent." Hanbury handed him a bag of coffee and a small ham, and a lamp with some dry matches. "You've had a tough few days, losing your horses like that."

He had staggered, back up the hill again toward the camp, confused and aroused and laden with a stranger's clothes and food and talking in his head to his father: "Silly old buggar, see I made it. They saw me for what I was." Catherine would be impressed, too, she couldn't help but be. She'd tease him but her eyes would widen. Deio Jones, cavalry officer 13th Hussars. It was a turn up.

Later that night (it was frosty outside and stalactites of snow hung frozen on the trees) he was in his tent and it wasn't, for once, the cold that was making him tremble, but the sight of his new uniform on his bed. Gosford hadn't said whether its previous occupant was dead or a deserter, but it was his now. The cherry-colored jacket was edged with gold and pitted here and there with small gunpowder burns; there was a sash with a watery stain on it. Two pairs of flannel drawers, two shirts with a black ring around the neck. A shaving kit with another man's coarse black hairs in the soap. A pair of blue overalls, furred pelisses in which he would feel an absolute burk, a high fur hat, a pair of long leather boots with "Lobbs" written in the soles—too tight, he'd rather see if he could get away with using his own.

Chalk, who'd been ill again that day, lay on the floor watching him unwrap them.

"Quite sure you didn't nip them, mate?" he said.

Deio had climbed into the breeches and the red coat; he turned around, he looked good and he knew it.

"Watch out, Chalkie lad," he said, "I could get veddy veddy craws with you. Might even have to have you flogged."

Both were relieved to find themselves laughing together again. Deio's change of circumstance had thrown them all. Arkwright had gone completely silent when he'd told him and gone outside to stand with the horses.

"What's the matter, Arkie?" Deio asked, when he went outside to see him.

"I don't know," he said.

"Try to say."

Arkwright had turned his big tragic eyes on him. "If I hadn't lost them, you wouldn't be doing this."

"Maybe not, but I'd want to," he'd said.

"Then you've got a death wish," said Arkwright.

They lost no time in sending him out. Gosford spent a day briefing him and arrived the next day, all officiousness and maps, to tell him that Hanbury wanted them to the Fifth Redoubt the following night, and the night after that to get as close as they could to Sebastopol.

The next morning he got up early with Arkwright and tried to still his nerves by sticking to his usual routine. He groomed all the horses until they shone, polished their tack, and tried on the new regimental sheepskins he'd been given for them. Two were torn and muddy, but he couldn't help the swelling of his heart when he put them over the saddles: he felt he was conferring some power, and maybe making up for their other disasters.

He waited and watched more snow fall, drifting and then flurrying through the trees. In the early afternoon he went back to his tent and unwrapped his Minie from its case. He held the rifle loosely in his hand and caressed its barrel. He'd got it from a gunsmith he knew near Smithfield's and it had cost him a cow, but it was worth every penny. The French, who mostly had Minies themselves, laughed at the Englishmen's heavy inaccurate muskets—they wouldn't laugh at his.

He was not as calm as he was pretending to be. He'd had a bad night's sleep the night before, a semi-awake nightmare of worry about the horses, and about Russian soldiers lying behind the sand-bags and trenches of Sebastopol. The Russians had thick greatcoats and fat rosy faces, and they were smiling. Before dawn, he dreamed of Catherine. He held her again, put his face next to hers, and breathed her in. It was so sweet that waking up was like being torn from heaven.

Chapter 60

The ship had stopped moving, they knew they could put it off no longer. They must look at Balaclava for the first time. They put on their cloaks and bonnets, went out in the face-slapping cold, walked to the top deck of the ship.

Porter, who'd been up earlier, had warned them to brace themselves for some terrible sights, the worst she had ever seen. The air was thick with bad odors, putrid and sickly, and when she looked down Catherine saw piles of blue and gray men, dead or writhing in agony, lying on the decks of the jammed ships, bathed in the light of a weak winter sun. In the gaps between the ships, what looked at first like buoys or sandbags, were dead bodies, bobbing in a suppurating froth of pink and yellow water. She could feel herself detaching from reality and going into a softened fuguelike state.

"Why pink?" She heard herself say.

Porter, clutching her hand, said that because the corpses had been buried at sea without proper weights, they'd come to the surface of the water again. Now she saw that between them floated pieces of people: a head decapitated on an anchor chain; a leg, purple and shiny; a man's trunk in a sodden uniform. The smell of sulphated oxygen they gave off was so sweet and so meaty that, after one inhalation, Catherine went down to the cabin and was violently sick.

When she came round, Sister Clara sat on the bunk opposite her sponging Miss Pruitt's head with eau de cologne.

"Fainted," she said, "dead away. I'm not surprised. The Sanitary Commission was supposed to have cleared the harbor up, but if anything it's worse than I remember. Have a sip of water dear, but try not to take too much."

"I'm sorry," said Catherine, "I'm so sorry." She was crying, yet she felt separated from herself as she listened to her teeth chattering and drank the sherry-colored water. "I'll get used to it."

"No, you won't dear," said Sister Clara briskly, "not this. Why should you?"

They were told to stay in their cabins for the rest of the afternoon while their ship jerked and bumped onwards toward the landing quay. A lump of salt pork and some biscuits arrived but none of them could eat. Miss Pruitt got on their nerves by crying a great deal and repeating that she never should have come. Nancy Porter bit her fingernails until they bled. And Catherine tried not to think about Deio, maybe so close and maybe hundreds and thousands of miles away. Death, once so terrible, such a big thing, now felt so ugly and ordinary, almost inevitable.

"Where are the Russians now?" she asked Sister Clara, who took an interest in military strategy. They were in bed together sharing a blanket, trying to keep warm. The other women had fallen asleep.

"Ah, well, the rumor is that close to one hundred thousand of them moved into Sebastopol a couple of months ago," said Sister Clara. "It may only be a rumor."

"How far away is Sebastopol?"

"About ten miles north of us here."

"Of this ship?"

"Of this ship."

"And how many are we?"

"I can't say exactly, nobody knows. My guess is twenty thousand if we're lucky and if you count the allies." Catherine shook her head, and heard herself pant. Sister Clara was renowned for looking on the bright side.

"My God," said Catherine, "aren't you frightened?"

"Forget I said any of this, won't you, dear?" Sister Clara was whispering. "I'm talking too much. I must miss going to Confession." They closed their eyes, but Catherine couldn't help herself.

"Why on earth did *you* come back?"

Sister Clara gave her an anxious glance. "I was sent back to do God's will. There is no other choice."

"Are you all right?" The nun's face was as pale as her wimple.

"God asks a lot," Sister Clara's voice was monotonous, "but he doesn't ask for more than you can give."

"I'm so sorry about Clancy," said Catherine. The trumpet player had died in the night. "You gave him so much pleasure."

"I think I killed him," said Sister Clara. "I reminded him of everything he'd lost."

Three days later, at ten o'clock at night, they were taken in a bullock cart up the hill toward the General Hospital. They lay in the back of it, their cloaks encrusted with frozen snow and bullock droppings, their limbs so cold they were locked into one position.

"This is nothing," said Sister Clara, who had tried to get them to sing to keep warm, but their lips were too cold. "This is nothing," she repeated through juddering teeth. "Every few weeks here there is a spell of what the soldiers call 'Russian cold,' when the temperature sinks to ten below zero. Then, if you put your hand on metal, it will stick to it."

When they reached the top of the hill, a large and beautiful moon was riding on top of some dark clouds. It shone down on the hard snow and on the four wooden huts that comprised the hospital, washing everything in a silvery, bluish light, and making their first view of the General Hospital, Balaclava, almost romantic.

The door was opened by a clearly exhausted elderly woman with a storm lamp in her hand. She told them her name was Miss Weare, that she was the superintendent of the hospital, and that they should follow her down to the kitchen for a bowl of negus and then go straight to bed.

"Oh God, not another woman," muttered Porter to Catherine. "I'd far rather take orders from a man."

Down in the kitchen was a Welsh cook, Miss Davis, about sixty years old. "Sit down here," she told them, "and get this down you."

She gave them a glass of what she called Crimean wine, sugary and hot and pinched with cinnamon, and then she put some bread in the bottom of four white dishes and ladled meat broth over it.

The women whimpered with pleasure, and although their hands still felt like boulders, they put their heads down and ate like animals. The cook had the good sense only to fill their bowls and leave them to eat and thaw and not think.

When the scrape of their spoons stopped, they were sent to bed: Sister Clara to share with the two other nuns on the first floor, Catherine and Porter to follow Miss Davis's stout outline up the stairs to the nurses' room. At the top of the stairs she took a key from a bundle around her waist and gave the keyhole a vicious stab. "The flamer's iced over again," she told them, and Catherine, still shivering with shock and cold, found herself smiling. It was good to hear a Welshwoman again, just comforting like the soup.

A kick opened the door onto the dormitory: a long narrow room with four beds, one already occupied by a sleeping woman who did not stir. There was a blackboard at the end of the room with Russian characters written on it. (Davis had explained on the way up that the hospital had once been a school.) Catherine's bed had a pile of children's crutches and an old wicker wheelchair on one side; on the other was a sleeping woman, whose mouth was wide open, air streaming from it like smoke. She hadn't stirred.

All of them undressed without a word. The day had finished them.

Grateful for one good thing, she lay down in a proper bed again, limbs still rocking from the motion of the ship. She was longing for oblivion, to shut down, to stop caring, but there was a new noise outside to try and ignore: the whirr and crump of distant artillery fire. On a night as light as this, the enemy could attack as easily as in the middle of the day.

Before she went to sleep, she rubbed some cream into her face and hands. The little pot of lemon and glycerine that Eliza had sent her from home was running out.

"It doesn't matter," she thought, "I may not live long enough for wrinkles."

She was calm in the thought, but as soon as she closed her eyes black thoughts flew about her mind like bats: the harbor, the swollen corpses, the staring eyes, the bits and bobs of human flesh floating around.

And then, she couldn't help herself, she thought of Deio.

What had made her so sure that he would live when so many others had died here? And if he had lived, how? How in God's name could you land horses in that terrible harbor? Or feed them? Or house them? This felt like a place with an infinite variety of ways to kill you.

Frozen and heartsore, she tossed and turned under the prickly blanket. Her fault—her foolishness, her pride had led him here: into all this squalor and hopelessness, and here she was herself, in the eye of the storm.

Chapter 61

Olive Purdey, the sole occupant of the dormitory the night before, woke first and looked at her new companions without interest or surprise. Most of her life had been spent in the St. Giles Rookery in London, where she'd worked as a maid, a whore, and a cook in a brothel; rats, lice, and cold were taken in her stride, also the sudden appearance of strangers in her room.

It was minus ten degrees indoors and she'd worn her shoes to bed to stop them icing up. She took a nip from the small flask of brandy hidden under the mattress and put her dress over the bloomers, chemise, and petticoats she'd slept in.

The creaking of her bed woke Catherine, who sat up in hers and looked around her with her heart pounding.

"Good day." She extended her hand toward the large woman, now struggling into a selection of gray woolens.

"Morning."

"Did we give you a shock when you woke up this morning?"

"No," said the woman, "I was told you was coming. All right, are you?" Her tone implied she didn't want Catherine to go into any detail.

"Yes, thank you," she replied politely. "It will take us a while to learn the ropes, but quite well thank you. Are you on duty today?"

"Yes."

"Can I ask a question before you go?"

"Yes, you can."

Her heart was going like a hammer.

"Is there— Do you— You see, we've come from the Barrack

Hospital at Scutari," Catherine whispered, "and there are people we know who are here and who you might know."

"No, there's been no women come yet from Scutari but you lot. There's been some from Miss Stanley's lot, but they've been sent away again. Yes, that's right." Any moment now Olive's foghorn voice would wake the others up.

"Oh no, hang about, some of the ladies did stay," repeated the stolid Olive, "and some is already gone." There was a malicious gleam in her eye. "Some of them thought us nurses would work for them as lady's maids so we had to sort that one out."

"The thing is, I'm not really sure if the person I'm talking about has been here and gone home, or not come here at all, or has stayed here. Are there lists with the dead on them?" She turned away.

"I dunno," said Olive. "I've never thought to ask. But it's needle in a haystack time, you'd be lucky to find her if she isn't here."

"It's a him."

"Well, you'll have to get more information than that." Olive put her knuckle in her nostril to dislodge a piece of frost. "Where's he from?"

"From Wales."

"So many have gone I've lost track of their names." Olive's eyes were vacant, she'd given up trying to help. "Ask Miss Davis in the kitchen, she's Welsh and she's a know-it-all."

And so no cheese there. Nothing. It was stupid to expect news so quickly she told herself. After breakfast (hot porridge and some good homemade bread) taken in the kitchen, the superintendent, Miss Weare, arrived to show them around.

Neatly dressed and middle-aged, she seemed, with her nervous darting manner and quick smiles, very anxious not to be shown up in front of people who knew Miss Nightingale. She spent a good hour in what she called a "getting to know you meeting," in which she questioned them keenly about their experiences in Scutari: What kind of work had they done on the wards? Had any nurses been sent home? What improvements had been made? "They're like cocks in the ring underneath it all aren't they," Porter said later.

They were taken down to ward two, a long, airless, narrow room where Miss Weare briefed them. The hospital had space for two to three hundred patients and beds for only half that number. There had been some local skirmishes during the night, she said, and thirty new patients were expected later in the day. Fifteen of them were on the operations list.

"Most of our patients are in for bowel problems," Miss Weare's pale eyelashes blinked rapidly, "and of course the low circulation that comes with dysentery has led to more and more frostbite. Our numbers for scurvy are also rising far more quickly than we would like."

Catherine was surprised to see Miss Pruitt and Miss Hibbert hold hands in evident terror. None of this shocked her any longer.

At the end of ward, two young orderlies were throwing a packet of bandages at each other. They stopped to look at the women.

"Could I ask you to move those?" Miss Weare's voice was high, breathless. She pointed toward two bloodstained stretchers propped against the wall. "Someone is bound to trip over them soon."

She blinked rapidly at the nurses as she said this as though surprised at her own audacity. Not a born leader, thought Catherine.

They spent the rest of the day being shown the workings of the hospital: where to line up for food, where to collect the supplementary diets, where dirty linen was stored and so forth. After lunch, she helped one of the nurses, a Sister of Charity called Sister Veronica, change the bedding of a man in the last stages of typhus who was suffering from a continuous and profuse hemorrhage of the bowel. Then they were sent to find beds, bedding, and a hot meal for four men who had come in that morning with frostbite.

Sister Veronica, although she was plump was quite comely; she went from bed to bed with a male orderly, undressing the half-conscious men with a minimum of fuss and false modesty—a task that would have been considered unsuitable at Scutari. That done, she put them into clean shirts and bathed their lips with warm water and vinegar. No coyness there, just ordinary decent, human helpfulness.

Thank God for work. Catherine plunged herself into it again

and again that day. She told herself it was stupid to have expected news of Deio so soon.

After a drink of water and some bread and cheese at lunch-time, she and Nancy Porter went back on the wards and, because it was so busy, were trusted with the delicate task of unbinding the foul, curious selection of articles—bandages, old haversacks, bits of shoes—embedded in the men's frostbitten feet.

"Some of the men haven't taken their shoes off for months," Sister Veronica told them. "They were frightened their shoes would ice over, or their feet would swell, but it's done their circulation no good at all."

She introduced them to a young man lying in bed wearing a woolen hat, and with his blue and white toes all stuck together. Gently, carefully, she separated them with warm water, then rubbed them briskly with her hands, even though the young man, who lay with his eyes shut, said he could feel nothing at all.

Again, the quiet competence of her gestures showed Catherine that this nun was not one of those helpless, spiritually flirtatious Roman Catholics that Miss Nightingale had warned them about. Another huge exaggeration, a lie even. This was a woman with years of experience, a professional nurse, someone like Lizzie, compared to whom Miss Nightingale was the rank amateur. Catherine was bewildered by this. Why had so many hardworking women been sold so short, and how many other lies had they been told?

Work. Sleep. Eat. Work. That was the pattern of her days for the next month. In early February, the temperature had dropped by another ten degrees and she understood what Sister Clara meant by Russian cold. Locks froze, the mud in the trenches froze, beards stuck to men's faces, great lumps of snow hardened under horse's hooves, turning them into ball bearings. When you went outside, cold smacked your face, made your ears ring, froze the roots of your hair and made it hurt. Everybody suffered from chilblains, from mild frostbite, from chapped skin. And when it wasn't snowing, it rained steel needles of sleet and the streets became muddy ravines lined with the bodies of drowned animals.

This was the month when hundreds of men lay down quietly in the snow outside their tents and closed their eyes. Even for brave men, enough was enough. The month she had to accept that if she went out on her own to look for Deio, she would die. Rushing from bed to bed she learned to survive in a world in which there was only the moment—no past, no expectations of a future. Each day she helped young men face the loss of friends, of courage, of faith. False dreams died, but not hope or love, or something close to it. Extra sources of power seemed released in all of them, and although hysteria was never far from the surface, they were a team as they hurtled, frozen and exhausted, from bed to bed.

She knew that from now on whatever happened to her in her personal life—and oh, how she grieved quietly sometimes, seeing a man in a bed that could be him—there was another place that she could go where she felt competent and necessary. Sometimes—and this was the oddest, most disturbing thing—it even felt as if looking death in the face day after day made you feel startlingly alive.

And then, one afternoon, she was helping Sister Veronica in ward two with the same young man she'd seen three weeks ago with the woolly hat and frostbite. He'd been readmitted, and this time Sister Veronica thought his wounds were so bad that his leg might have to come off. The nun had gone to find a doctor; Catherine had stayed and was straightening the soldier's bed when she turned round and saw him walking toward her.

He looked at her with the blank eyes of a man staring at himself in a mirror. The same stained frock coat, too, with the bunch of silk ligatures threaded through the top button ready for use. The desire to run or to scream was so strong she had to move away.

"Dr. Cavendish." Miss Weare had appeared by her side. "Have you met our new nurses?"

"I am very pleased to meet you all," she heard him say. "You look better Nurse Porter. Miss Carreg," he bowed his head slightly.

They'd covered the man's wounds with loose bandages. He laid them aside and peered at his gray and blue feet. He was so close to her, she could hear him breathing. He told Sister Veronica to go and mix up a linseed poultice, which he thought might raise the temperature in the man's feet, and then, to her relief, he begged their forgiveness for rushing off, but he had two patients in the theater, chloroformed and waiting, and five others to do that night. "Thank God for some new helpers," he said amiably.

Miss Weare started to twitter as if he had paid her a very great compliment. He looked through her, and looked directly at Catherine.

"We've lost eight doctors in the last nine months from fevers alone," Miss Weare explained as he walked off. "We are so very grateful to him for stepping in so promptly. He is a very fine surgeon indeed. Did you meet him at Scutari?"

"Yes," said Catherine, "I met him at Scutari."

Miss Weare waited for some other comment, but a loud bang from outside the hospital made them both gasp.

"What was that?" said Catherine. All her movements felt stiff and unnatural.

"So very silly of me to jump after all this time," said Miss Weare, "it's only target practice."

Late in the afternoon, a message came to her via Miss Weare: at six-thirty, she and Sister Veronica were to report back to the bed of Private Willis, the young soldier with frostbite. She had no option but to do as she was told and, at the appointed time, stood by the bed. It was bitterly cold now, even though the fire and the lamps had been lit; Willis's lips were blue. While they waited, he slipped in and out of sleep, talking to her when awake about what had worried him for days: his parents were tenant farmers from Warwickshire. He was the eldest and only son and if he lost his leg, they'd lose their livelihood.

"What's this? What's this?"

Cavendish, in a black muffler, and with the arms of his frockcoat sodden with blood, was walking toward them, determined as usual to take center stage.

"He's frightened about losing his leg," Catherine warned him.

"Well, nobody's said he would yet," he grumbled. "Let me have another look."

He unwrapped the bandages. Willis was asleep again, his calves black and ulcerated, his toes as white as candle wax and looking about as useful. He sent Sister Veronica away for a bowl of warm water.

"And so, Nurse Carreg," he said when she was gone, "how did you contrive this?"

"Contrive this!" She leaped away from him.

"To follow me here."

She gave him such a look of dislike that even he looked startled.

"That's a lie," she said, "and you know it."

He drew in his breath. "Still so fiery. How interesting." The sight of his damp mouth made her flesh crawl.

He drew a curtain around the man, and brought his lamp closer. "I've thought about you, Catherine," he said in a low, urgent voice, quite different from his facetious one. "I really can help you, just be a little bit nice to me. I have a house, quite close to the hospital, and Miss Weare is a pussycat compared to Miss Nightingale. No one will know or care. I want this," he said flatly. "I don't have time to argue about it. I'm tired. I have it all set up for us now."

"What are you talking about? What are you doing?" She looked down pleadingly at Willis, but he was semiconscious and had no interest in either of them. She was shaking. "Please, please stop this."

"Oh, don't worry about him"—he followed her eyes—"he's gone or nearly. Worry about yourself, Catherine." He straightened up, and all the light had gone out of his eyes.

"You don't know how things work here and I do, so don't make me cross, Catherine, or I will do things I might regret later. Do I make myself clear?"

Never clearer, only this time, there was no Lizzie or Barnsie to confide in, only herself in a new room and in a new bed and with a new set of colleagues, who probably wouldn't believe her anyway. The only good bit of news came later that week when Sister Veronica told her that Cavendish had been sent to assist at a frontline regimental hospital opposite the defenses at Sebastopol. It was about as dangerous a position to be in as could possibly be imagined, and for the first time in her life, Catherine hoped that another human being would die.

Then, when the duty rosters were put up for the next week's work, came something else that seemed like a fortuitous change of scene. It was part of every nurse's routine to go down every five weeks to the kitchen and do a stint with Miss Davis. Her turn had come.

Chapter 62

On her sixth day of working in the kitchen, it occurred to Catherine that, for the first time in a long time, she felt safe, and that this was entirely due to Elizabeth Davis: she ran the kitchen with a rod of iron and was, in her own way, every bit as powerful as Dr. Cavendish.

In a world where food meant life or death, Betsy Davis, with her genius for culinary improvisations, her sudden furies, her dimpling smiles, and her astounding energy was as treasured and pampered as a goddess. They worked together, with two other orderlies, with barely a break from five-thirty in the morning to nearly midnight, when Miss Davis retired to her "room" near the kitchen: a cubbyhole with a calico curtain between her and the supplies she trusted with no one. Nobody entered her kitchen without her permission, or left without her noticing.

Fortunately, and maybe because she was from Wales, too, Davis seemed to take a shine to Catherine from the start. She told her she was a good hard worker, and that she could make a decent "Cry-am-mean" cook out of her.

Her first lesson was to show Catherine how a few onions, a scrap of cabbage, some water, and bones if you were lucky, could, with clever seasoning, make a passable soup or a stew. The stew varied according to what was available: high meat went into it and game; even, when needs must, horses and dogs, and once, in desperation, rats. Spices, of which Davis had her secret supply (she'd been a nanny once in the West Indies) were jealously guarded. Nothing was thrown away, nothing wasted.

And when kitchen staff weren't cooking, they cleaned. As far as Davis was concerned, the mucky, unpredictable world outside stopped at her window. In her kitchen, glass shone, curtains were clean and pressed, and, after fierce fights with the purveyors, she had stoves that worked, five glowing braziers, a large scrubbed table, and, best of all, food. No wonder the men fought to work down here.

Catherine, turning up for her seventh day of kitchen work, found the usual anxious crowd of pensioners and young boys standing outside the door with their bowls, pails, and tin cups, praying that when the door opened—at six-thirty sharp—Miss Davis would have no nasty shocks for them. Sometimes even this Welsh wizard could not conjure supplies out of thin air.

Inside the kitchen, the trays were neatly laid, the porridge turned and flopped with a lazy sound inside a large copper pot.

"Stir that, love, would you?" Davis handed her a wooden spoon. "There's no milk for it mind," she added. "It was sour as junket when it came and there are no greens: the bullock cart tipped over from Ballyclava, but you cut the bread up and tray up the porridge, then we'll see what's in that lot." She pointed toward four wooden crates standing in the corner, with General Hospital Balaclava written on the side.

There was a strict order for doing everything in the kitchen: at eight o'clock soldiers' breakfast, nine o'clock officers' breakfast, lunch at one. Davis had taught the orderlies punctuality the hard way: if they were late for no good reason, she refused to cook their food.

After the breakfasts had gone upstairs, Davis took off her apron, Catherine wiped the table, and, as she had done every day for the past six days, dared herself to ask the question. If anyone knew, Davis, who knew everyone in the hospital, would, which was why her heart was bumping in her chest even at the thought of it. Asking the question felt like jumping a ravine: a final thing that could in one second obliterate her.

Several times, she'd lined up the words in her mind and almost said them, but the time never quite seemed right, and even now, a quick glance at Miss Davis—focused and looking furious as she held a large chilblained finger on the tip of a knife while a pile of onions exploded into small fragments—was enough to put her off.

Around ten-thirty, when the kitchen got quieter, they both sat down for a bowl of porridge and a cup of black tea, and she almost came out with it, but then an old orderly, a stretcher-bearer, came into the room with an empty bowl. He kissed Miss Davis and called her his darling and his heart.

"Now don't you cooch up to me," she warned him with a mock blow, "see those over there?" She pointed toward the crates. "This young lady and I are going to open them this afternoon. They're gifts sent by the good people of England to nasty old men like you."

The man, cackling happily, seemed to love this ritualized abuse. She sent him off with a dried apricot and a prayer book, and when the door closed, pushed the crate toward Catherine and gave her a carving knife to cut the string.

Opening the free gifts with Miss Davis normally held all the fun of forbidden things, because in Scutari, where the boxes went to the purveyor and got lost along with boots and wooden legs and other useful things, they'd been the source of such enormous tension. Miss Nightingale had made lists of them in triplicate and kept telling the nurses that if they ever *ever* touched them they would be accused of stealing and be sent home. But, on this morning, she almost exploded with nervous tension. She *had* to ask today; next week she might be sent back to the wards. They carried on unpacking a mad assortment of goods: knitted muffettees, a box of dried peas, some bacon wrapped in brown paper, two ancient linen shirts with tide lines around their necks, the head of a doll, a smart leather case with a pair of scissors in it, a bag of tea.

"Oh, the ragman could make his fortune from this lot," said Miss Davis, throwing out a broken egg timer and a few lines of knitting. "But as far as the food is concerned, I've told Mr. Fitzgerald that unless it's actually crawling, I'll use it."

She opened the lid of the stove and stabbed around viciously, making sparks fly, and then dived again into the cartons, this time coming up with a ham and a packet of sago.

"Shall I do that, Miss Davis?" said Catherine. They were alone together at last.

"No, love, you sit there, and as I said before, call me Betsy. I can't have a Welshwoman bowing and scraping to me."

Now or never! Now or never! Ask her quickly.

"Thank you, Betsy. Betsy?"

"Yes, love."

"I want to ask you something."

"That ham will cook up lovely." Betsy's face was glowing from the stove. "All right, so it's only enough for a mouthful for most of them, but that might be the last mouthful a man will get and the sago's very soothing to the stomach cases. Innit?"

She often ended sentences with "innit," a sharp question needing no reply.

"Betsy?"

"Yes, love."

She took a deep breath.

"I'm looking for a man. A young man, a drover from Wales called—"

"Deio Jones," said Betsy.

"You know him!" Waiting for Betsy to tuck a carrot around the ham and some onions and some weevily corn, was the longest few seconds of her life.

"Yes I do. Poor love."

"Why poor love?" Her voice was trembling.

The door opened and an orderly, looking green and colicky, came in. He told Miss Davis he was very sorry but he'd been "taken bad with the runs" and would have to stop working for the morning; if someone else could take the lunches upstairs, he'd be very glad.

Waiting for Betsy to finish what she'd been saying about Deio made her believe, as she had as a child, in a real hell again, with crackling flames and the cries of the damned.

This time, she grabbed Betsy by the collar. "Betsy, please," she said. "Tell me where he is."

"Ward six I think," she said.

"What happened to him?"

"He was blowed up," said Betsy simply. "It was a horrible thing. He was a handsome lad—so how *am* I supposed to get my dinners up to the ward?" She suddenly snapped at the orderly.

"When did he come in?" she said.

"I'm not sure," said Betsy. "Was it last week or the week before? You get confused, don't you. Oh dear, you do look pale. Stay down here for a while and help me tray up the veg and then, if you want to, take some to him—although I don't think he's eating mind," she said as an afterthought.

Betsy consulted her lists; she said there were four others on ward six, the officers' ward, who hadn't had their lunches either so she could take up some ham and sago to them as well if she liked. She raced around in a daze, lifting trays and emptying soup pots, until at last Betsy handed her the tray and the covered bowls and said she could go.

The time was just before one o'clock, but it was dark as dusk outside the kitchen; there were purple shadows on the snow and a bitter wind darted through the trees. Ward Six was about two hundred yards from the hospital, up an inclined path. It was treacherous underfoot and she and the orderly kept slithering into the dirty snow on either side of the path. The wind caught the corner of her cape and flung it around; as she was wrestling it down she saw a Turkish man and his mule standing in their path blocking their way.

"Move aside, you silly bastard." The orderly directed a shaft of pure fury toward the man.

"Don't worry," she was worried the two of them would fight, "we've got time."

Her voice sounded reedy and unnatural.

"There we are, miss, he's moving now," he told her more gently, for she had started to shiver. "It's only over there."

He pointed toward a long, battered wooden hut with a plume of smoke coming from its chimney. There was a row of frozen bandages hanging on a washing line outside. When they'd reached the front door, the orderly wiped his feet ceremoniously on an old coconut mat. She stared at him blankly; what a pointless thing to do: the floor was as dirty inside as out. She could hardly breathe as they walked up a narrow corridor, smelling the sulphurous mixture of smoke and night soil. Through one door, then another, and then into a long narrow room with eight beds crammed on each side of it. Each bed was separated from the next by about two feet, and an occasional torn calico curtain to give the illusion of privacy. In this gloom she saw only dark figures huddled under bedclothes, all bathed in the same copper-colored light. There were murmurings and occasional cries of pain, and then laughter from two officers sitting in their dressing gowns playing cards, one with a smeared bandage around his eye, the other with his trouser leg pinned up.

She walked up the ward, banging her leg rather painfully on a washstand. She could hear her heart beating and felt a sour sickness in her stomach.

"I'm going off now, miss," said the orderly. "But if you see him tell him I brung you. Ash is my name." He put the tray quickly in her hand and rushed off, green-faced. She stood there, dazed, half listening to a sudden commotion in the hall and doors banging. Some new patients were being carried into the ward. She could hear one crying and saying his leg had been broken and the cries becoming more anguished as the orderlies tried to bundle him faster than he could manage.

She waited for them to pass; her tray was heavy and awkward.

"You're going to be popular." The senior orderly gave a swooning look at the food.

He led her between the beds and told her who to feed. First, the chinless wonder from the Household Cavalry who had insisted, pathetically, on laying out some tattered bits of lace and a dented sword at the end of his bed, as if these scraps of uniform would give him the dignity his body lacked. She put his bowl of food beside the bed and tried to smile. The orderly said he was not expected to last the day.

"Here's your next customer," he told her, leading her to a high-ranking Russian officer who had been captured and put in the un-healthiest bed in the room, near the latrine. He had an ugly bayonet wound on his neck and a large bloody bandage where his ear had been. She was handing him food when she heard shouts from the hall outside. The door had opened again and a new patient half dropped from his stretcher.

"Don't! Don't! Don't!" he was shouting.

The Russian refused to stop eating; he was groaning and begging her with big goggle eyes to stay. Then the orderly put his head around the calico curtain and said if she had another bowl to spare the new chap could do with it.

The Russian had fallen abruptly asleep, his mustache covered in sago. She cleaned him up, drew the curtain around his bed, and found the orderly again.

"Where is he?" she said. Her mouth was absolutely dry. "I was told to bring a dish of food for Mr. Deio Jones."

"Haven't the foggiest love," he said cheerfully. "I'm new on this ward. I'll go and see, but don't move, else I'll never find you again."

She stood and waited; it took him ten minutes to get back.

"He's over there."

He pointed to a bed in a haze of grayish smoke near the fire. She walked up to it and stopped. There was a pair of bloodstained riding boots under the bed. A thin arm, bruised and ugly, lay outside the mound of bedclothes.

"Deio," she whispered leaning over him. "Is it you?"

When he turned, she tried not to flinch. His face seemed almost entirely a beard, matted and disgusting with flecks of blood and mud in it. In the middle of the beard some black lips glistened.

"It's Catherine," she said. "I've brought you something to eat."

She watched his eyelids squeeze tight shut and the corner of his mouth tremble.

"Oh God," he said. "Catrin."

While she stood there looking at him, another ambulance party came into the ward, carrying an unconscious man on a wooden hurdle.

"Easy now," said one orderly. "Down he goes."

"Is he a goner?"

"Dunno."

The two of them bounced the hurdle up and down a few times to check. Deio glanced at them, shut his eyes, and seemed to pass out.

"Two down and one to go." The older man winked in Catherine's direction. He said his name was Jim and that she was a sight for sore eyes. She was so shocked she couldn't move.

"I know this man," she said. "That's why I'm here."

"He's been asking for someone called Catherine."

"It's me."

"Are you his wife?

"No." Tears were pouring down her face. "Who is the duty officer on this ward?"

"It's Dr. Smetheren." The orderly had a kind, beery face. "So, where'd' you know him from? Scutari?" She waved his question away, fighting for control.

"A friend," she said eventually, "from home." She was surprised to hear her own voice. "I want to stay for a while and help him."

The orderly was folding the blanket and putting it back on the stretcher.

"They often call out for someone." He gave her a quick glance. "I didn't pay it much mind."

"How long has he been here?"

"Don't have a clue, love." He consulted a chart at the end of the bed. "Let's have a look. All it says here is they found him in a ditch. He was in ward four and they moved him here today."

"But has he been seen to?"

"They must have done something, but he doesn't look very special. I'll help if I can."

She winced. The orderly had large, beefy hands. He went away and came back again with some gray lint, some brownish water in a bowl, iodine, and a pair of scissors. He put one of his big hands on top of Deio's head, and began with the other to dab away impulsively with his cloth.

"Let me do it . . . please! Please. *Stop!* . . ." She felt at that moment as though she could have shouted and screamed or gibbered quite easily.

"All right then." Jim was not offended. "Calm down. Your hands will be gentler than mine. I'll undress him from the other end, then if they find us you won't be accused of straying off the path of virtue, unless of course we meet in the middle."

Another saucy wink. His lack of sensitivity was almost a comfort. "Deio," she whispered. "Deio." She brought her face close to his eyes. His eyelashes were singed, the lids blackened and puckered with frostbite. There were shreds of flesh in his beard.

"Stay still. Stay still! I'm going to try and clean you up."

She took a deep breath and clasped her hands together, they were trembling violently.

"Still as you can," she whispered. "I'll try not to hurt you."

As she cut away the hard dirty clumps of beard around his mouth, some brightly colored bits of skin came away in her hands. Someone had been blown up beside him.

He was breathing with his mouth half open, his gums pale with shock, his pulse weak. She heard the splatter of blood on the floor as the orderly took off his socks, then they took off his breeches, which were stiff with dirt and blood.

No, no, no, no, part of her protested inwardly as the orderly wrinkled his nose and held the breeches as far away from himself as he possibly could. He said he would be back in a tick with some clean clothes, if any could be found.

"Why haven't they undressed him before?" she said.

"There's over a hundred in ward four waiting for a bed," he said. "He was one of the lucky ones."

"How bad is it?" she said, almost inaudibly.

He said, in a tactless boom, he wouldn't really know until they'd got him properly cleaned up. That everything was still there—two legs, two feet, all the other bits and pieces (another appalling wink), but there was some mucky stuff in the middle, perhaps a bayonet wound, and his feet were nasty.

"Thank you for helping," she said.

"Think nothing of it. Nice for him to wake up and see a friend."

"To see a friend . . . to see friend . . ." As she tried to untangle the grizzled beard from the bright pieces of skin, the words buzzed senselessly in her head.

"Catrin." He opened his eyes, but they swam in his head and went blank as though he had died. "What are you doing?" he whispered.

"Cleaning you up, Deio," she said in as normal a voice as she

could manage, "You've been hurt—try and lie still! I'm almost finished. There! One more bit."

"I don't want it." If he hadn't been so weak he would have
jumped out of bed.

"You'll be all right. Not as bad as we thought."

"I know." Now that the mud had gone his lips were swollen,
berry-colored. "The man next to me was blown to bits."

Looking down at him she felt nothing but a desperate sorrow.
"Poor Deio."

He didn't answer.

He opened his eyes briefly again; the slight cast in his eye, always more pronounced when he was tired or in pain, began to wander. He was looking at her so strangely.

"You have a gash on your chin," she said. "I . . . I was trying to
clean it off and put some iodine on it."

Her voice sounded meek and uncertain, as if the very sight of
him took her back to a time when she doubted almost everything
she did and wanted.

He lay still for a moment, and then felt below his bedclothes
with his hands.

"Oh my God, Catrin," he said, in the same faraway voice. "I
don't know."

"Don't know what, Deio?"

He looked at her. "I don't know," he said, his eyes glittering back
at her, unreadable, lost, and full of fever.

"Did you undress me?" He closed his eyes and cursed. "Breeches;
everything?"

"Breeches and everything!" She tried to do her auntie Gwynneth voice but it didn't come off and he was too ill.

"No, Deio, the orderly did that."

"Ouch." A stab of pain hurt him.

"Let me see where you're hurt, please."

She pulled back the bedclothes, took a deep breath and looked.
There was a diagonal cut above his belly button, about seven inches
long and still pulsing blood. His rib cage was hugely swollen; judg-
ing from the shallow breaths he took, it might be broken.

"You need a doctor, Deio."

"Um."

He gazed blearily at her—the skin around his eyes looked so painful.

"I can't take all this in, Catherine," he mumbled, "it's too funny."

He looked like a cornered animal. All she felt was terror of him dying that made her limbs feel heavy and her heart pound. They were in a black boat together, in a black sea, about to disappear over the edge of the world forever.

Chapter 63

*I*t had stopped snowing and the sky was full of pearly brightness as she ran back toward the kitchen, her shoes crackling on the snow, her coat flapping. She was panting with fear; she knew now how quickly you could die in a place like this and what Deio's best chance of life was, but the solution seemed so risky.

She had to tell someone; she knew that now, so she went down to the kitchen, sank into a chair, and told Betsy everything—or almost everything. It felt like defilement mentioning Cavendish and Deio in the same breath, but she had to.

Betsy stopped mashing her potatoes and did something unexpected: she took Catherine in her arms and hugged her. She looked at her as though she was her own, and said she'd guessed at a secret and was glad it was out because it was no sin. It had happened once or twice before at the hospital, she said, a nurse recognizing a man she knew.

"How wonderful it must be to see a familiar face when you are ill." Her plain, mannish face lit up at this thought. "Especially a girl as pretty as you."

She put a dollop of potato on a plate and carved a few slivers from the ham joint.

"So that's for your young man tonight."

"I don't know if he can eat it." Betsy's optimism was making her heart sink. "His mouth and tongue seem very swollen. He's so ill."

"Take it," said Betsy. "Show it to him, it will give him hope; pass it on if he can't eat it."

"And he's in a very strange state of mind," she blurted out.

"It felt like it was the last thing in the world he wanted, seeing me there."

"Oh, good God, what nonsense!" said Betsy. "If he hadn't wanted you, he wouldn't have called out for you—it's shock, or fever."

"In books and things, you might think it was romantic," said Catherine. "It wasn't."

"Oh, romance be buggered," said Betsy with her usual vigor. "This is a war and men can be awful silly babies about things like that, especially those who like their women to be ladies. They've never seen nurses at war before, and maybe it does feel all wrong, but he'll come round, Cath. Wash his clothes, slip him a few tidbits, he'll soon find you useful."

"Useful?" Catherine felt a moment of confusion. "Do you mean like a servant?"

"Now don't you dare talk to me like that." Betsy almost smacked her with her spoon. "You'll never keep a sweetheart if you talk like that, and when the war's over, which they say it will be soon, you'll want to go home and do what's natural for a woman. So don't stand around talking rubbish to me, that meat's getting cold. Take it up to him nice and hot, and if he can't eat it like that, cut it up small."

Walking back to his ward she tried hard not to think, she was too tired and it was all too confusing. All she knew was that he had to stay alive.

Betsy arranged time off, and for the next four days she was able to be with him in the ward. She fed him scraps of food; held water up to his swollen lips, and when he would let her, tried to brush some of the burrs and mud out of his hair, which was still surprisingly glossy as if this part of him refused to die. He drifted in and out of consciousness. Sometimes, waking and seeing her there his eyes lit up, and other times he muttered angrily as if she was responsible for this ordeal. While she watched and waited, she fed on him: his hair; the beautiful brown hands; the points of his teeth; the simple, marvelous fact of him being there and still alive.

Sitting with him, she quietly accepted her happiness and her helplessness. What if there was in the end no decision she could make, if love, this kind of love, formed when you were young and undefended had its own momentum and terrible power. You were innocent and thoughtless when it took root, and now here it was: something as simple and natural as a tree, and here it would stay, whatever she tried to do or think about it.

But she was also living on reserves of energy she did not have, and one freezing night she went to the wards, put her head, briefly, on the pillow beside his and fell asleep. She woke suddenly in the early hours, looked up and saw Cavendish looking down at both of them.

"What a pretty scene," he said.

She jumped up quickly, braced for his anger, but he was smiling in a gentle and understanding way, swaying slightly.

"I know him," she said. She forced herself to stand tall, to look him in the eye. "He's my friend."

"I can see that." He looked yellowish with fatigue in the morning light. "Heavens, you *are* nice to your friends."

"A friend from home I—" something in his expression stopped her.

"Don't." He held up his hand. "I am very, very tired and have no interest whatsoever in your . . . in your . . ." He swayed on his feet as though about to propose a toast.

"You've kitted him out nicely I see." Cavendish touched the red hat and the muffler that Betsy had given him. "Where do you find such things? Oh don't bother to tell me, I actually don't give a rat's arse. What's the matter with him?"

"I don't know yet."

"Well, we can soon find out." He was starting to sound impatient.

With a ripping sound, he drew the calico curtain around the three of them, stared down at the bed and then began to unwrap Deio's nightshirt, ignoring his weak protests. She helped him fold the woolen blanket down, saw him feel inside the wound with as much emotion as Betsy would stuff a chicken. His hand was covered in pus and blood and Deio was groaning and trying to push him away.

"Be careful!" she wanted to shout. "Don't hurt him."

"What kind of friend, I ask again, Carreg?" he said, feeling around. "Oh don't answer, I've never met a nurse yet who wasn't a . . . wasn't a . . ."

"Please don't." She looked him straight in the eye. "Not now. He was a drover. I knew him in Wales; I think he was given a commission out here, but I don't know. I haven't seen him for months."

She was trying with every ounce of her strength not to give in to the terror she felt at how much worse his wound was looking. Deio had fallen asleep again; it seemed to her that his face on the pillow grew more and more serene.

"Is he going?" She couldn't hide her panic.

"Probably. I don't know. I can feel something inside the wound, maybe shot, maybe some metal."

"Can you help him? Please help him."

He seemed to go off in a dream, focusing on a point above her head and then rocking himself backwards and forwards on his feet.

"No, I'm sorry but I can't," he said at last. "Too tired. I've been up since four this morning, and quite honestly, why should I, there are a hundred other men in this hospital I won't get around to seeing for days."

"No?"

"No. Sorry." He didn't sound a bit sorry. "Don't take this personally. I must lie down before I drop."

"In the morning then? Please. Can I at least come and ask you again?"

"You are very keen to see *me* suddenly," he grumbled. "Well, perhaps." He pushed out his lips. "Maybe."

"Thank you."

"*Thank you,*" he mimicked her. He was looking at her very strangely. "The odd thing is, Catherine, I really did want to help you."

"You can."

He shook his head. "No. Not like this"—he yawned showing all his teeth—"I'll talk to you tomorrow," he said.

When she went on the ward the next day, she could hardly believe her eyes. Though Deio could barely walk, they'd made him line up against the wall with the ambulatory patients; he was waiting for a teaspoon of the chalk, honey, and peppermint water, routinely dispensed for diarrhea. She watched him from a distance, furious with the orderlies who should never have got him up. The miserable nightshirt they'd given him only just covered his knees and was already a map of watery bloodstains. And he looked cold—cold and shriveled; he held his hands around his ribs as though to stop them bursting.

My poor love. She knew how much he'd hate to be seen like this.

She watched him make his agonizing way back to bed, and although she wanted to box the ears of the silly old pensioner who had led him there and who was now collecting the spoons, she went to him and, instead, tried to sweet-talk him into emptying the tubs in the room; the stink was so strong she guessed they'd been standing for several days. The old man, stooped and bleary with tiredness himself, said he was too busy, but if she would shave some of the men that afternoon, they could swap jobs. While she was agreeing to this, she could see, out of the corner of her eye, Deio's fingers feebly plucking at his blankets, trying unsuccessfully to pull them up. She went to him.

"Deio," she said, "did you sleep at all?"

"No." He glanced at her and carried on staring at the ceiling. His beard and hair were wet with sweat. His pillow was jumping with lice.

"Deio." She touched the tips of his fingers. "Do you know how this happened?" she asked him.

"Don't." He closed his eyes. "I can't."

The black skin around his eyes creased.

"Did you know I got a commission?" he said suddenly. "Did you know that? What a fool."

"I'd heard, Deio, and I felt proud of you. Lewis and Meg will have been, too."

"Ugh, I don't know," he mumbled. "Can't take this in, Catrin. Don't ask me questions or I'll act the girl."

"Then I won't." She would have liked to hold his hand, but felt him go away from her to some place where she wasn't wanted.

While he muttered and explained things to himself, one of the cuts on his lip cracked open and began to ooze.

She sat beside him. Nothing in her training had prepared her for the shock of seeing someone she knew in this much distress. Now she knew how quickly—a cough, a blink, a sigh, a sweet, sudden smile—it could all be over.

She glanced up to see if the orderly could see them.

"Look!" she whispered. She took the lark's wing he'd carved for her out of her bodice. She'd hung it on a piece of leather. "I wear it all the time."

"Don't." He closed his eyes again, tight.

"Your lip's bleeding," she told him. "Use this." She handed him a clean rag from her apron pocket

"I'm sorry," he said suddenly.

"What about?"

"I wish I'd understood . . . Now I can't."

"Can't what?" She watched him swipe away at his chin. "Oh for God's sake, Deio, please let me do that, I've brought you some food. Try and eat some."

He ignored her.

"Catherine." His hand was burning in hers. "I've never felt so strange." He gave her a sudden smile of inspiration. "I saw the Water Horse."

"Listen, you silly bugger." Her lips were at his ear, and she was whispering, fiercely. "Hold on! Please hold on!"

There was a rattle of wind across the roof and the entire flimsy hut shook like a piece of paper. The man in the next bed sat up like a ghost, looked at them, and lay down again.

"Deio, I've brought you some food; if you don't eat it I'm going to wallop you one."

"Too tired. I'm too tired."

She poked a tiny morsel of ham between his lips, wincing at the pain it evidently caused him. The cast in his eye was wandering wildly. She talked to keep the thread of life from snapping.

"What was the name of your first pony, Deio? Come on, remember! Come on."

"Gray Dawn, twelve hand, fast."

"How did you first learn to ride a horse, Deio?"

"Always, always . . ." he murmured.

"Not true. You had to gallop for the first time, jump for the first time."

"Why are you here? You should never have come," he said.

"Damn you, Deio." For a moment she was a furious little girl again, about to brain him with her whip. "Don't you dare go to sleep. I'm here because I damn well want to be. I wanted to try things for myself, to see if I could do this."

The man in the next bed was calling for her. She rested his head in a more comfortable position and tucked his blankets around him.

The wind rattled the doors again, moving the stench of the latrine tubs around the ward. She went back to Deio's bed and, while he was asleep, did what she'd dreaded doing all morning and pulled up his nightshirt. She listened to his chest, she looked at his belly. She could smell the coppery odor of his blood; feel the heat coming off his chest wound. The skin around the wound was a dark red and angrily inflamed, and it was so deep she could see the faint pulsations of his lungs breathing. She thought of her mother; of herself, standing by the window in her white dress watching her bleed. *Tell me what to do.* And she still didn't know. The dark wave was coming again; waiting to fall.

She went back to the kitchen where Betsy was standing by a new wooden crate. "Idiots!" she said. "They sent a cartload of wooden legs this morning and more winter boots than we'll ever need. If we'd had those boots three months ago we could've had a bonfire of these." She was waving the wooden leg around her head, when she saw Catherine's face.

"What's happened?" she said. She pulled out a chair and pushed her in it.

"He's dying," she said. "He has a fever. He's stopped talking. I think his lungs will give out."

"Oh God," said Betsy, "poor love, you go back to him and cooch him, we can manage; just stack them boots for me in the scullery before you go."

"Betsy. There's something inside his wound. He needs an

operation to get it out. If you were in my shoes, who would you get to do it?"

Davis moved her lips around with her tongue while she thought.

"Last month I would have said Meredith, he was the best, but Stead is good and so is Carter, but he's at the front. I think I'd have to say your friend Dr. Cavendish for the simple reason that he's here and you know him."

"He knows about me and Deio, will that make a difference?"

"I don't think so . . . I don't know . . ." It was the first time she'd ever heard Betsy sound unsure about anything. "I mean, we're all of us a bit peculiar at the moment, so maybe he's not such a bad man."

Catherine gave a low moan. "Do you think he's the best doctor? Tell me the truth now."

"I do." Betsy turned away, shook her head and sighed. "You'd better let them men in," she said, "before we have a mutiny on our hands."

She had nothing more to say about an impossible situation.

Lunch was a thin onion and goat stew; its dispatching and clearing up seemed endless, but Betsy had told her to wait, because if Catherine thought it would help for her to talk to Cavendish, she would. She said he would listen to her, and if he didn't, she would threaten to starve or poison him, simple as that.

Catherine tried to smile but she couldn't. She sensed there would only be one chance to ask him the question and that the way they asked it would be of paramount importance. She made a conscious effort to check her usual impulsive nature and think of him objectively: to read him without emotion as one might try and read an unpredictable animal. His bad temper must always be reckoned with, those moments when his rocklike face darkened and his eyes blanked, but then she remembered the almost old-womanish care with which he had wrapped her in her cloak in Constantinople.

She tried to think dispassionately of his better qualities: the deftness of his hands, the single-minded care with which he carried out even the most mundane of his medical duties. Cruel, controlling, professional, fastidious, which part could you rely on? He was definitely a fight animal, dominant and resourceful, determined to stamp himself on any situation, but did that make him a bad surgeon?

She thought about it off and on all morning and decided there was nothing constant about his nature except his vanity. The glances he'd given her over his patients—*Aren't I the clever one;* his self-conscious habit of smoothing his whiskers; she'd even seen him checking his own reflection in a knife in that hotel in Constantinople. He was a man who at all times preferred an audience, even if it was only himself.

At the end of the afternoon, Betsy returned with the news that he was on duty that night. "They've been told to put no more patients on his list. He's full up to the eyeballs."

"Betsy." She had decided. "Thank you for offering to see him, but I must do this myself. Then if he says no, I will only have myself to blame."

Betsy, who was as unshockable as Barnsie when it came to men and their ways, put her hands on Catherine's shoulders, and then pushed her away, considering.

"If you go, you must make the most of it. Go away and wash your face and brush your hair, and when you get there, be nice, be sweet—look, put a dab of this on." She got out the bottle of rosewater a Turkish man had given her to flavor her junkets. She put it behind Catherine's ears and on her pale wrists.

"Good luck, love."

Half an hour later, she was outside his hut. He opened the door in his shirtsleeves and slippers. Behind him, she caught a glimpse of a cluttered table; the bones of a fish on a dirty plate.

"Nurse Carreg. Come in. What a charming surprise—no, don't worry about your boots."

He took off his slippers and put a jacket on. "I'm afraid I have no servant at the moment," he said. "It's a bit of a shambles."

As he swept a chairful of books and clothes aside, a case of medical implements clattered onto the floor.

"Ooops," he said looking at her. "I should be more careful."

She'd expected arrogance, anger even, but it was clear from the jerky speed with which he buttoned his jacket that he was nervous, also, from the hopeful gleam in his eye, that he wanted her still. Deio's early training had made her sensitive to human and animal signals. If he'd been a horse, you might say he had stopped his posturing, was confused to see her here, but was bending an ear toward her and was ready to be caught.

How awful, but how helpful, too. She took a deep breath.

"Are you well, Dr. Cavendish?"

"No, exhausted since you ask, and you?" He gave one of his bright, insincere smiles.

"Moderately so."

"Moderately well or moderately exhausted?"

"Moderately well, or as well as anybody can be here at the moment," she said.

"This war is hell," he countered pleasantly. "Far worse than Waterloo I hear, but they say it will be over soon."

He was watching her as carefully as she watched him. She could see his unmade bed in the corner of the room; the jumble of muddy boots underneath it. She breathed the staleness of his air, his dirty clothes, his socks.

"The reason it's so untidy," he was drawling now in a slightly affected way, "is I had to fire my man this morning; I found him drinking my brandy. Actually, I'm getting rather sick of all kinds of people here for letting me down."

"I've been thinking about that," she said. "About how very different things are in a war. You think people are one thing, and they are very much the other—or can be."

"Yes. I'm glad you're coming round to that way of thinking."

He nodded his head toward her and put up his hands. "You're quite bright for a nurse," he said jauntily, then whispered. "I'm ready to forgive you, Catherine."

She couldn't do it.

"I've not come to say I'm sorry, but to see you and to ask a very great favor of you."

"Ah."

He sat down opposite her, his legs spread-eagled.

"Oh! *She* wants a favor of *me*." He opened his mouth wide to show how cheeky this sounded.

"My friend in ward six, Deio Jones, did you have time to think about him? He's very ill."

"And a diagnostician now as well." His eyes were sparkling.

"You saw him. You know. Would you consider putting him on your list?"

"Why should I?" He put his legs up against an unlit stove and made an important face.

"I feel he may die without it."

She heard the popping of his oil lamp.

"The first answer that comes to mind is very much no," he said at last. "I can't. They're stacked up there like sardines. I'm a week behind at least."

"Please."

"Why should I?"

"He is someone I knew as a child, a friend of my family. Please." He was waiting for more. "And," she lowered her voice and forced herself to look at him, "I want you to."

"Ooohhhh." He pretended to be frightened. "She *wants* me to. Do you know you were very rude to me before you left Scutari? Come over here and sit on my knee—I should put you over it—can't hear you at all over there."

She felt a complete revolt of her nervous system as she sat on his knee. There was a piece of food still in the corner of his mouth, and though his lips smiled, his eyes only looked at her.

"Would you like a drink, Catherine?" he said. "That little bastard did leave a little brandy."

"No, thank you. I don't have much time."

"Oh," he grumbled. "I thought all nursies liked a little drop."

God, how she wanted to strike him.

"If you do the operation"—she made herself look at him again—"I would like to be your assistant. I know you are a very fine surgeon and I could learn a great deal from you."

"I haven't said I'm doing it." He was tapping her waist with his fingers.

"This man needs your help. I think he might die tonight without it." Her voice trembled, but there was no change in his expression.

"Ah—" He bit at the quick of his nail and rubbed his nose. "I am on duty in twenty minutes time," he said. "But I've got a good idea. Do you see these?" He held up the first three fingers of his right hand and waggled them. "You were right to come to me, because they are clever hands and do you know what they'd like to do now?"

He shifted her weight on his knee and she tried to stand up, but he held her down.

"This." She felt one of his hands slither, cold and dry as autumn leaves up her petticoat and under the leg of her bloomers. "And this."

His voice was calm as he drew aside her apron, and then, grumbling at the amount of material in her uniform, he took her breast and squeezed it hard, all the while staring at her, daring her to cry out. "And this . . ."

She was sweating with the effort of concealing how deeply she loathed and despised him at this moment. The same doglike expression as before crept over his face as he rubbed himself against her, the same harsh breathing and sharp cry and sudden dopey look when he was finished. It was over in a few minutes. He said he wished he had more time.

While it was happening, she closed her eyes and wished she could die and never ever remember this again. But at least, she reasoned, as she straightened her uniform and tried not to cry, he hadn't tried to penetrate her, or even to kiss her.

The light in his room was already breaking up and cloaking its corners in shadows. It seemed she was free to go now; he was getting dressed, grumbling again, and looking for his instruments: his needles, his knives his sutures. He was not quite finished with her. He did want a kiss—a wet, fishy-tasting kiss, a mouthful of damp whiskers. *Please, God. Please, Deio, forgive me for this.*

She took herself to the chair on the far side of the fireplace. She sat, a frozen statue, while he drank a small glass of brandy.

"All right," he said at last. "I'll do it tonight."

Chapter 64

He was unconscious when they went to collect him later that night. Two pensioners bundled him on a hurdle; they told her to pick up his blankets and follow behind. They gossiped as they wove around the corridors: about the war and the Russian patient, who they agreed was a surly bleeder considering how nice they were being to him, and about who was operating that day. As they left the ward, they bumped him hard on the doorjamb; then they took him out of the hut and into a biting wind.

A misty moon lit up the squalid collection of hospital buildings and the half mile or so of path that lay between them and the operating theater. It was bitterly cold and, as they slithered and slipped up paths treacherous with mud and half-melted snow, they saw that day's crop of rotting corpses, some left in stinking piles on the ground, others stuffed unceremoniously into a bullock cart.

The blankets kept sliding off Deio. He looked so pale that if his teeth hadn't been chattering like castanets she would have feared him already dead. She tucked the blankets around him and felt his pulse, which was faint. "Hold on," she whispered, "you must hold on." He gave no indication that he'd heard.

It was ten o'clock by the time they reached the operating hut. A soldier with a gun told them they'd have to wait outside. The surgeons, he said, had been going since early morning and would be working all night. They waited for what felt like an age in the freezing moonlight, then the front door opened and they had to stand for more than an hour in a corridor smelling like an abattoir. Here, men were stacked in stretchers and on the floor and she had to close her ears to their requests. For water or extra blankets or medicines. It was her first time in the operating theater and it seemed to her like the outer reaches of hell: a hospital with desperate patients and practically no staff, operating in a sea of mud in the middle of a freezing night, and with the barest minimum of supplies.

She could not believe the quiet patience of the men around her. The man next to Deio had a fearful head injury. His eyes flicked back and forth as though he wanted to flee, but he managed a polite smile and a greeting to her. Others lay absolutely still with their severed legs, or partly missing stomachs, torn ears, and mashed heads. An orderly was holding a candle and reading to a young man with half his hand gone and the rest wrapped in a filthy bandage.

The Lord is my shepherd. I shall not want. He maketh me to lie down in green pastures: he leadeth me beside the still waters.

While he read, the queue shuffled slowly toward the end of the corridor where a sliver of light showed from beneath a closed door. When the door opened, everyone looked at one another: *Is it you now? Is it me?* and watched another body being taken in to murmurs of "God bless," and "Good luck, mate." And when the door closed again, the entire line of waiting men listened intently, either to the silence—for apart from the groans and murmurs it was very, very quiet—or to the sounds of sawing and swearing and occasional brusque shouts from behind the door. The orderly told her Cavendish was doing three amputations that night.

The door opened again. "Next!" called the orderly. An emaciated boy clutching a haversack with a hare's paw sticking out of it, moved up beside them. "We won't be long now will we, miss?" he asked her.

"No," she said, trying to smile, "not long now. Where are you from?"

He told her in a speedy gabble about his home in Kent, his mother, his girl named Marjorie.

"Move up!" The orderly pointed and waved him forward. "You're next."

The door opened and Dr. Cavendish appeared, gaunt and hollow-eyed and covered in blood up to his elbows.

"You can come in now yourself, Nurse Carreg," he said. "I think you'll find this an interesting case."

The orderlies gave her an odd look, and she hated leaving Deio, who was fast asleep, but she had no choice. She followed the boy into the operating room. It was a cramped space—about twenty feet by twelve—hot after the freezing corridor and bathed in a greenish, coppery light from five hanging lanterns. Her boots sank into about two feet of soft sawdust impregnated with blood; and the heat of the room seemed to cook its rank odors of living and dying flesh to a point where it was so sweet and rich and bad and dreadful, that it was almost impossible not to vomit.

In the middle of the room was a rough table, covered in blood-stained sheets and a careless jumble of bloody instruments: knives, probes, saws, needles. A wooden crate underneath was filled to the brim with amputated limbs, human parts arranged with as much ceremony as dogs' bones. She felt her mouth fill with liquid and only with the greatest effort did she stop herself from fainting.

When the room swung back into focus, she saw Cavendish standing over the boy.

"Come over here, Nurse Carreg, it's an interesting case."

The thin boy, who was having his jacket removed by an orderly, lay on the table, rigid with fright. His hands had to be prised from his haversack and his hare's paw. They held the chloroform rag over his face, and then Cavendish got a laugh by picking up a knife, neatly lopping the mascot's paw in two and dropping both parts into the basket under the table.

"I can't resist," he said, and two orderlies tittered obediently. His eyes looked huge and exhausted.

Out in the corridor, one of the stretcher-bearers had told her Cavendish was the man he'd choose if, God forbid, he had to have his leg off. The ratio of men to medics, he said, was now one doctor to one hundred men. Kimberly, the other surgeon on duty, was "a nice man but a numbskull" who was learning on the job, with agonizing consequences. Before the war he'd been the kind of village apothecary for whom the setting of a bone was a medical emergency—the men begged not to have him.

The boy, awake again, trained his petrified eyes on Cavendish as if they would never leave him.

"Damn," said Cavendish, "another bad batch of chloroform—is this your friend by the by? I can't remember what he looks like."

"He's outside," she said.

"Oh, I saw you talking to him and thought this was the one. That was why I said he was interesting." She shook her head at him, how could he play games with her at a time like this?

"We'll have yours in next."

"He's not mine," she said.

"Well, he's next." She felt her body go rigid and cold. Should she try and convince him again that Deio was nothing more than a family friend? And if she did, what difference would it make? He was bending over the boy now, totally absorbed in the messy wound he found on the boy's upper thigh. Straightening up, he told the boy that he wasn't going to operate after all because there was about a quart of maggots in his wounds and that they would do the job of cleaning up better than he could. He could go away, have a good night's sleep, and hope for the best.

The boy's face went slack with relief. Tears came into his eyes. "God bless your eyes, sir," he said. "I was prepared for the worst."

Cavendish's strange, blank eyes swept over the boy, and she longed to be able to read his mind. When he was working, everything about him—his strutting walk, his brusque voice, his manner—seemed less offensive, less self-conscious. He was a professional. Now he yawned and said, "Well, good luck, sir," and then, in his barking voice, "send in the next one."

"Stay here," he ordered Catherine. "The men will bring him in," and stood beside her, waiting.

Deio's hurdle was moving through the door. His eyes were tightly shut, and his face beneath his glossy black hair wore a look of strained anguish. The wound had bled again and stuck to his nightshirt. When they'd tipped him onto the table, Sister Clara was told to cut the nightshirt off.

"Deio Jones, Thirteenth Hussars, sir." The orderly ticked him off his list.

Cavendish looked at her briefly and then, holding a candle high, looked down at Deio. He rarely spoke when he worked, and apart from the tinkle of an orderly arranging the surgical tools, the room was silent. She heard him take a breath, and he put his hands on Deio's stomach, a young man's belly, hard and brown where it wasn't torn and bruised. He felt the whole area with his fingertips.

"Broken ribs," he murmured, "seventh, possibly eighth." Deio gave a gasp of pain and tried to push him away, but an orderly held him down. "Lie still, sir," snapped Cavendish. "Bayonet wound; query gunshot wound near spine. He's lucky not to be paralyzed," he said to her. Deio was deeply asleep again, and deathly pale.

"Those lamps are hopeless," he grumbled, and told her to bring the candle closer. "I can't see a thing in this."

She rushed to get the candle; under its flickering light she saw that part of the wound had split and was leaking blood.

His fingers probed for the track of the bullet. "Lacerations to abdomen caused by Christ knows what. I'll work on the spine first, but I'll need help to turn him over."

The old orderly gripped Deio's arm.

"Be careful!" The words were out before she knew she'd said them.

"It's her friend," said Cavendish. "She's going up in the world."

His eyes met hers over Deio's exposed belly and the other medical staff smirked as they did at any banal joke that came out of his mouth. She didn't care; every atom of her being craved for his fingers to be careful. He was frowning again, deciding what to do.

There was a popping sound from a lamp. She could feel her body wet with sweat, but struggled to look calm; Deio's life depended on it. Cavendish was usually decisive but tonight he was fiddling, first picking up a curved knife from a bowl of rusty water, then a straight one; he stared at it. Then, at last, "The narrow probe," he told the orderly. "It's second from the left in my case."

Deio's legs were starting to twitch and he was groaning. His lips, were pale with shock; his stomach wound oozed brackish blood. Catherine wiped his lips with vinegar and water; she looked at Cavendish and felt herself close to pleading with him.

"We need more charcoal for that fire." Cavendish was holding the wound together now, his hands covered in Deio's blood.

"This won't take long," he told them. "I'll get that bullet out and then do the ribs. Nurse Carreg"—he nodded toward the chloroform bottle—"a small amount on the rag, please.

"You'll feel drowsy, and then you'll fall asleep," he told Deio. He took the bottle from her hand. *All good surgeons need a touch of the murderer in them,* he'd told her once.

"Here, let me do this. A friend," he asked pleasantly under his breath, "what sort of friend?"

The pensioner orderly was out of earshot; an exhausted Sister Clara sat like a broken puppet in the corner.

"He's a neighbor from home," she told him. The rag was soaking up the green liquid. "Nothing more."

"Are you sure?" His voice was a playful whisper. "When I asked you before you wouldn't say."

"Please don't do this."

"Why not?"

"You know."

"No, I don't. I wish I did."

"Please go on, you're better than the others at this."

His great big, exhausted, blank eyes swept over her and he suddenly smiled, sincerely and warmly. "I'm very tired though; I don't know how I've got so tired."

"But the good thing is you go on working, and your work is good. Finish the operation and I'll come round; I'll tuck you in." She added, "Thank you for doing this."

It nearly killed her to say it, but time was running out for all of them.

The orderly was now looking strangely at them, something had to be done. As Cavendish held the chloroform over Deio's face, she inhaled the dense perfumey smell and saw Deio's face become white and clammy. His breathing became deeper and more even and, for a moment as she watched, she died with him.

"I'm glad it worked," Cavendish said to one of the orderlies. "The new lot is about as useful as shit." She heard their voices as though from a distance, coming and going. When Deio was sound asleep Cavendish, who had stopped to light up one of his cigars, put it out. He adjusted the lanterns and swiftly felt along the tracks of the bullet, first with his probe then with the tip of his index finger. As he flipped the mucus- and blood-covered bullet out, it bounced along the floor and was caught in the corner by the orderly.

"Howzat?" he said. "That's a good one, sir."

His teeth bared under the lights and he gave her a little wink. Then, when he'd checked there was no other bullet, he took a curved knife, laid it against Deio's belly, and sliced off a piece of rotten flesh, staunching the blood as he did so with a bundle of rags. He took the needle he kept in the lapel of his frockcoat, got her to thread it, and sutured the jagged wound, working deep through the skin and cellular tissue. The surrounding abrasions were treated with a lint dressing doused in vinegar. Finally, he looked at Deio's ribs again, which, after careful manipulation, he bandaged. The relief when he stopped, looked up, and said, "It's done," was so great she almost fainted. "The fractures," he said, "are quite straightforward, but it's important to check the tension of the bandage tomorrow."

"Deio! Deio," Sister Clara was gently tapping his face, "you've had your operation, you can wake up now."

"Catrin," he murmured, "Catrin," and went to sleep again.

"That's nice." Cavendish lit his cigar. "He remembers you."

Chapter 65

After the operation she went outside with the stretcher-bearers. A man with a thin gray horse was waiting. He said his name was Arkwright.

"Is he going to be all right?" he asked anxiously.

"I think so." He said he was Deio's friend, and could take him back to his hut if he was well enough to travel.

She asked the two stretcher-bearers to wait for a moment, then asked what kind of hut and how far away?

"A tidy one," he said. "Bring him home."

To her surprise, the stretcher men agreed, saying an officer could do what he liked, and that he'd probably be better off in his own hut than in hospital anyway. She asked him to guard Deio for as long as it took her to get back to the hospital and collect her things.

Running back to the kitchen through a clear and starry night, she was aware of an immense sense of relief, of an exultation so strong she felt she could fly. Deio was alive; he hadn't died. She could hear herself gasping with joy.

In the nurses' quarters, she crept around in the half light, taking some money—twenty pounds—from the loose floorboard under the bed where she had hidden it in a tin. She put on as many clothes as she could wear, bundling the rest into a carpetbag, and went barefoot downstairs, her boots in her hand, to slip a note under the kitchen door for Betsy. She'd made up her mind now: Deio was safer away from the hospital, and so was she.

*   *   *

When she got back to Deio, Arkwright and the stretcher-bearers had wrapped him in four blankets like a mummy and covered him with a tarpaulin. All you could see was his hat, pulled down to his nose, his lips already purpling with cold.

They set off toward the hills. It was hard going under foot with the track rutted and colandered with shot-craters, and deathly cold; every now and then a tree unloaded a packet of snow down her collar. Arkwright told her to get in the cart with Deio, but the horse, a shambling collection of articulated bones in the moonlight, looked so exhausted that she chose to walk behind him. She thought of hanging on to his tail, but it was so gnawed and pathetic, she feared it could be pulled off as easily as a rag doll's arms.

Halfway up the slope, the horse stopped, its head nearly on the ground. It was gasping for breath. She kneaded its neck and thanked it for trying so hard. Then she saw with a terrible sense of foreboding, the white snip between its eyes.

"Moonshine." Hearing his groan, made the tears pour down her face. "What's happened to you?" She pulled at his freezing ears; let him rest for a while in her hands, then she went back to check on Deio, tucking his hands deeper under the blankets.

His lips were bluer now, and his teeth chattering. There wasn't much time.

She thanked God that dawn was coming—it was creeping over the horizon, lighting up inky puddles and trees—and that soon the temperature would rise. In the distance, Balaclava Harbor was a vaporous pot of silver and blue light.

"How much farther?" she asked Arkwright. They'd already been out in this deadly weather for over an hour.

He pointed vaguely toward the hill ahead of them. "The other side of that," he said. "Not far if nothing happens."

Her ears rang with the cold and her feet were soaking blocks of ice. She knew this was a risk, too. The hospital was dirty, and Deio's position there precarious, but this was cold, too cold.

He should have been coming around now from the chloroform

but he'd only opened his eyes once, when the cartwheel jammed in a rut, and she'd seen a brief blink, the gleam of his irises in the moonlight. He'd gone straight back to sleep again.

They came to the top of the hill and then, going down on the other side, she had to run so fast to keep up, she got drenched in muddy water. Finally, she saw a line of muddy tents, where a few men were moving around in the early dawn. One was stropping his razor; others just lay there smoking their pipes and looking at them. About a quarter of a mile past the tents, the cart stopped outside a modest log cabin. It was built into a hillside with a makeshift corral outside.

"Here we are," said Arkwright. "Home sweet home."

She saw the silhouettes of four horses, munching from frozen hay nets. When they whickered at Moonshine, he looked back blankly. He was exhausted; they all were.

They lifted Deio, a frozen bundle of blankets, from the cart into the shadowy hut. Arkwright, who hadn't said more than two words to her on the way up, told her there was a stove inside; when they'd got Deio into bed, he'd light it for them. He came back with some wood, a little pile of charcoal, and some tongs and laid a fire. She unwrapped Deio from his crunchy-sounding shroud and put him to bed. Arkwright blew on the fire; he showed her the container where the water was and a small side room behind a torn blue and white curtain; he said there was a mattress there she could sleep on.

Before he left, he mashed his forage hat in his hands and looked at her with his large, appalled eyes.

"Will he like— Will he— Is he all right?"

"I'm hopeful" was all she could say.

He said nothing. He seemed fresh out of hope.

Deio's bed was in the corner of the room, flush up against raw planks of wood stuck together with daubing. It had a collection of goat and sheepskins on top of it, some saddles and a gun underneath. It was wide enough for two, so, when Arkwright was gone, she took off her cloak, lay down beside Deio and fell asleep, still wearing her boots.

She'd never slept like that before, and never did again. It was like falling through a gap in time into some place of vast pillowy ease, for ten, then eleven, then twelve hours. Deep and sweet and hungry.

When she woke at three the next afternoon, she had a thumping headache and Deio was staring at her.

And then he slept again and while he did, she crept around the hut. She poked at the fire, which had gone out, then sat in a chair and looked at him. He was still deathly pale and had lost a lot of weight. He almost looked like a stranger with his odd expression and all that wild hair poking out of the red hat, and his beard still matted. She suddenly realized she was frightened of him—and of herself. What had she agreed to by being here?

To stop herself panicking, she got up and made an inventory of the hut so she could decide what she needed to bring back from the hospital.

Behind the curtain, she found a collection of cooking pots, a large skillet, some flour, a glass jar full of tea, some dried peas, a jar of nails, and some molasses, all carefully stored in a wooden box and with a rat trap nearby.

On the floor beside the mattress were some blankets and dirty shirts, a whip, a pair of cracked but well-oiled riding boots stuffed with paper, and some gaiters, so stiff with horse sweat they stood on their own.

The sight of his uniform hanging on the wall above his bed disturbed her. How unreal it seemed: those bits of braid, the cherry-colored jacket, blotched here and there with mud and blood, the gold epaulettes. Nothing to do with him really. Her wild boy with one foot permanently out the door.

Her own uniform was still soaked with the fear she'd felt during the operation. The ugly dress with its crude sash had been her mirror. Wearing it, she'd seen every bad thing about herself—her vanity, her snobbery, her cowardice, her weak moral character—for surely, and this must be faced soon, she had used herself to lure Cavendish, even to trick him.

She had to cling to simple thoughts about herself. She could make a proper fire. She would melt some snow and make some tea.

She would clean him up, and steel herself to look at him again carefully and dispassionately. If he needed to go back to the hospital, she would take him.

The fire roared into life in a crackle of flames. While she was putting water on to boil she saw, above her head, a squirrel and a couple of rabbits hanging from a hook in the ceiling. She'd skin them later and paunch them. "At least I'm useful now," she thought with bleak satisfaction. "I know what I'm for."

When the tea was made, she took off her boots, worn for the past twenty-four hours, and put her wet and purpling feet in the rest of the water. Wonderful! She soaked them, dried them, and put on a pair of Deio's clean socks.

During her search for socks, she found, in his saddlebag, an oval pebble she'd picked up years ago on the beach at Whistling Sands. She'd painted a wobbly version of Gray Dawn's face on it. He'd kept it.

He rolled over, groaning a little; she flew to his side. He'd wet his bed. She didn't want to shift him in case she burst his wounds, so she packed some towels around him, and wedged him against the walls with two sandbags. His color was a little better, but he still looked shriveled, much older. She wanted him awake soon and walking around.

After she'd washed her feet and made tea and set about preparations for dinner, she was shocked to find herself slightly at a loose end. Everything was so quiet now and she'd been so very busy. She wondered if it would be possible ever really to go home again now, to a house with only one or two other people in it, to a family.

This thought made her angry. How impossible she was: she'd only just found him again and she was already a little bit homesick for friends like Barnsie, Sam, and Betsy, for their company as well as their moral support. She'd never had friends like these; people you could tell anything to because you'd shared so much. Could one person ever replace all that?

She shivered and shook her head. Why was nothing in life ever really clear-cut and straightforward once you thought it through?

Finding what you wanted, what you were for, was the hardest question of all—you had to meet it head-on, make some mistakes and some hard choices, and then, perhaps, if you were very lucky, you might understand in the end why you made the decisions you did. No wonder Eleri had said it was a life's work.

She opened the door and stepped outside. The light was fading, but there was still a faint golden sheen as if there had been sun during the day. Craning her eyes, she looked toward the distant hills and the harbor, romantically shrouded in a veil of pink light. Betsy had told her what a pretty place this was before the war began; seeing it like this you could almost believe her.

Then Arkwright appeared again, shambling shamefaced through the door with a piece of foreign-looking bread and some goat's cheese for her. She was starving and wolfed it down. He said if she needed to go back to the hospital for a while, he would sit with Deio.

"Do you feed the horses?" she asked him.

"I do, miss," he said. "When we've got forage."

"Can I groom Moonshine when I get back? I like the horses."

"If you like, miss."

She wondered why every time she mentioned the horses, he looked like a whipped dog.

Before she left, she boiled some more water, found some salt in the supplies box, and, lifting Deio's nightshirt, looked carefully at his wounds. The circle of skin around his broken ribs was still black and blue; the stomach wound was leaking blood and pus, but Cavendish's neat stitches were still in place, regular and perfect.

What a mystery Cavendish was: lifesaver, perfectionist, bully, and liar. Her mother had once instructed her never to use the word "hate." "Such a strong, ugly word dear, say, 'don't like very much,' or 'dislike.'"

But no, only hate would do for now. Apart from what he had done for Deio, she *hated him*. His soft voice, his creeping hands, the memory of her head jammed between the railings of a bed in Constantinople.

Now she knew that if Deio and she were to have a chance, she had to face up to Cavendish, or else be his quarry for the rest of her time here. Every time the door knocked, she'd expect him. When she drew the curtains she'd see his blank eyes staring in. But *no more*. She'd made up her mind now. Tomorrow, she would go down to the hospital and would ask to see him. She would thank him sincerely from the bottom of her heart for treating Deio, and then she would threaten to blow his head off if he ever tried to touch her again.

On the wall above the table was a gun-rack holding a rifle and what she recognized as Deio's prized Minie.

"Mr. Arkwright," she said, "would that be too heavy for me?"

"No," he said. "But he won't let you borrow it."

"Well, he won't know," she said. "Unless you tell him."

He actually smiled. "So, are *you* going to join up now?"

"I might do," she said, and smiled back.

When she finally got back to the hospital, a week later, Betsy told her Cavendish had gone to a hospital station near the Fifth Redoubt, so she never had to point that gun. She was so flooded with relief, she had to sit down. She'd been dreaming about him, horrible dreams, for nights on end. In one, he was drinking water from a canteen when a bullet went straight through the canteen and into his jaw. She kept seeing him coming toward her smiling—that rocklike face all mashed up and wanting a kiss. So now there was a new flaw in her nature to consider: she hoped he would stay there, even die there, although she wasn't sure she was prepared to go that far.

"Good God, woman," Betsy had said, when she'd arrived back and was sitting in the kitchen. "You look terrible. I hope you're not thinking of coming back to work yet."

Catherine asked if it might be possible to go to Deio at night, but to work at the hospital during the days. Other women did it and spring was coming, so it might be.

"Catherine"—Betsy put both hands on her stout waist—"you may have a fight on your hands with Miss Weare."

"I know."

"But the war *is* winding down, and spring *is* coming, and my guess is they'd rather have you on those terms than not have you at all. But here's a question: How long since you had a day off?"

"Not for over a year. Longer if you count my training at the governesses' home."

"Well then, it may not be a big problem, because you're owed leave. Do you love him?"

She slipped the question in so quickly it caught her off guard.

"Goodness Betsy, I . . . I . . ."

"Well then, that's fine then," said Betsy serenely. "Isn't it?"

She took the rest of her clothes back to the hut, including the breeches Deio had given her what seemed like years ago. On her second morning there, she found a sack of bran for the horses. She boiled it, bulked it out with some cooked split peas and bread—beggars couldn't be choosers—and took the whole mess out in a steaming bucket to the five horses, watching with satisfaction while they scoffed it down. Moonshine ate so fast that some food got stuck in his throat; he choked and spat helplessly for several minutes before gobbling it up again with pathetic groans of pleasure. He and the others licked their bowls so clean they shone.

With a dandy brush from Deio's kit she brushed Moonshine's neck, belly, flanks, and rump, marveling at the amount of mud and sweat that could stick to a horse. He lapped up the attention, butting her with his hollow-eyed head, and pointing with his nose to the bits on his side where he itched. She curry-combed his tail, dunked it in a warm bowl of water, rinsed it, and rubbed it dry. Last, she picked out his feet, and then gave him what he loved most, a head rub between the eyes. Half an hour later, she was covered in grime but he looked halfway presentable. She felt peaceful for the first time in a long time.

Little by little, and without really discussing it, they settled into a routine together. Every morning she rode Moonshine up a hill toward the small stream that flowed down the hill to the east of their hut. Along with Deio's nightshirts and bedlinen, she took her old clothes—the blue-sprigged dress still smelling faintly of citronella, the awful black dress that Gwynneth had given her—and she washed them with Deio's things. If the water was too cold, she carried it back to the hut and did the clothes there.

And then, one morning, two weeks after she'd come, she was packing the soap and the dirty clothes into her pannier when a robin came and sat on the posts of the small veranda outside their hut and sang. Later, while she was washing, she saw a lark singing above her head in a tree peppered and scarred with shotgun bullets.

Spring had crept up on them and caught them by surprise. Now you saw it, it was everywhere: a clump of violets poking around the sandbags, some small, pink flowers beside the track. She rushed back home to tell him, said they should think about making a garden on the flat bit of land between the corral and the hut. He smiled politely at her and said that sounded like a good idea, but he thought the ground was still too hard, and also, how much longer would she be here?

Trying hard not to cry, she unbuttoned his shirt and bathed his wounds. Being young and fit, he'd healed remarkably well considering. The angry skin around the sutures had already faded to a dark pink, and although the swelling around his ribs had gone down, she warned him it would be six weeks at least before they were properly healed. He thanked her as usual, but still, things were not going as she'd planned. He was so quiet with her. He was now well enough to get up, and would walk around for a monosyllabic hour, but she often wondered whether he wanted her there at all.

Being by nature impatient, she found this hard on the nerves, but she knew better than to try and force the pace. She had to sit and pay attention, try and learn him again. It seemed the only thing she could do now. There was life as it was, and life as you wanted it to be. This was life as it was. She didn't even know yet what had happened to him, only that it had been bad, and that he'd smashed through the invisible safety net that the young and careless carry with them, and was in pieces. This hut was no love nest; it was more like a lair where two hurt animals must rest and lick their wounds and wait.

She knew it. She knew it. But here she was—such a fool!—sitting beside him in her blue dress, daring to hope again.

One afternoon when she had got back from her shift at the hospital, Arkwright and Deio jumped up in a guilty way when she walked into the hut. Around them were saddlebags, sleeping gear, a water container, and some rolled-up tarps.

"What's going on?" she said.

Arkwright just hung his head. He looked as white as a sheet.

"Out." Deio was scowling at her. "We're going out."

"Where?"

"I can't tell you that."

"Are you well enough? Those ribs aren't properly healed yet."

"I'm well now. I've strapped them."

He was handsome again, and with his old air of authority.

"Will you be all right here?" he said. "We'll be no more than a day."

"I'll be all right."

"So we'll see you, then?" He gave her an extra look of concern. "We'll try and catch some hares while we're up there."

"Up where?" she wanted to ask, but she held her peace.

For three days they went out in the morning and came back at night. Each night when he returned Deio looked more emptied out, and she was in despair about him. She was pretty sure he wasn't out fighting, because that had gone quiet, too; also, his commanding officer had sent a message, via Arkwright, that he should let the wound heal before he reported back to work.

She grew lonely in the hut on her own, and resentful. He and Arkwright seemed suddenly part of a club that excluded her. Finally, after two nights when he'd come home to sleep and hardly said more than four words to her, she let him have it.

He was smoking and brooding in a chair in the corner of the

hut. She was cooking some bread in a skillet on the stove. She heard herself say, "Are you ever going to talk to me again, because I'm getting heartily sick of it?"

He looked at her and got up and walked away. She warned herself to calm down, then walked across the room and smacked him squarely across the face shouting, "Don't you dare walk away from me. I hate that."

He held her eyes briefly. "Don't shout like that," he said. "I don't like it, and it's not safe."

"I don't care. I'm so angry I could, oooh—" He had put his hand over her mouth, and she looked at him, and he looked at her.

Later, when she'd stopped breathing heavily and they'd calmed down, she got the bread out of the oven, and a piece of salt pork, and they sat down and ate miserably together, both of them staring into space.

"You must say something," she said. "I can't live like this."

He put down his knife and fork, and said in a low voice, "What do you want me to say."

"Anything would be better than this."

His eye was wandering and she glimpsed his great distress, but she was remorseless.

"Tell me. You must tell me. I feel as though you're starting to hate me."

She heard him catch his breath.

"Here is the truth, Catrin," he said. "I've thought about you every single day since you left, and now I'm worn out with it."

"What has happened to you? *Tell me now.* I don't know you anymore."

There was a look in his eyes of a man too young to have seen so much. She wanted to hold his hand, but he shook it away.

"You won't like it."

Tell me. You must tell me.

He told her about the storm and how the horses had flown away like bits of paper: Nobby, Conker, Duke, a nice little bay he'd bought outside London, Cariad, and all the others, all smashed and bleeding, mostly dead.

"Cariad!" His words were sinking in.

Now it was his turn to hang his head.

"I should never have brought her; I was so angry with you."

"Is she dead?"

"No. Arkwright found three of them just a month ago, she was one of them."

No don't. Please don't. His eyes warned her to avoid excitement.

"You've never seen anything like it, Catrin. They'd been running wild in a valley near the Causeway Heights and the vultures have been at them and God knows what else, and it's my fault; you must never see her like that."

Now he wept.

"Why don't you bring them here?"

"They're too weak; she is in particular. She had a foal at foot when we found her and it died."

"Poor mare."

"Don't try and see her, Catrin. If she doesn't get much better, she'll need a bullet through the head."

"Deio! You are the biggest muff in the world sometimes. What I can't bear is being shut out of everything, and don't forget, I'm a nurse now, I've seen almost everything and I might even be able to help her."

She'd missed his smile, even one as wan as this.

It felt like home.

Chapter 66

The next day they packed up the saddlebags with sleeping gear and the shotguns, some fishing lines, water, hard cheese, and bread. They rolled up the tarpaulins and lashed them to the front of their saddles. An hour later they were away, riding through a dazzling spring day up the winding road toward the hills.

It was heaven being out on a horse again and she would have been very happy if Deio hadn't looked so drawn and deadly pale. After an hour, she asked him to stop for a while; his wound was so recently healed and he had taken little exercise recently.

"I can't stop, Catrin," he said. "I'm always worried they'll be gone when I get there." Now they were following a small stream uphill. There was a tang of sage and pine in the air and the horses were side-deep in long grasses. In a clearing halfway up the hill, they passed a heap of human bones scattered carelessly over some sandbags. She saw a hand poking out from the earth as though beseeching.

Around noon they came to a bridge and, below it, some cypress trees and a dell where the grass was as soft and as green as a lawn.

"This is it." Deio shot her a warning look. "We're here now."

He led her into a makeshift corral near the water's edge, camouflaged by branches of sawn-off trees. Inside the railings she suddenly saw four sorry-looking horses; they were restricted by hobbles around their front legs and were grazing.

She let him go ahead of her, watching him walk between them caressing them, calling them by their names, checking their ropes. He was in his natural habitat again and so was she. Her eyes fell on one horse that was nothing but a pitiful collection of sores and hollows and bones; it stood separate from the others as though ashamed of itself. Its front legs were bandaged and its coat was mostly black skin with the occasional clump of mousy fluff. A deep gouge in its side had been painted with thick orange-colored powder.

She went to its side. "What happened to you?" She gentled its ears while it stood with its head low to the ground. She ran her hand softly down the back of the animal's legs and then stopped breathing as she saw the distinctive white markings shaped like piano keys.

"Cariad!" she said. She bent down and looked into large tragic eyes. "Oh my God!"

Cariad made no sign of recognition. She could just about stand up. Catherine touched her horse all over, speechless with shock. When she looked up, Deio, who was watching her, looked quickly away. Her Cariad, her horse. They'd both been so proud of her once: the silly, knock-kneed filly who'd found herself on the drove.

"What happened to her legs?" she asked him when she could speak.

"She got lost and was stolen," he told her in a monotone. "Then she went lame and the bastard who took her bandaged her in wet bandages and when they dried they rubbed her raw."

There was an open wound in Cariad's rump.

"Vultures?" She touched the edges of it gently.

"Yes."

While they were talking, Cariad seemed to perk up a little and to listen to them intelligently. And then to remember. She shifted her shoulders so she could be closer to Catherine, sighed, and put the whole weight of her head in her hands as if to say, "You work this out."

"I'm so sorry," said Deio. "It's my fault."

"It's not your fault." Tears poured down her face. "None of you would be here if it wasn't for me."

She asked Deio to hold Cariad, and got out her lint and her scissors and a bottle of the Griffith's ointment Betsy Davis had given her and swore by for skin problems. She sent Deio down to the stream for some water and then they cleaned the wounds together. When they were finished, both of them put their arms around Cariad's neck. So many days they'd spent like this before: washing ponies, schooling them in the ring, filling their water buckets, settling their beds—playing house with live animals in the most satisfactory way. For him, a tenderness that had no other expression, for her—everything.

"We went out on the plain every day after they went." He was already saying more to her than he had in the last six weeks. "I thought I'd go mad. I behaved like an arse and was being punished for it."

"Punished for what? For looking?"

"No. Not for looking. For being myself. I hated myself."

When they were finished with Cariad, they gave her a handful of fresh grass mixed in with some of the gruel they had brought, and then they fed the other horses who were watching them covetously.

Now he was reeling with fatigue, so she was firm with him and made him sleep, on a bed made of saddle blankets in the shade of a juniper tree. When he woke, she was washing her hair in the stream and he came over and helped her rinse it, his hands as firm and as perfect as you'd expect from a man who understood animals so well.

He rubbed her hair in a towel and combed it for her strand by strand, spreading it out to dry.

"Did you get nits like everybody else, Catrin?" He was teasing her again. "Oops, there's one, and another—David and Llewellyn and Flora."

She cuffed him around the head, and pulled his hair. They laughed, for the first time in a long time.

It got cooler later. He put a rug on Cariad and built up the fire and put the camouflaging leaves back over the corral. Then he sat by the stream, and Catherine stared at his back marveling at him. He had picked out a branch from the kindling, attached a line to it, and caught a couple of beautiful trout, their sides silvery and speckled with gold dust. He put the bedroll beside the fire, and when the flames had burned down to pale and powdery ashes, he cooked the trout and they ate them together while the light faded from the day and the stars came out.

After their meal they sat with their backs against a rock and he looked straight ahead and told her everything. He knew how hard he'd been with her on that drove, but he couldn't do much about it: he'd loved her for so long; had this dream of her, and it wasn't of her dressed as a man and living like a man.

He'd come out here to find her, and felt very high on it all for a while, with his equipment and his horses.

"The horses flew away like bits of paper." He looked at her intently to see she'd heard and understood.

She put her hand out to him, but he wasn't ready for it yet.

"There's more, Catherine. I'm not who you think I am now."

"What do you mean?" She listened to the fire crackle and waited in the silence that followed.

"I don't know who I am now," he repeated.

Then he told her about Chalkie, his friend, and the night he'd persuaded him to go up to the front and fight with him, and how, half an hour later, Chalkie was blown to bits and he'd walked around caked in him for hours.

"Deio!" She saw his expression. "Deio, don't!" she said, frightened.

"I must finish this," he said. "I liked it at first, the fighting. You're not supposed to say that are you? But I *really liked it*. I was trained for it, I was good at it; it was like going hunting but better. The first time I shot someone, I felt great, almost as great as—"

"Lying with a woman?"

"Catrin! I didn't say that."

"No, but a young soldier in hospital did. You wouldn't be the first man to find war wonderfully stimulating at first."

"At first, but then you feel like scum . . . like the lowest worm. I killed a young Russian, and there was a picture in his wallet of a sweetheart. And before I killed him, I thought of you, and then I thought, 'Once I lived for her, now I kill for her.' And then I grew to hate what I saw and what I became and I do now and I don't know how to stop it."

"Deio." She held him tight. "Please listen to me. *Please!* I'm not who I thought I was either . . . all the bad things you worried about happening to me have happened."

"What bad things?" He sat up, ready to fight her corner.

"Not now. Deio"—she put her arms around him, she could hear her heart thumping with fear—"Please let me in. I've missed you so much."

He looked at her then squeezed his eyes shut.

"Catrin," he put his head next to hers. "Catrin."

They went down the track toward the stream.

The night was full of noises: the silky sounds of the water; the horses munching grass; and every now and then, the swish and whirr of shells being fired in the distance.

When he kissed her, she knew she'd never properly been kissed before, not like this. First the tender probing of his tongue, then a firm and urgent inquiry, a question needing an answer from her, which she gave in a blaze of pure joy. He smoothed her hair; he stroked her face, the points of her ears, her neck. A promise and a claiming all at once. And then they lay down on a quilt on the bank near the river and laughed because Cariad, looking like a peevish old ghost in her bandages, was jealously calling out to them.

She forbade him to do more than kiss her in case he burst his stitches or damaged his ribs, but as she lay behind him in the dark, holding herself against him, she was aware of relief breaking over her body in wave after wave. There he was, her miracle, and here was she. One day she might tell him everything, but maybe not. You didn't have to say. Not everything. Some secrets might stay like dark sediment at the bottom of a bottle, and would not improve with shaking. Either way, they had to meet as adults now: complicated, flawed, full of untamable longings. They had no other choice. But if she let him go now, she knew that a darkness would fall on her and she would miss him for the rest of her life.

In the middle of the night he woke with a start and sat bolt upright.

"Are you all right?" she said. "Are you in pain?"

"No," he smiled. "I'm not in pain."

She stroked his back, waiting.

"If I haven't asked you much about yourself, Catrin, it's not because I don't care," he said suddenly. "I know you had friends, like I had Chalkie, didn't you?"

"One day, Deio," she said, "not now."

It was good, lying there and hearing the water, seeing the stars break intermittently through the canopy of leaves.

Sometime during the night, he woke again and warned her that he couldn't ever imagine himself living in one place and that there was no one on earth who he could imagine wanting to spend twenty-four hours a day with him.

It was strange to hear herself laughing again.

"Heavens, Deio, you sound as if I've just insisted on . . . on . . ."

He took her hair in his hands, and held it at the nape of her neck.

"Well, I am asking you now," he said. "Because if I don't, I'll spend the rest of my life missing you."

It was still and quiet down at the water's edge. The horses, hearing their voices, pricked up their ears and carried on eating. He put another log on the fire, and wrapped her up in a rug.

Cariad was looking back at her from the fringes of the pool.

Her face was serene. She was back with her herd.

And now dawn was breaking over them, a flush of light falling on the broken earth and the remains of the fire, the new trees and the hills beyond. She looked at Deio, and then at the glowing light; once it might have seemed as fleeting as their youth, now it felt like a future.

Band of Angels

For Discussion

1. While on the drove Catherine thinks to herself, "life, for all its brutality, was a journey, an adventure" (page 92). Discuss how this reflects the overall theme of the novel.

2. Catherine has a multitude of men in her life. In what ways do her interactions with men help to shape her journey?

3. Throughout the novel heartache, loss, and disappointment often propel Catherine into action. Talk about those pivotal moments in the book. How do they help Catherine learn about the world?

4. Deio's mother Meg describes him as "not bred for captivity," (page 45) and his feelings for Catherine vacillate between his desire for her and his desire for freedom. How does this reflect some of the conflict between Catherine and Deio?

5. Deio seems both attracted to Catherine and repulsed by her while on the drove. What does this reveal about his attraction to her? About his personality?

6. During her interview with Lady Bracebridge, Catherine is irritated by the line of questioning and says to herself: "she wants a band of angels, not nurses" (page 191). How does this particular scene illustrate the class roles of the time period? What were some of the markers of class? How are people treated differently because of their class status?

7. Discuss the variety of women in Catherine's life. What kinds

of reactions does she have to them? How do these women impact the woman Catherine wants to become? How do they help her learn about herself?

8. Describe the experience of "droving." What are the sights and smells the author provides? How does it begin to prepare Catherine for what's ahead?

9. In leaving her home, Catherine leaves the comforts she's accustomed to. While at Scutari her living quarters are often filthy and the food and water rations limited. What other physical discomforts has Catherine had to face? How do her experiences reflect the brutality of war?

10. The hospital is described as "a large and icy pond where soon all the faults and the weaknesses would join up with one almighty crack and drag them all under." (pages 300–301) The author creates dramatic images of wounded soldiers, poorly stocked and staffed medical wards, and common illnesses and treatments. How do the hospital scenes both further the plot and affect the character's state of mind?

11. Catherine's sexual naiveté leaves her in a state of constant confusion. Through her friendships, particularly with Barnsie, Lizzie, and Miss Davis, she comes to some understanding of the nature of romantic relationships and sex. What does this say about the responsibility of women to each other in that particular time? What does the novel say about the role of female friendships?

12. Compare and contrast Deio's and Dr. Cavendish's possessiveness over Catherine. Both are intense, yet very different. How does the narrative describe the depth of feeling—both negative and positive—each of them has towards her?

13. "Learning to think for yourself is one of the most important things in life, even if you think wrongly sometimes," (page

297) says Lizzie to Catherine. The narrator affirms that "freedom was dangerous." In what ways are the ideas of freedom and independence in constant conflict?

14. Dr. Cavendish is callous and harmful and yet ultimately a necessary component for both Deio and Catherine. How is his character both a negative and positive force in her life?

Your last novel, *East of Sun,* took readers through India. What prompted you to tackle the Crimean War and the world's introduction to modern nursing?
In 2005, I went on a long-distance horse ride across Wales, along the drover's routes and the foothills of the Snowdon mountains. On my way home, I stopped at a place called Pumpsaint in mid-Wales where I saw, outside a tiny church, a plaque commemorating a woman called Jane Evans. She'd run away with the Welsh cattle drovers in 1853 in order to nurse with Florence Nightingale. I was completely intrigued. What bravery! What madness! What kind of woman would do this? At first, I thought I might try and write a biography of her, but could find almost nothing on her. Attempts to find first-hand accounts from other nurses in the Crimean War drew a blank—most of them were illiterate. I decided to write my first novel.

Elizabeth Herbert has a very minor role in the novel, yet the scene with her husband Samuel is poignant because of the way she manipulates his ego to acquire a task. Do you think women still have the task of managing male egos to achieve what they want?
I think many women learn, almost instinctively, to manage and massage the male ego in order to get what they want; but it's dangerous to generalize about this. My daughter and her friends are far more straightforward in their approach. They have grown up with a greater sense of entitlement, because, generally speaking, they are better educated and more confident than women of say, my mother's or Catherine Carreg's generation.

As written in the novel, and in historical records, Florence Nightingale seemed particularly sexless. Do you think that's attributed to her success? Does her lack of patience for women make her less of a feminist icon?

Florence Nightingale was an aristocratic, beautiful woman, who had love affairs and a marriage proposal before she dedicated herself to nursing. As a reformer, she used her considerable feminine wiles to get what she wanted from the politicians in power; at the same time she was incredibly tough with the nurses. I see no paradox here. Many of these women were rough and undisciplined; they had a poor reputation as slatterns and drunks. This was the first time in English history that nurses had been asked officially to go to war with men. Their behavior had to be seen to be beyond reproach.

The idea of the physical journey, moving from place to place, is a common narrative thread for you. What intrigues you about that element of the coming-of-age tale?
One half of my family has stayed put in the island of Jersey in the Channel Islands: a warm, closely knit, old-fashioned, extended family strongly rooted in one place. The other side of my family are globe spinners. They've traveled, endlessly between England, Canada, America, and Australia. They've taken weird and wonderful jobs en route, lived apart from their families for years. The contrast interests me. What is lost? What is gained? What is learned by leaving home?

You often contrast the dangers of freedom and the desire for independence with the securities of convention. Catherine seems to struggle with these two concepts. While writing, were you conscious of those elements? Do you think this is still a common conflict for women?
I recognize in myself a split: I like frightening myself, I like feeling free, I also like home and hearth and family. I wasn't particularly conscious of these conflicting desires while I was writing the book, because they are part of me.

You include detailed descriptions of the drove, horses, the war conditions, and nineteenth-century medical facilities. How long did the research take? Did you get your

information from primary sources? From books? The internet?

The research took the best part of a year. One of the best bits was actually riding along the old drovers' routes on a retired show jumper called Fred who seemed to love it, too. I also went to Turkey and then Scutari, to check out the hospital, now a military barracks. Amazingly, there is still a room in the nurse's tower that must have been Florence Nightingale's office. There was a dusty chaise longue still there and her desk. It was almost exactly as I'd imagined it. I also read as many histories and personal letters and accounts of military hospitals as I could. I hardly used the Internet at all.

Were you able to include everything you learned about nineteenth-century medical treatment?

No, sadly! Very tempting because it was riveting and often thrillingly gory to read, but I didn't want to overload the book with medical details.

The nature of Catherine's childhood—the lack of parenting from her mother, the rides with Deio—seem to aggravate her desire to take the expected position of wife and mother. Is that the juxtaposition readers are meant to take from the book? Does Catherine's childhood plant the seed for her journey?

One of the greatest traumas of Catherine's childhood was that she felt she had let her mother down when she was dying in childbirth because she was too squeamish and too ignorant. This made her long to grow up, to be better educated, less useless. Her other strong impulse was to be Deio's mate, and these twin desires caused, for years, a split in her.

Like Catherine, you live in Wales. How much of the setting is based on the area you live in?

Wales is a beautiful part of the United Kingdom, very wild in its center with lots of rivers and mountains and wide green tracks where the drovers once rode. I live in an old farmhouse that's been on this site in one form or another since the fifteenth century. From my window, I can see two huge pine trees, a traditional sign for the drovers that they could bring their animals here. So, yes, I'm hugely influenced by where I live.

Are you working on anything new? Any particular time period?
My new book, *Jasmine Nights*, is set in the Middle East during the war. I went to Cairo a couple of months ago to do some research.

There are many variations of the Water Horse legend. How did you come to the legend of the Water Horse? And which one did you have in mind?
The Water Horse, sometimes called the kelpie, is a supernatural creature that appears in Celtic folklore and was thought to inhabit the rivers and lochs and seas of Ireland, Scotland, and Wales. In some versions, the Water Horse is a terrifying all-consuming creature that rises out of the sea, which wants nothing more than to drown you. In others he is a more benign presence who will let you ride him and share his powers. In some versions of the legend he is a handsome young man who wants to lure a woman into his trap.

Also, the Scottish version of the legend seems like a metaphor for Deio and Catherine's relationship. Towards the end of the book they seem to settle in a comfortable acceptance of each other. Have they in essence tamed each other?
In my book, I saw the Water Horse as a creature on which Catherine and Deio could project the wildness, the terror, the longing for mastery of youth. It was only after I'd finished the book that I read that in the Scottish version of the legend the Water Horse rises out of the water seeking a wife. I loved that and would have used it had I known about it earlier!

Was in difficult to plot a romance in the face of war and maintain those elements throughout the writing process?
I was aware that Catherine and Deio's overwhelming need to see each other again might feel selfish in the face of all the catastrophes that were going on around them. However, the truth, uncomfortable or not, is that war is a great aphrodisiac: it intensifies desire, it makes people understand what really matters to them. I held fast to this idea.

"I always wish for books like this, but they are rare—
**a beautifully written compelling
saga that is impossible to put down.**
It's about ambition, love, survival, and the friendship
of three women who leave England for the exotic
and sometimes frightening adventure of India.
Reading this is an escape to another place and time
where friends and romance are waiting."
—DELIA EPHRON

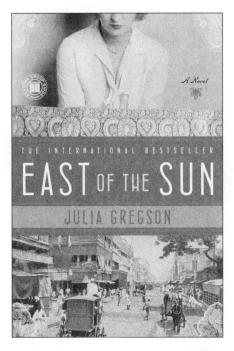